GW00726858

ONE SPOILT SPRING

ONE SPOILT SPRING

by

BEATA BISHOP

SEVERN HOUSE PUBLISHERS

This 1985 edition from SEVERN HOUSE PUBLISHERS LTD of
4 Brook Street, London W1Y 1AA
First published in Great Britain 1960 by Faber and Faber

Copyright © 1960 by Beata Bishop

British Library Cataloguing in Publication Data

Bishop, Beata
   One spoilt spring.
   I. Title
   813'.914[F]   PR6052.I796/

   ISBN 0-7278-1191-6

Printed and bound in Great Britain by
Butler & Tanner Ltd, Frome and London

The chestnut casts his flambeaux, and the flowers
  Stream from the hawthorn on the wind away,
The doors clap to, the pane is blind with showers.
  Pass me the can, lad; there's an end of May.

There's one spoilt spring to scant our mortal lot,
  One season ruined of our little store.
May will be fine next year as like as not:
  Oh ay, but then we shall be twenty-four.

A. E. HOUSMAN

Permission to include this extract from one of the Last Poems *has been granted by the Society of Authors as the literary representatives of the Trustees of the Estate of the late A. E. Housman, and Messrs. Jonathan Cape, Ltd., publishers of A. E. Housman's* Collected Poems.

CHAPTER ONE

The old French nun on the dais was reciting Corneille. Her magnificent voice rolled forth in a pattern of rhythm and modulation, playing up every clear vowel and ringing consonant until her speech turned into music and the meaning of the words faded behind their sound.

Gitta sat stock-still in the back of the class-room, not even trying to follow the text. She could re-read that at home as often as she liked; to hear it spoken by Mère Edwige who, besides being French, also seemed to be a direct descendant of Corneille's heroes, was far more important.

Did all French people talk like this? Were they all as brilliant and articulate as Mère Edwige and the Mother Superior? Or, for that matter, was Mother Agnes a typical Englishwoman? Never having been outside her own country, Gitta observed her foreign teachers avidly as if they had been the precious fragments of a large, infinitely remote whole. She was in her twentieth year, the war in its fifth, and it was impossible to guess how much longer it would last. The frontiers were sealed. One could not go abroad. The longer the isolation lasted, the more she resented it. To travel abroad—not in Germany, Austria, or any of the Nazi-occupied neighbouring countries which somehow did not qualify as abroad—was a wildly exciting idea which she reserved for special moments and, not being able to work it out in detail, hid again with a delicious sense of guilt. To talk in public about wanting to visit the West would have amounted to high treason.

"*Rodrigue, as-tu du cœur?*" Mère Edwige exclaimed, suspending her voice in a well-timed pause that sounded as weighty as the question. I must remember the intonation, Gitta thought, although she was not at all sure that that kind of question ever occurred in ordin-

9

ary conversation. Yet that seemed beside the point. There was nothing ordinary about the convent school, either. With its foreign nuns and international atmosphere it was like Europe in a nutshell in the middle of Budapest, the nearest thing to being abroad; it hardly mattered whether the curriculum had any bearing on practical everyday life.

Gitta found this cosmopolitan make-believe a heady stimulant. She liked to walk the length of the stone-flagged corridors, admiring the big pictures of Greek ruins, French cathedrals and Italian palazzi. Every day in the chapel she was fascinated to hear how each nun pronounced Latin according to the intonation of her mother tongue so that an ordinary *Ave Maria* sounded like a study in comparative linguistics. She loved the replica of the Notre Dame Madonna on the altar. Although years of convent education had immunized her to the visual side of religion and she was seeking for God alone, ignoring the other inhabitants of the Catholic heaven, she still responded warmly to the Madonna of Paris. Like everything else in the convent, the statue was different and slightly exotic, part of a pattern which she was happy to accept. The only thing that worried her was that in another two months the post-matriculation course would be over, leaving her with a diploma and nothing to do; but then what was the point of thinking as far ahead as that?

Turning towards the window she watched the bare plane trees shuddering in the March wind. It was a damp, fresh Saturday morning, the kind of day when almost anything might happen, and all of a sudden she lost patience with Corneille and wanted to dash out into the open. But then the tinny bell in the turret began to ring. The lesson was over and after a long break and a short lecture on text analysis the morning's work would end, too.

During the break Marta Péterffy steered her to the far end of the corridor where they could talk in peace. They leant against a glass case containing the scale model of Florence, a brown, skyless toy of a city under layers of fine dust. In the music room a few doors away a Polish refugee nun began to play Chopin. Gitta sighed and gazed at the tiny Palazzo Vecchio and minute Baptisterium under the glass. She felt unaccountably depressed.

"I'm the one to sigh," Marta said. "I'm in a mess."

"What, again? Same old trouble?"

"Yes, only worse. Will you stay behind with me after the break?

10

The last lesson doesn't matter. I think Papa might come along to tell the Mother Superior that he won't let me finish the course and I'd like to intercept him."

"What for? You can't stop him once he's here."

"No, but I can make it awkward for him. We had another terrible row last night. He was furious. He said he won't let me stay in this hothouse of Anglo-French-Judaeo-Marxist propaganda. I honestly don't know which is worse, his views or his terminology. At any rate I think he meant it."

Gitta frowned. It was one thing to hear about Marta's skirmishes with Count Péterffy who was rich, dumb and fanatically pro-German, and another to be directly involved in a family quarrel. She loathed violent scenes and would have liked to refuse, but to sound cowardly seemed equally detestable.

"What difference does it make if I'm with you?" she asked. "Your father won't take any notice of me."

"Oh yes, you might inhibit him, and that would help. He's been odd lately, terribly temperamental and bitter. I wonder if he's had some confidential news that upset him."

"For instance that the Allies are coming to occupy us? What would he do in that case?"

"Go to the conservatory and shoot himself."

"God forbid," Gitta said politely.

"Oh yes, he would. He couldn't live without his theories—you know, Hungary's mission among the lesser nations, back to St. Stephen or Attila or Nimrod, the older the better, down with all foreigners except the Germans because they can cope with the Russians, and so forth."

"Can't you get your mother to talk to him?"

"She doesn't care. She's too busy working out people's pedigrees before inviting them to dinner and looking at old copies of the *Tatler* when Papa isn't about. Not that she likes the English, but she thinks the *Tatler* is *très* snob. What's the time?"

"Quarter-past twelve."

"Let's go over to that window and watch the street. If he doesn't turn up pretty soon, he won't come today. I know his habits."

Reluctantly Gitta moved over to the window, scanning the empty street. She held herself straight, for Marta's tall, slim body made her self-conscious about her own plumpness; once again she felt terribly

11

plain, squat, gauche, a parody of what she would have loved to look like, and dramatic moments such as this made her feel more diffident than ever. She longed to be beautiful or at least striking, with blonde hair and fine eyes, preferably aquamarine, like Marta's; but all she had was a round, childish face with too much forehead and a strong jaw, straight brown hair, hazel eyes, not one feature matching her wishes. She did not even look her age, she looked about sixteen, and one of her worst fears was that she might float from late adolescence into middle age without ever looking like a real adult.

"It's getting late," she said to Marta. "Hadn't we better call it a day?"

"There it is, look, our car! We must have got some supplementary petrol for urgent war work."

The big black car stopped outside the convent. Gitta watched it in awe: privately-owned cars, especially large ones, were a great rarity. She very much wanted to see Count Péterffy in the flesh but the only person to emerge was the flat-capped chauffeur who hurried towards the entrance with an envelope in his hand.

"Oh, honestly," Marta cried, racing to the staircase, "how typical of Papa to back out at the last moment and do it in writing! I thought he had more courage than that. Come along, quick!" Gitta followed her with dazed loyalty and they reached the entrance at the same time as the chauffeur and the doorkeeper nun.

"Any message for me?" Marta asked.

"I'm to take you home in the car," the chauffeur said, thrusting the letter at the doorkeeper as if he thought Marta might try to snatch it.

"All right. Wait for me outside." She turned to the doorkeeper. "Please tell the Mother Superior that I'd like to see her urgently."

"Well, I'd better leave you now," Gitta mumbled, but Marta shook her head, saying she wanted a witness and the meeting might be instructive for both of them. So they stood around in the hall, waiting and wondering and staring at the big volumes of ecclesiastical history in the glazed bookcase, and then the doorkeeper returned and showed them in to the Mother Superior's study.

It was a bright room with whitewashed walls and two big windows, and in the few seconds that elapsed between dropping an awkward curtsy in the door and walking to the desk in the middle, Gitta fleetingly took in the ivory crucifix in the corner, the framed

12

crest of Paris on the wall with "*Fluctuat nec mergitur*" picked out in gold, a map of Europe and group photographs of former pupils. She smiled shyly at the small old woman behind the desk, a frail figure with a deeply lined face and brilliant dark eyes, and hoped that Marta would do all the talking.

"Gitta, *ma petite*," the old nun said, "surely you aren't leaving us, too? I thought it was Marta who wanted to see me."

"Yes, but I'd like her to stay," Marta explained. "It's for a personal reason which I can't explain just now, if you don't mind."

"As you wish, my child. Did you come to say good-bye to me?"

"I came to apologize for whatever my father wrote to you and to say that I dissociate myself from him in every possible way. In spite of that, I'll have to stay away for the time being. You see, I live at home and can't do as I please."

"But of course, you must obey your father. In fact I don't really like the way you talk about him." The nun spoke her own brand of rapid, French-flavoured Hungarian, presumably to stress the private nature of the conversation—normally it was considered foolhardy to use any language except French in her presence. "Whatever his views, you are his daughter and you must obey him."

"That raises a difficult point," Marta said. "If I obeyed my father, I would have to reject everything you yourself have taught me over the past eighteen months. I happen to prefer your outlook. Oh, *ma Mère*, you know what I mean, please don't try to defend him, we've got beyond that stage. Did he write anything objectionable to you?"

The nun shook her head regretfully. "Perhaps I should not discuss it with you but I must admit his note is not pleasant. He condemns everything we do here. He thinks we should teach German instead of French and English, since in his opinion those languages amount to enemy propaganda. He also feels we should not admit Jewish girls. It so happens that all our girls are Roman Catholics, some of them fairly recent ones, but then Our Lord was not baptized at birth, either. I fear your father is wrong. It doesn't matter, *ma petite*, I am not hurt, only sorry to lose you."

"I'm sorry to go, too. *Ma Mère*, what's going to happen? How long can this last?"

The old woman smiled sadly. The same question worried her day and night, although she never admitted her anxiety except to God. She was seventy-six, she was French, and France seemed a great deal more remote than Heaven. She did not expect to live much longer, but the expanding Reich terrified her on account of her small flock. Many of her nuns were refugees from Nazi-occupied countries; the rest were French and English, enemy aliens in the Germans' eyes. She had many Jewish or half-Jewish students and several Gentiles who came from anti-Nazi families. In spite of the convent's apparent peace, every second person around her was a potential victim, certain to be persecuted the moment the political situation deteriorated, and she knew she would be powerless to save them.

"We must not be afraid," she said. "God's will must be done, the rest doesn't matter. Don't forget what we taught you here, *ma petite*, even if we don't meet again."

"How could I forget?"

"I am sure you won't. Except that our ideals are so unpopular at present. To be a good European is unfashionable. And all the other things we believe in, fairness and tolerance and respect for the truth and the need for mental discipline and concise thinking—you will not hear much about all that in the outside world. Still, one day things will change. We must try to survive until then. Had you not better go now? We must not irritate your father by keeping you late."

The old woman rose and traced a cross on Marta's forehead. "*Au revoir, mon enfant,*" she said, "try to pray for your father. He needs it." She turned to Gitta. "I shall see you on Monday, but let me bless you, too. One never knows these days."

The girls curtsied and went out into the deserted hall.

"Well, this is it," Marta said. "Can we meet one day in town?"

"Of course. Ring me any day after lunch and we'll arrange something. By the way, I still don't understand why you wanted me to be present just now."

"Never mind, you will one day. Good-bye."

Marta ran down to the car and was driven away. Gitta gazed after her, suddenly realizing that she had forgotten to give Marta her telephone number.

Oh well, we're bound to run into each other, she thought, and hurried on towards the main road that linked the town centre with the City Park. The air was spicy and exciting; low clouds raced across the sky and puffs of wind tore in from all sides. A cat flashed along the kerb, chasing an air current.

14

Walking briskly to the nearest underground station, Gitta hopped down the short stairs to the platform and waited. The station was tiny and intimate, and the train that emerged from the tunnel consisted of one carriage, just as the entire underground system comprised one line only.

She sat down near the door. The carriage happened to be the one in which Francis Joseph had travelled along the line in 1896, opening what was then Europe's only underground railway. After a long spell in a museum, the coach, complete with commemorative plaque, was re-requisitioned for normal service. Every time she travelled in it, Gitta felt vaguely satisfied, as if participating in the triumph of democracy.

She was anti-Hapsburg, mainly owing to the influence of a republican history mistress whose condemnation of the dual Monarchy outweighed the legitimist leanings of Gitta's mother, whose childhood before the Great War had passed in the security of a long, perfect summer, or at least so it appeared in retrospect; but her wistful recollections only inspired Gitta to irritable attacks. With the heartless objectivity of the young she countered Mrs. Balogh's personal memories with sharp political arguments. To her mind the Monarchy and Vienna with its never-blue Danube and imperial splendour were props out of an operetta that deserved no revival. She hated operettas. They were phoney. She hated current politics. They were even phonier. The country needed a fresh start, a new way of life that combined those of Britain, Scandinavia and Switzerland, without obliterating one iota of native character. As she was not quite twenty yet, this Utopia seemed simple to achieve provided that those in power stood aside and the rest of the world did not interfere.

Political thought came naturally to Gitta. She belonged to a generation whose school curriculum had been heavy with political implication. World geography pointed to the balance of power, national geography to the country's mutilation in 1920. World literature spread cosmopolitan ideas; national literature was a long stream of stirring protests against tyranny. History taught its own lesson, however falsely official policy tried to interpret it. Since the beginning of the war politics had become a daily business, like the weather.

The train rolled comfortably from one tiny station to the next. A

15

few people got out at each stop, others strolled in to take their place. There was no rush, no crowd, no urgency.

Dismissing her political worries, Gitta thought of the morning at the convent when Mother Agnes had given an improvised talk about London. Homesickness had prompted her to by-pass the Ancient Mariner; her memories of London, infinitely remote behind the barriers of war, had rushed out spontaneously. The girls had listened entranced. London was the least familiar of all the Western capitals. Paris, or even Brussels, was easier to visualize with the aid of textbook illustrations, but London remained veiled. The old-fashioned postcards that were sometimes passed from hand to hand only showed busy, bitty scenes in varying shades of sepia, so that several girls imagined London to consist of sepia houses under a sepia sky, abnormally coloured by permanent fog. London seemed to lack the unforgettable patterns of Paris; no Etoile, no Concorde, no evidence of perfect proportion sprang to the eye.

The descriptions of Mother Agnes had therefore been truly welcome—at last a first-hand account of that puzzling city. She had talked at great length about the underground railway, and Gitta had listened incredulously to the intricacies of a network where a line could branch off in mid-town, taking intelligent people like Mother Agnes to Marylebone when they really wanted to go to Swiss Cottage.

London had sounded a bit frightening, and now as she got out at the mid-town terminus she was glad she knew her city as thoroughly as her own room. London appealed to her curiosity, Paris to her emotions, but this was Budapest, hard fact as one's normal habitat always is, and it was time to hurry home.

She cut across the streets that represented the glamorous heart of the city where everybody who counted appeared at least once a day. The small area was rich in interesting detail. Here were the shops that set the trend in fashion, in books, in furniture and flowers. Their windows were a vocabulary of taste and new ideas which one could accept or reject but not ignore. Gitta scanned the displays expertly. Everything looked elegant, positive, untouched by war-time drabness. Thanks to a strange local brand of logic emergencies and hard times caused the women to dress better and look more radiant than ever, shop windows to vie with each other in discreet opulence, and rare commodities to appear miraculously from no-

16

where. The paradox was not entirely frivolous; it sprang from a characteristic kind of resignation that was not without courage. The really important events were beyond anybody's power: the next best thing was to pretend normality in small things and hang on to the illusion doggedly even if the world went up in flames and there remained no one to admire the quixotic gesture. And so, in a city of choosy coffee drinkers, espresso bars only began to flourish when, logically, coffee should have been unobtainable; new English and French writers enjoyed a colossal vogue, although in principle their books should never have reached the country; clothes and shoes were rationed, yet the men and women one met in those streets still went through the moves of an informal *concours d'élégance*.

Gitta crossed herself on passing the Franciscan church with its permanent parade of busy pigeons and turned into University Street. Two students in flat green velvet caps talked loudly about the treacherous Jews. A baroque spire pealed out the hour. She rounded the vast yellow building of the Municipal Gallery and ran the rest of the way. She was ravenously hungry.

After lunch she was sitting with her mother in the drawing-room, drinking coffee and talking about the Péterffy incident, when Rozália, the maid, came in to say that she was running out of lard—could Miss Gitta go and fetch the rations, since she was the only one who could get the best pre-war quality from the butcher? Rozália was short, broad and bovine; she made even the simplest domestic information sound ominous, and her thick eyebrows, almost meeting in the middle, gave her an air of permanent ill temper. Mrs. Balogh only tolerated her because it was so hard to get a decent cook-general—all the bright, pleasant girls had gone into the factories or become conductresses on the rowdy yellow trams. Rozália was second-rate, the labour shortage her main asset.

"All right, we'll see about the lard," Mrs. Balogh said. "Although I wish the butcher didn't have a crush on my daughter."

"He says Miss Gitta is such a healthy-looking young lady."

"Oh, for goodness' sake, I know I'm fat, no need to rub it in."

Rozália withdrew with a shrug. She did not like Gitta who had at first treated her with grave courtesy, asking her about her village, her family, their way of life and their grievances. The maid resented this curiosity. She did not realize that Gitta was trying to turn her into

17

the ideal peasant girl full of wisdom, dignity and all the elements of a folklore manual. Saturated with sociology and anti-bourgeois revulsion, Gitta wanted to identify herself with the People, the nameless toiling peasantry who needed new champions if they were to save the nation, while Rozália wanted to sever the last links that still tied her to her class. Gitta's romantic approach met with stony opposition. The maid knew no ancient folk-songs, she remembered no local customs, nobody in her family ever wore traditional dress, and when Gitta once made an affectionate reference to the long-suffering peasants, Rozália flushed and said that in her village there were no peasants, only citizens. Since then relations had deteriorated fast. Neither could forgive the other for frustrating her secret ambition.

"Darling, don't snap at her," Mrs. Balogh begged. "I know she's awful, but if she gives notice we're sunk. The others we've had before were even worse, like that immoral person who used to wave to strange men from the balcony, or the gloomy creature who kept telling us how cruelly her granny had died."

"Isn't the current one always the worst?"

Mrs. Balogh picked up her embroidery without replying. She was a slim, attractive woman with an oval face and a good figure of which Gitta was very proud: a shapely mother meant a token of hope for a shapeless daughter. She worshipped her young, elegant mother who outshone her friends' mothers in every respect. Normally their relationship was happy and harmonious, but if the slightest thing went wrong, their very closeness turned them into fierce opponents who could make each other thoroughly miserable.

"We must take more stuff down to the cellar," Mrs. Balogh said. "The bombing can only get worse. Tomorrow I want you to help me rearrange the pantry, we must make room for the provisions I've ordered."

"Are you getting ready for a siege?"

"I'm just getting ready. I don't want to be caught empty-handed."

"Why worry about food when the world is going to pieces?"

"Don't be silly. Watching it go to pieces on an empty stomach makes no difference to the world. I'd rather hoard food than let the Germans have it."

"I was thinking of those who can't afford to hoard."

18

Mrs. Balogh glanced at her daughter. Her warm eyes were the colour of sweet sherry held against the light.

"If you're well stocked, you can feed starving people. If you aren't, you can't. A spare bag of flour can do more good than all your social indignation."

That was final. Their arguments always ran along parallel lines, yielding no absolute victory to either side, but Mrs. Balogh's practical approach invariably crushed Gitta's theories.

"You've never stood in a bread line," she added more gently. "I have, after the last war, and I want to spare you the experience. And since this beastly Government forbids hoarding, I consider it my duty to break the rules."

That, of course, was correct. Gitta went to the window and looked out. Their street consisted of a single row of mansion blocks facing a pleasant park with old trees and a sunken flower garden that sent up clouds of sweet scent on warm summer nights. She could see far over the roofs of Budapest, a patchwork of rose pink, red, grey, black and buff roofs, no two of them alike. In the distance a triple-peaked mountain rose into the pearly sky. On the left she saw the flat round citadel squatting on the top of Gellért Hill across the Danube.

"One gets so confused," Gitta said. "Automatic opposition is negative. All it does is make you think along two lines all the time. There are the official rules—not to hoard food, not to hamper the war effort, to admire the Germans, to hate the Jews, to pretend all is well when you know everything is rotten. And then the unofficial rules—but what exactly are they? To do the exact opposite of what you're told isn't enough."

"Surely you can feel what's right and wrong and choose for yourself?"

"Ah yes, as long as there's no conflict. But supposing I were in a position to blow up a trainload of Gestapo-men and I believed that it was wrong to kill——"

"But you are in no position to blow up trains. Oh, don't complicate life even more. I wish you were more down to earth—for instance, what are you going to do with yourself when your course ends in May?"

"We may all be dead by May," Gitta said gloomily. "I wish you ere a bit more down to earth."

"Don't be impudent. Heavens, the news, quick!"

Mrs. Balogh dropped her embroidery and rushed to the wireless that stood at the east wall of the drawing-room: the people next door listened to the B.B.C. as zealously as the Baloghs, and keeping their sets back to back either side of the same wall gave both parties a sense of security. Mrs. Balogh twirled the knob expertly but reception was bad and only a few snatches came through.

"The Russian Army has today entered Bessarabia." The voice drowned in atmospheric noises. "The invasion of Rumania. . . ." It faded out again.

"Coming pretty near, aren't they?" Gitta asked.

"And the faster the better."

The screeches grew so loud that Mrs. Balogh switched off the set. Reception would be better at night, she thought, and by then something else might be announced, too. The Russians from the east, the British from the south-west, the Americans from mid-air—things did not look too bad.

"Well, I'd better do some work before I go out," Gitta said.

"Where are you going?"

"You know. The usual place."

"What, on a Saturday?"

"Mihály is out of town. I must stand in for him."

"I see." Her mother sighed. "Try and keep your voice a little softer. Sometimes you sound too stiff and unmodulated."

Gitta smiled. "It's not acting, you know, it's straight stuff."

"Even so. You aren't lecturing them, are you? And darling, I don't want to interfere, but are you going to do it for much longer? It worries me. After all, it's terribly risky."

"Honestly, Mother, it isn't. You are imagining things."

"That's not a very good answer," Mrs. Balogh said impatiently. "People have got into trouble for merely listening to forbidden radio stations and what you do is a million times worse."

"But that's entirely different. Sometimes a minor trespass is riskier than a major offence. That's a fact."

"Why? Because Pali says so?"

Gitta ignored the ironical tone. "Yes. And he's quite right. Don't you see? As long as part of the Government wants to break away from the Nazis and the others don't, we're safe in the vacuum, unofficially tolerated, as it were. And probably the Allies will arrive

20

long before we've had a chance to get into trouble. Please don't worry."

"It's no use," her mother said unhappily. "I wish you'd stop."

"I can't. You promised you wouldn't interfere."

"Of course not. You know that."

"Well, then? Don't frown, darling. We're very careful."

She blew her mother a kiss and went to her room. In one corner stood the polished school desk littered with papers and books. She had used the desk for the past fourteen years; its adjustable seat and footrest were now set at their farthest limits, and even so she could only just squeeze herself into position. The rest of her room was elegant and adult; the desk looked out of place, a last reminder of childhood which Gitta would have loved to discard. But her mother would not hear of it. The desk was in perfect condition, it had cost a lot of money, and unless Gitta wanted to work on the floor, the desk would have to stay.

She spent an hour reading French history, trying out shorthand abbreviations and doodling initials on an old envelope. But she grew restless and at half-past four she left the house, forgetting all about the lard she should have gone to fetch.

CHAPTER TWO

~~~~~~~~~~~~~~~~~~~~~~~

Pali emptied his cup. In the last few drops the black coffee,
the sugar and the brandy struck such a perfect balance that
afterwards even the brutal cigarette tasted better. There was
something to be said for tracking down minute pleasures,
he thought, the precise gastronomic, intellectual and emotional
answers to one's needs. He twirled his cigarette and gazed across the
quiet café. Nothing much was going on between the mirrored walls
and Moorish columns: a few solitary men read the papers, chess
players ruminated over their boards, and here and there an old waiter
in black leaned against the wall, waiting for orders.

Pali put away his notebooks and stifled a yawn. It had been a
mistake to come to this place, the most relaxing among the six coffee-
houses that served as his second home. He had chosen them carefully, earmarking each one for a special purpose. One was for con-
centrated study (brown walls, weak lemon tea, no noise), one for
animated discussion (literary waiters, good brandy, muted excitement from the adjoining card room), one for pleasant melancholia
(*fin-de-siècle* fittings and the best croissants in town), one for romantic dates (quietly cosmopolitan, cyclamen lampshades), one for
writing (vast, splendid, the smoky temple of intellect) and, lastly,
this one, for contemplation and peace. Too much peace, he thought,
paying his bill. His basic laziness was not to be encouraged.

He walked along the street deep in thought, a slight, dark young
man who moved as if he enjoyed ordinary walking. There was something fluid and effortless in the way he carried himself, completely
in command of every limb and joint, pouring himself smoothly
around corners and getting through crowds without touching anybody. It was as if he had trained his body to achieve maximum
results with as little effort as possible, and then let it get on with it

while he was thinking of something else. Economy of action appealed to him. He never made a superfluous gesture or talked for the sake of talking, and this disciplined manner together with his face that was ironical, smooth and vaguely oriental, often gave him an air of indifference. He was twenty-five, looked thirty and never thought of himself as being particularly young.

Turning into a side street, he entered a big grey building where the air smelt of freshly washed stone floors. There were two young soldiers lounging against a door on the left, covering up the notice that said "NO ENTRY WITHOUT SPECIAL PASS" in fierce red lettering, with "Central Board of Folk Education" below.

"I hate to disturb you, boys," Pali said, "but could you look a trifle more military, not quite so relaxed?"

"Sorry," the taller man grinned, "it's only because you crept in so quietly. As a rule we can hear people coming and there's time for us to look fierce. Here are your papers. I had quite a time getting them from Captain Bajó's assistant—he said the Captain wouldn't be back tonight."

Pali took the envelope, entered the flat and settled down in a small, bare room. The big tile stove was hot but he shovelled on more coal until the fire roared loudly. His spirits rose with the temperature: to sit in shirt-sleeves in a smouldering room, basking like a lizard, stimulated his mind.

If only Mihály were back, he thought. The day's rumours were wilder than usual and he did not quite know what to make of them. Mihály's private reconnoitring under the pretext of an official car trip to the western border might clear up a few points, but not before the morning; meanwhile some line had to be found for the evening's job.

The envelope he had received at the door contained the verbatim transcriptions of news bulletins broadcast by Allied and neutral radio stations, for confidential and official use only. Confidential, yes, and as unofficial as can be, Pali thought contentedly. After all these months it still gave him pleasure to see how well his theory had worked out: provided one had an unexpected formula, he maintained, one could get away with murder.

His formula was pretty unexpected. Here he was, in the middle of Budapest, running a minute broadcasting station with a daily programme of forbidden news and anti-Nazi propaganda that, done on

23

a less daring scale, would have meant prison or worse. It could still come to that, but the risk seemed small. The political tangle favoured his formula. He knew that his private campaign would be tolerated and shielded by certain powers who felt unsure of Germany's victory and wanted someone to say so in their stead; he also knew that this tacit protection would cease the moment the Government fell or he himself got into trouble with some minor authority. His position was that of a spy operating in foreign territory who is assisted by his employers as long as he is successful but is disowned and forsaken in case of failure.

So far success had come easily. He had befriended an anti-Nazi Army engineer who had diverted the complete radio equipment from official channels and was looking after the technical side without a hitch. Mihály Bajó, a reserve officer attached to the Ministry of Information, supplied the texts of monitored broadcasts, besides providing two soldiers for sentry duty—a finishing touch that appealed strongly to Pali's sense of humour. The rest of his team consisted of two or three young people with writing ability and good speaking voices on whom he could rely blindly. The game suited him down to the ground. Like a good chess player, he always thought simultaneously along several lines, planning the next move but two, taking calculated risks and getting out of tight corners without anxiety or effort. He knew that the game would be up one day, but he trusted his sense of timing; it would have been foolish to refuse to do a good job simply because it might end badly.

Gitta burst in, shaking her windswept hair into place and swooping on the news bulletins. Watching her, Pali joined his finger-tips and rotated his wrists, as if testing their flexibility. He liked to underline his mental acrobatics with miniature physical exercises.

"Aren't things speeding up?" Gitta exclaimed. "The Germans can't even slow down the Russians, let alone stop them."

"Rumania is next door."

"Knowing the Rumanians, they'll capitulate the moment the first Red soldier dangles a leg across the border."

"Which means that we'll be expected to shield the Reich from the —what's the official term?—the barbaric hordes of the East," Pali said.

"Oh, don't you think the Allies ought to come now? Surely this is the right moment, they're holding Italy, Yugoslavia could be

24

cleared in a flash, this country would be easy to occupy——"

"Let's assume the Allies know what they're doing. Look, darling, don't lose your head. I'm a bit chary of too obvious solutions. Remember, the Allied forces are not led by Nelson Eddy on a white steed and they won't simply march in to the strains of *Lilac Time*. Not tonight, anyway. So I suggest we take a cautious line in the script and——"

The door flew open. A young officer rushed in and flopped on a chair. "You can lock the shop right away," he said, "they're coming!"

"Who, the Allies?" Gitta cried. "How do you know?"

"What's up, Mihály?" Pali asked. "I didn't expect you before tomorrow."

"The Austrian frontier is thick with German troops on the ready. Quite a few divisions. We'll soon know how many."

"But surely they needn't actually come in?" Gitta protested.

"No, they only want to inspect the Customs shed," Mihály snapped. "Come, come, use your head."

"That explains why the Regent has gone to the Fuehrer," Pali sighed, "or perhaps it doesn't. When do you expect the troops will arrive?"

"I don't know. They may already be on the move."

"Have you told anybody?"

"No, I simply left the car at the Ministry and came here. We'll have to pack up fast."

"How fast? Do you think tonight we're still safe?"

"Oh yes. Even if they've already started, they wouldn't get here in time to shoot you over the microphone."

Pali settled back to his desk. "Mihály, you'd better go and alert a few people while we get on with the job. Famous last words—I used to wonder whether people ever realized that they were uttering their last words. Unfortunately we can't say much just in case things turn out differently."

"Look here," Mihály said nervously, "we must talk."

"Of course. But we must talk to the nation first. Come to my flat after dinner."

"Oh, drop your mock-English sang-froid," Mihály stormed, "can't you see it's urgent? If they catch us, we'll be shot. We must work out something fast."

25

Pali looked at him patiently, bending his head to one side like a friendly dog. Mihály was flushed, tense, ready to leap, kill, die, anything as long as it meant action, whatever its consequences, and Pali understood his mood without sharing it. Genuinely incapable of losing his head, he found that other people's excitement made him calmer than ever; an observer rather than a fighter, he liked to think quietly instead of running round in circles.

"Of course it's urgent," he said soothingly. "Why not go and clear up your desk at the Ministry? It's probably bursting with compromising material. Find out how fast this place can be dismantled, pass round the news and meet us after dinner. You'll have plenty to do on your own."

"Oh, all right. Half-past eight, then," Mihály said and rushed away.

The room was very silent except for the hot roar of the stove. Gitta pushed aside the news bulletins that were already somewhat behind the times. She waited for thoughts to race through her brain, but apart from the knowledge that something dreadful and inevitable was happening, nothing penetrated the blankness. She had felt this kind of paralysis at children's matinées when on stage the villain was about to strike and, however loudly the audience shouted their warnings, the drama rolled on relentlessly.

Pali stroked her hair. "Come on, little one, soon it'll be much worse. Could you do the news while I do the commentary? We can't say anything about Mihály's news, we'd only create confusion, and anyway the whole thing may come to nothing. Ready?"

They worked wildly for half an hour and then raced to the converted bathroom studio where the walls were covered with hessian hangings and the microphone stood between the bath and the handbasin. The red bulb flashed twice and stayed aglow.

"This is the Voice of Freedom. Here's the truth behind the news," Pali began. He sounded relaxed and conversational, an individual talking intimately to other individuals. He had perfected this technique by listening to B.B.C. broadcasts in English; although much of the content had been lost on him, he had learnt the value of a casual manner. In eastern Europe the mere sight of a microphone made people strike a pose and burst into oratory; tired clichés were woven into endless sentences, mixed metaphors exploded bombastically. Most broadcasters talked down to their audiences, most listeners

26

despised the broadcasters and believed the exact opposite of what they said. Under the circumstances a conversational manner had great propaganda value.

"The invasion of Bessarabia only leaves Rumania between the Red Army and ourselves. Rumania will be taken, next week, next month or the month after. Now if you look at the map——"

He quoted distances, routes, the respective chances of strong German resistance and equally strong Rumanian efforts to secure a separate peace. Impromptu analysis was his strong point.

"You'll be told again and again that we share a common destiny with Germany, and just for once the official line happens to be correct. Germany is losing the war, and the way things are going we'll certainly share her total collapse. The past year tells its own story. Think for yourself and you'll know what to do."

Gitta followed with the news. After all these months, the first few words still cost her an effort: the studio had no recording equipment and she kept wondering what her voice sounded like.

When the red light went out, Pali patted the microphone. "What a shame to have to stop now when we're getting into our stride," he said. "You no longer breathe in the middle of a long word and I'm beginning to get the hang of commentary writing. Damn."

"Besides, our listeners! Last week three people asked me whether I ever listened to the Voice of Freedom—they said it's really good."

"What did you answer?"

"The truth—never heard it in my life. Then I started wondering whether they would recognize my voice."

"Not when they see you in the flesh. You sound so different from what you look like, nobody could identify you easily. You sound lean, mature, bespectacled. . . ."

". . . and I look fat, dumb and immature. . . ."

"If that's the way you see yourself——"

They returned to the overheated room. There was nothing to dispose of; the shelves only contained standard reference books, the desk drawers were empty. Pali put their scripts in an envelope and burnt the monitored material in the stove, stirring the ashes into the embers. At the door he handed the envelope to the tall soldier.

"Put it where the others are, János."

"Sure. They're keeping nice and dry under the potatoes."

27

"Fine. I think you'd better go, both of you. Report back to Captain Bajó, he'll tell you what to do."

They strolled out into the dark street. A short cloudburst had left the pavement shiny; a warm breeze blew along the canyons of houses, rustling like a flight of silk scarves. The air was sharp and spicy, carrying a whiff of petrol and a touch of staleness, as if the windows of every unaired, overheated room in town had been opened at the same moment.

"It smells of spring," Gitta said.

"It smells of decay, decomposition, epidemics. Oh, I know, decomposition is also a part of spring, although one shouldn't mention it. But then you're a lyrical writer, I prefer leaders and commentaries."

She smiled and nestled her elbow in his cupped hand. The spring evening filled her with exultation. This was the time of year when being alive became an absorbing activity, when a mysterious rhythm which she felt sure was that of the cosmos ran through her body so powerfully that she stretched out her fingers like so many antennae to receive the invisible waves. It was the kind of evening that normally sent her on long walks along the Danube, sometimes half-running under the chestnut trees with sheer joy. She held her face into the ambiguous breeze.

"No, it's not epidemics," she murmured. "Snowdrops, one fat blue crocus blowing up and then bursting like a balloon, white narcissi with red eyes, oh, I don't care, it's spring, it's starting now. Perhaps Mihály was wrong, you know what a Cassandra he is, perhaps they aren't coming in at all."

"You and your elemental outbursts! One minute it's politics, I can hear your little brain ticking over at the double, the next moment you take a couple of sniffs when there's nothing worth sniffing in the air, and off you go in a spring rapture, Germans or no Germans. Basically you're right. It should be a real spring."

"This is as real as it'll ever be," she said dreamily.

Pali chuckled. In spite of her quick, logical mind, Gitta's blind spot was very blind indeed, he thought. She was far ahead of her years, grasping ideas quickly and commanding a sabre-sharp technique of argument. It was only in relation to her own self that she was backward, boyish rather than feminine, gravely polite like a medieval page and so obviously pure of heart that in her presence doubtful stories remained untold even at free-speaking café tables.

28

Strange child, Pali thought, doesn't she notice? For months now they had been close companions, meeting every day in a mood of intimate understanding that thrived on half-sentences and shared thoughts; she was closer to him than anyone else and he had waited for her to realize just what this closeness implied, and yet here she was, sailing into spring on his arm without noticing that he loved her.

The tram stop was around the corner. He bought a bunch of violets from an old woman and pinned it on Gitta's coat.

"See you after dinner. And not a word to your mother about this latest thing. Tell her you may be late."

The tram arrived, clanging, rattling, vibrating in every joint. She waved from the platform and watched him getting swallowed up in the dark, a slim, hatless figure in a belted raincoat.

"I don't believe it," Mihály cried, hitting the piano with both fists. "Even if the Government is hopeless and the Army is stuck in Russia and nobody is properly organized, we can't be occupied just like that."

"Who brought the news, you or I? Considering the number of times it has happened to other countries, I don't understand your surprise," Pali said. Gitta stared at the floor, squatting against the round pillar that divided the long room into two. Mihály, who had shed half his age with his uniform and now looked absurdly young, all fair hair and long, thin neck, walked up and down unhappily, bristling against Pali's composure. Living at a high pitch of intensity, he had no shell to protect him from the world, and when disaster came he took its full impact. Compromise was impossible, life meant little if it was not worth living, the second-best was worse than nothing. The possibility of a German occupation filled him with rage and personal shame.

"If you're hoping for a national uprising or wild resistance, forget it," Pali said. "There won't be any. Isolated incidents perhaps, but nothing to go down in history."

"Why not? Less than a hundred years ago we showed the world how to make a revolution."

"I was afraid you would use that argument. Well, it won't happen now. Don't judge by ourselves. We're maniacs about principles, and there must be many others like ourselves all over the country, but the majority are indifferent. This war isn't their war. The moral

29

climate is wrong for action, it's been wrong for years. People are so used to double-crossing the authorities and being clever and managing nicely on the quiet that you can't expect them to turn into heroes overnight."

"An awful lot of people get profoundly moved at the sight of the national flag," Mihály snapped. "If half of them did something definite——"

"They won't. They won't even realize that once the Germans arrive they might just as well burn the flag. And the mast, too. But look, supposing the Germans arrive tomorrow, what do we personally do?"

"The first question is whether they get us or not," Gitta said. "They certainly know about the radio. Whether they can trace us is a different matter."

"We've received many protests against the radio at the Ministry," Mihály said, "rather strong ones, too. I had them filed and then sent memos to the wrong people. That side is covered. They'll pounce upon the transmitter, but that in itself doesn't give us away."

"And if they still catch us?" Gitta insisted.

"We'll deny everything," Pali said. "The most important thing is to have plausible occupations and good alibis. Mihály is all right at the Ministry, my medical grading protects me from the Army, although I've never felt fitter in my life, and working for my finals is another excuse. And, believe it or not, I even have enough money to last me for a while."

"If this goes on much longer, you'll be the oldest man ever to sit for exams. But supposing they don't catch us, what are we going to do?"

"It's no use making plans. We must live from day to day and do what we can, without hope or heroics. Mihály will despise me for this but I'll do my damnedest best to keep out of concentration camps. Seriously. 'Behold,' " he quoted, " 'I send you forth as sheep in the midst of wolves: be ye therefore wise as serpents, and harmless as doves. But beware of men: for they will deliver you up to the councils, and they will scourge you in their synagogues; and ye shall be brought before governors and kings.' Now if you read Gestapo cellars for synagogues and gauleiters for kings, you'll see how excellent the New Testament is—immensely adaptable to contemporary wconditions, especially in small countries."

"But even serpents and doves can get organized," Mihály said unhappily. "Why don't we link up with the opposition parties? Or the Communist underground? And if the studio really becomes useless, why can't we have a mobile transmitter?"

"Any radio technician will tell you just how long it would remain mobile under the circumstances. And I don't want to link up with anybody at present. The opposition parties, worthy as they are, talk much and do little. And I refuse to get involved with the Communists. I'd rather have my democracy the Western way. What's the use of curing a cold if you catch cholera instead?"

The telephone rang three times, stopped, rang again. Pali lifted the receiver. He frowned, said: "Yes, we can leave at once," and rang off.

"Any news?" Gitta asked.

"We must dismantle the studio tonight. The others are on their way. Mihály, you'll come with me."

"May I come, too?" Gitta asked.

"No, we'll take you home first. There's no hurry, the boys only want us to supervise the final effect. How sad—ashes to ashes, studio back into bathroom."

They strolled down to the river in the keen wind that blew the words back into their mouths. The Chain Bridge was deserted. Pali began to hum, the others joined in and they sang all the way, going through their entire opposition repertoire to let off steam. They sang Tipperary, Auld Lang Syne, John Brown's Body, the Marseillaise, and as a reluctant gesture to the anti-Nazi alliance, the Volga Boat Song. But none of the occasional passers-by paid them any attention, and Pali kept wondering whether anybody would have recognized Auld Lang Syne as a political manifestation.

CHAPTER THREE

~~~ooooooooooooooo~~~

On Sunday morning Mrs. Balogh woke up at eight and
began to plan her day at once. Unlike Gitta she woke
up quickly, completely and without distress. Night and
day were like intercommunicating rooms; she needed no
twilight passage to travel from one to the other. Sunday stretched
ahead, a fine, empty day waiting to be filled with action, with the
special chores Rozália could not or must not do.

Mrs. Balogh was a brilliant housewife who attacked domestic
problems with zeal and solved them with intelligence. Having lived
in many different settings, she could tackle almost any crisis. Her
upbringing had been erratic; as a young girl she had either been told
that the servants would look after everything and that she must on
no account ruin her hands by dipping them into cold water, or else
that she would never be able to control her own staff unless she knew
all about household work from the humblest job upward. Perfection-
ist by nature, she had followed the second principle, and as a young
wife she had run a large household and a trio of servants without a
hitch. Since her husband's death ten years before, the smaller flat and
one general maid had required less supervision, but war-time
difficulties made up for the difference, and Gitta was no help at all.

Gitta was undomesticated, uninterested, unwilling to learn.
Household problems and young men irritated her equally. She did
not seem anxious to get married or fall in love. She even hated
dances, partly on account of the pale pastel evening dresses that were
de rigueur for young girls; she said they made her look bulkier than
ever. But even recently when at long last she had agreed to go to a
ball, the evening had been a flop: Mrs. Balogh had found her
daughter discussing sociology with the scruffiest, most ineligible

32

young man in the whole glittering assembly, and she had felt like crying.

Gitta should have been born a boy, Mrs. Balogh reflected, deeply worried by her daughter's lack of girlish ambitions and her indifference to men. There had been an innocent but distressing episode with a married man which Mrs. Balogh still remembered with anger. Since then Gitta had become worse, spending all her leisure reading, writing and listening to music.

And, more recently, meddling in politics. That was the last straw, Mrs. Balogh thought, getting out of bed; although of course she knew she could not stop Gitta from putting the right principles into practice. Yet sometimes, listening to her voice on the Freedom Radio, a stiff, clear voice, as serious and youthfully pompous as the intent face that went with it, she felt alarmed at her child's illegal activities and would have liked to slap her in motherly indignation.

She opened the window and pushed the Venetian shutter outward. The grey spring morning was thick with silence, except for the distant rumble of heavy vehicles crossing a bridge. The leafless trees in the park stood out in clear black patterns, the freshly dug flowerbeds were the colour of cooking chocolate. If all went well, she thought, the china dinner service and the best glasses could be moved to the cellar before late afternoon.

The telephone rang ten minutes later. Pali apologized for the early call, he had to speak to Gitta, it could not wait.

"But she's still asleep! She gets so nasty if I waken her before nine on a Sunday!"

"Never mind, she won't be nasty for long."

Resentfully she entered her daughter's room. More resentfully she saw her come to life at the mention of Pali's name and rush to the telephone in abnormal animation.

"Yes? What's happened, Pali?" she asked.

"They're here."

"I see." She took it calmly, like a dreamer who accepts a flying locomotive or a talking rock as a matter of course. "Well, it's not entirely unexpected. Can we meet?"

"Not now. I want you to go out and look around. We'll need a story—you know, Budapest in the spring, atmospheric but factual. Be at home by two and wait for me."

"Please, Pali, I'd like to——"

33

"Good-bye. See you later."

She replaced the receiver disconsolately. How was she to wait until the afternoon?

"Well, what is it?"

"We've been occupied by the Germans."

Mrs. Balogh's eyes grew big, her lips narrowed into a white line. For once she had no answer to a situation. Gitta looked stubbornly at the carpet. She felt that at least one of them should remain unemotional.

"It's been in the air for some time now," she said. "They'll go out again, they'll have to, it's just a matter of time."

"And meanwhile? What about the Jews, the Poles, the escaped French prisoners of war, all of us except the Nazis? What's going to happen to us all? Oh, this poor, wretched country, being stabbed in the back once again!"

Mrs. Balogh blew her nose. She felt outraged on the one hand, frightened on the other. Being a person of strong habits, she had come to terms with the local version of the war; her attitude had been scornful, angry, indignant, but not entirely pessimistic, since the cataclysm had not affected her immediate environment. Now that the storm had forced the door open, her latent patriotism, individual pride and hatred for the Nazis fused into one catastrophic emotion, and when Gitta caught her in her arms, she was sobbing loudly.

They held each other for a while in the quiet room. Gitta felt relieved. At last the situation was clear, with all the cards on the table. The uneasy ambiguous spell had ended, there was no more need to wonder whether the Government would break away from the Axis or sink deeper into it. A real, tangible occupation presented real, tangible problems.

Mrs. Balogh wiped her eyes. "We'd better get dressed," she said tearfully. "It's half-past eight and God knows what else may happen today."

She sent Gitta off to the bathroom and went to the kitchen. "Good morning, Rozália, terrible news," she said. "The Germans have occupied the country."

The maid gave her an insolent look. "Good morning, madam. I know. The baker told me when he brought the bread rolls."

"It's a tragedy! These beastly Nazis, how I loathe them."

34

"At least they're Christians, madam."

"Are they indeed? Now look, I won't have any nonsense in my house," Mrs. Balogh cried, "and if you don't like my views you can leave at once."

"Please don't be angry, madam. Everything is ready except the coffee."

"I'm not angry," Mrs. Balogh said furiously. The threat of losing the maid was more than she could bear. "I only expect more common sense from you. We'll have breakfast at nine and lunch at one, so that you can get away early."

Breakfast was constantly disturbed. The telephone did not stop ringing; eventually Mrs. Balogh moved it to the table and sipped her coffee between bursts of conversation. Friends appeared on the line in quick succession—it was like holding a reception for disembodied voices coming from untidy rooms with unmade beds and half-drawn curtains.

Few callers had any information to pass on. They wanted to know whether she had heard, what she thought, what she would do, what it would mean in the long run. Questions and answers flashed to and fro, smoothly worded in the fashionable code language that never called a spade a spade and could express any views and rumours without using one incriminating word.

Gitta finished eating and left the room. Her mother found her fully dressed in the hall.

"You aren't going out, are you? This is no time for a young girl to be out on her own!"

"There must be thousands of people in the street. If they can——"

"You'd better lie low for a while, you little fool. Supposing they're after you and the boys?"

"Then they'll find me here even sooner. Don't overrate us, though, I daresay we're very small fry. Anyhow, I must go out. I'll be back for lunch. And Pali will drop in at two—you don't mind, do you?"

The street was quiet. Two small boys in navy school uniforms ran towards the church on the corner. The park resounded with birdsong. Gitta turned into a side street. The houses wore an air of Sunday blankness: the Italian restaurant, the cobbler's shop, the wigmaker's workshop, the coal merchant's padlocked basement, the seedy night club all looked deserted and unchanged. The change began at the next corner. German cars and lorries surrounded the big hotel, S.S.-men swarmed through the revolving doors, the pavement was covered with large crates and office furniture. The ground-floor tea room where Gitta used to dance on Saturday afternoons was being emptied of its red plush and gilt furniture. It seemed unwise to stop and stare. She walked down the broad street towards the Elizabeth Bridge.

She had expected large crowds but the streets looked no busier than on an ordinary Sunday. There were small German units everywhere, keeping to the middle of the road. Few of them measured up to Gitta's expectations. In the past visiting troops had strolled around with the steely splendour of German warriors on propaganda posters; these troops seemed second-hand, short, thin youngsters with badly modelled features and darting eyes, ill-tempered rather than ferocious.

It hurt to see them rounding corners and eyeing shop windows with the air of new-comers who intend to stay. She preferred to look at the people around her. Strange faces were a secret writing waiting to be deciphered: often she could sense the true person behind the façade, the microcosmos within the shell of flesh and bone. It was no pleasant experience and she submitted to it as if to a short illness that left one sad and exhausted. Faces floated past her, flashing signals of despair, fury, meanness, frustration or indifference; faces that complained, accused or sulked. Overcome once more by this clarity of vision, she moved on like a sleepwalker, battered by other people's emotions. A dumpy woman, standing forlornly with two Semitic children, sent forth waves of animal fear. A soldier's face was rigid with contempt. He limped badly and had the faded look of those who had grown old before growing up; there were many like him, veterans of the Eastern front. Gitta saw him turn, stare and spit: a few men in green shirts and black breeches, bedecked with Arrow Cross emblems, were cheering some Germans who looked away and marched on without taking any notice.

Gitta felt cold, sick and lonely. She longed to slip her hand into Pali's and hold on to him for comfort; she could not believe that a foreign military occupation could happen so smoothly and unsensationally under one's very eyes.

Sweet country, sacred land of heroes, the posy on God's hat (since God, of course, was Hungarian), what next? The thread of history had snapped; this could only be a vile extra-curricular mistake.

36

History was full of heroes, martyrs, champions, brave women, courageous mothers, a congregation of splendid ghosts whose reflected glory made even the worst calamities look moving and sadly noble. But this was different, this was all wrong, not a barricade, not a shot or the dry swish of a sabre; no virile voice to shout "Let life perish if honour can be saved!" or words to that effect, the improvised slogans that make history. Gitta swallowed hard. The currency of flag-waving patriotism had been devalued in one morning, the official brand of veneration for one's country, dished out at school and at innumerable public functions, made no more sense. In future one might have to cheat, lie, kill and commit all kinds of crime out of patriotism, but one must not talk about it ever again.

Somebody touched her arm. "Oh, good," Marta said, an elegant, well-made-up Marta looking so different from her class-room self that Gitta blinked twice before getting her into focus, "I was wondering where to get in touch with you. I've run away from home and it's marvellous. Come this way."

She led the way to the river and did not stop until they reached the cobbled lower quay, separated from the riverside road by a wall. They were alone. Marta held out her cigarette case.

"Thanks, I don't smoke. Mother's dead against it."

"What a baby you are. I suppose my family would rather have me smoke opium if only I conformed otherwise. Well, listen. Yesterday Papa hardly spoke to me at all and I kept quiet, too. In the afternoon he got the wind up about the occupation—somebody had sent a code warning from Austria—and he worked himself up into a terrible state. He must have realized that to be occupied isn't quite the thing."

"Thank goodness for that!"

"You don't know Papa. This morning he declared that much as he deplored the occupation, it was the lesser evil, and the sooner we won the war, the faster our allies would go home."

"Our allies have already earmarked this country as their permanent soya-growing colony."

"Quite. So I blew my top and stalked out. It felt great."

"And where will you stay?"

"At my aunt's. She's the family rebel but her pedigree is stupendous and Papa loathes and respects her. I can also stay with Gyuri, my boy friend, he has plenty of room."

37

"You can't do that. There would be a frightful scandal if your parents found out. Or do you want to marry him?"

Marta sat down on an iron bollard near the water's edge. The Danube looked sluggish and disconsolate, as if the dull green water had grown tired of reflecting the sky. She threw her cigarette in the water.

"No, I don't. I want to be free, not tied down again in a different way. Besides, Gyuri is a Catholic with four Jewish grandparents which technically turns him into a Jew, too. Not only can't we marry, we aren't even supposed to have an affair. The law about race pollution, you know."

"You do complicate your life, don't you?" Gitta asked, suppressing her shock. "Now that the Nazis are here he'll be in trouble."

"Oh, I'll try and get him out of it somehow. But look here, I didn't mean to discuss my family woes with you. I want to work with you."

"Work with me? What on?"

Marta peered around. They were alone. "This is the Voice of Freedom," she said teasingly. "Here's the truth behind the news."

"What's that?"

"Come, come. I was one of your devoted listeners. I think you did a fine job. Will you be able to carry on with it?"

"I don't know what you mean."

"Don't be silly. All these months at the convent I've heard you talking, reading aloud, reciting poetry. Believe me, it wasn't difficult to recognize your voice on the wireless."

"All right, you win," Gitta shrugged. In spite of the shock she felt rather pleased. "And where do we go from here?"

"I want to join your group. You'll need more people now."

"I haven't had my own instructions yet."

"Pass me on to your chief, then. Oh, I don't want to embarrass you, you obviously don't know what to say. Never mind, tell me when to contact you and I'll obey, just to show you how disciplined I am."

Gitta tried to think. Pali had once explained how the cell system worked, but this situation did not fit the theory: Marta knew too much, she herself knew too little.

"Go to the *confiserie* in University Street at five today," she said at last. "I'll try to arrange a meeting. If we don't turn up until five-thirty——"

"Fair enough. Meanwhile I'll enjoy my independence. You see, I've been wanting to join you for some time now; that's why I dragged you along yesterday to *notre Mère*. I wanted to make my views quite clear so that your people should trust me in spite of Papa. Well, do your best for me."

They parted at an obscure restaurant that sent whiffs of brown ale and paprika sausages through its open door. "I've never eaten out on my own—what a gloriously sordid place!" Marta said, stepping inside like an alert explorer.

Gitta hurried home and found her mother in the drawing-room. "What's going on?"

"Depressingly little. There are Germans everywhere and the people just watch them. Did you listen to the news?"

"Of course. Nobody said anything. They can't possibly know yet."

"They" always meant the forbidden stations. The local radio annoyed Mrs. Balogh so much that she never listened to it.

"I've had a flood of visitors," she went on. "That silly Suzy Tóth dropped in and made me quite cross: she'd been so sure about the American occupation that she'd got herself a new dress and a perm —frivolous hen. Still, I can't help liking her. The Weiners came next, then Nora, then old Mrs. Blum. Rozália looked most disapproving. The poor things all fear the worst. I told them it couldn't last very long but they all know how little time it takes to die. I almost burst into tears. They want us to keep things for them. Look, here they are. . . ."

She opened the steel strong-box that served as her home safe for documents, jewellery, a few unset gems, Gitta's baby teeth and snippings of her golden hair. Now the box was full of unfamiliar objects which she unwrapped from layers of tissue paper: several gold cigarette cases and men's watches, a platinum bracelet set with emeralds, a pearl necklace, a roll of golden sovereigns, several rings and pendants.

"Good Lord, this is worth a fortune!"

"Not quite that. The poor things want to have something tucked away. They have no illusions about being able to keep their property. The Weiners will also bring along some cameras and rugs."

"Good idea, except that it's a frightful responsibility. Supposing we're bombed out?"

"Now don't you start again. I'll keep their stuff together with our own, no preferential treatment. I can't do more, can I?"

In spite of everything, lunch was excellent. Under Mrs. Balogh's guidance Rozália had shed the coarser characteristics of provincial cooking and she no longer drowned their food in spicy fat. She served giblet soup with small liver dumplings, tender chicken fried in blond breadcrumbs with new potatoes and home-bottled French beans. The chocolate *gâteau*, bristling with sliced almonds, was flat in the middle, Mrs. Balogh complained, but clearly her mind was not on the food and she only grumbled to create an air of normality. Gitta watched her with a surge of affection. Her mother was rising to the situation splendidly.

Pali arrived in time for coffee. He looked subdued and drank four small cups of strong mocha in quick succession.

"Well? Tell us everything," Mrs. Balogh said eagerly.

"We're in a mess. No, I don't mean us personally, at least not yet. We dismantled the studio completely last night, our chief technician even got an army van to remove the equipment. The transmitter was taken this morning. Mihály had sent out his two privates with faked orders to guard it. The Germans appeared at eight. They inspected the orders which they didn't understand, they talked a great deal which our soldiers didn't understand, then they signalled to the boys to clear out, which they did."

"Thank heavens for that," Mrs. Balogh sighed. "I hope you aren't going to use the studio premises again?"

"I don't know. It's a handy place."

"Children, do be careful. You don't know how it's going to end."

"We can make a pretty shrewd guess. The Gestapo headquarters is being established in your favourite hotel round the corner. This is going to be a thrilling neighbourhood."

"The devil take them all!"

"Oh, he will, but he may take us first. I gather the arrests have already started; suicides too. It's you who should be careful. Don't leave anything dangerous about. I don't trust your maid, she looks stupid and stubborn, a natural Nazi. Do you pay her well?"

"Far too well. And she gets presents on top of it. I know that a servant can be one's paid enemy, but what am I to do? I don't think there's anything dangerous here."

"Your wireless is permanently tuned in to the B.B.C." He twirled

40

the knobs and switches into a harmless position. "And that?" A smiling double portrait of the Windsors hung on the wall in a gilt frame.

"I'm a romantic," Mrs. Balogh said indignantly, "and theirs was a beautiful love story. I think they're wonderful."

"We happen to be officially at war with Britain. I'd remove that picture for the time being."

"Never," Mrs. Balogh said defiantly.

Pali shrugged. "What about your den?" he asked Gitta. "Still full of enemy propaganda?"

"Oh no, only Baden-Powell's photograph and that framed poem my pen friend sent me." The poem was "If", printed in red and blue Gothic type. Alongside the text there was a drawing of a young pilgrim, staff in one hand, lantern in the other, bravely climbing uphill.

"Bless your heart, stop being naïve. There will be enough trouble without inviting it. Put away your souvenirs for the time being."

"All right, I'll think about it." Mrs. Balogh did not resent Pali's stern tone but she felt unable to share his alarm. She did not see why any stranger should ever enter her flat and criticize her wall decorations.

"Don't leave it too long. Come on, little one, we've some work to do."

Gitta led him to her room. She put the typewriter on her desk and squeezed herself into the seat. "This time I suppose you'll do the news and I can do the commentary," she said wistfully.

"That's exactly what we're going to do."

"Hurray! Have we got a mobile transmitter after all?"

"No, my pet. I told you there wouldn't be one. All we have is a boy from the Polish underground who is off to Sweden tonight and I want him to take an eye-witness account to Stockholm."

"How is he going to get there?"

"Leave that to him. He seems quite happy about it."

She was ready to type but he grinned and shook his head. "You remind me of the Children's Crusade sitting in that outgrown desk, doing your first big story that'll appear in Swedish, without by-line, payment or complimentary copy. Bad luck. Never mind, one day you may do better. Right. The Voice of Freedom speaking from the mousetrap."

"Good title. Shall I put it down?"

41

"Please yourself. It may not sound so good in Swedish. By the way, you'll have to translate the text into English to save time at the other end. Can you do that?"

"Of course," she said indignantly. "But try and use short sentences."

He dictated a fair amount of information. At least nine German divisions in the country. All airfields taken. The Gestapo arrests several members of the Upper House, a number of deputies. The Prime Minister escapes. According to a German spokesman, Hungary's role is determined by her geographical position (an original observation, he added under his breath). The Gestapo H.Q. is being set up in the city centre. Isolated incidents reported from several military barracks. No large-scale resistance.

"That's all. We'll spare them the rumours, though they're a lot more interesting than the facts. Your turn."

"What do you want me to do?"

"The commentary. Why did I send you out at the crack of dawn? Put down your impressions and comments."

"Don't be silly. Who am I to make comments?"

"Make them on behalf of the resistance movement, junior branch."

"And how am I to know what the resistance movement thinks?"

"Listen, my little idiot, we are the resistance movement. We belong to it. I thought you knew. The trouble is, you always expect things to happen correctly, with introductions all round. Well, this is it and I'm afraid you'll have to get cracking."

It took her ten minutes to write her piece, an hour to translate both texts. She typed the final version on thin paper without margins or paragraphs to save space, wondering what the Swedes would make of it. While waiting for Mihály, she told Pali about Marta who would soon be waiting in the *confiserie*, smoking nervously against a background of infinite sweetness.

"Do you trust her?" he asked when she had finished.

"I do."

"Do you like her?"

"Oh yes. She's the kind of person I'd like to be. She seems to enjoy being herself."

"Don't you? I enjoy you being yourself. All right, let's have a look at her. The family set-up sounds gorgeous."

Mihály arrived, looking tense and haggard. He hid the typescript

42

in his wallet. No, he did not mind if they went to the *confiserie*. A new girl? Let her join. They were short of girls and girls made excellent decoy ducks.

So they trooped down to the *confiserie*, a venerable place with wood panelling and marble-topped tables that made girls giggle with shock when their bare elbows touched the cold surface; a place where generations of schoolchildren had enjoyed their end of term treat, gobbling down terrifying numbers of cakes with the still, solemn air they had assumed for the school festival and now found difficult to shed. The place had its traditions. Girls who were too young to be seen in coffee-houses went there to meet their admirers over a coffee and a *mille-feuilles*. Married women frequented it to exchange whispered gossip or to complain about their husbands. It was a sweet, frivolous place, extra-territorial behind its barricades of *gâteaux*, *éclairs*, *petits-fours* and *tête-de-nègre* cakes, an old-world sanctuary where a malicious tongue and a sweet tooth qualified as virtues.

They found Marta at a corner table, well away from the other customers. The *confiserie* was beginning to fill up: a noisy group came in from the street followed by a couple, two soldiers, a mother with three small sons. They all talked in loud Sunday-afternoon voices; the scent of the cakes hung overhead like a gossamer curtain of vanilla, chocolate and mocha.

"Gitta told me about you," Pali began. "Why do you want to join us?"

"I can't very well resist the Nazis all on my own. And I must do something or burst."

Pali dug his fork into a rum *gâteau*. "Supposing I tell you that there's nothing to do except wait for things to blow over?"

Oh dear, Gitta thought, he doesn't like her. She glanced at Mihály: he contemplated Marta with the rapt attention of an art-lover confronted with the original of a masterpiece he had only known from bad copies.

"I wouldn't believe you for a moment. You may object to me on account of my father's views, in which case I'll link up with some other group or form one myself, but it would be a waste of time."

"For goodness' sake," Mihály said, "can't you see she's all right?"

"Don't rush me. I don't possess your intuition."

Gitta blinked nervously: she resented any attack on Pali's

43

authority. But Pali played absently with his napkin, leaving Mihály to watch Marta's perfect face and slow smile that made her cat's eyes shine as if lamps had been lit behind them.

"I gather you've run away from home. What are your plans?"

"At present I'm staying with my aunt, Hanna Morelli, but I'll look for a place of my own."

"I'd like you to return home."

"Certainly not. Didn't Gitta explain? I'm free at last and I intend to remain so. That's my private life, anyhow."

"Not as private as all that. You don't seriously think your parents will let you get away so easily? What's more, at home you'd be able to collect information."

"You don't want her to spy on her parents?" Mihály protested.

Marta laughed. "Spying? Impossible. Papa and his friends can hardly wait to pass on their confidential news. Oh, but I don't want to go home. It's marvellous to be free at last."

"Freedom isn't as simple as that," Pali said. "It must come from inside so that even living at home makes no difference to it. As long as you're on the run we can't use you. Illegal work needs a foolproof façade. We can't afford to slip up on your father or the family detective screening you."

"Bother. Gitta, what do you think?"

"Pali is right. Why can't you stay permanently with your aunt?"

"I wouldn't like that. I'll have to think it over."

"You do that," Pali agreed, "and let me know. Oh, look! Here we go."

Four German soldiers marched in. Conversation died away like music on a running-down gramophone. A waitress dropped a plate. Unperturbed by the stir they had created, the soldiers conducted their visit with precision: placing their caps on an empty table, they went to the counter and ordered coffee and three pastries each. They ate and drank earnestly, exchanged a glance and ordered the same again.

"Swine. They've come a long way to eat pastries," Marta growled. "Shall I throw a glass of water at them?"

"If you must, do. We can always say it's a traditional welcome based on a fertility rite."

"I'd like to throw something else," Mihály said darkly.

"That stuff isn't available yet. Save up your primary emotions."

44

The carved clock struck twice. Slowly voices rose among the tables. The couple at the neighbouring table paid and hurried away. A girl turned her back on her companions to stare at the Germans. The family group returned to the pleasures of eating, elbows propped up, thick pink tongues removing the last sweet morsel from every fork-prong. The small collision between history and Sunday normality had passed, without affecting either.

Pali and his companions left. Mihály strode away to meet the Polish courier who would be waiting for him in the University Church at six.

"What about you?" Pali asked Marta.

"I'll ask Aunt Hanna to negotiate with Papa. If he agrees to certain conditions, I'll return home tomorrow. You're right, I'd be an awful nuisance if Papa decided to track me down."

They watched her walk down the darkening street, an elegant figure, her hips rotating to a fine rhythm. "Well, what do you think?" Gitta asked Pali. This was like presenting a capricious child to a stern judge.

"She may be extremely useful but I wouldn't choose her as a close friend."

"Why not?"

"I don't know. Pure hunch. Still, whatever's wrong with her hardly concerns us. Don't frown, little one, she'll do."

That night Pali sat up late in his flat, drinking brandy and getting colder and more sober with every sip. He tried not to worry about the Freedom Radio: if the next day or two brought no surprise, there was nothing to fear. And then? The rest was in shadow. He wanted to withdraw from everything, hibernate, hide or die. He drained his glass and picked up the *Discourses of Epictetus*. "If we are neither fools nor hypocrites," he read, "and all this be true, namely that good and evil depend on our own choice while nothing else matters, why do we then worry about anything? What can frighten us? Anytus and Meletus may kill me but they can do me no harm." He sighed. The crippled Phrygian slave of almost two thousand years ago knew how to comfort him.

The Baloghs listened to all the foreign stations they could get on the wireless. None of them mentioned Hungary and they felt more and more dejected. It was as if they had been finally cut off from the

45

rest of the world and nobody knew what was happening to them. At nine o'clock Mère Edwige rang and asked Mrs. Balogh not to send Gitta to the convent until further notice; she should, of course, carry on with her studies at home. Later Gitta stood at the window of her dark room, letting the night wind ruffle her hair. She felt determined and a little lost, like a child who sneaks out at night on some unspecified adventure with nothing but a small torch and a penknife to give her confidence.

Mihály lay awake half the night, thinking of Marta. Their meeting had shattered him: she shone behind his closed eyelids, in his bloodstream, in every heart-beat. This was final. She was the companion he had always longed for, the perfect partner incapable of treason. The world was full of betrayal. One needed a firm, unshakeable link to keep one from despair. Twenty-four hours earlier he would have gladly died in some brief, hopeless battle; now he wanted to go on living.

Marta lay still in Gyuri's arms. The room was dark except for the yellow glow of the lamp next door. His hand caressed her smooth neck and small ears, he murmured endearments into her hair, but she only felt triumph, the pleasure of achievement. For the first time ever there had been no need for them to make love early in the afternoon when she was supposed to attend a music lesson; she had stayed late, thinking more of her defeated father than of Gyuri. Still, it was time to return to her aunt's flat. Taxis were hard to get and she hated to walk in high heels.

CHAPTER FOUR

Countess Hanna Morelli saw the apparition early in the morning. She was in bed, a firm-fleshed, statuesque woman with masses of red-gold hair that surrounded her face in bold waves. Her enormous divan was a haven of well-being. Relaxation loosened the confines of her body, her muscular white arm was almost at one with the down pillow, her long legs were lost in the cool sheets. All her life Hanna had insisted on owning a large, luxurious bed, a last refuge to flee to, alone or in company, from the surrounding doom. She would rather have sat up all night than sleep on a single divan: a narrow bed was uncivilized, hardly better than a coffin. Her present divan was vast and beautiful, covered in an exotic damask; her silk eiderdown was wine red, her bed-linen richly embroidered. She had been sleeping alone for many weeks but the bed maintained its air of festive expectation.

Hanna's blue eyes, blond-lashed and round, were open, although she had only just begun to waken. The spell of peace and happiness was still unbroken, a precious, fragile state so quickly blurred by the first memory of all the sadness one had taken to one's sleep. She lay still, in complete repose. This was a precious moment, the kind of blissful halt that Hanna relished and collected as others collect first editions and rare coins. And then her nostrils dilated. She could feel a presence approaching.

The white monk appeared at the door, opposite the bed. Hanna's eyes fastened on him without alarm. He stood still, immensely dignified and lonely, a slim figure in a white habit, hood drawn over the eyes, arms folded. The pose had not changed since his first appearance on the eve of Hanna's sixteenth birthday, in the family chapel of her Austrian relations. Even then, almost thirty years ago, Hanna had received the apparition without fear. The next day her father had been killed in a riding accident.

The pattern never changed; all five subsequent visits of the white monk had been followed by a tragic event. Hanna, who combined lucid intelligence with respect for the supernatural, had come to regard her monk as a wise friend who, though unable to ward off catastrophes, could be relied upon for a warning.

She sat up slowly, pulling the bedclothes to her chin. Disembodied spirit though the monk was, she feared her nakedness might embarrass him. "Thank you for guarding me," her lips moved silently. "Who is it going to be this time?" The monk remained still. "Not Miklós?" He shook his head. "Perhaps I shouldn't ask questions," she wondered, "but you never come without reason. I suppose the things I want to do are risky, but there's no other choice!" The monk unfolded his arms. His long, almost transparent hand rose in greeting, then the tall outline dissolved.

Sinking back on her pillow, she shut her eyes in prayer. Being both religious and anti-clerical, she had worked out her private faith in a truly catholic taste. Her God was wise, understanding and universal, an expanding deity able to accommodate Jesus, Bacchus, Jehovah, Buddha and Osiris. Such an all-embracing God was easy to pray to: He had the right facet for every mood, every repented sin and despair. Now Hanna lent him the Gothic gentleness of the Amiens Christ and asked Him to help her bear whatever was coming. As long as Miklós did not die or discard her she was prepared to carry on.

She rose and forced herself through her morning ritual, splashing in the scented bath water, rubbing fragrant oil into her skin and brushing her incendiary hair until it crackled with sparks. Whatever links her soul had with the invisible world, Hanna believed in looking after her body.

After breakfast she settled down to do some thinking. Action was needed, and the monk's appearance had only strengthened her resolve. It was her niece Marta who had started this, her sudden appearance had been like an electric storm that had left Hanna disturbed and dissatisfied with her narrow life. But then she was an old-fashioned humanist who disliked action and feared violence. All her life she had felt that to build one's self, to strive towards some level of excellence and harm no one was as much as one could be expected to do: the rights and wrongs of human relationships alone were in-

48

tricate enough to take a lifetime of patient sorting out. All this remained true, yet she realized that passivity was no longer enough. Her carefully laid pattern was to be disturbed or destroyed; Goethe's collected works could no longer make up for the Third Reich.

She was fond of Marta, a rebel like herself, the latest dissenter to rise from the line of worthy Péterffy landowners, soldiers, politicians and courtiers, demanding freedom and self-expression. Hanna had won her own battle long ago. Now she was regarded as an eccentric, solely redeemed by the wealth and snob rating of her late Italian husband. But Marta was well on the way to victory, too; her father had agreed to grant her full independence provided she did not bring the family name into disrepute. Poor dear Lajos, Hanna thought, unable to refer to her brother without condescension—little did he realize that it was he who had brought the family name into total disgrace with his political blunders.

Hanna found Marta's new friends remarkable, a new breed developing independently of preceding generations. They seemed mature, wise and sound; also a little too resigned and dispassionate for their years, but how could one expect them to have illusions in times such as these?

After their first meeting Hanna had offered her services to the "cause", as she chose to call it, not noticing the pained expression of the young people who detested capital-letter terms, going so far as to make their rare religious references to Allah which sounded less solemn than God. But they had realized that Hanna's temperament needed verbal dramatics—flamboyance was a minor sin.

She had offered to put up eight Jews in her flat, should the need for hiding-places arise. Her villa in the Buda Hills was also available, but, as Marta had pointed out, in an emergency it was easier to get lost in a big city than escape from an isolated building. This reasoning had reminded Hanna of gangster films. Experienced hostess as she was, it had never occurred to her that hospitality must also include safe escape routes for one's guests.

She switched on the wireless. The B.B.C. came in as clear as a bell. "We appeal to all Hungarians to assist those who are persecuted by the Germans," a man's voice said. "Deny all help to the Nazis. Prove your national conscience, your humane feelings by helping all those who are persecuted for their political attitude or race."

"Of course," she said loudly, as if the voice had expected an

49

answer. To her non-technical mind the functioning of the wireless was more miraculous than the appearance of the white monk.

Leaning against his grand piano which he was using as a demonstration table, Pali shook the medicine bottle and held it against the light. The clouded liquid swirled around and burst into greenish bubbles. He poured a few drops on a used envelope and rubbed it with cotton wool.

"Look, no writing! All gone!"

"But it looks awfully stained and messy," Marta objected.

"Wait until it dries, you won't see a thing. The only snag is that the surface turns rough and unless you're careful the next lot of ink may run."

"But what's the purpose of it?" Mihály asked. "You can't erase one particular entry on a birth certificate—say, religion—and substitute something else, because you'll never match the ink or the handwriting."

"Of course not. The entire document must be cleansed and filled in afresh. Unfortunately the beastly ink they use in registry offices looks different from any other kind." He held up two more medicine bottles. "This is a genuine sample, I pinched it myself. But even stealing it by the gallon doesn't help, since it changes in time from deep black to greeny grey, and if we forge a birth certificate issued in, say, 1920, fresh ink may look fishy."

"Come on," Gitta said, "what's in the third bottle?"

Pali uncorked it and scribbled his address on the cleansed envelope.

"Perfect!" Mihály cried. "It looks like genuine old ink with traces of cobweb and rust. Brilliant work. Who are we to congratulate?"

"I found an extraordinary chemist who can produce this stuff in any quantity, together with the cleanser, which means that we can salvage any old document and fill it in with the right sort of name, religion and ancestry."

"That's fine for Jews who don't look it," Gitta said. "But if someone looks very Semitic it's no use changing Finkelstein into Forray and turning him into a Lutheran, together with his late parents."

"People who aren't helped by forged documents must hide. But we can't waste safe hide-outs on non-Aryans who look like Young Siegfried."

"And supposing we run out of cleansable forms?" Marta asked.

50

"Well, yes, that is a point. We can't give up our own papers because we may have to prove our own pedigrees one day. Do you realize that we must carry at least ten documents each, namely our birth certificate, plus birth and marriage certificates for our parents and both sets of grandparents? If only we knew someone who could forge blank forms."

"I've got it," Gitta said. "The cemeteries! People are buried according to their residential districts. If we look up recently deceased persons, we can get copies of their documents from the district registry offices and pass them on to people who tally in age and sex."

"You morbid child, what an admirable idea!" Pali beamed. "And how do we know that our chosen dead are—sorry, were—Aryans?"

"You can judge by their names, can't you?"

"To a certain extent. You may find that a man buried as Forray is in fact a late Finkelstein and therefore unsuitable. We'll risk that. But seriously, the things one is forced to do. This is hardly better than body-snatching."

"By the way," Mihály said, reluctantly shifting his eyes from Marta, "did you notice that all documents bear a serial number and a date at the bottom in tiny print? We mustn't register a 1925 birth on a form printed in 1930."

They nodded thoughtfully. Document forging seemed a fine art with many unexpected points. Marta took a bottle of brandy from her brief-case and handed it to Pali. "Let's have something drinkable at last," she suggested. "Documents are dry. I've had my fill of them. Papa got out ours last night and practically had a fit because he thought he'd discovered an undesirable ancestress."

"On whose side?"

"His own. His great-grandmother had a suspicious surname. Not quite Finkelstein but hardly better. And it occurred to him that perhaps she was not so much Transylvanian German as German Jewess. In those days the family was hard up and it stood to reason that they might have married money. Oh, we had real melodrama in the study. Papa scrutinized me and my brother for Semitic features, then he drove forty miles in the middle of the night to his mad uncle to find out the truth. Alas, no luck. The lady wasn't Jewish."

"You must be the only person in the land to regret not having a non-Aryan ancestor," Mihály said. "Why do you hate your father so much?"

She shrugged. "For a number of reasons. I want him to understand the accident of birth, and a Jewish great-grandmother would have been a good argument. I suppose I still want to save him in spite of himself. The more I think about him the more I feel that one ought to be born an orphan and thus avoid neurosis."

"That's a colossal subject," Pali said. "Let's save it up until after the war. We'll have a visitor any moment now and I want you to shut up about him. Officially he's a vet. We're going to work together."

"Curing sick pigs?" Marta asked.

"Yes. No. He's a British agent."

"At last!" Gitta exclaimed. "This is getting interesting. Does he look like Leslie Howard?"

The doorbell rang twice, then once more, Pali rose. "I hate to disappoint you, he doesn't. His name is Dr. Sas."

The middle-aged man who entered was thin and ugly in such an average way that it would have been hard to pick him out in a crowd. Amid his undefined features his small, hooded eyes looked bored. His clothes were shabby, his hands none too clean. He wore the preoccupied scowl of a busy man with no time to waste and nodded curtly to no one in particular. "That porter of yours," he said to Pali, "does he always hang about in the hall? He looks damn curious."

"Don't worry about him. A German soldier got his sister into trouble last year and since then he's been an ardent anti-Nazi."

"What about the back staircase?"

"The exit connects with the rear of a dairy. Quite easy to get out through there."

Dr. Sas grunted and accepted a drink. He glowered at the company and began to shoot questions at them in a cold, charmless manner. Pali, who had met him through a Yugoslav contact, watched the procedure with amusement. Dr. Sas was clearly determined to destroy the idea of the handsome secret agent who carries a gun and remembers to get flowers for the ladies. He spoke flawless Hungarian with barely a hint of an accent, but his slang was out of date. Obviously he was neither English nor Hungarian. The rest was anybody's guess.

Eventually he ran out of questions and surveyed them less malevolently. "You've been damn lucky to get away with your radio lark

—pure beginner's luck. The Nazis have probably expected more experienced characters than you. I suppose some wretched political prisoners have taken an extra hiding in your stead." He scratched his ear, creasing his face into a simian grimace. "I can see why you dislike the Nazis, but why the hell are you so devoted to the British? You don't know them, you've never been to England and you won't get anything out of this except a lot of trouble. The British will win all right, but you'll get no thanks. The British are snobs and you'll remain bloody foreigners to them even if you happen to have become bloody in their service."

"Let us have our weaknesses," Marta drawled. "Why do you work for them? Do you get well paid?"

"Leave me out of this. What I do is different."

"Quite!" Gitta was furious. "You're a professional, we're amateurs. We need some cause to be devoted to since we're against most things that go on. As our cook so wrongly says about the Germans, we've never had any trouble with the British. They may be snobs but then so are we in our own way. It's a pity you should be so unpleasant because we aren't impressed."

"You're a silly girl and you talk too much," Sas snapped.

Pali rubbed his hands. "Having successfully tried out one approach," he said ironically, "do you think we might get down to business? We're short of time, too."

"Make some decent coffee first. I don't get enough sleep and it begins to show."

He had plenty of work for them, he said, enough for twenty-four hours a day. He gave them a telephone alarm system with suitable code words, he set up a radio monitoring and typing service for postal propaganda, he explained the principles of document forging and ended up with a survey of the world situation. "In the end you may all have to skip down to Yugoslavia," he added. "One of you had better learn Serbian."

"That will be Gitta, our champion linguist," Pali said. "But when will she do it if she's to monitor, type, forge and act as courier as well?"

"We aren't on holiday," Sas muttered, taking up the subject of partisans. In spite of his unpalatable manner he was a good teacher and they listened to him with reluctant fascination. The heroic daydreams of adolescence were turning into reality, the romance of cops

53

and robbers and giant-killers was becoming a practical proposition, the only possible way to say "No". Then all of a sudden Sas broke off and asked them to go. He had some other business with Pali.

The other three left at once. Gitta shot off to the nearest cemetery to look for Aryan identities. Mihály took hold of Marta's arm and said: "Come to the river, let's count waves."

"I only do that when there's a gigantic crisis on."

"Life is a gigantic crisis. I love you and you don't love me. What's worse, you've no idea about yourself. You don't know who you are, nobody has observed or explained you and you live day by day, changing all the time, and it's all wasted. You need me to teach you to live. Tell me about yourself, I've twenty years to catch up with. Your voice is extraordinary, it's a cool water voice, it makes me thirsty."

She laughed and rubbed her shoulder against his arm but he did not put his arm round her waist. Things were not so simple as that. The cobbled street sloped, making her steps short and springy; she walked like a filly that longs to break into a gallop. A pair of ivory curtains billowed from a window. It was April. Across the street a dozen children were playing at air raids.

CHAPTER FIVE

～ↄↄↄↄↄↄↄↄↄↄↄↄↄↄↄↄↄↄↄↄↄↄↄↄ～

This was the height of spring. The growing days pushed the sky so high that even the winds rose to the upper regions, and sometimes the clouds raced wildly in the heights while the air below remained still. Warm showers were followed by mild breezes. The streets smelt moist and mysterious. The chestnut trees along the Danube held up their candles to light up lovers' faces, but the spring moon was in public disgrace, since clear, bright nights invariably meant heavy air raids.

Under the surface calm one lot of people were busy settling their affairs before committing suicide—"the only possible way to emigrate", one of them wrote in his farewell note; others were getting used to being frightened; a maladjusted minority scribbled denunciations to the Gestapo, seeking revenge for personal wrongs. There were many Gestapo establishments all over the city, several of them occupying former luxury hotels where even the night club premises were rumoured to overflow with prisoners.

The yellow stars of the Jews shone in the streets like daffodils. Some Jews who tried to cover up the brand-mark with a brief-case or a bent arm were threatened and insulted by German soldiers. And those who were not obliged to wear stars wore badges on their lapels, badges of political parties, groups, societies and fraternities, animal emblems, flags, crests and other symbols of allegiance to some collective body, because to stand alone was unbearable. One shop that normally sold paper lanterns and carnival masks cashed in on this collective trend by launching a general-purpose badge anybody could wear, since it did not signify anything. But even badges yielded little protection in the frequent street *razzias* in which passers-by had to prove their identities and their usefulness to the war effort.

Early in May Gitta received an official summons to report for war work, unless she was already in essential employment. Hanna immediately provided a suitable job. Ervin Wass, a lawyer friend of hers, needed a part-time secretary who had to be non-Jewish to be employable and anti-Nazi to be reliable. The lawyer himself was doing his war service at the Ministry of Justice, which automatically exempted his staff from war work.

Ervin was an excellent man, Hanna assured Gitta, an absolutely *comme il faut* person, a trifle dull but really charming, a man of taste. She felt sure Gitta would like him.

Gitta was more anxious that Ervin Wass should like her. To become a secretary at a moment's notice with no practical experience at all frightened her. How did one make a good impression? What did one say to one's first prospective employer? She went along to the interview in her best dress, wearing a little innocent make-up to give her confidence, but Ervin was too great a surprise and she was tongue-tied.

He was charming and courteous, offering her cigarettes, chocolates and a choice of liqueurs when she hardly knew how to sit gracefully in the deep armchair. The office was like a luxurious private study, with superb furniture, good paintings and oriental rugs; there was not one utilitarian touch anywhere, and she wondered whether his clients were worthy of the setting.

He ignored her shyness. There was little to do, he explained, but he needed someone round the place while he was wearing out his reserve officer's uniform at the Ministry, or calling on the firms for which he acted as legal adviser. Alas, he had been forced to dismiss his old, excellent secretary who was a Jewess; in fact, he had been fined for having employed her long after the closing date for the "cleaning up" of offices. Still, he was sending her money on the quiet; she needed it, poor girl.

He explained his work and office routine with an air of humorous modesty which suggested that he did not think much of his own activities. Were lawyers supposed to be dull? Everything about him, even the filing system, seemed novel. She had never thought an office could be run so pleasantly.

He was a lean, tall man with a boldly handsome face; forty, perhaps, but it was hard to tell. His hair was very fair, almost flaxen. He had light eyes and the golden tan of the inveterate sportsman who begins to row and play tennis a little before spring arrives. She watched and did not quite believe in him. Brought up without a father or any male relative, the only men she knew were under thirty. Really adult men of the more sophisticated kind were an unknown breed, of which Ervin seemed an attractive specimen. She accepted the job eagerly. This was a splendid alternative to packing ammunition in a factory.

After the first few days adjustment was easy, although she did not understand why anybody should pay her handsomely for doing so little in such luxurious surroundings. The simple secretarial work he left her every morning took an hour to do, and he was out most of the time. When he did appear, he made Turkish coffee for both of them and dictated one or two short letters. No clients came. Sometimes women telephoned in his absence, decidedly private callers wishing to leave no message. One of them spoke in a warm, caressing voice that Gitta associated with heady scents and daring clothes. Undoubtedly, her employer led an interesting life.

Confined to the office until the early afternoon, she got through an enormous amount of illegal work. Pali produced newsletters and anti-Nazi circulars which she typed, six copies at a time on thin paper, until her head swam. The real business started in the late afternoon. Dr. Sas kept them busy indeed.

One day she went out to the convent to see the Mother Superior. The garden gate was locked; after a brief wait, the doorkeeper beckoned her to the side entrance. There was singing in the chapel, thin, joyless singing in honour of the Virgin, the Queen of May. Once again, Gitta stood at the back, gazing at the Notre Dame Madonna's serene face under the massive crown, at her smooth Gothic brow and fine lips. In spite of the flowers and the golden candle-glow, the chapel looked wintry and dead, and she suddenly knew that she would never see it again, that Mère Edwige would no more analyse the texts of Xavier de Maistre or Mother Agnes talk about the lawns of England.

After the service she waited in the reception room, fighting her sadness. Two months had robbed the convent of its reality, another two months——

"*Mon enfant*, how brave of you to come and see us!" The Mother Superior's hand was hot and dry; she seemed to have shrunk even smaller. "We have had a great deal of trouble since the occupation. The Germans don't like us, I fear."

"What happened? Have they taken anybody away?"

"Oh no, no. But we have been investigated for a full week and questioned and cross-examined most horribly. They tried to make out that we were spies, especially poor Mother Agnes and myself. And of course my dear Agnes became a little angry and she started quoting Shakespeare, that beautiful passage. . . ." The pale forehead puckered, the small hand clung to Gitta's arm, and then the nun remembered the words and they came out in her sharply intoned Franco-English, ". . . 'and take upon 's the mystery of things, as if we were God's spies; and we'll wear out, in a wall'd prison'—well, you know the part I mean. One of the Germans understood enough English to pick up 'God's spies' and 'wall'd prison' and became even more suspicious. So in the end I showed him the quotation in the *Collected Works* and that put his mind at ease. Now we only have to report to the police every week."

"*Ma Mère*, aren't you thinking of going away from here?"

"Certainly not. We have no other home."

"But you are not safe here."

"Safe? We are safe anywhere. We can only die once. But I am not worried now. We have been investigated and I do not think we shall receive further attention. We are just silly old nuns out of touch with our own countries—why, I believe we should be more suspect in France and England than we are here, so the Germans could not even parachute us back there to make us spy for *them*. Imagine, old nuns floating around on parachutes! That is why I hope that we shall be left in peace. What about you, *ma petite*?"

"Nothing much, *ma Mère*. I have a job. And otherwise I do what I can. There is so much to do, one is driven by a sense of urgency, but sometimes everything looks utterly futile. David and Goliath is all very well, but a pebble can't do much in a landslide."

"Every effort counts, *mon enfant*."

Gitta shook her head. "I wonder. By the time we provide one Jew with suitable documents—why, yes, forged ones, of course— hundreds are being rounded up and taken away. One wants to do something big and effective and . . . one can't," she concluded lamely.

"David only had a sling," the nun said. "Go on providing people with papers and don't expect too much. You must do the best you can, here and now, nobody can expect more from you. I am glad you look so calm and determined. You have been happy here, haven't you?"

"Oh yes, very happy. It'll never be the same again. But it's only now that I know how happy I've been—why doesn't one ever know when it's actually happening? Why can't one be happy and be conscious of it? It's like being cheated," Gitta said vehemently, "the way things pass and the way one must look back at them to see what they were all about. Is one's whole life going to be like that?"

The old nun smiled and shook her head. To tell Gitta that what she wanted was only attainable in eternity seemed cruel.

"I am glad you lock your gate now," Gitta said to change the subject. "Not that it means much, but I hate to think of you all alone, with no one to help if you need protection."

"Oh, we are very careful now. We have some guests staying with us and they need privacy and quiet."

She wanted to hug the old nun and then scold her for being foolhardy. She could well imagine what kind of guests were hiding in the back of the building.

"*Ma Mère*," she begged, "promise me one thing. If anything happens, if for some reason you want to leave the convent or send your guests elsewhere, will you let me know at once?"

"Thank you, *ma petite*. I cannot promise anything, but I shall remember your kind offer. I am proud of you. Come again if you can. God bless you now, *bon courage*!"

Gitta curtsied and kissed the nun's hand. Passing through the garden she picked a dappled leathery leaf from an ornamental shrub and put it in her purse.

CHAPTER SIX

~~~ᴄᴄᴄᴄᴄᴄᴄ🌣ᴅᴅᴅᴅᴅᴅᴅᴅᴅ~~~

Hanna had been looking forward tremendously to the meeting. To put up Marta's lover and organize a hideout for him in the country was to be her first serious task and she wanted to fulfil it to perfection. Her need for action had pushed her into exaggerated preparations: the guest room was fit for royalty, with a pile of fresh English and Swiss books on the bedside table; she had got in special provisions and drinks and could hardly wait to receive her guest whom Marta had promised to bring along at four. Eventually she arrived at five, on her own.

"Oh, you're late," Hanna cried, "and where's your Gyuri?"

"I don't know. He's gone."

"Do you mean he isn't coming? Has he been taken away?"

"No, just gone. I'm sorry," Marta said, sinking into an armchair, "I don't understand it myself. We had a long talk yesterday, I explained our plan and told him not to hesitate any longer—he's supposed to report at the labour camp tomorrow morning, you know—and he agreed to come here with me today. When I went to fetch him he was gone. Here's the message he'd left."

Hanna read and re-read the note: "Gone away indefinitely. Please use the flat freely if you wish," and shook her head. "It doesn't make sense. Did you have a row yesterday? This note sounds very cold."

Marta looked away. "No, not a row, only a slight argument. I got a little angry with him; he didn't seem to grasp the situation and went on about purely theoretical difficulties when all he ought to have worried about was ordinary survival. He carried on about this business of having been brought up as a Catholic and now being pushed among the Jews with whom he has nothing in common, and when I said that to avoid the labour camp was more important than this hair-splitting, he rounded on me and accused me of being insensitive."

"But I'm afraid you are! And then?"

"Nothing much. Or rather quite a lot, but it was all so odd—I mean, there I was, trying to help him, and all he said was that he wanted no help from me because I didn't love him."

All right, perhaps I don't, she thought, but why rebel against it now? So far the affair had been civilized. Gyuri had accepted the need for furtive meetings and long separations, he had not missed the romantic props that normally lessen the tension between two strangers thrown together in the brutal intimacy of love, a link resting on assumption rather than experience; they had managed without long walks and sentimental meetings, without kisses in moonlight and music in small restaurants. Their physical and intellectual relationship had been perfect; why did he suddenly have to ask for more?

"Sometimes a caress and a bit of warmth are worth more than a battle plan," Hanna said, "but I don't think you understand that. There's something hard and perfect about you, something vaguely inhuman, and even if it's only a polished surface, it can be a bit chilling. I daresay you handled Gyuri the wrong way—otherwise he wouldn't have gone!"

But what was the right way? Marta wondered. How could she have given him what he needed without pretending? Men were impossible: they took things too seriously, wanting full emotional possession when all she wanted was to remain free, and they refused to understand.

It had always been the same, ever since the age of sixteen when she had her first brief affair with an Austrian boy who had come to stay with them in the country. She had quite liked him, he had adored her and almost killed himself when the time had come for him to leave. He still wrote to her from the Eastern front. She never replied. Even discounting the fact that he fought for the Germans, which made him as good as dead, there was nothing to say.

There had been others after him and before Gyuri. Family supervision could not stop her from having short affairs. She started them out of sheer curiosity and a sense of power, but nothing important happened, perhaps nothing ever would. The curiosity waned fast; all that remained was boredom, nausea, and a yearning for purity, for the white soaring of the spirit. So she broke off the affair and decided to wait for the real thing that was bound to come her way

61

some time, but the interval never lasted long, because the next man's admiration would rouse her curiosity, starting the vicious circle once more.

Sometimes she had two lovers at the same time without considering herself disloyal. She felt she could only be faithful to someone she really belonged to, and that was the one sensation she had never experienced. How could one break a non-existent link? The old tenets were untrue, a woman did not give herself to a man, a man did not take anything from a woman by seducing her. All that pious talk about surrender did not mean a thing. Love was a mutual conquest, a twofold effort like building a bridge from either side of an abyss in the hope of meeting in the middle, except that in her experience the meeting did not take place because her overwhelmed lovers were always building away in a different direction she could not accept, towards everlasting love, marriage, inseparability.

Gyuri had been different. Perhaps that was why the affair had lasted so long. Yet he, too, had wanted more than she could offer and had left her rather than continue on her terms.

What did love mean to other people? What did it mean to Mihály who pursued her with flowers and charming gifts, ignoring her emotional reserve and physical provocation? What did it mean to Pali and Gitta who seemed to have a close understanding and a personal code no one else could make out? Their souls must be wedded, Marta thought, because their bodies certainly aren't, yet that, too, looked like a kind of love.

"I don't blame Gyuri for vanishing," Hanna cried, annoyed by Marta's silence. "You're wrong. You can't discard one-half of a moral code and retain the other. If you choose free love, well and good, but then it must be both free and love, not just promiscuity coupled with the emotional coldness of a middle-class virgin! You worry me, you're going to end up as a man-eating neurotic. I understand Gyuri."

"I do, too, to a certain extent," Marta admitted. "But how can I help being what I am? All right, something is missing from my emotional make-up. What is it? And what can I do about it?"

"You can't love without submission. You must accept the other one completely and throw in your lot with him. More emotion, less logic, less of this odd reserve of yours that seems to say 'yes, but . . .' all the time."

"How can I submit to someone if he isn't my equal or superior to me? I know I sound like Mephistopheles and you may accuse me of devilish pride, but none of the men I knew was superior to me; in some respect or another I always had to find excuses for all of them. And so I went on saying 'yes, but . . .', sharing what we could and leaving the rest alone."

"Love is no duel, you know. You don't pit your strength against the other to see who wins!"

"I can't accept someone whom I vaguely despise because he's handsome but stupid, or makes social gaffes, or lacks intelligence or imagination, and all of them fell down on some point, making me feel ashamed of them. It was just as well that I had to keep my attachments secret. I've never met a man whom I could have proudly presented to the world as my own."

"My dear," Hanna said sadly, "you didn't love any of those men, you simply went to bed with them. And where did it get you? You're lonely and unhappy."

Marta swallowed hard. "And where did emotion and submission get you? Aren't you lonely and unhappy?"

"No, I'm not! Granted, if you count practical results, my approach got me nowhere. I'm forty-five, I've been a widow for ten years, men have caused me much sadness and I'm not getting any younger. And for a long time now I've been involved in an affair that looks catastrophic from the outside but keeps me happy in my own way. And I've been wildly happy in the past, happy without reservations, and that's the only result that counts. It may not sound a great deal to you, but to me it makes other things bearable. That sort of happiness piles up and stays fresh and I can draw on it whenever I feel like it. You need that sort of capital when you are no longer young. You won't understand it just yet. When I was your age, I didn't, either. I used to think that my elders had only themselves to blame for growing old. I felt sure they were guilty of negligence, and if they had taken more care they would have stayed young for ever. Well, I was wrong, although with care one can slow down the process."

"Come, come, you look wonderful."

"I'm glad you think so. You see, I don't worry any more. At one time I couldn't bear to look into the mirror, I dreaded to find a new wrinkle or to notice that my jaw-line had slackened a little more. It was dreadful but I accepted—here it is again—I accepted the fact that decay is a daily process and one must get used to it. The trouble is that the heart stays young long after one begins to tint one's hair."

"Why is your present affair so catastrophic?"

The pale, round eyes clouded over. How was she to explain what she herself hardly understood? "Miklós is wild and completely incalculable," she said. "He comes and goes as he pleases, I never know when I'll see him again. He's a bit like you, afraid of getting involved, but then in a man that sort of fear is more natural."

"Why do you put up with it?"

"Because I love him," Hanna said indignantly.

"But what do you expect from him in the long run? Do you think he may become tame one day?"

"I don't expect anything. I would hate him to become tame. I don't think of the future, I love him and I know that eventually he always returns to me for a while, and that makes life worth living. This is my last chance to be happy. If I miss it, there won't be anything to look forward to. At my age——"

"You sound like a dear old thing of seventy."

"No, it's not that. But even at seventy I hope to be more emotional than you are now! At least I've committed my sins out of conviction and without reservations, not half-heartedly like you. Oh, can't you understand?"

Marta nodded. Why argue? Hanna's approach seemed ludicrous to her: it was just as well to let her have the last word. Now that Gyuri had gone she refused to think about her problems. Her courage did not go very deep. She did not dare to admit herself how much she hated men.

CHAPTER SEVEN

~~~cccccccccc~~~

"I didn't think I could stand it," Mrs. Balogh said to Pali, "three more people in the house with no extra help or extra rations. Yet it's working out quite well. Of course the bathroom is never free, but we mustn't be petty. Tell me, is anything going on? What's the latest?"

"There's going to be a literary purge," he said. "Undesirable books will be eliminated from the nation's system."

"What undiluted idiocy! Have they nothing better to do? Do you think it's serious?"

"Oh yes. There will be a bonfire in a public square and the Minister of Propaganda, dressed in national costume, will burn books. A good omen. The side that burns books always loses the war."

"But surely this will only create a colossal demand for banned books?" Gitta asked.

"The moment the full list appears, all the best people will be reading forbidden literature. The black market is getting organized. Soon you should be able to get a kilo of coffee beans for a slim Thomas Mann. Unfortunately the best booksellers are Jewish and since they're no longer in business things won't run smoothly. Like butter, culture will be sold from under the counter."

"Even the gods fight vainly against stupidity," Mrs. Balogh burst out, touching the bookcase with the gesture of an angel guarding the gates of Paradise. Her beloved bookcase was a massive piece, discreetly carved around the base and the top, its glazed doors reflecting the rest of the room. On the four deep shelves the double rows of books wove a vertical pattern of red, brown, blue and gold stripes.

"If they're going to search people's homes for banned books, we may be in trouble. This is such a mixed lot, I don't even begin to know what to put out of sight."

"Considering your illegal guests who should be in the ghetto instead of hiding in your flat, you needn't worry about books," Pali said, but just to please her he rose and inspected the shelves.

"You'll need several large packing cases," he said. "This is hopeless, full of racially impure authors. Heine, Werfel, Mann, Zweig, Kafka, Asch—pack them away. You also have too many English books. Keep Shakespeare, the Germans claim him as their own, anyway, but Huxley and Russell and Woolf had better go to the cellar. The Russians ditto. I'm not sure about the French. You can always say they sympathize with Vichy. The gangsters who'll search private libraries won't know better."

"But what about the ones like Anatole France and Hugo who are obviously dead? You can see it from the bindings, they're so old-fashioned," Gitta objected.

"Goodness me, say they would sympathize if they were alive, be more inventive. Of course you can keep your books on Wagner, and all the Aryan Germans. They may even earn you a free pardon. And although most of your Hungarian books are anti-Nazi by implication, nobody will query those."

"But the bookcase will be half-empty! Surely I needn't put away all the Russians—what about Rachmanova?" Mrs. Balogh pointed at the anti-Bolshevik trilogy by a Russian refugee which was sensational enough to have seeped into every up-to-date bookcase in town. Pali shrugged. "That'll be part of the next round. You'll hide your Rachmanova if the Russians come in. Can't you wait?"

"You don't mean to say that the Russians burn books, too?"

"The real thing will start if and when the Russians arrive," he said. "They don't ban books, they banish the people who own them. Logically all you should have to do would be to have your books hauled up from the cellar and hide the Rachmanova instead. In actual fact it'll be more complicated. From what I gather, the Russians dislike the same books as the Nazis, although for different reasons. They'll object to Mann, Zweig, Werfel, Kafka and Freud, not because they're Jewish but because Mann and Zweig represent the *haute bourgeoisie*, Werfel has become an ardent Catholic, Kafka is anti-totalitarian and Freud maintains that people have certain components which are not listed in Marxist theory, although of course the cure for neurosis is classless society, not psycho-analysis.

And the English are corrupt and the French are decadent. Am I making myself clear?"

"Well, then, the best thing would be to have no books at all."

"That could be interpreted as a silent protest. You can't be too careful these days."

Rozália knocked and peered in sullenly. "The old lady is crying again, Madam, I wonder if you could come and talk to her."

"Oh dear, is she? I'll be along at once. It's dreadful," Mrs. Balogh added after Rozália's withdrawal. "I don't know how to console poor Mrs. Blum. She has three sons in various labour camps and she cries half the time. She's almost eighty. Heaven forbid anything serious should happen to her. And the laundress is sick," she reflected in the doorway, "and we're practically out of sheets."

The room was very quiet now. The slate-blue dusk was thickening outside; a church bell pealed softly. Pali's eyes were closed, his hands lay limp in his lap. He had not slept more than three hours a night for several days; weariness flattened and paralysed his body like an enormous paperweight, while his mind refused to relax, so that his waking state was like the familiar nightmare in which the wildest effort only produces the speed and strength of a snail.

"Talk to me, little one, otherwise I'll go to sleep."

"I want you to talk to me. Nothing has happened since last time," she said. He had not been in touch with her for two days and she had missed him. "The evenings are the worst. We either sit in the shelter waiting for the all-clear or else we sit here, comforting our guests. Either way one is never alone, which I find a strain. How long is this going to last?"

"The way I feel now it'll never end, although Sas assures me that I'm wrong and that things are moving. Sas baffles me. He vanishes for a few days and then pops up again with advance information which is confirmed by events within a week. Whether he flies a private plane to the Allies and back or runs a transmitter on a mountain crag, his forecasts are dead accurate."

"I'm glad he tells you things. The rest of us could be thin air."

"All of us are thin air to him. I'm sometimes useful, hence the extra courtesy, but otherwise all we're doing is kids' stuff. Sas is a political operative. We might have been valuable to him while the broadcasts continued. Since the occupation we've been lapsing into charitable activities and he has no time for that."

"Somebody must do that, too. Considering that he dumps his protégés in our flats, he might be more civil."

"He's neither civil nor civilized. Wait until he himself comes to stay—the man's a born wrecker. I've never seen anyone disorganize a place so completely in so little time as he does."

"Mother will tame him soon enough."

"I doubt it. Sas is a chaos-maker. He's untidy, he upsets things. Lock him up in a spick-and-span room, tie him to a chair, he'll still make the floor dirty and the furniture dusty. Even when he stands still he seems to gather fluff round him."

"He has probably never had a home of his own and he would be miserable if he had one."

"True. Sas wants no home, he only wants women. He has an eye on Marta."

"How absurd. Marta is otherwise engaged."

"Oh yes, in more ways than one. She's flirting with poor Mihály, she also tries to flirt with me and doesn't exactly discourage Sas, either. I'll have to tick her off. Otherwise she's wonderful. Yesterday she went to a small parish office and found only one clerk in attendance. She promptly sent him off to the archives to look for a fictitious document, and while the poor dazed man got himself covered in dust, she pinched a dozen blank forms. I admire her nerve, but the same nerve also turns her into an emotional bandit. I don't want Mihály to get hurt; he's already obsessed with the idea that the world is full of traitors, and if this girl lets him down, he'll probably have a breakdown."

Gitta sighed. Whatever one did, the human element broke in. Marta's weakness had come at a bad moment, although personally she was too depressed to care. Time flowed on slowly and so facelessly that sometimes she forgot what day it was. To exist from one day to the next making small and futile efforts was much worse than to rush into battle and die gloriously, or, better still, win and live.

He stroked her hand. "I know, little one, I know. One's nerves get rubbed away fibre by fibre. But there may be some movement soon. The moment somebody yells for an armistice, we'll fly into action. Still, all's bad that ends badly, don't hope for too much."

"Will nothing ever work out well?"

"No. Something always goes wrong at the last moment. Not

senselessly, though; every failure has its sound reasons, even if they aren't obvious at once. Get resigned to the worst and feel grateful if it doesn't happen. There's no other philosophy left."

They sat still, holding hands in the dusk. He did not want to depress her. His basic pessimism was deep and private, he wanted no sympathy or consolation; there was nothing to be consoled for, unless one's ability to recognize the hopelessness of life was a regrettable mental quirk. It was good to sit still with her, knowing that her cheerful fatalism made her believe in a cosmic order that always worked out well in the end. The cosmic order he believed in always worked out justly, and that meant tragically. But let her go on purposefully, let her attempt the impossible, move mountains, make walls tumble down, let her prove, if she could, that everything was happening the way it should.

Mrs. Balogh came in, exclaimed at the darkness, remembered the black-out and drew the curtains before flicking the light on. Dinner was ready, she said. They drifted over to the dining-room and joined the others—old Mrs. Blum, still trembling after her long cry; a plump young woman with a Socialist past whom Sas had smuggled in during an air raid and then had forgotten all about; and Suzy Tóth, Mrs. Balogh's silly friend who had been denounced to the Gestapo for listening to the B.B.C. in a ghetto house, had escaped, and now existed in a state of subdued hysteria.

Nobody spoke much. Rozália's face was enough to discourage conversation. The guests ate little and behaved apologetically, obviously unable to forget their predicament. The more Mrs. Balogh tried to make them feel at home the sadder they became. After dinner they retired to the two rooms they shared, Mrs. Blum to pray, the plump Socialist to read, Suzy Tóth to do her nails.

Back in the drawing-room Pali opened the gramophone and played some of Mrs. Balogh's old American records. "I can be happy, I can be sad," the Whispering Baritone sang, "I can be good or I can be bad, it all depends on you." Mrs. Balogh nodded to the rhythm. The tunes were dry, the triteness of the words was balanced by their foreignness that made even the most commonplace statements charming and significant.

"There's a rainbow round my shoulder and it fits me like a glove," the reverse side assured them. Before the war she used to dance to these very tunes in good night clubs and she always brought back some little souvenir for her small, pigtailed Gitta, pinkly asleep and problemless.

"Teardrops never dry, headaches multiply," the gramophone whispered, and although at one time Gitta had found the idea of eternal sorrow attractive, teardrops were no longer enough. All right, once bitten always afraid of being misunderstood, and love was a lush breeding-ground of misunderstandings, but one had to take a risk. She wanted to feel love, anxiety, happiness, anything as long as it was real and lasting. She glanced at Pali. His eyes were on her. Did he know what she was thinking? It suddenly occurred to Gitta that her everyday life was centred in him; even when they were apart, she addressed her thoughts to him, and the world only made sense when she tried to see it through his eyes. The relationship was new, just as he himself was different from any other man she had ever met. If only she knew how he felt about her—could it be . . . ? Outside the sirens began to wail.

"I bless your memory," the gramophone croaked as Pali lifted the pick-up. Mrs. Balogh rose wearily. "Pali, you might just as well come with us to that smelly shelter. We can't take the ladies down, it's too risky. The caretaker and his wife are Nazis."

"I'd rather stay here if I may, I'm reasonably bomb-proof," Pali said. Nazi caretakers depressed him more than the weird silence and occasional explosions of the nightly raids. There had been some bombing, but often the enemy aircraft only crossed the sky, and Pali liked to sit in the dark and listen to the hum of their engines.

CHAPTER EIGHT

~~~~ccccc6608888cccc~~~~

I t was the first real summer afternoon of the year, warm but
still fresh, the golden aftermath of spring. The trees along the
boulevards were only just beginning to grow dusty; the hills of
Buda looked emerald-green in the distance.

Gitta was ambling across the Margaret Bridge, taking a brief-case
to Hanna's flat for Sas to pick up at six. The shabby brief-case
weighed little; it only contained a few sticks of dynamite, blank
documents and suchlike explosive material, and if Mihály had not
been detained elsewhere, he would have taken it along himself. A lot
of fuss about nothing, Gitta thought. The courier service was always
in dispute: Sas maintained that it was madness to let military-age
men carry illegal cargo, since they were the first to be stopped in
street raids. Pali, however, insisted that while the girls were less
likely to be caught, they would not know how to get out of a sticky
situation. What did it matter? Gitta wondered. She felt sure that
nothing could happen to her, that, without any good reason, she was
immune from accidents, mishaps and death. As long as Pali did not
find out, she was quite happy to deliver risky parcels.

The air was sweet and warm. The river breeze ruffled her hair and
beat her light dress against her legs; she felt she was swimming against
a current of billowing air. Trams rattled across the bridge, people
hurried past her in untidy groups. On her right the rich, bushy trees
of St. Margaret's Island looked like beautiful old giants basking in
the sunshine.

The island had been her favourite place ever since she could remember. One of her earliest wonders—she was learning to walk at
the time—had been the rolling island lawn starred with tiny daisies
and the tame pheasants and peacocks mincing around disdainfully.
Later, one June, she had danced around the flaming red rosebeds,

71

watching the sleepy bees that gyrated in the thick wall of rose scent. City-born and bred, the island was her nature reserve; more than a park, less than the real country, it had become her magic grove. She visited it every Palm Sunday to savour the spring air and think about life, or what she thought was life, strolling around the ruins of the Gothic convent where St. Margaret had spent her brief life interceding with God for the country which then, too, had been in desperate straits. And God hath turned the vermin of her body into pearls. Perhaps one should have devoted one's life to God at an early age. Perhaps true happiness only came to the elect like St. Margaret or the Mother Superior. But then the search for happiness was the wrong reason for entering God's service; one should not try to haggle with Heaven, offering one's life in exchange for guaranteed bliss. To suspect that, God apart, there was no perfection in the world, did not equal true vocation.

No, she did not belong to the elect. The worst of adolescence, the frantic bouts of prayer and cosmic insecurity were over. Now she felt more interested in worldly perfection. Pali had brought a tremendous difference to life, he made her feel inwardly strong, secure and happy, he understood her so well that she never needed to pretend or attach verbal footnotes to her statements. She could hardly remember what life had been like before they first met ten months ago. If only they had a little more time for themselves, a little less work and worry, if it were possible—and honourable—to concentrate on themselves! The thought was selfish. She put it out of her mind.

She was only a hundred yards from the Buda end when all vehicles on the bridge stopped abruptly and the pedestrians in front of her slowed down. Near the bridgehead a dozen German soldiers had formed a cordon and were waving everybody to a halt. Gitta turned round, but the same thing had happened at the other end, and the branch leading off to the island had also been sealed. She pressed the brief-case to her side. What in heaven's name did they want? This was really bad luck. She felt trapped and annoyed, but there was nothing to do except shuffle on with the others towards the cordon, present her identity papers and walk away as fast as possible.

The crowd ahead of her had become so thick that she could not see the bridgehead. Things were moving slowly. She was certain to

72

be late, and Sas would be furious—supposing his plans depended on split-second timing, even this unexpected incident would make a poor excuse. Sas was unpleasant enough at the best of times; to make him cross seemed a foolish risk. She craned her neck nervously and peered ahead. Her heart stood still. The reason why the queue moved so slowly was that the Germans were searching people's bags and parcels.

It can't be true, she thought, this has never happened before. Her palms were clammy, her elbows felt sore with tension. Dynamite and documents. Dynamite and documents. Or perhaps something worse, only Mihály did not want to tell her? What excuse to give? Found the brief-case in the street and was taking it to the police? Impossible. The icy, heart-bursting fear grew worse every moment and her lips trembled, but she had to push on, because the people behind her were moving ahead, and to stop or run would be fatal. Drop the brief-case in the river? The police launch under the bridge was permanently on the look-out for suicides, the crew would fish it out in no time. And even if it sank like a stone, she would still be caught and questioned, her home searched, the three Jewesses found. . . .

She had almost reached the cordon. Empty-handed pedestrians waited sheepishly for the soldiers to examine their proofs of identity and then walked away with an apologetic air. The others took longer to be cleared. Parcels were opened, brown paper rustled to disclose food, shoes, light bulbs, three small picture frames, a length of blue material, school textbooks, all kinds of trivial, innocent objects. Gitta watched them enviously, no longer believing that this was actually happening. Wake up, it's all right, wake up, if only somebody would shake her by the shoulder and break the nightmare!

She stepped forward and held out her documents. The soldier who took them was young and bored; he frowned at her unrecognizable four-year-old photograph, handed back the papers and pointed at the brief-case. The fastening was unfamiliar. Fumbling with it she broke a finger-nail and raised her finger to her lips. "Come on, hurry up," the soldier said indifferently. She looked at him and felt all the blood rush to her face.

"I cannot possibly show you with all these people around," she heard herself say, "it is my underwear and other . . . personal things, I really cannot. . . ."

The soldier's thin eyebrows shot up. He guffawed, turning to his neighbour; he jostled the soldier on his other side, and then everybody was laughing and pointing at Gitta, making cracks about blushing girls and pretty lace pants, and when she no longer knew where to look in embarrassment, the soldier patted her shoulder and let her pass.

She held her breath and walked away blindly. Not to hurry. Not to look back. It was a quarter-past six. She did not care. The bridge was now out of sight. The panic began to lift and icy calm seeped into its place. Nobody followed her. The case was still in her hand. She had got away with it, all was well. Only the shock persisted. This time God hath turned the dynamite into a joke. Would He do it again? Or was she just as accident-prone as anybody else? Immunity was no longer a matter of course. The golden helmet had received its first dent.

She arrived at Hanna's flat quite late, but although there was no sign of Sas, Hanna seemed greatly distressed. "You must help," she said in an urgent voice. "A terrible thing has happened, I am at my wits' end and there is no time to lose."

Oh Lord, Gitta thought, must everything happen at the same time? In the drawing-room a desperate-looking elderly couple and an Army officer stood uneasily around the table. They shook hands without saying their names. The woman kept wiping her eyes with a crumpled handkerchief.

"It's all right, my dears," Hanna said. "This is a friend who may help us. Tell her the essential facts, we must hurry."

The officer rubbed his forehead. He was young and pleasant-looking, but his hand trembled and his face was greenish-white. "It's like this," he said. "These people are Jews, they live in a yellow-star house. They have . . . I mean their daughter Eva and I . . . we have been in love for a long time, but of course we couldn't marry because of the racial law. When the Germans came in, I wanted to save her. My unit is stationed in the provinces, I knew I wouldn't be around if there was trouble and she needed me. So I took her along as my wife. It was the best I could do under the circumstances, you see."

"Yes, of course. Go on, please."

"Everything went well," the man said. "Nobody suspected us, my poor darling felt quite happy and secure, and I managed to have food and money sent to her parents here—oh Mother, please don't cry, I cannot bear it. And then, two days ago she got a terrible head-

74

ache. At noon she collapsed, and an hour later she was dead."

The girl's mother moaned softly.

"It was a tumour on the brain. Nothing could have saved her, the doctor said it was a merciful end. But now we have to bury her!" the man shouted. "You cannot even die and get buried in this wretched goddam bloody place without documents, and if I produce her real ones, I will be court-martialled and her parents punished, and she will not even get a decent burial, my darling Eva. . . ."

"Pull yourself together," Hanna pleaded. "There's no time for this. We need the facts."

"Oh, I hardly know what I am saying any more. Yes, the facts. My C.O. called in yesterday to collect Eva's documents. I said I would drop them in later. That was a mistake, because when I didn't turn up he became suspicious and summoned me over. So I said I had found that all our papers were in town and I would have to fetch them. He gave me a day's leave, I must be back tonight with the papers."

"Time is terribly short," Gitta said. "Supposing we cannot provide you with suitable papers, could you possibly . . . vanish?"

"And leave her there, dead and alone? Who do you think I am?"

"Please don't misunderstand me, I only meant it as an extreme possibility. You really need a certificate of marriage and a birth certificate for her. Oh Hanna, where am I to get the forms?"

"Marta keeps her forging kit here, she doesn't dare to take it home, only I don't know how these things are done. Look, here it is!"

The large envelope Hanna tore out from her bureau contained a variety of papers, mostly copies of originals gleaned from parish offices, several blank birth certificates and one tattered marriage certificate form, washed down with cleansing fluid and worn thin at the folds. Worse still, Gitta suddenly realized that Marta's kit contained no special ink.

There was no reply from Pali's telephone. Marta was out. If the papers were not ready soon, the man would miss his last train and the dead girl would miss her funeral and nobody in the whole world could do anything for them.

Sas arrived at the height of chaos. He grabbed the brief-case and turned to go, but Gitta caught his arm and forced him to stop. "If I can get through a German cordon with your wretched case, you can jolly well listen for a second," she declared and went on to explain

75

the situation. Her vehemence surprised Sas; he had always considered her singularly passive.

"Oh, were you on the bridge this afternoon? Poor girl. Probably you were the only one with anything to hide. How did you get away?" But he did not really want to know; life was too short for details. "Here is the ink," he said, pulling out a small bottle from the brief-case, "but for Pete's sake hurry, because I can't stay long and I must take it with me."

"Couldn't you fill in the papers?" she pleaded. "My hand isn't steady, I'll make a mess of it."

"No, I never do this sort of thing myself. Come on, relax, breathe deeply. You know how to do it. Countess, I could do with a drink."

"Help yourself, everything is over there." Hanna drew Gitta to the table. "Come on, precious, you can do it, it'll be easy, I promise."

"Hey, use ordinary ink on the birth certificate!" Sas called out. "Those forms are brand-new, you are obviously producing a fresh copy, and nowadays they use plain ink and steel nibs for those."

Almost cross-eyed with concentration, Gitta penned in the data with the special civil service hand she had recently acquired, a rounded, childish style of writing with clear loops and simple capitals. The distraught officer watched her closely, dictating the names and birth dates of fictitious Aryan parents, while the real ones sat mournfully, witnessing the final loss of their daughter who now needed new parents on her birth certificate because she was dead.

Then came the change of ink, the change of texture from fresh, smooth paper to an uneven rag. "What do you think you are doing?" Sas barked. "We cannot have the same hand on both documents! Use your head, child. Countess, what about your handwriting?"

"It would never do, it's too big and untidy. Look, here it is."

He glanced at the sample. "No good. We need a small, fussy, angular style. This is supposed to be the original marriage certificate. Five years ago a middle-aged registrar would have written in that style; it was the accepted calligraphy all over the country."

"Let me try," the dead girl's mother pleaded. "I think I could do it." Slowly she wrote "Budapest, Hungary" on a scrap of paper and held it out to Sas. He nodded. "All right, go ahead. Hold the pen very lightly and write across the folds, even where they are worn away."

This was the second eternity within one day, Gitta thought as she watched the pinched grey face bending over the paper, the faded grey hand moving painfully up and down, hesitating and starting again. The officer's voice dragged out every syllable as he dictated names, ages, date and place of wedding, names of witnesses. "Witnesses! We must sign for them!" Hanna panicked, but all was well: both fictitious witnesses were to be dead fellow officers from a remote regiment, well past the checking power of authority.

"Not bad," Sas said when all was over. "It will be perfectly all right, nothing to worry about." He handed a pill to the officer. "Swallow this ten minutes before you call on your C.O., you'll feel calm and composed. I must rush now. Good night."

Nobody saw him out. They stood around numbly, not knowing what to say. The girl's father cleared his throat. "You had better go, son. Your train will be leaving soon. I don't think we shall meet again. God bless you for all you have done for our little Eva."

Gitta nodded to the room in general and hurried out. Hanna caught up with her in the hall and kissed her on both cheeks. "Thank you, my sweet. Pray to St. Rita tonight, she is the saint of the impossible. She will have to work overtime to get that tattered paper passed."

"St. Rita, is it? Sometimes I wonder whether anybody below God can do anything at all," Gitta said and hurried away, taking two stairs at a time.

At last the triangular display cabinet was empty. The white lace frills hung forlornly from the dark shelves which were now quite bare except for faint tracings of dust. The white china child's head, the Dresden shepherdess with her swain, the Alt-Wien fruit dish, the Copenhagen figurines and Egyptian carvings were all at rest in the packing case, protected by layers of tissue paper and blond wood shavings. Mrs. Balogh sighed. This was like a burial. More and more things had to go underground; ordinary life itself was retreating into the cellar, paying a dark price for safety.

The cellars of the big block were sombre, a maze of wooden partitions and damp earth floors, where in normal times maids wandered around with a guttering candle in one hand, a key in the other, looking for their masters' fuel store and hoping there would be no rats among the logs. Now that the air raids were getting worse, the cellars had become essential. The assistant caretaker made a tidy income from providing additional cellar space and carting down tenants' belongings in packing cases and tin trunks.

Mrs. Balogh threw another handful of shavings into the open case. Her back ached a little. All this packing without a journey wore her out, and the flat was getting so depressing, too. In its full splendour this place had been her means of self-expression, a blend of elegance, comfort and warmth. Mrs. Balogh believed that a woman's main function in life was to provide comforts for body and soul, to build little nests of well-being, whether in the form of an imaginative meal or by putting fresh flowers into a room and spraying the air with scent; or, above all, by providing a haven for a tired, worried soul. She performed all these functions supremely well, and her home had been her biggest achievement. But now, bit by bit, she was forced to dismantle her small universe, the perfect cocoon she had created for Gitta and herself. The flat was losing its identity. The silver cabinet was empty, the china and the big collection of glasses were gone. She had thinned out the bookcase. The splendid table linen and embroideries, carefully guarded for Gitta's future home, had been packed away, and now the display cabinet stood vacant, too. If it goes on like this, Mrs. Balogh thought, soon we shall eat bean soup out of a tin bowl; and the end was still nowhere in sight.

It was mid-June now. Apart from the summer that followed its normal course, everything else was going awry. Rumours swept the city every day, growing and changing as they spread, collecting crumbs of wishful thinking, political bias and personal theory until they got completely distorted; and then the next lot of equally unreliable information poured in, sweeping all else away. The Western Allies were going to land next Wednesday. By air, of course. Some people went so far as to list the actual landing places. No, the Russians were not coming, the British and the Americans were tackling the job on their own. Simpler minds fondled glorious visions of a great Anglo-American army occupying the land in the heroic mood of early Hollywood epics. Others knew for certain that the Anglo-Saxons, as they were generally called, were turning against the Russians in a gallant bid to save Europe from barbarism. But then the wind changed. They were not coming. Nobody was coming. Death, pestilence and famine were imminent, the country was to vanish from the face of the earth, there was no future and the very past would disintegrate, since there would be no one to remember it.

There was also the counterblast from the opposite camp, the prophets of Hitler's New Europe, and their rumours were just as colourful and ominous. But by and large the pro-Nazi and anti-Nazi rumours rarely clashed, since people of both camps preferred to swap information with their fellow sympathizers, and the lurid threats were more likely to please their originators than scare their opponents.

Mrs. Balogh sat down wearily, dropping her beautiful hands in her lap. This was her second great war. The first one had ruined her youth. The present one was spoiling her best years and Gitta's girlhood. Her daughter's brief season of pink gowns, *Crémant Rosé* and long waltzes already seemed remote and dead, a small Atlantis in time, never to be recaptured. Gitta was changing so rapidly, Mrs. Balogh reflected; she would never be the same again. Even the worst of adolescence was better than this fast, forced maturing, this quiet acceptance of tasks and responsibilities which should never have presented themselves. Sometimes Mrs. Balogh felt that she was the younger of the two, less exposed to real danger, and she was a little jealous of Gitta's friends who knew more about her than she did.

Above all, Pali. Was he just the pack leader, the wise, precocious commander of these wise, precocious children, or had he a personal hold over Gitta? Sometimes she intercepted their glances. Their eyes were calm and tender, flashing messages of some private harmony that remained unconfirmed by word or gesture. They could not be in love, she decided. Love was wild, confused, uncertain; Gitta had never been able to handle her emotions, they had always raced away with her until she was the blindest, clumsiest thing on earth, hurting herself and everybody around her.

Outside, a siren blew the alert. Another one blasted out the all-clear. Idiots, Mrs. Balogh frowned; they could not even handle an alert properly. She shook her head. Her pauses never lasted more than five minutes. It was time to think about food, see how the rations were going and, if necessary, order some black supplies. Six people could not exist on three ration cards.

Dr. Sas had taken his plump Socialist away. Old Mrs. Blum and Suzy Tóth were still in the flat, and there was someone else coming, the sole survivor of a Gestapo raid. A few months ago such overcrowding would have been unthinkable. Now it did not matter. The saddest thing was that whatever one did, however far one went in personal sacrifices, deep down the guilt for other people's crimes never stopped nagging.

CHAPTER NINE

O ne sweltering afternoon late in June Gitta stood at the tram terminal near the Margaret Bridge, waiting for Pali. She looked around nervously. Her moment of horror had tainted the innocent bridge and she still approached it reluctantly, like a horse that shies at the spot of an old accident.

Pali suddenly stood in front of her; he always seemed to materialize out of thin air. But this time he looked different, a younger and more informal version of himself in a white sports shirt and summer flannels. Instead of the eternal brief-case there was a rolled-up towel under his arm.

"Heavens, I've never seen you without a tie!" she exclaimed.

"Only the first of many surprises." He grabbed her hand and broke into a gallop: the outward-bound local train was already whistling.

"But where are we going? Is it a secret?"

"You'll see. Quick, it's moving!"

The little train pulled away from the open platform. It chugged northwards, past shabby buildings, warehouses, stretches of waste land and dusty gardens. The old houses of Óbuda huddled under the bulbous tower of a yellow church, and behind them the hills curved away in lush chaos. Gitta looked around in the crowded compartment, savouring their separateness from those around them—red-faced men wiping their foreheads and tugging at badly knotted ties, plump women with dark stains under the sleeves of their summer frocks, a deaf old lady trying to read lips with eager bird-eyes, a boy munching an overripe apricot. Everybody was loud and full of earthy summer, and Gitta watched them happily from a bubble of silence. Pali's fingers were cool on her wrist. She would have followed him anywhere, contentedly, without asking a single question.

81

They jumped off at a deserted stop and turned into an avenue of silver poplars whose glittering leaves trembled in the still air like fingers on a keyboard. They were beautiful trees, rising over the flat landscape like tall exclamation marks. The sand crunched under Gitta's red sandals; her canvas beach bag jerked to and fro. The end of the avenue twisted round the corner and ended abruptly at the river bank. Released from the stone quays of the city, the Danube lay idly in the blazing sunshine, green, slow and enormous.

A narrow path ran along the water's edge. Some five hundred yards away the willow shrubs formed a small niche, almost concealing a boat-house. Smiling mysteriously, Pali unlocked one set of doors. There was a double scull inside, a fine, fair boat, elegant as a swallow.

"Whose is it?" she asked. "May we use it? Oh, tell me, I can't bear the suspense!"

"It's mine for the duration. The real owner is a doctor friend of mine who is at present busy making bricks in a labour camp, but he transferred this place to me at the last moment to save it from confiscation. He's absolutely determined to survive and take up rowing again, so we must keep the place in perfect order."

"Oh, we will! What a splendid, wonderful place! I'm glad it's not a gold-mine or something stupid like that. Look, there isn't a soul anywhere, only birds and mosquitoes. Isn't it marvellous?"

Her voice broke with excitement. She could hardly control her delight, but feeling too bulky for jumping up and down for joy, she only shifted her weight from one foot to the other in a clumsy penguin dance, and when Pali unlocked the cabin door, she rushed in to change.

The cabin was spacious, a sparsely furnished twilit room smelling of timber and damp sand. Putting on her blue shorts she thought that this was the primitive sketch of a home, an adventure-story hideout where one might arrive furtively after a long journey and cook dinner on a spirit stove. She ran her fingers along the wooden bench. Even the thick cobwebs in the corner did not matter. Every detail was unique and important, and she memorized them as if her future happiness depended on remembering them correctly.

Outside the sunshine made her blink. "One could make curtains," she said shyly, "and some cushions, and bring out a stock of tinned food and two plates. . . ."

82

"That's exactly what I thought when I first came out. I wonder how my guitar would react to the humidity?"

He stepped inside and came out a minute later in shorts and sandals. His skin was smooth and golden, he looked like a young warrior from an unknown Gauguin.

They pushed the boat into the water and rowed slowly upstream. The tall-treed green shore looked mysterious from the river, an unexplored forest where even the gaps in the foliage held wisps of green haze and the promise of solitude. Above them the clear sky curved up luminously, endlessly.

"Happy?" he asked after a while.

"Tremendously. How do you know?"

"Your back looks happy. And your elbows. Couldn't be easier— don't we always know how the other feels?"

"Oh, we do. Though often I think it's sheer imagination and you are in a completely different mood. But then you aren't. How does it work?"

He answered three strokes later. "Do you remember when we first met? You brought your first article to the office before I retired from the paper and you looked so scared I wanted to wipe your nose. You even accepted a cigarette from the features editor and then didn't know what to do with it."

"I hadn't realized it would taste so foul. I held it at waist level to keep the smoke out of my face."

"Well, you sold your article all the same. It was a good piece. If there were still papers for which one could write without losing one's self-esteem, you would make the grade in six months—and of course I would be the greatest leader-writer of all. Oh, our wasted talents. But what I am getting at is that someone opened the door and a sheet of paper flew off the table. Do you remember?"

"No, I don't."

"Foolish child, that was a vital moment. We both reached out and caught it together in mid-air without even creasing it. Do you know how few people can catch things like that? It needs alertness, quick reactions and good timing. You had them all, and you hardly noticed what you were doing. That was when I got interested in you."

"Funny, I never thought of that. I took it for granted that you could catch things the same as I can. And then?"

"And then? Nothing. I've been interested ever since."

The water sparkled under their oars. Little swishing noises flew out from either side of the boat, pearls of happy sound. The sun shone in melting ecstasy, pouring down golden heat in large waves; after a long rehearsal, high summer had just begun in all seriousness.

"You call it being interested. I don't know what to call it. I just accept the fact that we . . ."

"Well?"

"It's a sort of basic similarity, I think. Not just holding the same opinions, that means nothing. We are synchronized. Yes, that's the word I wanted, synchronized. At first I thought that, as you impressed me so much, I was simply aping you out of sheer admiration. So I tried to contradict and disagree, and it was as impossible as contradicting myself. Now I know that we really are similar. Other people have a shell which must be penetrated before making contact, but with you there is none. Not for me. It's rather like . . ." The boat moved idly over the cloudy water that looked emerald in mid-stream, olive near the bank. "It's rather like recognizing one's own self in somebody else," she said. "It saves a lot of explaining."

He steered towards the bank, tied the boat to a gnarled grey root and helped her out. The sand felt warm as they sat down. Her heart beat so loudly that she was sure he would notice it. They had never discussed themselves before. Far away, across the water, a man led a horse along the road, and two birds waltzed over his head.

"Yes, we are synchronized," he said. "You've found the right word. But now you will have to think further, as I did. I used to wonder about perfect harmony between two people, long before I met you. I used to watch people falling in and out of love, lapping up bad excuses and false pretences, hurting and getting hurt, never stopping to wonder what it was all about. Oh, they did stop between two affairs to say a few platitudes and get a little drunk. Lord, the clichés they always produced! The war of the sexes is inevitable. The moment you get what you want you don't want it any more. Anticipation is better than fulfilment. Intelligent people cannot remain faithful. And so on. All the things they had heard from their parents who did not know the difference between sentiment and emotion, all the rubbish they had read in bad novels and heard in operettas, set to music and made to rhyme."

Gitta, who had often heard and sometimes used the feminine

84

equivalents of these clichés, blinked nervously. "But surely some of it is true?"

"No doubt most of it is true for people who don't know what they are looking for, and as a result never find it and console themselves as best they can."

"What are you looking for?"

He picked up two pebbles and placed them on her bare feet.

"The golden age. You know that myth which says that the basic human being was both male and female, until the jealous gods split it in half, rather like dividing a walnut kernel. Well, one spends one's life looking for the missing half-kernel, the one and only person who can restore the old unity. To my mind, that unity—it must have been an enviable state, otherwise the myth wouldn't harp on it so wistfully—the original unity means complete togetherness of body, soul, spirit, everything."

She picked up the two pebbles and pressed them together. They matched. "I see," she murmured. "And we . . ."

"We come from the same nutshell."

She pulled up her knees and laid her cheek on them. The sun was as bright as ever, but the air seemed to have grown cooler. She felt overwhelmed. There was so much to say and she could not speak. To get rid of the inhibiting lump in her throat was as difficult as levitation is to the uninitiated.

"I have known it for a long time," he said. "One warning came after another. Not just emotional things, although those would have been enough by themselves. When we were still broadcasting, before I began to send our scripts to the potato shed in János's garden, sometimes I looked up the stuff we had done a few days earlier, and I never knew which bit was yours and which was mine. It was uncanny. We react identically to outside stimuli, not only catching things in mid-air but also interpreting official bulletins and sensing Mihály's latest conflict from the way he enters the coffee-house. I realize that looking for similarities in someone you love is an old pastime; the more things you believe you share, the less lonely you are. Well, we've never had to look for similarities, they were there, waiting to be recognized. I have known this for ages and I was hoping you knew it, too. If the Germans had not come in, I would have tackled you about it earlier. But one cannot decide on one's fate between forging two birth certificates."

"Is that why we are here?"

"I wanted to be alone with you at last, on neutral territory. (Stop trembling, little one, because I'll push you in the water.) We are so busy resisting the Nazis that in the end, out of sheer habit, we may resist each other, too. One mustn't resist love."

"But are we in love?" she asked wildly. "Are we?"

He put his hand on her shoulder. "We are not. This is more. If you accept the half-kernel theory, the idea of being in love means very little, a temporary link between two people who are separated by everything else. We are not in love. You've said it, we are synchronized. Of course, we also love each other, because we recognize our basic sameness, and it would be a fine thing if one did not love one's self, even if it was once removed."

"This is so difficult," she sighed.

"Of course. Hellishly difficult. We begin by plunging into the middle of things—most people go through life without even brushing it in passing—and this cuts out the prelude which is normally mistaken for the real thing. We had no opening movement, we never wondered what the other one was really like because we knew right from the start. We are not going to have any surprises, disappointments or fights. There is nothing to fight about."

"What is it we'll have then?"

He kissed her cheek. "Freedom. Love is a kind of freedom—freedom from aloneness and restrictions. Freedom from one's identity. One has a key to the other, one can leave one's own limitations and expand a little and bask in the warmth. It's like building one's life around a double cocoon of happiness."

She dropped her head on his shoulder. "What's going to happen to us?"

"It has already happened. The essential part has. The rest is detail. I think we should get married so that we can expand ourselves in peace—when all this is over, of course."

"Are you so sure we'll survive?"

"Absolutely."

"Funny, so am I."

"Oh, we'll survive all right. We may not be able to get together. All I know is how happy we could be, I'm not saying it will actually happen. But if it doesn't, if we don't ever meet again——"

"Oh don't!"

"Oh yes, even if we don't ever meet again, the situation will not change. Even if both of us marry six times and go off to the opposite corners of the earth, it won't alter anything."

"Why, is there only one real half-kernel for everyone?"

"Yes. Only one."

"What a terrible risk." She edged away from him and turned towards the river. Neither of them spoke or moved. The landscape and the warm golden light were suspended in a timeless moment that could have gone on for ever, a little eternity captured in a drop of amber. He watched her patiently. This was the crisis, the moment of transition from one stage into the next. How would the Sleeping Beauty react to the daylight? At last he leant forward and looked at her face. She was gazing at the water with a sad, forlorn air.

"What's the matter, darling?"

She did not reply. Her eyes were suspiciously bright.

"Little one, if something is wrong, out with it!"

"I don't know," she said wretchedly. "I'm frightened. This is so big and so important, I don't want us to spoil it."

"Spoil it? How?"

"Oh, I don't know. Don't ask me, not now. I love you terribly but I'm terrified." She was almost in tears and clutched his hand.

"But surely you must know what you're frightened of?"

She blew her nose. "It's . . . too big for me, too final. So far I have simply accepted what little we had and dreamt about the real thing when there was time. But everything was always in the present, the farthest we ever thought ahead was next week. And now you take this whole thing and place it against eternity, and final things terrify me."

"Is it marriage that terrifies you?"

She nodded.

"Why?"

"I've never known a happy married couple," she said hesitantly. "My parents used to quarrel. My mother's friends used to quarrel with their husbands; one even ran away from home and came to our place with her lover. There was an awful lot of trouble. Later she married her lover and then they quarrelled just the same. I wasn't told about all this but I sensed the atmosphere at home, and my mother's friends talked in a jargon which they thought I didn't understand, and they all looked so disillusioned and bored. Oh, and quite early on I noticed that fairy tales always ended when the hero married the heroine. Once I asked why, and my governess said: 'Because there's nothing else to tell.' So I concluded that marriage was the end. Once people got married, nothing else happened, there was nothing to say or do."

"But you are perfectly right! What you say is the exact summing up of bourgeois wedlock, from which Allah save us both. Darling, I don't insist on marrying you. I only suggested it as a practical device. If you weren't so obviously unsuited to it, I should be delighted to live in sin with you. But just imagine what your mother would say. Look, I can promise you that half-kernels like us can survive even marriage and remain happy. We belong to those rare people who never degenerate into mere husbands and wives. Cast away your fears. Now that you understand what it's all about, there's no need to be afraid."

"No, perhaps there isn't. But one doesn't grow out of one's confusions so fast. Sometimes I still think that Allah has a beard, for instance."

"How do you know he hasn't one?"

Her hand slipped into his. He caressed her shoulder and she wriggled closer, like a child in need of comfort. Then she was in his arms, clinging to him as he kissed her cheek, her neck, the tip of her nose. She shut her eyes and smiled. His touch on her warm skin was wonderful, it seemed that her body had only sprung into full existence because his fingers had touched it. But when his arms tightened and the kisses grew more intense, she panicked. Resistance welled up inside like a wave. She was frightened again: they were slipping on to dangerous ground where misunderstandings could have fatal consequences, she did not quite want this, not yet, she loved him so much that there was no need for this wild physical closeness. She kept quite still lest she offend him, but he sensed her change of mood and released her immediately, hiding his face in her hair.

"All right, darling," he whispered. "I seem to rush you from one shock to the next. Forget it."

"No, no, it's my fault, it has nothing to do with you. It's just that . . . oh, I'll tell you one day, it's rather stupid."

"Wouldn't you like to tell me about it now?"

"No, no." She shook her head so vehemently that her hair flapped from side to side. "Not now. Oh Pali, we are so happy already, even though I behave so idiotically, won't it be absolutely marvellous later on when I've come to terms with all this?"

He nodded. He felt closer to her than ever: she was new, fumbling, worth waiting for. The fact that he wanted her hardly mattered. The temperature of love had remained steady and he felt grateful and contented. This was happiness: to have at last found someone who would not fail him, who would justify his dogged faith in personal happiness as life's one saving grace, and provide an escape from solitude. There was no collective salvation for any man, only one person could bring it, one atom of unshakeable love, loyalty and understanding. He had found her, half the battle was over even if she needed time to catch up with him. He would wait. There was so much to look forward to, shared peace, eternal curiosity, the laborious search for truth, the small joy of having a late dinner in spring and waving a radish at the stars, the twin cradle of their bodies, the deep trust that makes two people fall asleep together. All this would come. She only needed to grow up a little more.

Over the purple-specked water the boat floated easily to the boat-house. They dressed in silence. She had kept the two matching pebbles and cradled them in her hand as she waited for him to lock up. Birds were calling in the trees. A cloud of tiny white flies circled overhead, a snowstorm of beating wings and baroque gyrations.

"Let's go, water sprite. The trains are a bit unreliable."

But she did not want to leave. She looked at the boat-house, the willow shrubs, the water, the enchanted corner which should not be abandoned lightly. At last she handed him one pebble, put her arms round his neck and kissed him.

CHAPTER TEN

~~~~~~ᴄᴄᴄᴄᴄᴄ᳁᳁᳁᳁᳁᳁᳁᳁᳁᳁~~~~~~

I've never been so happy in my life, she thought. They were
walking together without speaking and that, too, was a way of
communication. Their arms were linked, their hands inter-
twined, their legs moved to the same rhythm. Sometimes she
glanced sideways to see whether he was really there, sometimes he
nuzzled her cheek. She felt reborn, almost transfigured. Everything
had acquired new significance; the world was not the same any more.
If they had suddenly taken off and flown up into the blue summer
sky, she would not have been at all surprised.

They were crossing an old part of Buda, a sleepy district of small
houses surrounded by contemporary streets and streamlined blocks
of flats. The scene was like an architectural siege, a petrified battle of
styles in which the encircled old minority seemed completely indifferent to the modern menace around.

The cobbled streets were narrow and twisting. The small houses
had sunk deep in the course of centuries. Many ground-floor windows were at knee-level; several steps led down to the low entrances.
They were lovely, crotchety old houses with thick yellow walls and
steep tiled roofs overhanging the windows, giving them an air of
secrecy. Here and there flimsy ivory curtains parted to show heavy
brown cupboards with winter apples lined up around their tops; in
some rooms one could see old people resting in velvet-covered arm-
chairs; green-tubbed oleander trees blossomed in the small court-
yards with summery abandon.

Much as she loved old houses, Gitta was too deep in thought to
notice them. When was she to tell her mother about Pali? It did not
seem fair to spring a surprise of such magnitude on her just now—
but was it fair to keep her in the dark?

She had always shared everything with her; the events of her life had only half happened until she was able to report on them. Mrs. Balogh's attentive brown glance, the tilt of her head, were essential to make facts real and valid, it was she who supplied a profane *nihil obstat* to Gitta's experiences. Now, feeling a little guilty, she lavished affection on her mother to make up for this temporary betrayal.

"It's the wrong psychological moment," said Pali who had once again guessed Gitta's thoughts—it happened so often and so mutually that neither of them was surprised any more. "Your mother is tired, worried and harassed, I don't think she would welcome another shock. And besides, darling, I can't bear conventional procedure. No long engagements, please. Much as I want to spend the rest of my life with you, I absolutely refuse to sit through long family meals and talk about bath-mats. Or anything else, for that matter."

She nodded eagerly. The only civilized thing to do, she thought, was to leap out of a taxi, get married in five minutes and go off for a stroll as if nothing had happened. Unlike most girls she had surrendered to the idea of marriage for Pali's sake, not the other way round, but the difference had to be stressed to keep up her courage.

They turned into a contemporary-looking street and entered a brand-new block of flats. The entrance hall was white and blue, the lift shot up to the third floor where Pali produced a latchkey and ushered her into a flat.

There was not a stick of furniture in the two large rooms; the gleaming kitchen and bathroom were also empty. Between the windows of the larger room there was an absurd round porthole.

"Well, what's this place?" she asked.

"I thought of taking it. It's quite reasonable."

"What's wrong with your flat?"

"I've lived in it without you. I want this place for us. Don't you like it?"

"I do, especially the porthole. It's quite mad."

"Good girl. I particularly want the flat because of the porthole. What with that and the boat-house, we're having a rather nautical romance for a land-locked country. Hey, what are you thinking about now?"

"Nothing."

He threw his thin macintosh on the floor, sat down and pulled her to his side. "Darling, you have a fairly expressive face and I'm not

91

quite dumb. Please don't have secret thoughts, it's not fair!"

She slid down and put her head in his lap.

"I think it's time I told you something," she said, looking at the porthole. "I can face it now. Down at the river when I behaved so oddly I should have told you something that had happened to me two years ago, but somehow I didn't have the courage to talk about it."

"Is it something to do with the chap who caused you a breakdown? You mumbled something about that a long time ago. Well, tell me."

"Is there time? Aren't Sas and Marta expecting us?"

"Not for a while. Come on, let's have it out."

She made herself comfortable. His closeness did not frighten her any more and she did not flinch when his hand settled on her waist.

"He was married but I didn't find out until it was too late; by then I was completely infatuated, the whole thing was like a dream, down at the Balaton. One should never fall in love on holiday, it's quite wrong. There was the lake and a beautiful park and we went sailing and dancing—oh Lord, this sounds so corny, but it wasn't then."

"What did your mother think?"

"She was glad. He was quite marvellous and she thought it was time I got interested in someone at last. Then the bombshell came."

"Poor darling. He sounds a bit of a——"

"Oh no, no, it was all my fault, I took it too seriously. He was probably flattered and amused, and when he realized how I felt about him, he immediately told me everything. He did it so charmingly, it only made things worse. And then he returned to town. We had three more days to go—poor Mother, I don't know how she stuck it with me, I must have been hell. Then we came back, too, and that was worse because I knew he was around, perhaps only two streets away. Half the time I wished I would run into him, the rest of the time I prayed I wouldn't. Of course I did. We were both alone, it was raining hard and I stopped and stared at him like a fool. He smiled and said how much he had thought of me, and I was quite speechless, imagine that. The next day he sent me roses and a wistful little note in French. That was too much. We used to speak French, you see, just for fun. So I took to my bed and howled for three days and didn't eat or drink. I thought it was the end of everything. He had a wife and two children but he loved me. I had no one and I loved him—well, I thought I did—and the only thing to do was to die. Of course I didn't. One doesn't, not since Young Werther, and even he had to shoot himself."

"And then?"

"That's all."

"Come, come. It makes no sense. That's not what you wanted to tell me. When did you last see him?"

She shuddered. "But it's so awful," she faltered. "All right, then —we met again in the street some months later and it was just as upsetting as ever. I don't know what it was about him that paralysed me every time we met. He was very attractive, but there was something else, something commanding—I don't know. Anyway, he seemed very happy to see me and begged me to meet him the next day."

She shut her eyes and went on in a small, weary voice.

"We met at a café. He told me he loved me and said a number of absolutely wonderful things. Then we went to a flat, I think it belonged to a friend of his. He said he wanted to talk to me in private. I went with him quite happily, but——" She shook her head miserably. "He was furious when I refused, he called me a stupid kid and asked me what I thought I was doing, and his face looked so different, I was really frightened and at the same time quite heart-broken. I suddenly realized that all the time we had misunderstood each other completely and that was the worst part of it. I simply ran away. And afterwards I discovered quite by accident that he had chosen the precise moment when his wife was in hospital having their third child. Oh Pali, this sounds so tasteless and melodramatic, I'm terribly sorry, but at least I'm not responsible for that."

He bent down and kissed her. "You poor sweet traumatic thing. On the strength of this you may be as difficult as you like for the next six months or so; after that, Allah have mercy on you. Don't let's talk about it any more, not just now. Look, I won't cancel the flat for the time being. If we survive and it doesn't get hit, I feel we could be very happy here and use the porthole for crystal-gazing. Well, time to go. Sas will want his dreary meal pretty soon."

But he was mistaken: this time Sas wanted nothing less than a real evening out. He was in a state of joyless excitement, his hooded eyes looked bright and he insisted on going to a popular open-air restaurant. So off they went on a tram, disregarding their usual rule of not travelling in groups. Sas kept patting Marta's elbow. He had the air of an unsuccessful commercial traveller.

They chose a table behind a tree, separated from the others by serving tables and, beyond them, the orchestra. Sas ate loudly and enthusiastically as if he had been fasting for a week. The clouded wine was too sweet, the meat tasteless, the pastries looked faded, but the tables stood under green trees and the air smelt of linden flowers. Everything looked so peaceful that Pali was growing restless. These days apparent normality filled him with apprehension.

The gipsy band appeared on the dais. They hacked their way through a number of sickly, mediocre melodies that sounded all alike and could only be told apart by the words—bad lyrics about brown maidens, high-flying cranes, poplars and graves. These tame, sentimental pieces have been cherished by generations of operetta fans who liked a bit of music to accompany their wine and lighten their sorrows. There was a song for every sentiment, loosely worded for easy self-identification.

Normally Gitta would have made acid comments on this syrup. Now she felt uncritical, and at least the tone of the band was perfect. The first violin rang out in sweet, hysterical lament; its voice was tremulous, clear and appealing, and the rest of the strings sighed together, a composite of sad, deep tones, tearful and resigned. Love, Gitta thought, made one tolerant.

The first violinist stepped down among the tables to take orders for songs. The first few requests were as unimaginative as the set pieces until a few tables away somebody showed better taste and the band broke into an old folk-song. Gitta's eyes lit up. It was one of her favourite songs, a slow, simple tune, monotonous in its sadness.

"There's no forest without green branches, my heart is never without sorrow," she hummed. "Sorrow is like the good wind, wherever I go, it follows me." Sas cast her a moody glance; he did not care for this peasant stuff. But she continued with the second verse. The people opposite sang loudly.

"The sun came out over the plain, it shone on every girl's window. My Lord, why should it be that it never shines on mine?"

"Come, come, you aren't doing all that badly," Marta said.

"My justice lies buried in the Rumanian king's chest," Gitta hummed. "Whoever would redeem it for me, God would bless him."

"Play it again!" a man at the table opposite ordered, and he

94

yelled out the words: "My justice lies buried in Adolf Hitler's chest, whoever would redeem it——"

"My, my," Sas said, "there's going to be trouble. The man's either drunk or stupid."

"Or brave," Marta suggested.

A stout man shot up, yelling protests. Others rose to their feet. The gipsy ran back to the rostrum, but the stout man ordered him to repeat the tune once more and then bellowed it out, substituting "Stalin-Roosevelt" for "Adolf Hitler". The noise grew infernal. Waiters rushed around, the band fled into the restaurant building.

"This is how civil wars start," Sas commented, gobbling down Marta's untouched pastry. Two policemen appeared from the street. By the time everybody had returned to their seats, the opposition table stood empty. Pali handed a cigarette to Gitta. She had started to smoke lately.

Sas lit a thin, mean-looking cigar that made Marta flinch: his cigars were too smelly even for the open air, and he smoked them with gusto, tormenting their wrinkled bodies between his stained fingers. He hunched over the table.

"The Germans are preparing to clean up Budapest. They've finished with the Jews in the provinces, now they want to do the same here. On the other hand protests are rolling in from the Pope, the Red Cross, the neutrals and the lot, and although they can't help those wretched two hundred thousand Jews who have already been taken to Poland——"

"As many as that?"

"At least. And I'm afraid very few will come back. But now there may be some resistance to a further drive. Didn't you notice that the place is full of gendarmes from the provinces?"

"Why, yes," Gitta said, "but surely those are the worst of the lot?"

"Not necessarily. They'll obey their orders, and if the Germans persist against the old man's wishes, there may be armed fights. The next few days will be sticky. I want you to get as many Jews under cover as you can. To hell with comfort, put them under the piano—it doesn't matter. Things will go one way or another within a week. If they go badly, well, it's too bad. If they don't, you can send your boarders home."

Slowly the band drifted back and burst into Viennese waltzes, the safest music under the circumstances. Thin strains of jollity floated under the trees, lulling melodies devoted to blue waves, women, song, gold and silver, the innocent music of a dead world. Gitta wondered what her mother would say to another influx. Marta added up Hanna's rooms and decided to put Gyuri's empty flat to good use.

"Cheer up," Sas commanded. "You can't do a thing now, and God alone knows when we'll have another night out." He twirled his cigar and hummed a few notes off key.

But even a second litre of wine failed to cheer them up and after a while they left the restaurant. They were quite close to Gitta's home when Sas steered them towards the entrance of the park.

"But it's out of bounds after dark," Gitta protested. "There's an A.A. gun in the rockery!"

"Never mind, I must pick up something from under a bench. You two go ahead, Marta can stay with me."

The park was very dark. Pali took Gitta's arm and guided her along the path. She rubbed her face on his shoulder. It had been a full day, and the bad news had depressed her. Their brief spell of peace and happiness had made her selfish: she wanted to stay happy and concentrate on Pali. Happiness was habit-forming, she thought; the more one had, the more of it one wanted.

"I think he's got it," Pali said. "I know where his bench is, he uses it regularly as a letter-box. Oh, look, what's that over there?"

A torch flashed out from behind a tree some twenty-five yards ahead. The faint steps behind them stopped dead.

"It's a cop," Pali whispered. "Make a scene, quick." And he said loudly: "Really, I wish you didn't carry on like this, it'll do no good at all."

"Well, I have to, haven't I?" Gitta replied uncertainly. "I must tell you what I think, although you won't budge, you're selfish," her voice rose, "you don't even listen!"

"Of course I do," Pali half-shouted, "but you're really impossible." He stopped in the middle of the path. "I don't object to your mother in principle, but——"

"Leave my mother out of this!" she snapped.

"What's going on here?" the policeman asked, shining his torch into their faces.

"You see what a row you're making," Pali said reproachfully. "I'm sorry, officer, my fiancée and I are having a little argument."

96

"Go on, put the blame on me," she said venomously. "Most gallant!"

"You aren't supposed to be in this park after dark. It's against the rules. Says so on all the gates—can't you read?"

"I'm afraid we didn't look—oh, what an evening," she wailed. "Please let us cut across, it's getting late and the last thing I want is trouble at home."

"Your papers, please."

In the weak light of his torch the policeman examined their documents at great length while Gitta kept up a flood of hysterical conversation to drown any noise the retreating Sas and Marta might make. Only after five minutes and a serious ticking-off were they released. Then Gitta wailed that she was frightened in the dark and the policeman saw them to the far end of the park before returning to his beat.

The street was deserted. Pali put his arm round her. "Oh, you were so convincing—I love you, little one. Isn't it marvellous what a lot of things we need for a row, a park, a policeman, plus Sas in the background, making off on his big flat feet? We won't be able to have very many quarrels, the ingredients won't always be available. Do you mind?"

She smiled, feeling numb with exhaustion. "I'm like the devil's grandmother who needs matchsticks to prop up her eyelids," she murmured. "I love you, too. I wish we were in the boat-house."

CHAPTER ELEVEN

T he office was hot. Behind the lowered Venetian blinds Gitta typed away languidly. A bluebottle droned around the curtains; its metallic buzz grew aggressive every time it circled nearer the lamp. Gitta contemplated her white lawn dress and blue sandals. Summer was boiling away outside, the gaunt trees along the avenue were coated with fine dust, and at noon the asphalt felt soft under one's feet. This was her first summer without a holiday, but she did not mind. Spending a few quiet hours in the office was as good as a holiday. Although the mass deportation Sas had feared had not taken place, the flat was still unbearably crowded with five extra people crammed into very little space, two of them practically sleeping under the grand piano, as Sas had suggested. Mrs. Balogh kept chaos at bay, but the strain was beginning to tell and she often snapped at Gitta since it was impossible to snap at anybody else. They had both expected Rozália to hand in her notice; the maid, however, said nothing. She went about her business very much as usual, shooing people out of the room she wanted to clean and sending them back the moment she had finished. When Mrs. Balogh offered her a handsome sum to compensate her for the extra work, she refused it brusquely.

It could not go on much longer: Pali said so. Sas was expecting a change any minute. Gitta sighed and typed another sentence. If it had not been for Pali, she would have long ago succumbed to one of her black depressions that paralysed body and soul until she felt she would never smile again. Now things were different. She only had to think of him and everything came back into focus. Every hour brought nearer their next meeting, and once they were together nothing ever went wrong.

The telephone rang. "Four-two-three-five-five-eight," she said.

"Miss Gitta, will you please come home," Rozália said.

"Why, hello, Rozália, what's the matter? Something wrong?"

There was a brief silence, then the flat, wooden voice said: "You must come home at once, Miss Gitta. It's important."

"But I can't leave the office just like that! What's the matter? Is my mother ill?"

"No. Will you come at once," Rozália repeated, and then her voice went shrill and she shouted: "No, no, don't come, go away, I meant no harm!" A man's voice bawled something in the background, Rozália screamed and the telephone went dead.

Gitta dialled her home number at once, but nobody replied. She replaced the receiver. It was easy to guess what had happened, but she had no idea what to do next. Her body was tense with apprehension. Pali's number did not reply. Where could he be? Apart from keeping their dates meticulously, he was as elusive as Sas. Hanna was out. Her maid thought she would not be back until late. Mihály? He had warned them about every telephone in the Ministry being tapped by the Germans. Hell, she had to risk it, they had rehearsed the alarm code often enough.

"I think I'll have to go away for a while," she said. "Don't get in touch with me for the time being, not until you hear from me."

"Good God, are you sure?" He had understood.

"Looks like it. Very much so."

"Where are you now?"

"In the office. But I must go home now."

"Is it wise? Shall I meet you somewhere?"

"No, thanks. Mother is unwell, I can't leave her on her own."

"Gitta, think hard. Wouldn't your mother prefer you to stay away?"

"It's no use, I must go home."

"We'll try to . . . send you magazines and books."

"Thanks." She held the receiver so tight that her knuckles went white and the finger-nails cut into her palm. "Tell Pali to look after himself. Give him my love. I must go now, Mihály—isn't it stupid?"

The journey home was interminable. She stood on the front platform of the tram, near the driver, and watched the gleaming tracks rolling under the wheels. She knew what to expect and she was scared.

As she let herself into the flat, a strange man grabbed her by the arm and flung her into the middle of the hall. There were two more men standing near the wardrobe and another two shot out of the drawing-room.

"So you've come home at last," one of them shouted. "You ought to be ashamed of yourselves, you and your mother."

He grabbed her elbow and pushed her into the drawing-room. Everything was upside down, the furniture had been shifted around, the rugs were crumpled, doors stood open, drawers had spilt their contents. It was as if a spasm of sickness had upset the immaculate room. Mrs. Balogh stood in the middle with immense dignity, her arms folded, her face contemptuous. She nodded to her daughter. The door to Gitta's room stood open. She could see all their guests standing in a cluster inside.

"Right. Now we're all here," Mrs. Balogh said. "What next?"

"Wait and see," a short man said darkly. "Get on with the search, boys, we've wasted enough time already."

Well, this was it, Gitta thought—the scene she had so often imagined, knowing for sure it would never happen and therefore not bothering to think up a satisfactory conclusion. The thought of being caught had only troubled her as a half-pleasurable fantasy, in the manner of children who think up horrors to frighten themselves and then shiver with joy because after all it's only a game. But this was real, five plain-clothes men wreaking havoc in the flat, five frightened Jewesses trapped next door, and nobody to help. Still, the fading of the fantasy made her fear vanish, too. Now she was only angry and full of fight. She glanced at her mother. Mrs. Balogh answered with an unmistakable wink.

"Who are you, anyway?" Gitta turned to the nearest detective. He was busy peering under the carpet; his shiny trousers stretched tightly across his seat.

"State Police," he snapped.

"Oh. And what are you looking for?"

He looked as if he wanted to strike her. "It's not you who should ask questions. If I were you, I'd shut up."

"You obviously don't know what you're in for," another man said. "Wait until you hear the charges."

"I can hardly wait." This was true: she very much wanted to know how bad the situation was. Was it just the Jewish guests or worse? And how in heaven's name did the police come to be there at all?

100

"Fehér, take those Yids away," the man in the shiny trousers said to his youngest colleague. "They'll be questioned at H.Q."

"I'm responsible for those women being here," Mrs. Balogh said. "They didn't want to come, I insisted that they stay with me."

"Look here, must you make things worse for yourself? Shut up and don't stick your neck out."

Mrs. Balogh looked him up and down with immense contempt.

"You're a traitor!" the man shouted. "A traitor to your race and your country! You worship our worst enemies!" He tore the gold-framed portrait of the Windsors off the wall, but Mrs. Balogh stamped her foot and snatched it from him.

Now the five women were coming out from Gitta's room. Slowly, reluctantly they passed through the door, keeping close to the wall. Old Mrs. Blum came last. She shook her head, muttering to herself.

"Quiet there!" Fehér growled. He was a thin young man with wavy hair and a silver-white silk tie. But as Mrs. Blum took no notice of him, he tapped her shoulder and shouted: "I said, be quiet, do you hear me?"

"Young man," Mrs. Blum said, "I'm old enough to be your grandmother. I had seven sons, four were killed in the Great War, two were wounded, so I think I have more right to talk than you."

"Why don't you claim immunity?" Fehér asked crossly. "With that sort of war record——"

"Why should I? My three surviving sons are in labour camps. Why should I have it easier? I'm seventy-six, you know."

"Take them out and for Christ's sake stop nattering!"

"Come this way." Fehér opened the door. Suzy Tóth burst into tears and waved to Mrs. Balogh. "Can't you do something?" she wailed. "Can't you stop them?" But Mrs Balogh frowned and said disapprovingly: "Pull yourself together, it'll be all right," and then Fehér jostled everybody to the hall.

Pali, Gitta thought, what would he do? He would talk himself out of most situations or, if that were impossible, he would deny everything that was not irrefutably proved. Failing even that he would fall silent and make things awkward for his captors. That was the line of most resistance.

The other detectives came in.

"You've hoarded an awful lot of food!" one of them said.

"Didn't you? The only difference is that I can't search your pan-

101

try." Mrs. Balogh smoothed her hair. "Really, I do wish you'd tell me what you're looking for."

The man in the shiny trousers ignored her. "Leave the food, boys, we've enough evidence. Take that strong-box, the picture and the papers and let's go. Is the car ready?"

"Fehér took it to run the prisoners in."

"Damn Fehér! I wanted the car, he could have made them walk. He knows how short we are of transport. Now we must go by tram. Are you two ready?"

"Just where do you want us to go?"

"To prison, of course."

"By tram? Don't be silly!" Mrs. Balogh exclaimed. "Do prisoners pay full fares on public vehicles? And what about handcuffs?" She turned to Gitta. "Darling, go and change. You can't go to jail in a white dress."

The jewels, Gitta thought, the jewels and valuables belonging to half a dozen people—were they marked with names and addresses? And what papers were there? Had she kept anything compromising in her desk? She could not remember. The last batch of leaflets had been posted two days ago but she had been a little careless lately, too happy to worry about risks——

"She'll damn well come as she is." The man was furious. "Your flat will be sealed for the time being, you needn't worry about your property. Come along now."

"I'm not leaving this flat until that beastly creature clears out."

"You've no right to call her beastly, she only did her patriotic duty. Anyhow, she's ready to go,"

"I want to see her leave. And I want her keys."

Rozália stood in the hall surrounded by two battered fibre cases and a number of parcels. There were red patches on her face; her chin trembled. When she saw Mrs. Balogh and Gitta being escorted out by four detectives, she threw up her hands and began to wail.

"Forgive me, forgive me, I meant no harm, you've been like a mother to me, say you aren't angry, it's only that I wanted those women out of the way!"

"Be quiet. And clear out," Mrs. Balogh said.

"It was the Yids, madam; you don't know what they're capable of!" The maid's rough hands shook. "All my life I've had nothing but trouble with them. They aren't like us, madam, I hate them!"

102

"It's all right, my dear, don't upset yourself," the man in the shiny trousers said. "You've done the right thing, there's nothing to worry about."

"Leave me alone!" Rozália shrieked. "Leave my lady alone, she's a fine person, she's always been kind to me. Oh Jesus and Mary, what have I done!"

"Stop it, you stupid girl, before I get angry. You should have made up your mind before getting in touch with us. Now give me your keys and go, I must get this place sealed."

Rozália thrust the keys at him and picked up her baggage. Half-blinded by tears she staggered out of the flat, her long wails echoing from the staircase. Mrs. Balogh averted her face. Pali had been right: the maid was a natural Nazi.

Mrs. Balogh watched the flat door being locked and sealed and it occurred to her that the ice-box would soon need fresh ice, otherwise the butter would go off within a day. But she said nothing and they left the house, the four men surrounding them unobtrusively— there was little glory in escorting two women in summer dresses down a sleepy street. In the tram all six of them kept quiet, hardly looking at each other. Gitta wondered whether to kick and scream and appeal for help, but the likely results did not seem to justify the effort. She looked at her mother's large handbag. It looked pretty full. Had she stuffed in a few useful things when nobody was looking? But then what was useful in jail?

Before entering the police headquarters, Gitta took one last look at the indifferent street. They were marched along cool corridors, past drab doors and heavily barred windows, and there were ill-tempered men rushing around in rubber-soled shoes. Gitta wished her high heels did not ring out so gaily. Her spirits began to flag: defiance had been easier at home.

After a lot of administration—one could not even go to prison without paper work—they were pushed into a large, crowded room. The door slammed behind them. Men and women were standing about or sitting on the dirty floor. The air smelt heavy. Mrs. Balogh took hold of Gitta's hand.

"Surely, they don't expect us to stay here?"

A little man rushed forward, grinning broadly. "Welcome, gracious lady, make yourself at home. This is the first dormitory one gets into, they're awfully short of cells. It's all right, really, except at night, but you needn't worry about the people, they're a nice lot."

"I'm sure," Mrs. Balogh said politely. "Who are they? Have you been here long?"

"Couple of weeks. Oh, we're a mixed bunch, mostly larceny and theft and black market, nothing serious. Are you politicals?"

"Why, yes, I think so," Gitta said. "Any others here?"

"Only one. That thin chap in the corner. Bit touched, I think, he walks up and down reciting poetry. They say he's a Commie."

"I see." Mrs. Balogh looked around uncertainly with the air of a woman in a shop who does not think she will buy anything but has not got the heart to say so. "But look here, where are we going to sleep? I mean, my daughter——"

"It's very decorous here, truly, nobody undresses," the little man assured her. "And I'll see to it that you get proper seats. Hey, get up, mates, we want those chairs for the ladies," and he presented two ancient wicker chairs with a grand sweep of the arm, dusting them with his grubby handkerchief.

They sat down. The brown walls were peeling, the only light came from a fly-blown bulb high up, since there were no windows in the room. After a long while the door was unlocked and two men brought in a cauldron of soup which they slopped out into enamelled mugs.

"When I was packing away the other day," Mrs. Balogh reflected, "I thought we might soon be eating bean soup out of tin mugs. Well, here it is. Darling, I wish I could have spared you this. It's wretched not to be able to protect one's child from this sort of atrocity."

"Atrocity? May nothing worse happen to us. At least we're together. And all the best people are in jail—oh, sorry, I didn't mean to be frivolous. But the whole thing is so unreal, don't you agree, I can't take it seriously."

"It may be serious, especially for you. Oh, baby, I so wanted you to have a good time while you're young and now I can't even give you a decent dinner; and God alone knows what comes next."

"Please don't let's become tragic. After all, this is mostly my fault. I'm responsible for an awful lot of things, not you. Look, we simply must try this soup, I bet we've never eaten anything like it. We'll get off lightly, you'll see. Above all, please don't cry."

The soup was dreadful. They ate it and sat silently. Time stood still, it was impossible to tell the hour. Much later a policeman came

104

in to take out those who wanted a wash. Gitta joined a group of women. The row of dark, sordid lavatories had loose doors with no handles or bolts. "But this is impossible," she said sharply to the policeman who stood two yards away. "I want to shut the door!" He shook his head. "I'm not going to hang myself," she pleaded. He shrugged. He had his orders. But then he moved away to the far end of the corridor.

Mrs. Balogh welcomed her back with an enormous bottle of eau-de-Cologne and some cotton wool. "Have a little wash," she suggested, "and rub some into your hair. I fear the worst; these people don't look too clean and the last thing we want is vermin. You know," she went on less briskly, "I was thinking how unprepared one always is in life. I've seen *Fidelio* at least twenty times, but I've never thought about prison as such—it never occurred to me that Florestan might have been troubled by lice, for instance, the scenery always looked so antiseptic."

"The light will go out in a moment, lady," said the little man who had first welcomed them. "Better get ready."

"How?"

"Well, you can't sit up all night! Look, here's a State blanket, quite clean, too. Now if you put it down on the floor, like that——"

"Later, thank you. We'll stay put for the moment."

Around them people were lying down, one after another, wriggling uncomfortably in search of the least painful position. The room had turned into a wilderness of legs, arms and crumpled clothing. Two women argued shrilly about a sheltered corner, then a man separated them and they curled up, muttering furiously. Now there was only one man standing up, a short, birdlike man with blazing eyes and thick red hair. He spoke softly to himself until a fruity voice from the floor demanded silence; and then the light went out.

CHAPTER TWELVE

"Their flat is sealed all right," Marta said. "I went right to the door to take a close look. There was a man watching me from next door, but I had Papa's *Mein Kampf* under my arm and I felt quite safe. Then I went down to the caretaker's flat on the ground floor, and the maid was there, having a colossal row with the caretaker's wife. The maid knows me, she saw me once, months ago. I said I had been in the country and where was Gitta, and then both women started yelling and eventually the maid rushed out with her luggage and I followed her."

"But what was the row about?" Mihály asked. He was badly shaken.

"Apparently the maid had complained to the caretaker's wife about the Jewish refugees in the flat, and the wretched woman, who is a fanatical Nazi, incited her to report the Baloghs, because she said they would both get a reward. Rozália only came to her senses when it was too late, and she's terribly conscience-stricken."

"I should like to strike her with something sharper." Pali's headache was getting worse. It felt like the beginning of a full-scale migraine. They were sitting in Hanna's drawing-room, knocking back stiff drinks and glowering at each other.

"But at least their flat is safe!" Hanna said. "Such an enchanting place—at least they'll have somewhere to return to."

"Countess, don't be naïve," Sas said. "We don't know whether they will be able to return to it. And the State knocks off its own seals as easily as it puts them up. Did the maid say what exactly she had written to the police?"

"Mainly about the Jews. But I'm afraid she had also enclosed a copy of our last leaflet. She had pinched it from Gitta's desk."

"Hell and damnation!" Sas roared. "Why in God's name did that idiotic girl keep the stuff in her desk? She was told to be extra careful on account of that maid and the other people in the flat!"

"That will do," Pali interrupted. "Spare us your tantrums. I daresay that under similar circumstances others would be caught napping, too."

"All right, all right, I know you have a soft spot for little Gitta, but if she spills the beans we will all be in the biggest mess. Don't you realize what it means? We may all have to clear out and lie low for months or go to Yugoslavia, but I happen to have some work to do here!"

He banged his fist on the sofa table and the glasses protested with a tinkle. Hanna leapt to her feet.

"Dr. Sas, behave yourself!" she cried. "For one thing, don't smash up my furniture. For another, we may be a bunch of soft-hearted morons, but that poor girl and her mother are in trouble, and if you can't be more decent about it, you may just as well go."

"I apologize, Countess. We don't see things in the same light. But I can't go just now. I am involved in this, too."

Pali swallowed two aspirins. There was a persistent purple flicker in his left eye, and several thin steel blades rotated slowly in his head.

"Look here," he said wearily to Sas, "Gitta won't spill the beans. I know her. She's no fool, she knows what is at stake. So let's get on to the next point."

"People do talk under great duress, and I don't think she has ever been slapped in her life. If they give her the full treatment, she will get a colossal shock. You may swear by her character, but how do you know whether she can or cannot stand pain?"

"Surely, third degree is highly unlikely!" Marta said quickly. "After all, she's only a podgy child with the most innocent face in the world. I personally feel that whatever they do to her, she'll shut up. That girl can be obstinate, she'll dig her toes in and just stand there like Luther, with no alternative. The point is—can we do anything to get her out?"

"Terribly difficult," Sas said moodily. "At one time I had splendid contacts with the police, but they are useless now. What about you?"

"Unless Hanna tackles my father, I can't do anything. If I asked him, he would turn me down automatically."

"Can't you blackmail him by saying you'll be in trouble unless the

107

Baloghs are released?" Mihály asked. "Surely he would stand by you!"

"Not necessarily."

"Let's leave him out altogether," Sas suggested. "We'll try some other means. But even if we succeed, they'll be under observation for some time, which means that nobody, you understand, nobody must get in touch with them. I want this to be absolutely clear; no sentimental nonsense on anybody's part," he said sharply, looking at Pali. "Meanwhile, all activities suspended. Destroy every shred of evidence, wherever you keep it, and don't meet too often. We've got to sit out the next few days. I think I'll be able to get some information soon."

"All right, you old bully," Marta said. "I should like to meet you in peace-time and see what you're like. Probably madly neurotic and frustrated, with nobody to order about."

Pali was no longer listening. Behind the screen of pain he saw Gitta's face, trusting, open, eager, the cheek childishly rounded, the mouth determined. Were they going to hurt her? The pressure was mounting inside his head, he could hardly bear it. He was to blame for her predicament. He had assumed full responsibility with the first instruction he had given her, and she had always obeyed unquestioningly, implying by her soldierly submission that whatever he commanded was right, correct and safe. She probably still thought so. He knew that she would not let him down and that she still believed in him as unconditionally as he did in her; but that would not stop the police from beating her up.

Little one, he thought, it should be me, not you, and I can't do anything for you now. We were too happy. Whatever happens, something is going to be destroyed. The jealous gods have separated the half-kernels again, the gods, not Allah—He is detached and lets the minor powers get on with the dirty work. There are dark powers, call them accident, destiny, coincidence, bad luck; Saturnus rolls across the sky and destroys a delicate pattern, and we are left with a pebble each in our hands.

Hanna touched his shoulder. "You look ghastly," she said. "Why don't you go home? There's nothing we can do now."

"I have a headache, that's all. I'll ring you tomorrow."

In the street the air smelt of dry dust. The sunset stretched a purple banner across the sky, and the cobbles seemed to rise and fall under his feet as he walked home. He went to bed immediately with a strong sleeping-pill and woke up at midnight in the cold grip of a nightmare. He went back to sleep and the same dream returned: he saw Gitta through a thick green wall that moved like water but felt solid when he tried to break through it; she was in difficulties, crying and shaking with fear; and when at last he found a porthole in the green wall, he was unable to smash it.

CHAPTER THIRTEEN

~~~~~~~~~~~~~~~~~~~~~

It was their fourth day in prison. They had acquired the knack
of lying on the floor at night without becoming stiff and sore
half-way through; it was mostly a matter of changing one's
position at regular intervals and distributing the body's weight
between hipbone and shoulder. Personal hygiene depended on the
eau-de-Cologne which they used twice a day, rationing themselves
to a few drops at a time. Gitta's white dress was turning greyish. Her
mother's, dark blue with irregular white circles, still looked reasonably crisp.

Prisoners came and went, but for every two who were taken away
three new ones arrived, and now there were some gipsies among
them, three unlicensed prostitutes and a small, frightened barber
who had accidentally cut a German soldier on the chin while shaving
him and had immediately been arrested. The red-haired, birdlike
man was still there, though, keeping very much to himself and pouring forth a wealth of poetry in a soft, even voice. Gitta would have
loved to speak to him, but Mrs. Balogh had laid down the rule of
not talking unless talked to, so she only strained her ears in his
direction. But once when she opened her compact to put the last
remaining powder on her nose, the red-haired man strode across the
room and said: "How wonderful to see a woman bothering about
her face. Don't put your mirror away yet—won't you comb your
hair?"

After that they often sat together, mostly in his corner. He said it
was the best point for watching the door, yet the most awkward for
any assailant to reach. Having been in and out of prison for some
years for being a Communist, he had developed a trauma about
doors that burst open suddenly. His name was Lázár, he was a poet,
homeless, penniless, father of two illegitimate children by two differ-

ent women, ready to die for his beliefs but much more anxious to live for them. Gitta spoke to him gently, with the reverence due to a mild lunatic, because although Lázár's mind functioned with the precision of a machine and the flamboyance of a Roman candle, his complete lack of social responsibility struck her as somewhat insane. He sensed her restrained curiosity and misinterpreted it vehemently.

"Pity you are such a little *bourgeoise*," he said. "It always upsets me to see people like yourself who are bright and full of good intentions and yet completely useless—you are so rigid and conventional, your upbringing has crippled you for life. I bet you have ready-made ideas. I bet you think that the Englishman who changes into a dinner jacket in the middle of the jungle is doing an admirable thing."

"Yes, I do. He does it to maintain his balance and self-respect."

"Piffle. He does it out of snobbery and to remind himself of his class prejudices."

"If that helps him to maintain his balance, all the better. But you are illogical. To me, powdering my nose here means the same as the dinner jacket means to the Englishman in the jungle, yet you were glad to see my compact. And what about you? You go on reciting poetry and some people here think you are mad, but to you that's the equivalent of a dinner jacket."

"Poetry is a thing of the mind, dinner jackets and compacts are not. You see how weak your judgement is, not noticing the difference."

"All right," Gitta said equably, "mine is weak, yours is rigid, and I am not sure which is worse, except that a poet shouldn't be dogmatic. Anyway, why do you pity me as if I were lost for ever? I have no intention of dying young."

"No, but you will be a dead loss in our future society. There will be no room for *bourgeois* souls in it."

"Everybody is trying to eliminate me. I don't fit into the present, you don't think I shall fit into the future. Well, where do you want me to exist, in the past?"

"That's where you exist all the time. The past means conventions, and you are full of them. You are twenty, but you haven't lived yet, and you feel no urge for it, either!"

"How do you know whether I have lived yet or not?"

"You are a virgin, aren't you?"

111

"What has that got to do with it?" She was too shocked to blush.

"An awful lot. Take a lover. Have a child. Bring it into the world and love it, and then you will have started life, not before."

"I suppose if I do the same in marriage, it doesn't count?"

"There you are, another convention! Don't you see the difference between having a child by your lover because you want it, and having a child because you are married to a chap and it's the thing to do? Your type of person horrifies me. You are half-dead, killing your impulses, always wondering about the outcome. I am surprised that you have managed to get yourself into jail at all."

"Why are you here?" she asked sharply.

"Out of sheer habit. I haven't done anything this time, they just brought me in for security reasons. You don't happen to have a pencil?"

"No, they took mine away. Can't you write in your head?"

"I've been doing it for too long. Some parts get mixed up."

"I should like to hear some of your poetry."

"Not yet. I don't know you well enough. And I don't feel like it just now. What are the things you are thinking about? When you can't sleep at night, for instance?"

"Oh, mostly wondering what's going to happen to us. I hate this waiting. Do they always do it? And when something does happen, what is it going to be like?"

"I don't know. Your case is different from mine. But be prepared for one thing: these cops are astoundingly stupid. I call them the Unintelligence Service. You'll see for yourself."

The summons came the same afternoon. A glossy-haired man poked his head round the door, bellowed out the Baloghs' name and marched them along several corridors to a long, gloomy hall furnished with desks and chairs. They were made to stand in front of a desk. The middle-aged detective sitting behind it scrutinized their papers for a long while.

"You are guilty of illegally sheltering five Jewesses in your home," he said. "How much did they pay you?"

"They didn't pay me, they were my guests."

"Answer me. How much did they pay you?"

Mrs. Balogh did not reply. She shrugged and looked away.

"I must warn you that obstinacy won't help."

"I invited them to stay as my guests," she said, "because I had

112

hoped to keep them in safety as long as necessary. Unfortunately, I failed."

"You are an intelligent woman. You are a Christian. The Jews are our worst enemies. Why do you stand by them?"

"Because as a Christian I believe in being kind to my worst enemies," she said sarcastically. "But look here, this is a waste of time. I am not going to discuss my moral tenets with you. Let's get on with the job."

"As you wish. I daresay you'll soon stop being impudent. You are also guilty of hoarding food, undoubtedly purchased on the black market, and of being in possession of Jewish property which should have been surrendered to the State."

"Nonsense. All the property in the flat belongs to me."

"Indeed?" He placed the family strong-box on the desk. "Let's go through the contents together, shall we? I want you to check them against our list."

Out came the small parcels, anonymous in their white tissue paper wrappings. Gitta's heart jumped. If the man asked Mrs. Balogh to enumerate and describe the contents, they were lost. She knew how hastily the valuables had been put away, practically without looking at them, almost four months ago. But Lázár's forecast had been correct. The detective began to unwrap the parcels, laying them out tidily all over the desk.

"An awful lot of fine jewellery," he said. "Highly valuable stuff. You aren't a rich woman, you are a widow, how do you come to own all this?"

"My late husband was well off. He thought jewellery was a good investment."

"Have you any receipts to prove it?"

She laughed scornfully. "Even a good investment must be presented graciously, don't you agree? If my husband had given me the receipts, I should have been mortally offended."

"Indeed. Interesting. And what about these things? Three heavy gold cigarette cases—men's cases, aren't they?—and four men's wrist-watches of the most expensive kind. What's more, they are almost brand-new, and your husband died ten years ago, did he not? So how did you acquire these?"

Mrs. Balogh gave him a level look. Her normal nervous blinking had stopped; her gaze was steady and crystal-clear.

113

"They were given to me as presents."

"You don't say so! Who by?"

"By my men friends. As you've said yourself, my husband has been dead for ten years."

Gitta almost choked. She bit into her tongue until it hurt. The detective glanced at her, noticed her burning face and decided to drop the subject. But Mrs. Balogh was not satisfied.

"Is there any law forbidding a widow to accept gifts from friends?" she asked. "I want to know my position. You see, all my life I've been on the right side of the law."

The detective was already wrapping up the exhibits. "This needs further investigation. But you'll be asked to name your . . . benefactors."

"Oh, I couldn't do that," she said girlishly. "There would be some high-ups involved, including a German dignitary."

"Sign this list, will you?" But now she insisted on checking and secretly memorizing every item, putting them back into the strongbox herself. Gitta watched her with pride.

The detective signalled to a man in the back of the room. "Take the woman back. The girl stays here."

"Oh no, my daughter is a minor, I'm not going to be parted from her."

"Tut, tut. A woman of your character has no right to fuss. Your daughter will be safer here than she was with you."

Bang, Gitta thought, Mother as the original Scarlet Woman. "Don't worry, darling," she said solemnly, "I'll be all right."

Mrs. Balogh was led away. The detective stared hard at Gitta; his round eyes contracted with the effort. She stared back. It was a game she had excelled at as a small child.

"I have a daughter of your age," he said at last. "I want to help you, you need it badly. Tell me everything and then we'll try to find a way out."

"Tell you what?"

He wagged his head, then his hand shot into the file, tore out a sheet of paper and thrust it at Gitta. "What's this?"

She recognized their leaflet. They had been so proud of it; a masterpiece of persuasion, Pali had called it.

"Oh, that? It came in the post."

"It did nothing of the sort. It was done on your typewriter."

114

"I doubt that very much."

"Oh, cut the cackle, you stupid kid: do you want to go to a concentration camp?"

"Not particularly. But I'm telling you, it came in the post."

"You belong to an underground group. We know. Tell me the names of your accomplices and we'll drop the charges against you and you can go home with your mother."

She looked away, just as Mrs. Balogh had done, and did not reply.

"Several young people have been visiting your flat lately. We have their descriptions. You don't stand a chance, you fool!"

She kept her mind deliberately blank, as though even thinking of Pali might give the detective a clue. She remained immobile when his fist crashed on the desk, right under her nose, but her stomach contracted nervously.

"We are going to find them! You'll all be shot like mad dogs! High treason is no trifling offence, you stupid girl, and in wartime being a minor doesn't count!"

He was shouting at her, his fist flailing the air, until every noise died away in the hall and she was conscious of unseen eyes focusing on her back. The man's violence frightened her more than his threats, his voice was harder to bear than what he was shouting, and she clenched her teeth and looked away stubbornly. A rough hand pulled her up. She was being pushed and jostled back to the communal cell.

"Don't cry," Lázár said.

"I didn't cry when it happened," Gitta sniffed, tears rolling down her face, "but I've got to cry some time." Her handkerchief was drenched, so she folded it in four and wiped her nose with the driest bit. There were red finger-marks on her cheek.

"Why did he hit you?"

She shrugged. "He made a row the very first time. Next time he shouted and swore at me even more, but the desk was between us and I felt fairly safe. This time he stood in front of me, and when I told him for the tenth time that I knew nothing and had nothing to confess, he made as if he wanted to slap me—you know, that silly trick schoolboys do, swinging a hand towards your face and then stopping half an inch short of your cheek. Well, I lost my head and

115

kicked him in the shins, and then he slapped me right and proper, the brute."

"At least he didn't knock your teeth out. They like to do that. Still, I'm glad you kicked him. Where's your mother?"

"Oh, probably being questioned somewhere else. They waste an awful lot of time on us. What's going to happen in the end?"

"Your mother will probably get away with a fine. I don't know about you, they are much stricter with youngsters who won't confess than with adults who are caught red-handed breaking a regulation. I don't know what advice to give you—carry on being cheeky and annoy them, or shut up and try to get released fast. Both have their drawbacks."

She did not reply. The novelty of being a prisoner, of sleeping on the floor in company with thirty-odd unknown men and women, had worn off, and now she only felt anxious and distressed. Physical discomfort hardly mattered; it would have been petty to long for a hot bath or fresh clothes. But she was mortified to realize that such a situation such a complete loss of self-determination, could actually happen to them, and the last shred of her childhood fell away with the knowledge that her strong, invincible, resourceful mother was just as helpless as herself. Until now she had maintained a secret core of trust and dependence, sampling life with the unspoken certainty that, if anything went seriously wrong, Mrs. Balogh would be able to sort it out and only chide her for getting herself into such a silly scrape. Now that they were in a scrape together, she recognized the loneliness of every human situation and the limited nature of her mother's power, and she felt desolate.

"I thought dinner would always be at half-past seven," she said.

"What's that?"

"Oh, nothing much. I was having a *bourgeois* thought, you'll probably laugh at me, I don't care . . . it's only that if you're brought up in a well-organized way, you think that the whole of life will be like that. Ever since I can remember we always had our meals at the same hours, and I thought it would always be like that. When I was small we lived in a vast flat—Father was alive then—and on winter afternoons I used to play in the big *salon*. It was a lovely room, with tobacco-brown silk draperies and large yellow wing-chairs and an enormous Oriental carpet. The piano stood on one side, Father's violin lay on top, and on the walls there were small engravings

116

showing scenes from operas. I used to play there with my dolls and picture books, and the stove purred in the corner and most days it snowed outside. Well, every afternoon at four the clock in the dining-room next door chimed, and the fourth chime wasn't quite off the air when the door opened and Mother or my governess brought in my hot milk. It came in a tall porcelain beaker with circus animals painted all over it, a seal balancing a red ball on its nose, a clown with a hoop and I think a girl on horseback. I sat down quickly on the floor, grabbed the beaker and drank until I was breathless."

"Go on."

"That, of course, stopped when I grew older. But meals were always on time, obsessionally so. Dinner was always at half-past seven, and I had to allow time for washing my hands and tidying up. Sometimes I would have given anything for another ten minutes on the ice rink, I was very much in love with a little boy there, but he rarely spoke to me. And when he did, I had to interrupt him when the last moment had come for me to leave. I suppose he needed two hours' skating to pick up enough courage to talk to a girl, that's why he always left it so late. Once I went home crying. I felt he would never notice me again. But I mustn't be late for dinner, even if it broke my heart."

Lázár rested his head on his knees and looked at her gravely.

"Perhaps these things don't really matter in life," she went on, "but they make such a good framework. They give you ridiculous security. Your heart may break, you may be hurt by people, you may lose your faith in God or discover that your favourite poet is a silly, sentimental rhymester—but dinner will still be at half-past seven. Now I know that all sorts of things can happen. One may even go to sleep without dinner."

"Yes, all sorts of things are possible. In the end you only have yourself to hang on to. Render down what you are to a minimum, a capsule, as it were, to contain the essential, and discard the rest. Question every single belief you hold. Have the courage to admit that half of them are phoney or hypocritical or second-hand, and throw them away. Lose the details, they don't matter a damn. You must only retain the things you absolutely believe in and cling to them through everything. I remember hearing a story when I was a boy—I lived in a village, there was no wallpaper or piano, and only one meal a day, I bet you've never met anybody who had spent half

117

his life barefoot or at least without socks. Yes, this story has stuck in my mind ever since; it was about a young lad who went in search of some symbolical nonsense—the tree of eternal youth, I think—and reached the river of Death. As he crossed it, the water washed away his clothes, his hair, his flesh, everything until only the nice clean bones remained. The essential, if you like."

"And then?"

"Oh, he clambered out on the other side, and suddenly his flesh and his clothes returned and he was stronger and handsomer than ever. And, not knowing any better, he continued his journey."

"A comforting moral."

Mrs. Balogh was brought in. She made her way across the room and sat down next to Lázár.

"They're mad, completely mad," she said wearily. "We went through those beastly jewels again, same questions, same answers. Then they said—there were two of them today, the new man looked like a water-flea—they said we were suspected of working for the Russians, and he kept asking me about a radio transmitter."

"Did you ever have one?" he asked.

"No, we didn't. The last contact we had with anything Russian was when my daughter read Merezhkovsky at the age of thirteen and became violently ill for a couple of days. But how can you prove anything negative, that you have no transmitter, for instance?"

They sat in silence. It was very hot. The stuffiness grew unbearable. The gipsies smelt bad, everybody moved as far from them as possible. Mrs. Balogh furtively inspected her nails. She would have given almost anything for a cup of strong coffee.

The next morning—they were in the middle of their eau-de-Cologne ritual—a tall, cross-eyed man strode in and shouted: "Politicals, come along and bring your belongings." The Baloghs and Lázár scrambled to their feet. The cross-eyed man let them pass through the door. It was a sparkling morning. The sunlight streaming through the windows hurt their eyes. There were two more men waiting outside and they were marched off to the main entrance of the building. Outside a big open lorry stood loaded with office furniture, desks and chairs piled high, with some filing-cabinets thrown in.

They were made to clamber right on top, not without difficulty. Mrs. Balogh abhorred gymnastics. But at last they were safely perched on a big desk, and their escorts hid discreetly in the back.

118

Gitta was overjoyed to be out of doors again. She lifted her face into the sweet summer air, relishing the faint breeze and the silken sky with its staccato clouds. The lorry drove across a bridge, rattled through cobbled streets, heaving and creaking at every turning.

"Imagine if anybody saw us now," Gitta whispered to her mother. "They would probably think we'd gone stark raving mad to travel on top of all this furniture! Oh, isn't the air stupendous? I'd forgotten it smelt so nice!"

She began to sing, drunk with comparative freedom. After the evil-smelling, windowless room the light and the air were overwhelming, and she turned her head ecstatically from side to side to see everything. She hummed and chatted with her mother and teased Lázár who perched wanly on the edge of the desk: his empty stomach did not take kindly to this dizzy type of transport.

"Be quiet," one of the detectives warned at last. "You're making far too much noise."

"But it's so lovely up here," she said. "Where are you taking us?"

"You'll see."

The lorry drove up a sloping road, past the Meadow of Blood and the Southern Railway Station. More and more trees and gardens appeared with fewer houses in between. They were leaving the town behind, climbing towards the hills.

"Damn," Lázár said softly, "we're going to the Svábhegy and that can only mean the political police. Better stop singing."

CHAPTER FOURTEEN

ard as she tried, Hanna Morelli could do nothing for the Baloghs. The once influential people she approached were unable to help. Traditional nepotism no longer functioned, and bribery had become difficult, since nobody knew whom to bribe in the first instance and how to proceed to the higher channels. The retired civil functionaries and former Secretaries of State shook their heads sadly: these days people had to work out their own salvation. But, talking about salvation, one of them added, would she care to join them at a spiritualist session that night and ask a few questions from their guiding spirit who spelt out messages with a glass?

The session took place in a dusky room. Hanna was asked to join her hand to the half-dozen anxious ones hovering over the writing glass. Eventually the glass began to move over the alphabet board; messages poured out for those present, brief, cryptic messages which everybody interpreted differently. Hanna's turn came at the very end. She was greeted by her dead father who strongly advised her to go abroad (did he not know that travel was impossible?) and then said that he was very happy, receiving higher tuition from Lin Yutang. But, as far as Hanna knew, Lin Yutang was still alive, and she decided to withdraw her support from the group. Uninformed spirits were worse than no spirits at all.

But there was no escape. The air raids, unexpected deaths, privations and chaos forced people to flee from reality and turn for consolation towards the occult. Most of Hanna's friends had taken up some supernatural hobby and she received a multitude of invitations to weird meetings.

The anthroposophists were quite promising and perhaps she would have joined them in all seriousness, had it not been that one of their leaders had an uncanny eye for reading astral bodies, and Hanna felt bashful about being so unilaterally exposed. After all, she wanted to read the occult, not be read by it. She tried a second spiritualist group which consisted of naïve, gushing members who failed to conjure up any spirit, however ignorant. Much to Hanna's dismay a newly formed Oxford Group disbanded itself after only one meeting for fear of being accused of pro-British propaganda. How was she to choose? Astrology beckoned on one side, numerology on the other; Nostradamus was widely read in air-raid shelters together with Paracelsus and the Tibetan Book of the Dead. At last her Egyptologist friends put her on to one of their adherents, an accomplished sculptress who could establish anybody's past identity, several incarnations removed, and, in a trance, produce amazing clay likenesses of their past selves.

Hanna presented herself eagerly, hoping to emerge as the reincarnation of some great, passionate figure—Cleopatra, Francesca or Mary, Queen of Scots. But the sculptress came back empty-handed from her first trance. "I can't get hold of you," she admitted. "You are not entirely here in your present self, part of you is anchored down in the past as if it had not been completely transferred. Can't you remember anything?"

Oh no, not remember, but she agreed, there was a strange element in her somewhere, an unrelated fragment that often manifested itself in weird dreams and instinctive knowledge, and, sometimes, in waves of icy sadness that seemed to come from another existence. Would that be part of the mystery? The sculptress nodded and said nothing. It was like facing one's judge in a pitiless underworld.

Suddenly the sculptress moaned loudly. Her eyes closed, she went off into a second trance. Hanna tiptoed out of the room and waited feverishly next door; the thought of learning the truth both exhilarated and frightened her. The sculptress called her back after a while. "I still didn't get you," she said, "but I got someone who is linked with you very closely and is the instrument of Fate in your life, a man. You have sinned against him in a previous existence and you are now being punished for it."

She flicked a damp rag off a clay head. Hanna gasped: the freshly moulded face was that of Miklós, her incalculable lover, Miklós wearing a peculiar head-dress and long hair, but the wide cheekbones and slanting eyes were certainly his, and a scratch in the clay

lay across his cheek at the precise spot where in reality he had his duelling scar.

"Oh Lord, you're right," she wailed, "it's him, true to life! What have I done to be punished now? Help me, please help me!" She clutched the hand of the sculptress in great distress; the small clay face looked like a shrunken head, an unwanted trophy from another life.

"You treated him cruelly. You left him when he most needed you and he died soon afterwards. Worse still, you left him for no good reason, only a passing caprice, and there's no excuse for that."

"How dreadful," she stammered. "Perhaps I didn't understand the situation, just as now he doesn't understand it and makes me suffer—after all, it's fair and just, but I can't live without him. Oh, do help me, please. Shall I be able to make up for it? Shall we ever be happy?"

"Not in this incarnation," she said regretfully. "The balance is difficult to re-establish. There's nothing else I can tell you. Don't come here again, you are too intense, you disturb the atmosphere for my work."

Hanna went home and cried all night. It was heart-breaking to believe that she would have to die and be reborn before finding happiness with Miklós. Suppose he should miss the next incarnation and they should not meet again for several centuries? The thought was unbearable. The main reason why she did not contemplate suicide was that she did not believe in it; besides, the sculptress had at least confirmed her own secret belief that Miklós was not just another lover but a man of destiny in her life.

Banned by the sculptress, she found herself all alone with her soul, and took it around the seats of occult wisdom as if taking a precious patient to a number of specialists with only the flimsiest hope of a cure. Each new thrill faded quickly. The practitioners of multi-coloured magic had only one thing in common—failure.

One evening Miklós arrived unexpectedly. Preceded by a sheaf of red roses, he sauntered in with the air of a man who had only gone out to buy some cigarettes. She watched him with fascination. The handsome, arrogant face, the greying temples, the strong brown hands made her feel weak and helpless. Beyond a doubt he was her personal destiny; it was just as well for a woman to know when she was defeated.

122

Was there no hope? Over the past two years he had sought her out and abandoned her at regular intervals, always vanishing without a trace, never explaining or apologizing. Each time he came as a conquering hero, a contemporary Attila, the scourge of God, and two or three days later he left her in a blaze of emotion, devastated like a sacked city. But now, armed with occult experience, she thought there might be a way to break the karma. The only thing to avoid was telling him about their transcendental past. She knew he would roar with laughter and dismiss the story as idiotic nonsense.

His wife had died, he said. Oh, some months ago, but he had been too busy to come to town. There had been a lot of trouble on the estate. Crops had been requisitioned, troops quartered, half the labourers were in the army. Trouble everywhere, he said, running his hand through her flame-gold hair. Apart from occasional desire he disliked her and did not understand why she never slammed the door in his face. During his long absences he thought of her as a silly, overdramatized woman who read deep meaning into insignificant trifles. Yet he was unable to give her up. They were like the proverbial pike and fox who were found dead on the river-bank, clutching each other so tightly that nobody knew whether it was the fox who had caught the pike or the other way round.

After the third brandy she told him about the Baloghs—he knew so many people, could he not try to do something? He protested angrily. People who did wrong must be left alone, this was no time to break the law. Why bother about the Jews? The country would be better off without that scheming, mercenary minority. She listened in alarm: his words came in a furious torrent, he must have used them countless times in the conspiratorial air of provincial clubs where racial prejudice flourished and intolerance was regarded as a manly virtue. The warmth of the brandy left her limbs. She had never imagined that he could possibly belong to the enemy camp.

"Don't let us talk about politics," she pleaded. "That's one more point on which we disagree. There are too many, anyhow, and we may have very little time left, don't let us argue!" She rose to fill his glass, but he caught her in his arms and covered her eyes with his hand.

The summer storm that broke at two in the morning did not waken him. She lay wide-eyed, his head heavy on her shoulder. Brilliant shafts of lightning ripped across the half-drawn curtains.

There would be a storm as well, Hanna thought sadly. She loved him with every molecule of her body and with her entire misunderstood soul, and her love had always remained unrelated to its object. He had never offered her an anchorage. All her efforts ricocheted off the surface. It was like the dream she had often had in which she sat in a powerful submarine, watching the enemy approach; and when the submarine tried to submerge, it hit a shallow bed of sand and remained suspended, half in water, half in air, burrowing vainly for the depth that was not there.

She had never been able to get through to him, and now, although he was free from his wife, the situation looked more hopeless than ever. His wife had died but politics had put another barrier between them. To continue to love him meant a kind of treason. Sharing her luxurious bed with the enemy, she thought of Gitta, and her guilty imagination promptly produced the image of a tormented girl, lying in heavy chains on a slab of cold rock.

Hanna's shoulder had gone to sleep but she would rather have had her arm amputated than pull it away from under the sleeping man's neck. She loved him, she loved him, and there was no hope, not in this incarnation. Torn by guilt and immobilized by his body, she began to cry, quietly at first, then with increasing vehemence.

Her sobs wakened him. Any disturbance of his sleep made him feel murderous, so he turned away furiously and pushed a large lump of pillow between them. This was becoming a bit too much. Silly, hysterical woman, what the hell was she crying for? Just before dropping off again he decided it was time to leave her for good.

CHAPTER FIFTEEN

itting on the bare floor of what had once been a double bedroom in a luxury hotel, the Baloghs were straining their ears. Their first prison cell had been sound-proof, this place was humming with noise. Gitta heard rumbling conversations going on either side of their room; heavy footsteps shuffled past the door, men called loudly to each other, and then a scream rose over all other sounds, a shrill, desperate scream turning into a long wail, into silence.

Mrs. Balogh grabbed Gitta and pulled her close. The scream had wakened the tigress in her. If these brutes were going to harm her child, she would attack them with her bare hands, scratch their eyes out, fight unto the last. Gitta dropped a kiss on her mother's hand. Nobody had bothered them since their arrival a week ago. Three times a day they were fed by a morose youngster who brought dry bread and cherry-stalk tea with saccharine in the morning, thin soup and more dry bread for lunch and dinner. Gitta was growing slimmer. In spite of occasional hunger pangs and sick headaches she was delighted to lose weight.

After the discomfort and fetid air of the first communal cell this clean, empty room was a vast improvement. The parquet floor looked dull, the green shutters were locked and nailed into position so that the daylight trickled in thinly between the slats. There were two shapeless straw mattresses with no blankets lying on the floor. When Gitta first moved them, one mattress revealed a dog-eared book that looked like a grammar, and for one moment she thought it was a Serbian one from which she could continue her studies. But the book turned out to be the second part of a Polish reader for advanced students, and she did not understand a word of it.

Mrs. Balogh slept a great deal. At the police headquarters she had hardly shut an eye. The proximity of so many strange men had worried her, and she had kept perpetual watch over Gitta, listening to her even breathing in the dark. Here there were no strange men and the straw offered reasonable comfort, so Mrs. Balogh settled down to catch up on her rest. Her faith in sensible habits had remained unshaken.

As a result Gitta had plenty of time to herself and she began to enjoy solitude. This was the second time in her life that she had found herself alone, enclosed and isolated. The first one had occurred at seventeen, when she had gone to a place of retreat shortly before Easter. With some twenty girls from her school she had been taken to an isolated convent, miles away from everywhere. The long, bleak building stood alone in the midst of brown fields and sparsely wooded hills, the solitary road was soft with mud and a coven of crows circled around the bare trees. The withdrawn landscape forced the eye to turn inward and the convent offered no distraction, either. Whitewashed walls, plain furniture, simple meals and a modest chapel made a colourless background which encouraged the flowering of the soul. The resident nuns smiled often but spoke little, and it was not compulsory to attend the twice-daily meditations in the assembly hall. Gitta adapted herself quickly to this quiet black-and-white world, as holy and austere as a Spanish painting. She spent most of the day in her tiny room, gazing at the wooden crucifix on the wall or letting her eyes stray through the window to the slaty sky. She thought about God and the ultimate matters, trying to sort out the rights and wrongs of life in relation to divine demands. She failed to find the panacea. How was one expected to manage anything as personal as the good life with nothing but general directives for guidance? Her yearning for truth and integrity grew stronger; her bewilderment increased.

Now the yearning was as strong as ever, and once again she had ample time to think about her moral code that had led her, directly or indirectly, to prison and bewilderment. That in itself was bearable. But it had also separated her from Pali. She missed him desperately; nobody else mattered, or, if they did, they mattered on a different, more superficial plane. Pali's absence was insupportable, she needed him more than food or drink, she needed him as a limb needs the body to which it belongs.

She stared hard at the blank wall, trying to conjure up his face, but having very little visual imagination she only saw the uneven cracks in the paint. So she tried to imagine something less ambitious, a tree, perhaps. The tree obliged: spindly branches appeared faintly to her straining eyes, then a slanting trunk with one thick arm growing sideways then knotty roots—her imaginary tree grew from the top downwards—but in spite of its rugged appearance one blinking of her eyes made the image vanish and she had to start all over again.

The following afternoon she was taken to be questioned.

There was one plain-clothes man sitting at a desk; a German in Gestapo uniform paced up and down behind him. Her guilt had been established, the civilian said; all they wanted was repentance and the names of accomplices. They were mistaken, Gitta replied politely, she had not done anything wrong and she had no accomplices. The Gestapo man smiled and began to talk about secret transmitters. She understood no German, she said. Nonsense, of course she did, a girl of her education with all those German books at home—but no, she shook her head and said firmly, "*Nix deutsch,*" the ironical little phrase her ancestors had used against past approaches in the German tongue.

Who are your friends? Why are you against us? The civilian was quiet and self-assured. You are only a child, he said, we make allowances for bad influences, nobody blames you really, but you must mend your ways.

"I have nothing to say. I know nothing. However long you keep me here, I shan't be able to tell you anything. I'm afraid I'm wasting your time." She was no longer cheeky, only scared and sad.

"Oh, but we won't keep you here," he protested. "Unless you change your mind very soon, we'll send you to Germany, and nobody knows when you'll return."

"She's a waste of time," the Gestapo man said. "I know the type, as stubborn as a mule and more dangerous than she looks. Oh, well, she might just as well see the others who also refuse to talk."

The civilian grabbed Gitta's arm and marched her along a corridor. He stopped at a door. The guards opened it and he pushed her inside. She saw five pale, emaciated women standing in a row with their hands strapped to an overhead beam that was high enough to force them on tiptoe. Their faces were badly bruised. One girl, hardly more than sixteen, had two black eyes and a swollen mouth.

127

The man shook Gitta's shoulder. Did she want to join them? Did she want to talk fast or die slowly? Five pairs of eyes looked at her. She felt cold with nausea and pity and raised her head. "*Du courage, toujours du courage*," the woman in the middle rasped out with a strong foreign accent. "*Vive la Serbie!*" And the others repeated, "*Vive la Serbie!*" Gitta nodded, biting back her tears. "*A nous la victoire*," she heard herself say. The man hit her in the stomach and hurled her out into the corridor.

She staggered into their room, but hardly had she sat down on her mother's straw mattress when the burly policeman called her out again. He led her to the lavatory, handed her a cigarette and a box of matches and stood guard outside the door so that she could smoke in peace. Kindness was the last straw. Gitta leant against the partition and sobbed, puffing away at the same time until her head swam and the unaccustomed tobacco penetrated her body right down to her toes. "I want to go home," she moaned, "I want to be left in peace." Then she finished her cigarette, splashed cold water on her face and stepped out into the passage. "It'll be all right, miss," the policeman said, "you'll see, and meanwhile you can smoke every now and then, it's good for the nerves." She looked at him with overflowing eyes. "How kind you are. Nobody's been kind since we were taken away," and she started crying again, so he quickly led her back to their room and locked the door.

Mrs. Balogh did not know how to console her. She was still crying when the door opened once more. This time it was Fehér, the young, spiv-like detective who had taken away the Jewish refugees from their flat. He walked in awkwardly, hands apologetically spread sideways, his uncertain chin twitching over a gleaming silver silk tie. Mrs. Balogh rose and stood in front of Gitta. She was at the end of her tether.

"Oh, hallo, gracious madam, hallo, miss," Fehér beamed, "I'm so glad to have found you, this place is like a rabbit warren. Oh no, Miss Balogh, you haven't been crying, whatever is the matter?"

"What do you want?" Mrs. Balogh asked.

"First of all, your Jews are all right," he said importantly. "The old lady has been sent home, the others will be released today or tomorrow, but they'll have to live in yellow-star houses. Better than going to a camp, that's what I say."

"I wish I could believe you."

128

"It's perfectly true, madam, I swear. Please don't think that we are all bandits. I'm an ordinary detective and a good Christian, I wish you well, truly."

"These days you can't be a good Christian and an ordinary detective at the same time. What else do you want to tell us?"

Fehér wagged his head mournfully. His long, fox-like nose twitched, his crinkly hair smelt of walnut oil dressing. Mrs. Balogh surveyed him scornfully. She knew his type: he was one of those stupid young men who make loquacious shop assistants, inefficient clerks, fanatical demonstrators and champions of unworthy causes. This type responded well to haughtiness, so she looked him up and down as majestically as she could and waited for the reaction.

"I've taken the liberty of investigating your case," he said in a low voice, rubbing his manicured hands. "It doesn't look too good, for some reason Miss Balogh is regarded as a dangerous political agent, but somebody outside has started things moving for you, and Laci and me are also trying to help."

"Who is Laci?"

"My chum. He was with me that day in your flat and we're doing our best to get you out."

Passing a hand over her forehead, Mrs. Balogh sank down on the straw mattress. "I don't understand," she said wearily. "First you arrest us, then you try to get us out. Please explain. Of course if you're interested in a reward, I should be only too glad to——"

"Oh, really, madam, you don't understand." He was genuinely pained. "We don't do this sort of thing for money, Laci and I earn all we need. We just want to help you because you're . . . nice people. And because it's a shame for a young girl like Miss Balogh to suffer this sort of trouble."

Ah, is that it? Mrs. Balogh thought. Gitta's fatal charm, which she personally could not perceive at all, was working again; it must be, she decided, the sort of thing only men notice. She was about to say something non-committal when Gitta lifted her head.

"If you think we're nice people, you agree with us. If you agree with us, you shouldn't be doing this sort of work."

Little fool, her mother thought crossly. "What Mr. Fehér does is his own business, we're in no position to lecture him."

"I see what Miss Balogh means," the youth mumbled. "The point is that it's better for chaps like Laci and me to stay in the force and

129

do what little good we can than to hop it and let the tougher element take over. Now in this case perhaps we can get you out, see, especially if the outside pressure continues."

"But who on earth is pressing for us?"

Fehér's face wrinkled up to convey utmost secrecy. "I only know that the pressure comes from a high German source."

"Good Lord, not from the Fuehrer himself, I hope? Couldn't possibly accept it. Well, look, if you can really help to get us out of here, I should be very grateful, particularly for the sake of this child. They're very harsh to her, although she hasn't done anything."

"I know. Oh, I know. I hope when you're free you'll allow me to visit you," Fehér said, bowing stiffly like a beginner at a dancing class.

"Yes, do come and have tea or something, and bring your friend, too." The born hostess was never far from the surface, though it had flashed through Mrs. Balogh's mind that this simpleton and his chum would hardly appreciate the sophisticated meal she liked to call tea.

With two more bows and one idiotic smile for Gitta Fehér backed to the door. Then his features composed themselves into their official pattern of crude superiority and he banged the door hard, probably to establish his authority.

"Impertinent dog." Gitta was pale with indignation. "How dare he? What does he think I am?"

"Darling stupid child, don't worry about that. We must get out of here, and if he wants to come to tea, we'll have to put up with it. I prefer to feed him at home to eating the filthy food here."

"Oh, Mother, we can't have a secret policeman come to our home and sip tea and make small talk!"

"Don't be unreasonable. It may not come to that at all. I should like to know, though, who is intervening on our behalf. Have you any idea?"

"When I gave Mihály the alarm," Gitta whispered, "he said they would try to get us out. I imagine they've established contact, perhaps via the Germans. I knew, I knew all the time Pali would help, only I didn't know when, so I didn't say anything."

"Dear Pali," Mrs. Balogh said tenderly. "I don't put it past him. He can probably talk a Gestapo man into freeing political prisoners. Oh, he's extraordinary."

130

"Isn't he? Oh, Mother, darling, I think he's wonderful. There's nobody like him, nobody in the whole world."

"Are you in love with him?"

"We're in love with each other," Gitta corrected her happily. "I never had a chance to tell you, darling, I kept saving it up for a quiet moment, but there's never been one, and . . ."

"Just how bad is it?"

Gitta was astonished. "Bad? It is hundred per cent, and when the war is over——"

"Gracious me, you don't want to marry him?"

The sharp question surprised her again. Hadn't her mother urged her to fall in love and get married? She looked at her in bewilderment.

"Gitta, my sweet, Pali is a wonderful person, brilliant, witty, attentive, but in spite of all those virtues he's still a little nobody, isn't he, with no position, no money or prospects, nothing!"

"But one doesn't marry for those things; one marries because one can't live without the other. Oh, we're going to be terribly happy."

"How do you know, may I ask? Baby, you know nothing about life. Love is fine but not enough. You need a solid financial background and some social assets if you want to succeed!"

This is some dreadful misunderstanding, Gitta thought; they were talking at cross purposes and her confession was being turned into a trivial argument. Success did not enter into this at all; the only success worth seeking was the perfect fusion of the half-kernels. What had happened to her mother's fabulous generosity which normally made her deal out gifts, kindnesses, hospitality and help without hesitation, over and above her duty and, sometimes, her means, what made her mean and mercenary at the precise moment when Gitta presented her with her unique choice? After this, how could she tell her about the pebbles and the porthole? She stared miserably at her knuckles. Mrs. Balogh's young, pleasant voice flowed on relentlessly.

"You don't know anything about his background, his family. What about his parents?"

"They're both dead. He has no relations. What does it matter? The main thing is what he is, and that's good enough for me. Oh please don't ruin it, this is terribly important and I don't want you to

131

try and tear him to bits because you won't succeed, and you're only hurting me."

His background? She genuinely did not care whether he was a prince, a gipsy, or a foundling. But Mrs. Balogh, who was unable to sit through *Lohengrin* without feeling that, whatever the grounds, no woman should be expected to take a man on trust, believed in clear situations, and their conflict grew deeper every minute.

Gitta let the formidable attack take its course. Her career, her ordinary comforts, her studies, her standard of life were hurled at her by way of argument. How would she like to have to cook meals and go to the market with a basket on her arm, since Pali's financial prospects clearly made it impossible to think of a resident maid? How would she like to wash nappies all day and fade before her time? Ignoring the true issue, Mrs. Balogh went into fantastic detail, until her "child" stood up and sadly turned her back on her.

"Mother, stop it. All this boils down to one thing: you want me to be happy on your terms, and nothing else matters, not even what I want. I'm sorry, I can't alter our plans, so we may just as well change the subject."

There was no time to reply to this unparalleled statement. The sirens outside began to wail. The policeman opened the door. "You can't come to the shelter," he shouted. "We'll lock you in, and God help you if you try any stupid tricks." He dropped his voice. "Lie down on the floor, you'll be all right."

Doors slammed everywhere, footsteps scurried along the passage. Gitta pressed her face to the shutters and squinted through the slats. Planes droned overhead, anti-aircraft guns roared and popped loudly, the darkening summer sky was punctured by noise and flashing lights, and then the explosions began to rumble. In her excitement Gitta clutched a knob on the shutter that released a faulty lever, so that the slats shot up horizontally, offering a wider view. Down in the distance the city lay wide open, beautiful and vulnerable under a canopy of fire. The Danube displayed its mild curves, thinly spangled with bridges, the buildings on the Pest side held up their fluid skyline, a rhythm of chequered roofs, turrets, segmented domes, stout chimneys, hunching mansard roofs with fussy skylights, and here and there a spire standing up, brave and baroque, a badge of identity for God to see; and below this wavy, irregular and infinitely moving pattern countless tiny blank windows stared out of countless walls, the myriad eyes of a wary animal.

How I love it, Gitta thought in a hot rush of emotion, how well I love and know this city, the only place to live in, this familiar, mad, illogical place full of mock architecture and bluffing and danger and twisted people, and also full of constant challenge and love and the intensity of living and decent creatures and, well, everything, the microcosmos to which I belong. And now that it is being attacked from the air by the side I want to win, what do I wish for—success for the attacking pilots, or immunity for the city?

A hailstorm of bombs shot down on the Pest side. The explosions were followed by a wall of flame and smoke. The oil refinery in the north-east was blazing away in infernal splendour. Burning oil, Gitta thought, oil the Germans would take away; but there were workers' settlements nearby, and the fire was spreading. "Come away from the window," Mrs. Balogh said nervously. More houses were burning, all over the city little black pillars of smoke rose straight into the windless air; Abel's sacrifice was accepted, however involuntary the offering. Witnessing the devastation from above instead of guessing away about its extent in a deep shelter, Gitta felt hot loyalty towards the city, the solidarity of shared doom. Where in that ocean of houses was Pali? Was he thinking of her? Was her home still intact? She could not see that part of the city at all. If a fire broke out, there would be nobody to save the flat.

"What's going on?" Mrs. Balogh asked weakly from the straw mattress.

"Sheer hell." She tapped the slats shut and left the city to its destiny.

CHAPTER SIXTEEN

～～～～～～～

Whipped by bombs, bristling with conflict, the city began to show every symptom of war sickness. Supplies arrived unevenly; sometimes they stopped altogether. Basic commodities had vanished. To acquire a pair of decent shoes or a length of fabric was a herculean task that required good contacts, much patience and even more money. Business drained away from the shops. The people in the know made secret trips to obscure stockrooms, small workshops and slummy houses where passwords and references were needed before one was allowed to cross the doorstep.

Troops came and went, and in the absence of reliable information even the slightest military movement set off a wave of panicky rumours. To sharpen the tension a rash of posters broke out all over the city, showing Russian atrocities in gruesome detail. A strip of photographs recorded the terrible fate of a Hungarian watch repairer who, having got into Russian hands, had been cooked alive in oil for no good reason. The pictures were horrible enough to make people clutch their throats and bolt and then turn back manfully to read the victim's name and humble suburban address. The general shock was so strong that few people paused to wonder how the step-by-step close-ups had come to be taken.

One horror poster appeared on the wall of the dairy next to Pali's block of flats, and when he stopped in front of it the milkman joined him, clicking his tongue mournfully. "I know this man," he whispered. "Happens to be my wife's second cousin." Pali's eyebrows shot up. "How did it happen?" "It didn't," the milkman said. "This man is at home at Pesterzsébet, he's never seen a Russian alive or dead, he doesn't know why his name and address were used, and now he daren't leave his home for fear that there'd be trouble. They

134

should have warned him at least or paid him something for using his name! Shocking business, sir, I don't know what to think." Pali nodded non-committally and went on his way. Some days later he heard that the milkman had been taken away by the Gestapo straight from the dairy; at the same time they had also arrested the innocent watch repairer who, having escaped the Russian oil cauldron, received no mercy from those who had faked his death on posters.

Pali could hardly bear to see anybody. Human company made him ill-tempered and unpleasant, almost as bad as Sas, who, strangely enough, was the only person to leave his nerves unruffled. But then Sas was hardly human. He expected no social niceties, had no illusions and rattled out his summaries and news without fuss or emotion.

Sas rarely spoke about Gitta. He had traced the two captives to the hilltop prison and was reassured to hear that they were keeping quiet, but there his powers came to an end. Mihály had probed certain ministerial channels that led nowhere, Pali's own plan involving judicious bribery had foundered on one incorruptible link, while Marta, operating along unorthodox lines, was in no position to discuss her actions. So Pali watched the days roll past, suffering from remorse and depression. The dark forces were at work indeed, hammering out the implacable pattern by which no sooner had he found a solution to a problem than a totally unexpected event ruined everything, leaving him worse off than before.

The way things went he could not even submerge in private distress. The general doom justified his worst fears and he, unwilling Cassandra, dared no longer look ahead. His ability to foresee political events with reasonable precision gave him a ridiculous feeling of personal responsibility for the catastrophic situation. Until recently outside pressure had helped to promote inner freedom; the thicker the fog grew, the more his judgement sharpened. But now the pull of the opposites had become unbearable, and he found himself a Jeremiah without a voice, a Jonah with not even a whale for shelter.

Eventually it was Sas who jerked him out of passivity. Suicide could wait, he said. The banned opposition parties were stirring underground, armistice openings were rumoured, partisan couriers were seeping in from the neighbouring countries, there was work to do. Wearily Pali became active again and soon he found himself in endless conferences with blameless patriots whose goodwill normally outstripped their ability; and then he abruptly withdrew once more, because one of his student liaison men had been summoned to the offices of the political police on the Svábhegy.

The young man was lengthily questioned about political feeling at the University. Then, without a warning, he was confronted with Gitta. They looked at each other stonily; Gitta said they might have met at a dance a long time ago, but she wasn't sure; the young man shook his head regretfully and shrugged. The detectives admonished him to report dubious activities among his friends, and released him. He promptly reported to Pali, mentioning that Gitta looked thin, scruffy but unperturbed, and then he retired to the safety of the countryside.

After three more horrifying sessions the grillings ceased abruptly, and the endless summer days were only marked by Fehér's visits. He always brought them fresh hope and food—a surprising quantity of meat sandwiches, sweets, biscuits and fresh fruit emerged from the pockets of his natty summer suit. These offerings, combined with his clumsy compliments, made him resemble a courting village lad. The German pressure for their release was being stepped up, he indicated; he could hardly wait to greet his prisoners outside those walls. Mrs. Balogh treated him with condescending kindness, mainly to counteract Gitta's prim silence and obvious boredom. Laci began to call, too. He was older and tougher than Fehér, a short, muscular man with a small moustache and definite ambitions. He wanted to sit the war out in the service, he said, and then join his uncle who owned a travelling circus and was at present stuck in Ruthenia. A circus, Gitta asked, what did he want to do with that? Oh, mainly see the world, it was the cheapest way to do it, and he knew enough about horses and other animals to earn his keep. France, Italy, Spain, he said longingly, such a lot of countries to see, and a circus was welcome anywhere. "You must find this circus here pretty dull," Gitta commented, but Laci took no offence. A job was a job, and it could not go on for too long now.

New prisoners arrived. The Baloghs were moved to the former hotel dining-room that was crowded with captives, including the poet Lázár who greeted them indifferently. He had deteriorated since their last meeting, and was looking abnormally thin and deranged. Gitta had no opportunity to renew her friendship with him. An hour after their transfer Fehér took them to his office for questioning.

Laci was already there. Fehér locked the office door, produced a bottle of slivovic from a locker and poured out generous portions for all four of them. The mysterious German intervention—only semi-official, he added with a wink—had succeeded. The time had come to produce a suitable confession, get it passed and then, perhaps, be released. The slivovic was hot, sharp, delicious. Gitta smiled at Fehér who was ineffectually struggling with the typewriter.

"Let me do it for you," she offered. "I used to be a secretary before you caught me."

So the Baloghs set to work on their own confession, including all the points that had been proved and refusing to say any more. If only they could name one fictitious contact, Fehér pleaded, a mystery man, an elusive agent who had cajoled them into political crimes—but the captives refused, giggling under the influence of the unaccustomed drink, keeping their confession flat and unsensational. In an unguarded moment Gitta got hold of the confiscated leaflet that lay on the table, rolled it into a tight ball and pushed it into her brassière. True, it had been included in the confession in a rather hazy manner, but what did a vague reference mean without accompanying evidence?

More slivovic was passed round. Outside the unshuttered windows the trees swayed sensuously in the summer breeze. All they needed for perfect atmosphere was a gipsy band, Gitta suggested, and the two beaming detectives promptly invited her to an evening out, complete with wine, song and dancing, as soon as possible.

The situation was ludicrously informal. Clearly the detectives were most anxious to have the Baloghs set free and then enjoy their company and hospitality under happier circumstances. Pali had been right, Gitta reflected: the unexpected formula worked again, this time in the shape of two young detectives who wanted to rise socially and oblige members of the opposition who might become important the moment the régime changed. Even prison walls did not exclude the human element.

The same night, long after midnight, Gitta and her mother were hauled out of the hot, snoring hall. An unknown man led them up and down stairs, through darkened passages, to the entrance. He took them out into the road and handed Mrs. Balogh the wallet-purse that had been taken from her after their arrest.

"You may go now," the man said.

"Go where?"

"That's up to you. You're free."

They gaped in sleepy surprise. Mrs. Balogh was the first to recover. "I see," she said, "we can go home. But what about my jewels? Surely I can have them back?"

"Not before you've paid the fine on account of the Yids. You'll get a notification." He went back into the building. A guard slammed the gate behind him.

"Well, come on, baby, otherwise they'll think we want to stay."

The dark figures flanking the road did not move as they passed them. The August night was warm and unspeakably sweet, a pot-pourri of freshly mown grass, flowering basil, fragrant walnut leaves and the slow, aromatic breath of fir trees. Emerald glow-worms shone among the shrubs, giant stars crowded the black sky, and some-where far away a dog was barking, a plain, friendly domestic dog disturbed by a footstep or a low-flying bat.

They linked their arms and walked downhill silently. The shock of freedom was enormous; it felt strange to sneak back into the world in the dead of night, passing from the inner to the outer darkness.

At the bottom of the hill they found a taxi; Pali's flat was only fifteen minutes away, Gitta thought wistfully. The driver examined the bedraggled women. "Coming from up there, are you?" he asked, and ran them home at breakneck speed, refusing to accept payment.

As usual, the house entrance was locked. The caretaker's wife who came to answer the bell looked at them as if she had seen a ghost. Her panic confirmed the Baloghs' worst suspicions, and they treated her with cold contempt. Rozália was gone for ever, but that had not liberated them from all their enemies.

Mrs. Balogh knocked the seal off her door. The flat was undisturbed, still petrified in the chaos of the arrest. The kitchen smelt of decaying food. Mrs. Balogh rushed around with the feverish energy of someone returning from holiday. Gitta's sickly little orange tree, grown from a pip and nursed with the devotion due to an idiot child, had died of thirst. Mrs. Balogh put the flower-pot out of sight. She feared that the tiny casualty might upset Gitta more than all her recent experiences.

"Come along, darling, let's wash our hair, I hope it's not too late," she called out, and went to the bathroom to heat the water.

CHAPTER SEVENTEEN

~~~~~~oooooo6oooooo~~~~~~

The flowers arrived at ten in the morning. Marta unwrapped them indifferently, expecting them to be pinky-yellow roses and therefore coming from Mihály. But the roses were dark red, and the message in German read: "Your friends were released last night. When can I see you?"

Leaving the flowers on the marble console table in the hall, she ambled back to her room, gazing at the card. Triumph was tempered with dismay. The young, goat-faced Gestapo officer with whom she had brilliantly and progressively flirted throughout the past fortnight, had fulfilled his part of the bargain. How she was going to get out of hers was a different matter.

Still, triumph was sweet and never palled. Having recovered from Gyuri's rebellion and disappearance, Marta had returned to her old pattern. Every time she cleared a hurdle, she luxuriated briefly in the glow of emotional achievement and then, like a skilled head-hunter, looked around for the next trophy. The double rhythm did not change. Triumph was always followed by revenge as she conquered and rejected, conquered and rejected. Sometimes she amused herself by imagining her parents' reactions, should they find out about her secret life: her father who disliked her because he had wanted his first-born to be a boy and because Marta's complicated birth had delayed the arrival of a son by several years; and her cold, unemotional mother, absorbed in snobbery and the pursuit of eternal youth. Marta pulled a face at herself in the looking-glass. In spite of the familiar pattern, the conquest of the goat-faced German was different. She had undertaken it as a political action to get the Baloghs free, but the emotional score was still waiting to be settled, and she had to tread carefully.

So far, the Baloghs' freedom had cost her attending one of her

140

parents' regular parties for German functionaries to pick her victim, and two evenings at an exclusive night club before presenting her request. The Gestapo man was young, common and vastly sentimental; Marta's rank and beauty dazzled him into promising his help with the eagerness of a dog racing after a pebble. It occurred to Marta that if she could spirit the Baloghs away to the country it might be quite safe to kick the dog instead of patting him. Judging by the time it had taken him to make his semi-official influence felt, he did not seem a very important man, anyway.

Marta picked up the telephone and dialled Gitta's number. She heard two sharp clicks, and then the acoustics of the receiver changed slightly before the ringing noise began. She replaced the receiver at once. Gitta's line was being tapped.

Remembering Sas's thorough lecture on what to do when dealing with someone just released from jail, she got dressed and walked the short distance to Gitta's street. A bench in the park stood almost opposite the entrance to their block. Marta sat down, opened the morning paper and looked around.

The Baloghs' windows were open. She put on her sun-glasses and focused her eyes on the newspaper. People came and went. It did not take her long to notice the small, ugly man who kept crossing her field of vision, watching the Baloghs' house as eagerly as she did. He was flat-footed and anonymous-looking. So they are being shadowed as well, she thought.

Mrs. Balogh emerged at a quarter-past eleven with a shopping-basket on her arm. The flat-footed man became animated, followed her for twenty yards, then turned back and went on with his watch.

Oh Lord, Marta thought, it's Gitta they are after. She read the editorial that was resounding with the promise of final victory. Not unlike the war situation, the grammar of leader writers was deteriorating rapidly. She folded the paper and rose. The dog had not brought the pebble back very successfully.

She found Pali in a nearby coffee house and told him about her observations, without mentioning her Gestapo contact. Nervously he tore his paper napkin into fine shreds. The situation called for Sas, he said, and the sooner they found him the better. They toured the six or seven spots where Sas normally alighted between his mysterious errands, but there was no trace of him anywhere. Then, in University Street, Marta suddenly noticed Gitta in a freshly pressed pink dress,

141

followed at a little distance by the flat-footed man. It was too late to avoid her. She grabbed Pali's arm and dug her fingers in his sleeve.

Gitta saw them at the same moment. She stepped forward automatically, her eyes big and bright, her mouth slightly open, looking at Pali with the rapture of a lost pilgrim coming within sight of shelter.

Pali took in the situation in one glance. He raised his left arm and looked at his watch. "It's a quarter-past twelve," he said loudly and distinctly. "Not at all, a pleasure." "As a matter of fact, it's only ten past twelve," Marta countered, adding in a whisper, "you're shadowed, move on," and she was already pulling Pali away, turning to him with a dazzling smile, talking and gesticulating past the flat-footed man. She moved her hips provocatively to give him something to look at, should he turn to stare at them.

Gitta walked on, fiddling with her watch. The shock of seeing Marta on Pali's arm—the picture sank in only after they had vanished—was worse than the shock of being shadowed. All the elation of freedom had left her. The meeting she had so desperately looked forward to was already over; he had rejected her. She walked on aimlessly, straight into a gathering of blue-grey pigeons. The Franciscan church on the right was open. She entered and knelt down at the back.

She shut her eyes. The pleasing pattern of the altar, the softness of the flowers, were not to distract her. She wanted to think rather than pray, and now that God had irrevocably lost His beard, it was just as well to drop all visual comforts.

"What am I to do?" she asked the faceless power. "It's all such a terrible mess and I am no longer sure of anything," and she spurred on her mind to think clearly and sort out the police and Pali's shattering indifference and Marta's long, slim hand on his arm, the memory of the boat-house, and Lázár's parable about the essence of things; the new fighting aspect of Mrs. Balogh's personality that pitted its strength against the enemy and, alas, also against Gitta's tenderest dreams; and all these new experiences swirled around in an ever-changing light until she found herself explaining them to God rather than receiving guidance from Him. No, there was nothing to pray for, she decided. This was a patch of spiritual aridity which the Catholic Church treats with regret and concern, as if it were a bad, though not fatal, disease of the soul. She crossed herself and walked

142

out into the sunshine, taking a good look at the shabby man waiting outside the church. Was this her shadow? Two streets away she turned back. There he was, close on her heels, slowing down under her stern gaze and blowing his nose into a greyish handkerchief.

Wanting to be quite certain, Gitta crossed and re-crossed the street, she turned into an arcade, walked half-way through it and then retraced her steps; and the little man followed her faithfully if somewhat crossly, once even stopping in front of an empty shop window to contemplate it with interest.

Gitta accosted the policeman at the next corner; it appealed to her sense of irony to complain to one representative of the law about another. "Officer, I believe that man is following me," she said candidly, "can you please help?" But the flat-footed man was already there, flicking up his lapel to show the policeman the powerful badge beneath, and the young constable shrugged and scratched his ear; he was only on traffic duty.

"What do you want?" Gitta asked the plain-clothes man. "I've been released, haven't I? Am I supposed to stay at home?" Without a word the man walked away. The policeman was nowhere to be seen, either. There was nothing left to do except go home and help Mrs. Balogh in the kitchen; she had decided not to replace Rozália.

Fehér turned up in the afternoon with a large box of fabulous sweets. Gitta suspected that he had swiped them from a rich home in the course of his duties. The young man came meekly as a lamb, full of devotion and respect; an unworthy suitor, bent double under his ineligibility.

"Can't you send away that snooper?" Gitta asked wearily. "And if you can't, wouldn't it be wiser for you to stay away?" The thin youth protested vehemently: the snooper was not from his department and therefore he was powerless, although unafraid for himself. He peered down into the street and expressed anxiety. Obviously, the case was not entirely closed, although he could not see why. In spite of his distress he stayed far too long. Eventually Mrs. Balogh had to ease him out of the flat by pleading a headache.

As night drew on, their sense of isolation grew worse. The flat was quiet, the telephone remained silent. Mrs. Balogh sat listlessly in her favourite arm-chair with her unfinished embroidery over her knees. This kind of loneliness was worse than the isolation of jail where one could easily imagine the world—one's personal world—standing on

143

tiptoe outside the walls, waiting to welcome one back. Now it was like being at large, yet wearing handcuffs, being branded and watched, less free than ever.

After some deliberation they moved the wireless into Gitta's room, the most sound-proof part of the flat, and switched it on inside an acoustic barrier of cushions, rugs and blankets. Soon the familiar voice of a B.B.C. announcer floated in from space, and they listened religiously to the only human voice that still cared to speak to them.

"Nonsense. I want you to stay and carry on with your job as if nothing had happened," Ervin Wass said emphatically. Under his flaxen hair his face was deeply tanned. He looked healthy and cheerful, a figure from a chic holiday poster.

"I don't think you understand," Gitta protested. "Virtually we're still in jail. Our phone is being tapped, we're under observation day and night, the snoopers go through our mail every time the postman comes; obviously they're only waiting for us to make one wrong move to run us in again. More likely still, they want us—me—to lead them to my so-called accomplices. You don't want to get mixed up in all this."

"Oh, but I already am. The police were here the day after your arrest and I told them I wanted you back, so it's settled, isn't it? Precisely because you are under observation, the best thing you can do is to return to work and behave normally."

"How brave of you," she murmured. "You know, old friends with nothing to fear cut us dead in the street. We met one yesterday and she crossed over to the other side. Then my mother rang up a friend of twenty years' standing and the good lady stammered and rang off."

"Ah, yes, an old friend is more likely to come under suspicion. I, on the other hand, have only known you for a few months, and we have never met outside this office, which strengthens my position. But don't condemn your friends. People are scared of the Germans, the police, the bombing, the Nazis, the anti-Nazis, and they work it out of their systems by cutting you in the street because you have already paid a penalty which they hope to avoid."

"Aren't you scared at all?"

"A little. But my foolish optimism doesn't let it go too deep.

144

Things always work out in the end. Now the things you have done——"

"I haven't done anything."

"Hush, Hanna told me all about it. What you have done was extremely brave and very futile. For a while you made me feel quite spineless and decadent. Here I was, old enough to be your father, and while you went to jail, I went to row and play tennis in the afternoons. But in all fairness, my dear girl, what did you achieve with all this unpleasantness?"

She sighed and shrugged.

"Admittedly, you could have fared much worse, you could have been tortured or deported," the lawyer went on. "I know of some people who would give anything to be in your shoes, provided they are still alive. At any rate, they are politicians or at least adult men. But you of all people—the futility of it all! If there were a large-scale resistance movement, well and good, I would join it myself, as a matter of honour, but to be a lone guerrilla with no one to help when you are in trouble is utterly useless. I am not trying to belittle your efforts, but you must be more sensible in future."

She sat up in the deep arm-chair and peered at him curiously.

"But you are quite wrong! If you know that something ought to be done, you must do it and not wait for somebody else to begin! Supposing the others are also waiting, why, then nothing will happen! Know ye not that a little leaven leaveneth the whole lump?"

"What's that?"

"St. Paul. Don't you know the New Testament?"

"We were not encouraged to read it at school."

"Neither were we—funny how the Catholic Church prefers to keep the Bible out of the way—but I had a Protestant phase and read it very thoroughly. Also, my best friend at the time was a Protestant. She tried hard to save me. Then we were joined by a Jewish girl who wanted to be saved but didn't quite know which way. So the three of us met every morning at seven-thirty in the park and read the Bible and prayed. And then we went into battle, to school, feeling like God's own regiment with a private line to Heaven."

"And then what happened?"

"Nothing. I remained a Catholic, the Jewish girl accepted Christianity but refused to be baptized because she wanted to keep apart from all the opportunists who became converted for non-religious reasons. But all this is beside the point. What matters is that you—I don't mean you personally, I mean the people who think like you—send us to school, approve of our education which orders us to be honest and decent, and when we try to live up to it, you tell us not to be silly and to lie low. Why?"

"Presumably because we are twenty years older and we have spent those extra twenty years shedding the illusions you still have. Not all of us, though; I could just about stop Hanna from sweeping in to the Gestapo with a riding-crop and making a colossal, resounding scene on your account; dear Hanna is still a heroic adolescent. Don't despise me, my dear. I am still young enough to make a decent martyr under extreme duress, but I am too old to go out of my way to become a martyr."

"Nobody wants to become a martyr! I only want to do something, to protest, because to sit about and do nothing is dreadful. At any rate, I have lost all my usefulness now, unless I go south and join the partisans."

"And creep around on all fours with hand grenades in your belt? With those slim wrists? Besides, if you vanished, your mother would be in great trouble."

She had not thought of that. True, unless Mrs. Balogh joined her —a rather fanciful possibility—the partisans were out. Ervin Wass talked on soothingly, and as she listened, with a liqueur chocolate delectably melting in her mouth, she thought of the fall of Sodom where there were not enough just men to be found, even though the Lord had lowered his original demand from fifty to ten. Ervin Wass represented enlightened self-interest, his bland voice of reason recommended the line of least resistance, since all other lines were certain to lead to disaster. Yet he, too, had a kind of quiet, elegant courage, symbolized by his way of life and detachment, by his hand-made cigarettes and lovingly blended coffee. To him his personal style of existence was a creed that needed protection from the sur-rounding doom and vulgarity, and being too disillusioned to bang his head against a brick wall, he substituted his own bliss for that of mankind, guarding it jealously. Gitta watched his bold, brown face, his lightweight suit and dazzling silk shirt, and her mouth curved down wryly. ·

"Well?" he asked. "Am I talking utter rubbish?"

"You have no idea how dirty we were," she said inconsequentially.

146

"We had two baths each in the middle of the night, and Mother kept saying that when I had returned from the Girl Guide camp as a child, she had thought I had broken the record for grubbiness, but that had been nothing. Oh, I am sorry, this isn't a pretty subject, but a rather novel experience to me. I always forget that as a lawyer you know about all these calamities."

"Let me disappoint you once more. I specialize in company law."

"And you still want a jail-bird to work for you?" She rose and went to the window. "There's my bodyguard waiting for me. Won't you change your mind?"

He peered down from behind the curtain. "Swine, disgusting swine. I'll take you home."

"Nothing of the sort. If you want to help, tell Hanna what I told you. And ask her to give my love to the others."

"My poor little girl." He bent down and kissed her hand. "What are you going to do?"

"Walk home all the way. That's almost an hour from here, it'll teach him a lesson." She turned back from the door, pleasantly embarrassed by his act of homage. "I'll come in next week, if you don't mind. I want a little time to myself, at home."

He watched her from the window, a little figure in blue walking very erectly, head held up. The police spy followed her from a distance. He was stout and wiped his forehead before turning the corner

CHAPTER EIGHTEEN

"I
f he loved you, he would get in touch with you."

In her pink housecoat with her hair loose and soft, Mrs. Balogh looked young and girlish, and her arguments also carried a touch of adolescent illogicality. Pali's silence and Gitta's resulting gloom inspired her to motherly disapproval, mixed with a little malicious triumph. Romance, she believed, was the supreme power on earth; a man who failed in his romantic duties deserved no mercy.

"Considering that Aunt Alice who has never raised a finger politically doesn't dare to acknowledge us in the street, you can't expect Pali to march straight into the trap. The very reason why we are being watched and tapped and censored is to catch people like Pali. I thought that much was obvious."

"You always find excuses for him. The fact remains that he's brilliant enough to find some means of approaching you, except that he hasn't got the will or the courage for it. You can't mean very much to him, my poor child. To leave a girl in the lurch is unforgivable, especially as but for him you wouldn't have got into this mess. It's quite clear to me that your leaflet did more harm than our refugees. I should like to know what explanation he'll offer when you next meet."

Gitta looked pleadingly at her mother. The accusations hurt because they succeeded in twisting true facts into unjust barbs, and because she missed Pali so badly that any mention of him made her eyes hot and dry. She needed all her strength to justify his behaviour to herself; Mrs. Balogh's scorn did not help.

"Men have swum across the seas and fought with lions for the girl they loved," Mrs. Balogh went on. "He needn't do that much. A quick call from a public telephone box would do, or a bunch of flowers, something! I take a poor view of it, but of course it's none of my business."

The doorbell rang. Gitta leapt to her feet—a letter? flowers? what superb timing it would be for a token to arrive now! But there was only a tall man in a soft hat at the door.

"Are you Gitta Balogh?"

She nodded and straightened the collar of her housecoat; it was only nine o'clock.

"I must ask you to come with me at once."

"What for? Who are you?"

"Police."

"Oh no!" Gitta backed into the hall. "But we've had all that, we've been released a week ago, what do you want me for now?"

"This is altogether different. I'm not from that department."

"Well, then?" Mrs. Balogh moved swiftly in front of Gitta. The past few weeks had taught her to throw herself between her child and all strangers.

"State Security and Counter-Espionage."

"Oh, for goodness' sake don't be absurd. You don't mean to say that this girl", she shook Gitta's arm as if to demonstrate her mild disposition and helplessness, "endangers anybody's security?"

"Will you get ready at once."

"I'm coming, too," Mrs. Balogh decided. "If my daughter is an anarchist, so am I."

"You can't come, lady. And if your daughter isn't ready in five minutes, she'll come as she is."

"No need to be unreasonable," Mrs. Balogh said regally. She indicated the hardest hall chair to the soft-hatted man and hustled Gitta to the bathroom. "What shall we do?" she asked, pushing open the communicating door to Gitta's room. "We don't even know where he's taking you, this sinister brute—oh, baby, not the white dress again, I could hardly get the dirt out of it last time!"

But Gitta was thinking of Iphigeneia and insisted on wearing her white dress; it had already been degraded into a prison garb, she might just as well keep it as such. "Tell Fehér", she suggested, "he may know where this place is. Ask him to do what he can, which I expect will be very little. And nothing over the telephone!"

"Damn these brigands," her mother muttered, deftly preparing Gitta's sponge bag as if she had been going to a house party at short

149

notice. "One can't even lodge an appeal anywhere, no higher authorities, no legal protection. Once the police get you, the next forum is God, and His methods are notoriously slow. Look, here's an extra piece of soap, just in case."

"Are you ready?" the man called in the hall.

"I'll be back, darling," Gitta said weakly. "Don't worry too much, I'll come home pretty soon."

"I should hope so indeed," Mrs. Balogh said ardently. She did not realize that the Security Branch represented the deepest pit of Hell, the last but one stage before deportation. Or perhaps she knew, but it was part of her character not to acknowledge the possibility of defeat, just carry on, start again, try again, melting the impossible with the warm breath of confidence. How I love her, Gitta thought, kissing her mother's smooth, scented cheek. They found the man pacing up and down in the hall.

"Well, see you soon," Mrs. Balogh said bravely, shaking her daughter's hand. "Where are you taking her? Listen, supposing she falls ill and needs something, will she be able to let me know? Is there——?"

But he had already driven Gitta through the door. The staircase swallowed them up, and Mrs. Balogh's hand gripped the round brass door-knob so hard that a protruding piece of wire drew a small bead of blood from her skin.

The police car, driven by a flat-capped chauffeur, purred across the Francis Joseph Bridge, then along the quay to the north. The chestnut trees were turning yellow; always the first to betray summer, they already bore pale bunches of prickly, embryonic fruit. The spring night before the occupation when Gitta and the boys had walked under these trees appeared incredibly remote, almost prehistoric, yet the trees had hardly grown taller and the wooden benches were still the same. Some progress, Gitta thought, averting her face from her escort. Walking means freedom; going to prison first means a tram, then a furniture van, then one graduates to a black chauffeur-driven car, until only the cattle-truck remains.

Still bearing north, the car raced through unfamiliar districts, sleepy, provincial streets with dusty geraniums and ancient shops. Then there was no more town, only humble houses with gardens, large fields, vegetable plots, trees and willow shrubs—the boat-house must be near by, Gitta thought with a pang—and eventually they

150

stopped in a shadowy avenue of trees climbing up a hill, in front of a large, old-fashioned villa. The words "Workers' Holiday Home" were faintly visible on the stone gate. The garden was full of large oaks and walnut trees and the flower-beds seemed to burst with the Sunday-best colours of petunias, snapdragons, tiny begonias and the first early dahlias. There were gendarmes everywhere, tall khaki shapes wearing feathered black hats and carrying rifles on their shoulders; and the sinister glint of the rifles was echoed by the shining, black-green cockerel feathers, producing an impression of cold hardness that made the very flowers look like prisoners in their neglected beds. Reluctantly Gitta entered the garden. By now she had reason to suspect prisons that looked like something else. She was led to the rear of the house where a veranda jutted out into the shade, and ordered to sit on a wicker chair in the middle of it. A gendarme entered from the garden and began to walk round her. The soft-hatted man sauntered away.

Round and round and round, slowly, rhythmically the gendarme went, untroubled by his heavy uniform, hat and rifle. The heat was increasing; one could almost hear the temperature rising with a smooth golden drone, insistent as a singing mosquito, and then a bee appeared, tapping against the veranda's purple and green stained glass. Gitta closed her eyes. It was better not to think, just rest and wait and let things look after themselves.

"Open your eyes. It is forbidden to sleep."

The gendarme circled on, his left boot creaking with every step. "Is anybody going to see me soon?" Gitta asked, looking at the simple toy-soldier face. "It is forbidden to speak," he snapped. "May I breathe, please?" He did not reply.

The sun was blazing away in full midday fervour. No food arrived, only the gendarme was replaced at one o'clock. At three a child said inside the house, "Tony, Tony, come and play with me," and a man's voice answered: "We must do the potatoes first." There were kitchen noises seeping through to the veranda, the clatter of a pail on a stone floor, the dull clang of a tin spoon hitting the table, then the water began to run and the child laughed and squealed. Gitta strained her ears, but the man Tony and the child must have settled down to work, because all she could hear was the occasional plop of a potato falling into a water-filled basin. Then the child demanded a story. At first Tony murmured so softly that she could

151

not make out his words, but then he raised his voice a little and the child kept calling, "Wicked Scrowgay, bad old Scrowgay," and Gitta realized that Tony was reciting the story of Dickens's *Christmas Carol* from memory, pronouncing English names according to Hungarian phonetics; he was improvising where necessary, though not at the expense of hushed wonder or emotion. She felt like crying.

At five o'clock the gendarme stood to attention. Gitta glanced up from her reverie: a short, bald, doleful man in brown riding-boots was standing in front of her, rubbing a walnut leaf between his fingers. Behind his back the gendarme was signalling to Gitta to stand up. She remained seated.

"Any wishes, Miss Balogh?" the man asked.

"I want to go home."

"That, I fear, is impossible. But perhaps you would care to come for a stroll in the garden."

She stood up, shook her right foot that had gone to sleep and limped to the veranda door. Without a word the man paraded her round the flower-beds, still rubbing the walnut leaf which oozed heady sweetness from every crushed pore, then he led the way towards a wooden seat beneath an oak tree.

"Well, what have you got to tell me?" he asked.

"Nothing. I didn't ask to be brought here. I don't even know who you are."

"I am the chief here. I should like you to take this seriously, even though you made light of the previous questionings. I like plucky people, you needn't be afraid of me, but I won't stand for any clowning. You see, you really have no alternative left. You either tell me all about your group or you'll be sent to Germany."

"I don't belong to any group," she began, but the chief waved his hand with such weary resignation that she fell silent, clenching her teeth firmly together. She found her surroundings disturbing. The summer garden with its diffused green light and drunken scents was bad for concentration.

"There is a little child here," the chief said after a while, "a dear little lad of six. His parents were Communists. They are dead, we had to take the kid on. Tony, the man who looks after him, was a Socialist saboteur at Csepel. He's been sentenced to twenty years' hard labour, but as he is good with children, for the time being he works here in the kitchen and looks after the little lad."

152

"What has that got to do with me?"

"The child's parents refused to talk, therefore they were shot. Tony won't talk either, so he'll eventually go to Germany to serve his sentence. He won't last twenty years, though."

There were ants in the grass, lean brown ants following the rules of their mysterious choreography, and a glossy green insect balancing its paunch on a thick blade.

"What weak examples," Gitta said equally peacefully, ignoring her trembling stomach. "Why don't you tell me about all the people who were killed in France, Norway, Holland, Russia, Germany and all the other places? You probably think that two or three individuals make a better example than thousands of people, and you are quite right, except that I haven't done anything, so there's nothing for me to confess."

"Do you believe in God?"

"I do."

"What else?"

"Isn't that enough?"

"No. What else?"

"Freedom," she said in deep embarrassment. This was like naming one's secret love in public.

"Freedom indeed! What about order and obedience? What about building a little before trying to destroy? Now come on, be sensible. Who helped you to make those leaflets? Who runs your group? Who belongs to it?"

The seconds ticked by patiently. Gitta picked up a long weed with a ladybird on its tip and let the insect crawl over on to her hand.

"I made no leaflets," she said, remembering the feel of the soft paper she had crushed and hidden in her bodice in Fehér's office. It was gone, destroyed, nobody could compare its type with that of Gitta's typewriter, praise be. "You are the fifth person to accuse me of having produced illegal leaflets—I did nothing of the sort. Someone is trying to plant something on me. There's no group, no leader, no conspiracy. I tried to help a few Jews, that's all."

The ladybird flicked up its orange wings, the flimsy black underwings unfolded and the insect rose in the air. Gitta dropped the weed and turned to face the chief.

"May I see that leaflet, please?"

"It's in your file. You know the one I mean."

153

"I'd like to see it. I'd like you to prove that I had anything to do with it." The ladybird's take-off had filled her with hope. It was easy, you raised your wings or made some similar little movement without wondering whether it would work and you were off, up, away. Two men with files in their hands appeared in the veranda doorway. The chief motioned them to join him.

"A pity you don't respond to patience and goodwill," he said in the tones of a disappointed teacher when the two men sat down next to him. "I was hoping to save you, but since you refuse to take your last chance, we can waste no more time on you."

He cleared his throat and took a file from the man on his left. "You are guilty of subversive propaganda, of producing inciting leaflets and of generally endangering the security of the State," he pronounced, tapping the file for emphasis. "Since you will neither confess nor assist the authorities, you will be sent to a concentration camp in Germany as soon as transport is available. Do you wish to say anything?"

"Yes. I want to see that leaflet."

"Oh, don't be absurd. As if it made the slightest difference whether you see it or not. Here . . ." but no, it was only the typed confession, the list of valuables, Rozália's original denunciation, a few personal letters rifled from the flat, a sheet of headed police stationery with a few hand-written lines on it; Gitta was close enough to see the papers clearly.

"It must have been sent on to another department," the chief said at last. "It makes no difference at all."

"Oh yes, it does!" Gitta yelled. Something had snapped; the blood raced hotly to her head and she banged both fists on the garden table until they hurt. "How dare you? You can't even produce the evidence, you haven't even got a leaflet, how do you know that it ever existed? And if it did, how do you know it was my work and not something that came in the post? The only leaflet I ever possessed had arrived in a plain envelope; you can't send me to a concentration camp for that, can you?"

"Don't shout," the chief said.

"I'll shout as much as I like!" she screamed in rage, "and I don't care what you do. Aren't you ashamed of yourself, you stupid, arrogant little man? You can't prove anything, you haven't got a foot to stand on and you still carry on as if you were God's right hand, you make me sick. If you are so concerned with the security of the State, why don't you go and fight the Russians, not six-year-old boys and people like myself?"

A gendarme put his hand on her shoulder. Another came hurrying from the house. Gitta shook herself free and stamped her foot. "Soon you'll be sorry you ever set eyes on me—don't you know which way the war is going? You'll all hang, the lot of you, and I may be dead by then, but I'll still have the last laugh. Listen," she screamed at the three men who looked at her in amazement, "even if I had done the things you suspect me of, I wouldn't tell you a word, not one, I'd rather be cut into pieces and burned bit by bit, but I wouldn't speak. So how do you want me to speak when I don't know anything?"

The gendarme patted her arm. "Come, come," he said, "no need to make such a row, come back to the house, I'll get you some water." But she dug her heels in, shaking and sobbing, wild with fear and fury, and she went on yelling at the chief. She no longer knew what she was shouting, it was an incoherent rush of reproaches, threats and defiance, so that eventually the three men stood up and hurried away, leaving the gendarmes to comfort her, or, better still, shut her up.

Her knees felt weak. She slid down on the grass. Queer noises came from her throat as she went on howling helplessly, at last lamenting freely over everything that had gone wrong, everything that had changed so irrevocably over the past few months. Her distress embarrassed the gendarmes. They waited until she calmed down and took her back to the veranda.

She drank a glass of water and waited indifferently. Nothing mattered now, she did not care, she felt heavy and exhausted. An hour later the chief came in and sat down opposite her. "You are a damned nuisance," he said. "We have no time for hysterical females. Why, I think you ought to see a doctor; something is obviously wrong with your head. You may go home now, on probation."

"Why on probation?"

"Because I am not entirely convinced. Remember that."

She looked at him coldly. "I don't care."

"Why did you say we would all hang?" he asked.

"Think."

He shook his head. "I don't think we will. But I should be very surprised if you survived this war," he said, and left the veranda.

The soft-hatted man took her to the black car. It was getting dark. Another day like this, Gitta thought, faint with hunger and exhaustion, and I'll feel ninety years old, a Rip Van Winkle in reverse. At the Gellért Hotel the car stopped. "You can make your own way from here," the detective said. "You know your address and so do we."

She found Mrs. Balogh in the drawing-room, sniffing with tearful emotion. "Don't cry, darling," she pleaded, "I'm alive, I'm back, I shouted my way out of that place."

Mrs. Balogh locked her into her arms. "I knew you would come back," she faltered. "I could feel it in every bone and nerve. The Rumanians have capitulated, I've just heard it on the radio—my baby, it can't last very long now!"

CHAPTER NINETEEN

~~~cccccccð)))))))~~~

I t was one of Count Péterffy's days of sound and fury. He woke
up crossly, annoyed by the prospect of yet another torpid day
in town. The general situation had made him decide to spend
the summer away from his estates; with the exception of his son
they all stayed in town, and while the women did not complain, the
head of the family suffered intense frustration as the hot days came
and went, leaving their cargo of smelly heat, dust and disappointment. He was being cheated of his annual bonus, his ten country
weeks of riding, driving, touring the yards and stables, meddling in
everything with more authority than expertise, playing cards and
drinking with the neighbours, living up to his pet role of patriarchal
squire and old-fashioned gentleman. All this struck him forcefully
with his first waking thought, so he roared at his barber who was
three minutes late, he roared at breakfast over his unsatisfactorily
boiled egg, he broke into a hailstorm of oaths while reading his
estate manager's report, a longish account bristling with bad news—
the best buffalo of the herd had given birth to an albino calf, a
fabulous snow-white creature with pink eyes that died forty-eight
hours after birth, and the rose garden was in a bad way, too.

At this point the Countess retired to her suite, Marta sauntered
away to answer the telephone, and Péterffy took his wrath to his
study. Everything was against him, he decided, fiercely walking the
length and breadth of the large panelled room. He was infernally
lonely. His son and heir seemed stupid for his age, a frivolous
adolescent with no trace of responsibility; his wife was cold, loyal,
lifeless, bored by his political anxieties; his daughter represented the
spirit of opposition and her contempt hit him every time their eyes
met. This was no reassuring background for a man torn by doubts.
The war was going badly, very badly. Paris had fallen (to Count

157

Péterffy's mind Paris merely meant a lost German outpost), and the cowardly Rumanians had let the side down. Worst of all, he now had irrefutable proof that the Germans did not consider his country as a precious ally. In fact, they behaved as if they were dealing with a bunch of unreliable Bulgarian herdsmen. Bitterness welled up in Péterffy's heart. He was a simple man, a good-natured fanatic whose prejudices were as innate as his breeding; he could not help either. But when events swung away from what he considered normal, he was unable to adjust himself or reach logical conclusions of his own. Things were either black or white, with no margin for the countless shades of grey in between, so that when his fondest idea went bankrupt, his only reaction was to denounce it loudly and absolutely.

One morning paper was missing from his desk. He hurried out of his study to search for it. Why was Marta talking so loudly in the blue drawing-room—was there to be no peace and quiet in this house? He pushed the door open and saw his daughter struggling with a young, goat-faced German in Gestapo uniform.

"What's going on here?" Péterffy roared; at last he had a genuine reason for letting himself go. "My house is not one of your abominable pleasure camps! Do you want me to shoot you?"

The young man jerked to attention. He was terribly sorry to disturb, he had had the pleasure of attending such a charming party here, he simply thought he might call on the young Countess, he——

"Leave my daughter alone. Leave us all alone. No more charming parties for your kind," Péterffy shouted, putting his powerful voice and rolling diction to full use. "You are all traitors, the lot of you, leaving us in the lurch once again. We are always the last bastion to protect your flank, brave idiots that we are, stemming the flood from the East—what for, I wonder? Nobody ever thanks us for it. Shut up!" he roared as the German muttered something about the Fuehrer's promises. "This has been going on for a thousand years. We've always been the shield of Europe, shield towards the East, doormat towards the West, bleeding white between the two. You, you," he approached the young man threateningly, "you should be at the front, clearing up the Bolsheviks instead of murdering wretched little Jews who may have cheated over the counter but least they didn't steal the roof from over our heads!"

"Please, Papa, this man is our guest," Marta said as her father

158

paused for breath. She was enjoying the situation thoroughly.

"I didn't invite him! We didn't invite them!" Péterffy raged on, stretching his indignation to embrace the German forces *en bloc*. "At first you ask for military co-operation, then when we offer it you decide that our soldiers are unreliable—our soldiers!—and you demand economic support instead. Of all the gross, stupid impertinence! Should the enemy get here, which God forbid, we'll be left on our own as usual, without army, food or hope!"

The German clicked his heels and left the room. Marta followed him to the front door. "I'm most terribly sorry about this," she apologized. "My father is a bit odd these days. We're rather worried. Of course under the circumstances we can't possibly meet again."

The German, whose ambitions were mainly amorous and social, looked shattered. He was leaving in a week or so, couldn't the Countess meet him in a safe place to seal their friendship? But Marta shook her head. Family discipline was strict, she could take no risks. Perhaps one day, she implied, and shut the door behind him.

Count Péterffy called her in to his study.

"Thank you, Papa, I'm most grateful," she said, sitting down in the manner of a formal visitor. It was years since she had last entered her father's sanctum. "And I'm so glad about your change of heart. In the end we may see eye to eye."

"Who's that rascal? What did he want?"

"He'd helped to get two friends out of jail. I expect he wanted his reward."

"What friends? Jews?"

"Gentiles."

"They have no business to put Hungarians in jail. Damned cheek, trying to run the country."

"Papa, they've been running the country for years, didn't you notice?"

"Oh, leave me alone, you are an extremist. This country has a thousand-year-old tradition to follow. Neither your communistic ideas nor the German method will suit it."

"I'm not interested in the past. Look where it's got us. We are losing the war. I want to know what the future will be like. Why don't you let me explain what I mean? Why do you treat me as if I were an idiot child?" She longed to make contact at last. Her father had aged, his hair had turned an odd shade of grey, the light eyes lay

159

sunken in a network of fresh lines. He is going to die one day, she thought, I must try again, perhaps now——

"An idiot child? Certainly not. You have plenty of brains. But you are a rebel, a source of contradiction. Not very pleasant in the midst of one's family. You have never behaved like a daughter; even as a child you were difficult and stubborn."

"But did you ever wonder why?" she countered. "The very first thing I remember about you—I was about two—is the way you said, 'Never mind, she's only a girl,' as if I could have helped it. You never cared for me. You made the stable-master give me my riding lessons, but when Imre was old enough, you taught him yourself. I was only a girl, and by God, you rubbed it in all the time."

"You've always had everything you wanted."

"Oh yes, everything Imre didn't want, his discarded tutors, his old bicycle, his broken-down old mare that collapsed if anybody tried to mount her! And that summer we spent by the lake, every morning we went to the beach you warned Imre to look after himself because if anything happened to him, who would inherit the name and the land? Don't you remember? I do. I used to cry my eyes out. You didn't mind whether anything happened to me, I was only a girl."

"Of course I did," he said stiffly. "Why bring up all this old stuff? Naturally, a man is attached to his only son!"

Marta stood up. "Naturally. But then don't be surprised if I go my own way. I am sick and tired of always taking second place behind my inane brother."

"You can live your own life, after all, you're almost twenty and you've always wanted to be independent. All I object to is your lack of patriotism. You don't care a damn, do you?"

"I care a great deal. It wasn't I who welcomed the German occupation with a cocktail party for sixty people, was it?"

She shrugged and left the study. It was no use, he would never understand or accept her; she might just as well stop trying.

There was always Mihály to comfort her, dear Mihály, the only fixed star on her horizon since Gyuri's disappearance. Here was love indeed, steady and undemanding. He sent her flowers, poems and small, romantic tokens until she felt like a doll in a crinoline, all silky curls and whimpers. More important, he also made her feel like the young girl she had never been, dreamy and a little uncertain. She

160

liked him and for that reason refused to let the relationship turn into a love affair. Once that happened, it might be difficult not to hurt him, she thought; it was impossible to like and love a man at the same time.

But her latest failure with her father depressed her, and in the evening she agreed to accompany Mihály to his flat. His living-room was monastically simple, lined with bookshelves up to the ceiling. In one corner there was a low arm-chair facing a large Chinese drawing on the wall, a charcoal drawing of a waterfall beating and splashing against the rocks.

"That's my silent corner," he said. "It's thick with thought, you can feel it when you sit down there. I've been sitting and thinking there for years; sometimes even writing. There should be cerebral stalactites growing from the ceiling."

"What are you thinking about these days?" she asked.

"You." He led her to another arm-chair. The silent corner was unsuitable for conversation. He slipped down on the carpet and cupped his hands over her knees. His superior at the Ministry had been arrested by the Gestapo; as a result, his own exemption from front-line service would lapse any time now.

"Oh Lord, what are you going to do?"

"Go underground, the same as anybody else. It can't last much longer, and meanwhile Sas will fix me up; that man has a list of safe places as good as a hotel register, a hide-out for every taste. I am quite fond of the old stinker. I only hope he won't send me too far away."

"I shall miss you. Oh, what am I going to do without you?"

"What about me? I am the one who's worse off, I love you, you don't. Oh, Marta, I should like to take you away somewhere, to the sea or into the mountains, to have you all to myself. You don't know what you mean to me, you are a beautiful catastrophe and I would quite happily die for you—why don't you love me?"

"But I do," she said in a surprised tone. It was true, quite true, how could she have ignored it for so long? She slid down from the arm-chair and put her head in his lap, looking at him with large, searching eyes that grew more and more enormous, until he could see nothing else. The room around them vanished. Her eyes were two magnetic pools, drawing him into their blue-green radiance. This was the sea, the mountains, the weeks and months condensed

161

into minutes. There was nothing to wait for, catastrophes had their own rules of here and now.

"Will you always love me?" she whispered. "You won't leave me, will you? I am difficult, I need an awful lot of looking after. Will you help me to——"

He pressed his lips on hers. Ask me to be faithful, she thought, make me promise, break the spell. Love me well enough to hold me, make me feel secure so that I need not leave you before you get a chance to reject me. Break me in. Make me feel small and protected. Love me. Make me promise.

But Mihály did not speak. Later he put two cushions under her head, gave her a glass of wine and watched her with such glowing adoration that her eyes dimmed over with tears. Hanna was right, she thought, I was wrong. But now I know. Now it is going to be different.

He walked her home under low, oppressive clouds. "I don't want to leave you now," he said outside her house, "now or ever. If I should have to vanish, I'll let you know. Keep in touch with Sas, he'll always know where I am. Perhaps you could join me somewhere, if your family lets you leave town."

She pressed her face against his neck. Somewhere an anti-aircraft gun barked twice. "I have no family," she whispered, "I only have you." They held each other tightly, their hands refused to separate even when the alert sounded. He kissed her once more and vanished in the dark.

CHAPTER TWENTY

L ike a convalescent, Gitta took things easy, letting the time pass instead of spending it purposefully. Life seemed almost normal. The snoopers had vanished, the telephone was no longer tapped, the brave ones among their friends called again, spreading out conversational nets and sympathizing at great length. And yet, in spite of the apparent peace and calm, Gitta's feeling of being watched persisted: most of the time she found herself behaving in a restrained, lifeless way as if the slightest ebullience might provoke the unseen observers. The news was promising, people whispered hopefully about the impending end, but her own sympathies belonged to one old Jew who refused to be comforted; it was all very well for the Allies to be in Paris and Bucharest, he said, but he wanted them right outside, on his very doorstep.

The liberation of Paris came like a bombshell. Neither Gitta nor her mother had ever been there, yet they rejoiced at the news like exiles whose remote homeland has at long last been freed. To them Paris was much more than a city. It was the symbol of the unattainable West, the source of wit, beauty, elegance and creative intelligence. Paris was the altar where their favourite poets and artists had worshipped before returning to their sluggish, indifferent homeland, filled for ever with nostalgia or rage, according to their temperament. Paris was the shining opposite of everything that was wrong east of Vienna; a mystical shrine, it acted through its aura and one did not need to see it in order to grasp its full significance. In fact a visit might have destroyed much of the magic, since the transcendental idea of Paris was free of imperfections—a marvel of beauty, proportion and spiritual greatness.

It was this fabulous Paris that Gitta and her mother celebrated near the wireless with a bottle of red wine and fresh cheese biscuits. The wine sparkled to Gitta's head. She wanted to sing or shout or write—yes, she wanted to write, she had not written anything for months.

Her large blue notebook was only half full. That shapeless monstrosity meandering over four densely covered pages was the last piece she had written, early in the spring. No subject, no composition, a flood of lush adjectives with very little to hold them together. She left several pages blank to mark the beginning of a new phase in which nouns and verbs were to work harder, without the aid of padding. Heated by wine and hope, tempered by experience, she began to write about Paris and freedom, grabbing her pen chisel-wise. "Mind what you put down on paper," her mother warned. She did not like the wild look on Gitta's face.

On the last day of August, after lunch she found a message from Pali under the office door. He gave an unfamiliar address in the neighbourhood—would she please be there at 5 p.m.

She memorized the address and burnt the small piece of paper over the ash-tray, watching the perforated edge curl into brown ash. He was still using his spiral-bound notebook; at least that much was certain.

Almost two months had passed since their last meeting, two light-years in terms of lonely, horrible experience. Whatever he was to say or do could not fill the gap. Short of a miracle, how were they to return to their own brand of reality? Perhaps if they could stay together and sit out the rest of the war without further complications —but how?

She felt sick with apprehension, resenting every minute that stood between her and five o'clock. She kept planning the shortest route to the meeting-place, covering the distance at an astounding pace in her mind, so that when at last she was on her way, she could hardly walk for nervous exhaustion.

Darling, she thought, why have you waited so long? You let me down. You abandoned me. You were more frightened of the police than of hurting me. Every day was a little death, I woke up wondering whether you would ring and went to bed thinking it must happen tomorrow. Darling, darling, what now?

The old-fashioned block of flats was built round the kind of bleak, tiled courtyard that intending suicides like to examine from the top floor. The grey stone giant supporting the first flight of stairs had no nose and only one ear. Gitta walked to the third floor and rang the bell. Footsteps creaked in the hall, a door slammed, a voice called out a question, another voice said: "But it's five o'clock now." At last a woman let her in, an enormous woman in a mauve silk dress. The flat was vast. Gitta was led through five large rooms, furnished in the style of the *bourgeois* renaissance, before being left in a smaller *salon*. The blinds were down. The fussy looking-glass had a blind spot in the middle. She sat down, stood up almost at once, looked for something to look at, found nothing and remained standing at the stove.

Pali entered through a side door. His head was slightly bent to one side, his fluid way of moving was the same as ever. The wise, resigned face that she had failed to visualize in prison sprang into view with painful familiarity; how could she have forgotten it?

He took her in his arms as if to make sure that she was real. "Little one," he murmured, "I never knew you had a waist."

"I . . . I've lost weight. Oh, my darling, is it really you? It has been such an eternity. Where have you been?"

"I won't apologize for anything," he said. "It would be beside the point. I wish it had never happened, and there's nothing I can do about it now."

"Oh, never mind that. How did you get us out?"

"I didn't. My plans broke down."

"But then who did? Was it Sas?"

"No. What's worse, he owes you an apology. He was so sure you'd squeal that he wanted us all to leave town."

"To hell with Sas. It doesn't matter. But . . . the pressure from a high German source, where did that come from?"

"I suspect it was Marta's doing. She has been seen around with a Gestapo man, probably for the best possible reasons. How and what she paid for your release I don't know."

So it was not him, after all. She felt bitterly disappointed. "But where have you been all this time? I tried to imagine you in the places we know—oh, the agony of it. You must never leave me by myself for too long, I can't bear it."

He drew her to the sofa. "I'm afraid you'll have to, darling. You see, for a change I am on the run since Sunday and I may not be able to stay in town much longer. Oh, don't look so dejected, I am

165

not abandoning you, but we simply must keep out of each other's way. I would much rather miss you desperately in hiding than share a prison roof with you, several cells removed."

"Is that why we meet here? Who lives in this flat?"

"Nobody you know. It's a useful meeting-place since it has two entrances or, rather, two exits. These days it's the exits that matter."

"And why are you on the run?"

"They're after me—Allah knows why, there are so many possible reasons. Last Sunday as I was going home I found the porter waiting for me in the street. The Gestapo were in my flat, he said, would I please disappear. I haven't been home since, the porter smuggled out a few things for me on Monday. He says my flat isn't sealed. They obviously don't want me to suspect anything if I should turn up. Thank goodness there wasn't anything interesting in the flat. I had destroyed every shred of evidence when you were caught."

"What have you been doing lately? The usual jobs?"

"No. There was no need for it, the deportations stopped a little while ago."

"Well, then?"

His face assumed the shuttered look that normally stopped her asking questions. She touched his hand. "Don't lock me out," she pleaded. "I didn't ever let you down, why don't you trust me any more? Darling, don't be so remote. Let's run away together. What difference would it make? Let's go away and hide somewhere until it's all over, we can get married later. Or don't you want me any more?"

The boat-house, she thought, the half-kernels, what had happened to all that? But she could not say it, because the feeling of rock-like security she had drawn from loving him was no longer valid in this impersonal atmosphere and she did not dare to risk an open rebuff.

"Silly, of course I trust you," he said wearily. "Nothing has changed between us, but you must be reasonable; you are and you will remain a bad security risk until the end, and since you can't possibly help me in what I'm doing now, it's better for you not to know about it. You've had your share of trouble and I'm damned if I'll involve you in anything else."

"I see," she said tonelessly. "What you do sounds like sabotage or political work, but even if you weren't doing anything at all, I should still be a nuisance. Oh, I never thought this could happen to us. In

166

prison I used to think that everything was grim but you were there somewhere and that was what really mattered; you were my last ditch. But I can see that with you it's the other way round. You know I'm there somewhere, but everything else is grim and that's what really matters. Now I have nothing left, nothing at all."

"You little fool, don't you understand? I shall never live down the fact that you went to jail while I was free. Don't put me into an impossible situation. We are dangerous to each other, I refuse to cause you more trouble; we must stay away from each other until the war is over."

"You don't love me any more," she said.

He looked away in distress. He had overestimated her strength or her faith, she could not take the change. She did not understand that he only dared to dispose of her with such apparent ruthlessness because, to him, the basic link was intact and would—or so he thought—survive all hardships. Just for once he had been overconfident, or else her normal reactions were out of gear; and there was no time to reassure her.

"Sweet, darling idiot," he said, taking her pinched face between his hands, "you've got it all wrong. I love you as much as ever, only there's no room for it now. Please believe me. Have a little more faith. I know my record looks bad. To all appearances I left you in the lurch, I cut you dead in University Street because there was a cop upon your heels, I made no effort to see you until now. It really looks as if I were trying to get rid of you, but look, little one——"

The huge woman in mauve entered. "Time for you to go," she pointed at Pali. "They've just phoned."

"Thanks, I'll be along."

"Now," she insisted. "The car will be at the back in three minutes and you know they can't wait."

"I haven't finished yet," he said. The woman withdrew.

"Don't take any notice of this," he begged. "Everything is unchanged, but you must wait."

"How long for? When shall I see you again?"

He kissed her eyes. "I don't know, little one."

"Pali, Pali," she cried, "you won't just vanish without letting me know? Promise you won't?"

"I promise. I'll contact you as soon as I can. And I won't go away without seeing you first. Good-bye, half-kernel, so long."

167

The room was terribly empty now, an antechamber leading nowhere. The stupid wallpaper pattern irritated her, yet she could not take her eyes off it. After a while she opened the side door and stepped out into a long corridor. The mauve woman shot out from somewhere. "Not this way," she snapped, "you must leave through the front door."

The flat seemed empty but there were stealthy noises coming from behind every door. "Listen," the mauve woman said in the hall, "you've been waiting for the new dentist, Dr. Kabók, but he didn't turn up. Do you understand?"

She nodded. Dr. Kabók it was going to be, anything to oblige, and she wished she were dead.

CHAPTER TWENTY-ONE

~~~~~~~~~~

The road rolled gently across the woodland. On either side the trees flamed and glowed in the first rapture of autumn. Now and then mature leaves sailed through the air, obeying the deadly pull of gravity.

The car that bore Dr. Sas through this autumnal splendour was plastered with Red Cross emblems and labels proclaiming "DOCTOR" in heavy black type. He drove slowly, fighting the endless yawn that forced his jaws open and his eyes shut. I am getting old, he thought, bumping over a rough stretch. In the middle of a job the vision of a large, soft bed would suddenly appear to his mind's eye, a bed in a quiet room where he could sleep in peace for a week, and while the vision faded easily, the broken feeling of tiredness and the yawning fits grew worse. Retirement must wait, he reminded himself. People and situations were cracking up, everything was changing, this was no time to relax. He had few helpers left. Gitta remained in quarantine, Pali was difficult to reach since he now possessed several identities but no permanent address; besides, he was in a bad way, needing stimulants to stay awake and sedatives to go to sleep. Yet he is much younger than I am, Dr. Sas ruminated. These youngsters had no stamina, they were too nervy, too idealistic, debilitated by too much conscience and an exaggerated sense of responsibility. Mihály was the worst in that respect, a regular Don Quixote; now he, too, was in hiding. Marta stayed around, but Marta was in love and therefore not entirely reliable. Sas shook his head disapprovingly. Young love made him react with the vehemence of the Devil who finds himself caught up in a church procession.

Between two yawns he noticed the clump of three oaks and took the next turning into the wood. When the road became really bad he got out of the car, removed a vital piece of mechanism from the engine to frustrate thieves, and strolled along the path. The light was fading when he found the solitary grey house. A man came to meet him. His right hand was in his pocket, presumably gripping a pistol.

"I am the vet," Sas said. "I came to see those fowls."

"Which ones?"

"The two Orpingtons that fell off the tree."

"Oh, thank God you've come. We're going off our heads." The man bowed Sas inside and locked and bolted the door behind them. His fair-haired wife smiled wanly over a tableful of sandwiches, pastries and wine. How well people still live, Sas thought, applying himself to the food.

"I only got the message today and came at once," he said. "When did it happen?"

"A week ago during that heavy raid," the man said. "Normally nothing much happens out here, there are no targets. But that night things came pretty close. One plane was shot down at the far side of the woods, I guess there was little left of it when it hit the ground. Another plane limped out here from over the city. We could hear the engines cut out, then it crashed. It was pitch dark, but I felt sure somebody had baled out: it was just a hunch, and sure enough, at dawn I found the two chaps in the wood."

"Were they injured?"

"Scratched and bruised, otherwise fit. They went a bit wild when I suddenly turned up, and of course my English is very poor, but I quickly said 'God save the King' and brought them in here. I explained in sign language that they could stay here, since we had plenty of food and the whole thing couldn't last very long."

"It has already lasted too long," his wife said nervously. "You see, everything was quiet for three days, and then the Germans must have found the plane wreck, because they searched the woods. The first patrol only came to the door. I said we hadn't seen anybody and they went away. But the next day two S.S. men came, two rude types, and they insisted on searching the house. I slipped upstairs and warned the Englishmen while my husband kept the searchers busy." She shuddered. "He couldn't get rid of them, they wanted to see every single room."

"In the end they burst in on the two airmen and were shot dead," her husband continued. "It was inevitable, but we practically went

170

demented, what with two live Englishmen and two dead Germans in the house. At night we buried the bodies."

"Well, it was the only thing to do," Sas agreed. "Did you dig them in properly?"

"Yes. Used a little quicklime, too," the man said sadly. "But you see, we can't go on like this. Those Germans are bound to be missed sooner or later, and we can't go on shooting search parties, can we?"

The man stared at his feet. His wife looked unhappy. They are scared, Sas thought, and little wonder. He ate another pastry.

"Why don't you go and see the men, sir?" she suggested. "I'm sure they'd love to talk to someone at last."

The two airmen were sitting moodily upstairs. Sas explained who he was, speaking an accentless English that was as unidentifiable as his clothes. The pilot, a thin Londoner with the close-set eyes of an intelligent monkey, listened to him with relief. His navigator remained monosyllabic.

Sas outlined his plan: drive to town, deposit the two men in a safe place until the next secret convoy to Yugoslavia was ready to leave in four days or so. The rest would be organized at the other end. The men nodded. Anything suited them as long as they could get out of that house.

"Frightfully dull, eh?" Sas volunteered. "Besides, your hosts are worrying themselves silly. Decent people, though."

The pilot nodded. Very decent people, and the food was superb, positively pre-war; he had not eaten so well for years. Sas scrutinized him as he spoke and handed him a comb.

"Comb your hair back. Men of your age don't wear centre partings in this country. It looks outlandish. Are your pockets empty?"

They did not want to part with their sentimental possessions. Those meaningless letters and snapshots from home seemed more important than escape. But everything had to go. Sas burned the lot in the stove, together with an old newspaper, mixing the ashes thoroughly. They went downstairs to say good-bye to the unhappy couple. Outside the night was dark and moonless. The airmen shook hands with their hosts, muttering thanks and farewells. "Come to England after the war," the pilot said slowly and distinctly. "You can stay at my house, you and your wife." "Better bring your own food," the navigator added. "Yes, yes, England. God save the King," the man beamed. His wife wiped her eyes.

They reached town in pelting rain. The pilot lay neatly concealed under rugs and parcels in the back, the navigator travelled in the boot. Sas drove the car into a deserted courtyard, unloaded his passengers and led them through curtains of rain to Hanna's flat a few streets away. Hanna received them in an emerald gown and a blaze of hospitality; one glance at her preparations convinced Sas that the airmen would fall short of her expectations, since Hanna's mental image of the average Englishman was about as accurate as the average Englishman's belief that a typical Hungarian spends his life on horseback, playing the violin while racing with the winds of the Puszta.

"And remember, no visitors while the boys are here," he warned her in the hall. "I'll fetch them as soon as I can. Meanwhile keep everybody out."

"Even Marta? She speaks such excellent English."

"Above all, Marta. The boys aren't here to be entertained. And for Heaven's sake don't expect them to be fascinating. They're ordinary lads, and pretty dull at that."

The evening was a failure. The two men ate half-heartedly, not realizing what immense pains Hanna had taken over the exotic food at a time of shrinking supplies, culinary depression and no maid. They hardly drank or spoke and watched their flamboyant hostess with less than polite bewilderment. Hanna's extraordinary looks and swift, unidiomatic English, bristling with references to baffling subjects, depressed them. This refuge was more alien than the very ordinary house in the wood. They had not read any of the English authors Hanna kept quoting, they knew little and cared less about Druidism, and to talk about the war was out of the question. After a while the unsuccessful session broke up. The men spent many bewildered minutes in Hanna's lavish bathroom, looking for a piece of honest soap among the feminine paraphernalia, and then they retired to the guest room.

Hanna washed up pensively in the kitchen. Dull though her guests were, she was glad of a change. The weeks passed so slowly, so depressingly. Her Jewish guests had left when the deportations ceased. Miklós had kept away from her since that difficult night in July when she had wakened him with her sobs. Not a word since

172

then, not a message, although with his wife's death the only tangible obstacle had vanished, and she missed him with the accumulated pain of several incarnations.

It was this pain that made her try to forget their political differences. All right, he was right-wing, regrettably so, but as long as nobody suffered why should she stop seeing him? Why indeed, except for the fact that apparently he did not wish to see her, and so peculiar was their liaison that she did not even know where to reach him.

Two nights later, shortly after the airmen had retired, the doorbell shrilled. The Gestapo, Hanna thought resignedly; the end is nigh. She took off her high-heeled mules and crept to the dark kitchen. The glazed back entrance gave a good view of the flat entrance opposite. Raising one corner of the black-out curtain, she peered out.

It was Miklós, carrying his familiar overnight bag and a bunch of flowers. He tapped his foot and pressed the bell once more. Hanna could see his profile as he turned his head impatiently from side to side. She stared at him, her heart pounding loudly. The Gestapo would have been easier to bear. It was impossible to let him in: she felt desperately sure that he would find the airmen and have them arrested, even if it meant her death.

Darling, she thought, go away, go away, I can't open, don't wait there because I'll let you in, go away just this once. He rang once more; the bell resounded aggressively throughout the flat and she wondered what the airmen were thinking. Miklós glanced at his watch. He shrugged irritably, rammed the flowers into the letter-box as far as they would go and ran down the stairs.

She returned to the drawing-room and collapsed on the settee. What a terrible coincidence, what a loss. Tears rolled down her face; they fell on her dress, leaving marks on the green silk. She felt sure she had missed her last chance; after this he was not going to return ever again. Everything breaks up for the wrong reasons, she lamented, one is forced into situations instead of being able to choose them, and one grows lonelier all the time.

The sirens wailed outside like lost souls. Lost souls, we are all lost souls, she thought, and went to bed with a large glass of brandy.

CHAPTER TWENTY-TWO

~~~∞∞∞∞∞◯∞∞∞∞∞~~~

By early October chaos was complete. Air raids and bomb damage were changing the city's face day by day. Public transport operated erratically, if at all. To get from one point to another meant long, hazardous journeys and a great deal of walking, since few of the buses and trams followed their normal routes. There was a terrible sense of urgency in the air, the taste of impending change. Everybody talked about the unconditional surrender and the breakaway from the Germans that could not wait much longer. The optimists still believed in an airborne Anglo-American invasion—some even claimed to have seen Allied paratroops near the Western frontier. The pessimists watched the vast number of refugees flowing in from the east and insisted that it was only the Soviet soldiers who were pushing forward relentlessly.

Within the general chaos there was the personal chaos of all those who did not know where to spend the night: people in hiding, people on the run, Jews, deserters, resisters, priests, Poles, politicians, students, intellectuals, workers. It was a motley crowd of normally law-abiding citizens who, lacking the professional law-breaker's touch, needed all the beginner's luck in the world to avoid arrest.

Gitta still went to the office every day, although there was hardly any work left, and she spent most of the time going through old files and chatting with Ervin Wass who was becoming a very close friend. He would not accept her notice; he said he liked to have her around the place, and she agreed gratefully to stay, because apart from regular office hours there was nothing regular left in life.

Fehér, the crinkly-haired detective, appeared one morning in the middle of an early alert. Not having seen him for some time, the Baloghs had written him off with relief. There was quite enough to fray their nerves even without him. But now Fehér rushed into the hall in a state of great anxiety. He kissed Mrs. Balogh's hand, missed Gitta's, and almost fell over on the polished floor.

"You must go away," he panted. "I've come to warn you, you mustn't stay here for the time being."

"Why, whatever is the matter?" Mrs. Balogh asked.

His forehead shot up in even folds. "There's going to be the most dreadful trouble within the next day or two. The Gestapo have started picking up people who have previously been in trouble, and they're bound to reach you by tomorrow or the day after. There's no time to waste."

"Come, come," Gitta said, "what makes you think that they'll bother about us?"

"They're taking our files away!" he wailed. "All the political files must be delivered by tomorrow, and yours is among them. I've managed to delay it so far, but I can't spirit it away, because my new boss never leaves me alone in the office. Those were the days, in the summer. Please go away somewhere at once!"

"Come and have some breakfast," Mrs. Balogh suggested. "Surely there's time for that?"

"No, thanks, I must warn some other people. But I came here first, truly, I wanted to make sure you had enough time to get ready."

"You are too kind," Gitta said. "I hope one day we may——"

"I trust we shall remain friends?" He bowed in his provincial dancing-class manner. "When the war is over, perhaps you'll remember that I've always tried to do the right thing."

"Most certainly. When I am Secretary of State, I'll see that you get your reward," she said. But irony was lost on him. He kissed the ladies' hands and darted to the door.

"What I like about you, Miss Gitta, is your sense of humour," he said adoringly, and dashed out into the all-clear.

What now? Gitta rang Marta, her last remaining contact, and asked her to mobilize Sas. Marta felt sure that Sas would refuse to visit the Baloghs' home, so Gitta hurried off to her office to wait there.

They did not arrive until after lunch—Marta exhausted by the long search, Sas ill-tempered at this latest disturbance. Gitta's story depressed him even further. He had expected trouble at a later date.

Fehér's warning messed up his crowded plans. He scribbled a few lines on a slip of paper and handed it to Gitta.

"Go home right away, pack your bags and go with your mother to this address. There's a train after five, you must catch that. When you get to the *pension* tell the owner I sent you and stay there until you hear from me."

"But this place is miles away from town," Gitta protested. "Must we really go away? Is it absolutely necessary?"

"God, give me patience!" Sas exploded. "A real, live, genuine political detective warns you personally, out of the kindness of his heart, or else dazzled by your beauty and charm, and then you ask me whether it's necessary for you to go. Really!"

"I'm sorry. It's only that I don't like to leap in the dark, especially just now. Look, there's just one thing—I must see Pali before I go. Where can I reach him?"

"But Pali's gone away, didn't you know?" Sas sounded amazed at such ignorance. "It was a hell of a job to get him out of the country. I thought you knew that he might have to leave?"

She looked at him incredulously. Her lower lip trembled a little. Marta slipped a hand round her arm; she could not bear the look of naked heartbreak on Gitta's face.

"Christ, don't look so thunderstruck: he'll come back one day, we hope," Sas said irritably. "You women, honestly, you're hopeless."

"Yes, I suppose I'm hopeless. It's only that he had promised to see me before going away, and he's never broken a promise yet. I can't believe it."

"He probably had to leave in a dreadful hurry," Marta broke in. "You know how these things are, there's simply no time for anything except to take your toothbrush and fly. Isn't that so, boss?"

Sas nodded. He knew perfectly well that Pali was a mere five kilometres away in hiding and, at a pinch, could be reached without great risks, but he considered his own version more expedient. Gitta was a worse security risk than he had thought. It only remained for these romantic idiots to start playing Romeo and Juliet and tumble into a Gestapo car, holding hands. "My dear girl," he said, "I thought it was understood all along that work goes before personal affairs. You didn't seriously expect him to drop everything and rush

176

round to kiss you farewell? Don't be absurd. The real stink is still to come."

"Yes, I did expect just that. One needs something to believe in," she said, "although you would be the last person to understand."

Sas rose and brushed a few thin hairs off his forehead. "I'll be in touch with you soon. Make sure you catch that train and please don't write letters to anybody. Promise?"

Gitta did not even see him out. She collected her belongings, wrote a note to Ervin and prepared to go home.

"Cheer up," Marta said, "you take everything too much to heart. It's a mistake, unless you want to go through life collecting bruises."

"I know," she nodded. "I can't help it. Pali was the most important thing in my life, but obviously it wasn't mutual. A pity. Are you happy?"

"I am. And worried. Mihály takes too many risks. He's supposed to be in hiding, but he keeps popping in to town in broad daylight because he misses me. Oh, it's beautiful to be missed so badly, but I get nightmares every night, dreaming that he's been caught."

"Can't you talk him out of it?"

"No. Mihály is convinced that Fate is sparing him for some special purpose. He is like Orpheus, marching around in the wilds with a harp."

"Fair enough. Orpheus came back from the underworld!"

"Yes. Minus Eurydice. Well, you'd better go now. Good luck."

Rushing home, Gitta found Mrs. Balogh at the height of the situation. She had already packed their bags with skill and economy, preparing for an indefinite stay under unspecified circumstances. Gitta tidied up her own room, vaguely saying good-bye to her favourite belongings, but her strongest emotion was indifference, the indifference of all-round defeat.

They left the flat stealthily to avoid the caretaker's wife and took a tram to the station. Grey crowds milled round under the glass dome, the wet weather sharpened the taste of smoke and soot, and the train indicator was out of order. At last they sat in the north-bound train that crept through the black-out like a frightened worm. Sometimes they stopped between two stations and waited on the open track, sometimes grim faces peered through the glass partition with flattened noses and chins. The Baloghs sat in silence, squeezed

177

between anonymous, muffled-up passengers. At last they reached their station and got out. "Pension Dombos? But that's across the Danube, this is only the nearest railway station," a porter said. "Down the path to the river, the ferry leaves in ten minutes."

It was several degrees colder here than in town, and the rain whipped their faces from all sides. The river bank was pitch-dark. Mrs. Balogh, who was terrified of water and thought that nothing smaller than an ocean liner was really safe, stared desperately at the black Danube. Gitta held her arm firmly. More people came from the station, women in thick black woollen shawls, two young lads, a man with a mongrel. Eventually the ferry materialized out of the dark. It was not very big and the water made hollow noises against its sides. "Come on, darling, it's perfectly safe," Gitta whispered, helping her mother into the boat. Mrs. Balogh sank down on a narrow seat, ready to die. After a while the ferryman pushed off and began to row.

The Danube was wide. In the coal-black night, suspended between the river and the rain, Gitta felt as if they were floating across infinity. There was nothing to hold on to, not even a solitary star, and the water sang desolately. The last time she had been on the river with Pali did not bear thinking about. At last the ferry landed and Mrs. Balogh fled on to firm land, shaking violently. The two lads volunteered to carry their bags to the *pension*, fifteen minutes away in the stinging drizzle.

Dombos, the owner, answered the door. He had a bloated face and reeked of drink. "Dr. Sas sent us," Gitta mumbled. "Can you put us up, please?" Dombos winked, nodded and turned to lead them upstairs. The double bedroom was immaculate. Mrs. Balogh surveyed it with satisfaction, then she turned very green, clutched her throat and rushed out. The river trip was taking its toll.

They met the other guests in the morning. Dombos had acquired a distinguished clientèle, including several Budapest celebrities, all of whom were on the run for a variety of reasons, but whose political opinions were sufficiently homogeneous for them to ignore each other politely. At first, the *pension* looked disturbingly normal to Gitta, a well-appointed establishment such as upper-middle-class people might choose for a quiet holiday out of season; the food was superb, the service impeccable, and the red and gold autumn forest behind the building looked perfect for idle strolls. But then she discovered that Dombos, who seemed to spend the whole day in a jovial alcoholic haze, was in fact stone sober and very much on the alert. At regular intervals he emerged from his thickly curtained office to pass round the latest B.B.C. news among his guests. The commander of the local *gendarmerie* was a great friend of his.

The comparative peace irritated Gitta. She ate, slept and walked conscientiously, but it seemed criminally wrong to collect unusual leaves and wish good day to the occasional villager on the road. On their first Sunday in the *pension* she made her mother quite unhappy with her sullen temper: they sat down silently to lunch, interlocked in a clash of mute reproach and equally mute irritability. The wireless played jingling tunes. The news was due at one o'clock. "Attention, attention," a voice announced, interrupting the music. "We are now making an important announcement. Hungary is seeking an armistice. Here is the Regent's proclamation."

A dish crashed on the floor. Somebody hissed. The eaters froze into silence, holding their forks and bread rolls in the position in which the voice had found them. The words of the proclamation rolled out dramatically over their heads, sounding the more incredible because they came through the official mouthpiece they had learned to distrust over the years, so that although the proclamation fulfilled their secret longings, it was difficult to take in its full significance at the first hearing.

When the announcer finished reading, the people in the dining-room leapt up from their chairs, shrieking and shouting with relief, embracing each other, some women crying. "Darling, it's over, it's over, oh God—thank heavens we've been spared long enough to hear this," Mrs. Balogh burst out, but Gitta just sat there and stared at the tablecloth.

"What's the matter, baby? Didn't you hear what it said?"

She shook her head sadly. "You don't really imagine that this is the end? That the Germans will apologize and go home? Now I know what Sas meant when he said that the real stink was still to come."

"Really, you're quite unbearable." Mrs. Balogh rose and joined the excited guests. The noise grew louder until Dombos staggered in and yelled for silence.

"Ladies and gentlemen," he shouted, "you're my guests and you do exactly as you please. But if I were you, I'd stay the night at least.

179

I'll keep in touch with Budapest and keep you informed. Please carry on with your meal."

But now nobody wanted to eat. The declaration was read out again and again on the wireless, but the general ebullience was gone. After coffee the guests did not go upstairs as usual. Anxiously scanning each other's faces, they stayed in the lounge, engaging in quick whispered conversations and relapsing into silence with a worried look. At four o'clock Dombos ran out of his office. "You all stay here," he declared. "There's fighting in town. The Germans are holding the bridges, the Arrow Cross Party are busy taking over. Ladies and gentlemen, the picnic is over. God help us all."

Gitta left the lounge and took the path to the wood. The last hope was gone; there would be more blood, more shame, more terror. The ridiculous efforts of the past months had achieved nothing; there was no escape, the boy David had not even got a chance to raise his sling.

Failure, she thought, sitting on a tree-stump. We failed. There were too few of us and even we made a mess of things. She did not want to fight any more, she was scared, tired and empty. It would have been good to pray except that she did not even know what to pray for.

From five onwards the wireless roared out the threats and abuse of the new rulers. The Arrow Cross had taken over; no effort would be spared to carry the war to its victorious conclusion. The voices filled the air with evil and madness. Eventually Dombos turned off the set. "Be on the alert," he warned his guests mournfully. "We'll keep an all-night watch and give the alarm, if necessary. Sleep as well as you can under the circumstances." This time he was really and hopelessly drunk.

CHAPTER TWENTY-THREE

~~~ccccccc6Ŏɔɔɔɔɔɔɔ~~~

Count Péterffy received the proclamation of surrender manfully. Loyalty to some cause was vital to him at all times, so now he accepted the Regent's decision as the only possible alternative to total disaster, and said so, too, across the family dining-table. He then went to his study, pocketed his pistol and put on his overcoat. Marta was waiting for him in the hall. He refused to take her with him, so she followed him at a distance. It was easy. Péterffy never bothered to look behind him.

Had anybody asked him at that moment where he was going and with what intent, he would have been unable to give a coherent answer. Full of patriotic bitterness, he wanted to be at the centre of things, at the battlefield as it were, and he took aim at Palace Hill where his cousin the General had a house near the Regent's residence. The General had turned anti-German shortly after the occupation, and a violent quarrel at the Casino in April had put an end to their regular meetings, but surely this was the moment to make peace, join forces and do something heroic in the best tradition of their family.

Near the Danube he heard volleys of shots. German tanks rolled across the bridge to Buda, planes circled low over the Palace. A group of people with dazed, incredulous faces passed him and turned into a side street. Two men in cloth caps emerged from a house, shouting "Hurrah! The war is over! Down with Hitler!" and they ran along the quay with their coats flapping behind them. Péterffy frowned distastefully. He could not stand undignified behaviour at tragic moments. But then his frown deepened for a different reason. Arrow Cross men in green shirts, black breeches and shiny riding-boots burst into the main road, their arms swinging ominously from side to side, and Péterffy suddenly had the nauseating suspicion

181

that in final despair the Germans might link up with this band of political maniacs whom he had even in his previous phase firmly classed with the lowest sewer rats. More shots rang out. A dumpy woman yelled: "Dear God, what's going on?" He did not know, he went on grimly to cross the bridge, found his usual short cut up Castle Hill barred by Germans, so he took a detour, weaving in and out of narrow streets, until at last he got to his cousin's house.

The General was out. His wife was crying quietly in a drawing-room full of worried friends, all talking at the same time. Péterffy threw himself into the polite chaos. Nobody had any positive comfort to offer, but at least he was not alone with his doubts, and in the incessant noise he did not hear the rumble of approaching tanks.

Delayed by a large group of greenshirts, Marta had become separated from her father at the foot of the Hill. She did not know what to do—try to follow her father or go to Mihály's flat, just in case he had returned to town. Rounding a corner, she ran into S.S. men and was turned back. Now shooting started on the Hill. A convoy of German armoured cars drove up towards the Palace.

She stepped inside a vaulted doorway to think. There seemed little point in looking for Papa; the Hill was as good as besieged and the outcome was beyond doubt. She did not know who was firing the shots against whom, whether it was a straight fight between the Germans and everybody else, or between the Germans and several Hungarian factions of opposing views, but she did know that either way things were bound to end badly; being a true child of her time and place, she only wondered whether anything could be salvaged from the universal mess.

It was turning cool. She stepped out into the street and hurried back towards the river. The bridge was full of Germans, but they let her pass; some even whistled and shouted at her appreciatively. There were bigger crowds on the Pest side, quiet, dazed, indifferent people wandering around aimlessly, pointing at the low-flying German aircraft. Marta clenched her fists in her coat pockets. If instead of looking dazed these people did something, she thought wildly, if they grabbed kitchen knives or hatchets or chair-legs and began to fight, however hopelessly, perhaps something could be salvaged. But the creeping paralysis was now complete. The extremists were happy; everybody else stood back waiting suspiciously, not believing in any-

182

thing any more, except survival at all costs. She picked up a leaflet from the gutter. Emblazoned with the Arrow Cross emblem, it contained an ill-spelt tirade against the Regent's treachery—the ink was still wet enough to smudge her fingers—and a tornado of threats against all dissenters. What follows is always worse than what has gone before, she thought, slipping the leaflet into her pocket.

Still surrounded by arguing dignitaries, Count Péterffy was growing more and more restless. When a fresh arrival burst in to say that the Germans were besieging the Palace to take the Regent prisoner and that the Guard were powerless, he slipped out to see for himself. The solemn old street was packed with Germans. He turned back, cut across the courtyard and let himself out through a side door into a narrow passage that led along the backs of houses. There was nobody to stop him but he was not getting much nearer to his aim, and it went against the grain to hurry through back alleys like a common criminal. Eventually he emerged into the open. Germans on all sides, tanks, cars, lorries everywhere. One side street looked clear, but hardly had he gone twenty yards, when a posse of green-shirts appeared round the corner, chanting: "Down with the Regent! Death to the traitor!"

"How dare you?" Péterffy roared, planting himself in the middle of the street. "*Canaille*, rats, shut up! The Regent is the head of the State, his word is law!" He trembled with rage, planting his feet wide on the damp pavement, a thin, tall, ageing man in an astrakhan-collared coat, lifting one shaking hand to point at the giant replica of the Holy Crown that rested on the central cupola of the Palace. He wanted to shout something about the Holy Crown, the warm flood of heroic words was rising to his lips, but there was no time to give those bastards a lesson in patriotism. The gang surrounded him yelling abuse, and so great was Péterffy's indignation that he forgot about the loaded pistol in his pocket and attacked the nearest green-shirts with his bare fists; then several shots rang out and he fell to the pavement.

Marta staggered home at ten. Her stockings were torn, she had lost her cap and her blonde hair hung limply over her face. There was a smear of blood over her left eye where a flying stone had grazed her skin. She limped into the hall. Her mother came out of the drawing-room, her face deathly white, her lips compressed into a thin line.

"It's murder, murder," Marta said feebly. "I saw them breaking into Jewish houses and dragging people out and shooting them in the street. And shooting others on the quays so that they fell in the water when they were hit. Children and women and old people, everybody. They shot a hospital nurse who tried to save a little boy, and the Germans just stood there and laughed. Oh Mummy, it's . . ."

"Your father has been shot dead, too," the Countess whispered. "His body is in the study."

"Dead?" They stood motionless, staring at each other with identical blue-green eyes, their long hands folded in the same way, their chins tilted at the same angle. For once, mother and daughter looked alike. After an endless moment Marta stepped forward to take her mother in her arms, but the Countess shook her head and turned away. Marta went into the study. Her father lay on the enormous leather couch, under the buff sheepskin coat he used to wear in the country. His face looked sad, bruised, old; he was irrevocably disillusioned and irrevocably dead.

Marta looked down at him in the dim light of two small reading-lamps until her eyes filled with tears. Throughout the years of frustration and anger she had never cried once, and if she did so now, it was not so much the death of her father that distressed her as the complete futility of his life and death. She cried because he had always played the wrong role in a drama of his own making, because he had got himself killed for no good purpose on the same afternoon that hundreds of terrified people were also killed, for no better purpose, the only difference being that while Péterffy's dead body lay in his own study, covered with his own hunting-coat, the other corpses were floating in the cold, bloody Danube; and because, indirectly, he was responsible for all the deaths, including his own.

"I told you so," she whispered between two sobs, "Papa, I told you so," but the grey face remained stony, more unattainable than in life. Marta, who had never seen a corpse before, realized that this was no longer her father, this was a thing, a poor dead thing frozen into the final situation which everyone tries to avoid throughout life and which catches up with them none the less, and she sank down at the foot of the divan, overcome with pity and horror. "I so wanted you to love me," she whispered; it was all the same now.

Her mother fetched her an hour later. "Come, let me wash your face, it's bleeding," she said. Marta followed her into the bathroom, not even flinching when the iodine bit into her skin.

Countess Péterffy stared at the medicine cupboard. For the first time in her life she had washed her husband's and her daughter's face, all in the space of a few hours.

CHAPTER TWENTY-FOUR

〜〜〜〜〜〜〜

Three days after the ill-fated armistice proclamation Dombos lurched into the *pension* at two in the afternoon. His face was purple; he had some difficulty in focusing his eyes.

"You must go," he said to the guests who were sitting miserably in the lounge, waiting for something to happen. "I'm very sorry, dear ladies, dear gentlemen, you must all leave at once and not come back. My friend the commander's been sacked, they're sending some greenshirt bastard to take his place, the kind that eats Jews for breakfast and democrats for lunch. I can't have you here any longer."

"But where shall we go?" a woman asked anxiously.

"Just disperse in the neighbourhood," Dombos said. "Say you've been bombed out. Say you're refugees from the Russians, nobody can check. As ll . . . long", the l-sounds went first when he was drunk, "as you don't stay together, you'll be all right."

Gitta bent close to him. "Do you know of anybody who might put us up?"

"Go to Visegrád," he mumbled, "perhaps you'll find a room there. Lll . . . llissen," he said, raising his voice, "you'll have to be out of here pretty soon, all of you. I think we'll be raided before tonight."

Ten minutes later, all packed and ready to leave, Mrs. Balogh asked for their bill. "Next time," Dombos slurred, "not now. You may need the money, I won't." And when Mrs. Balogh took a deep breath to protest, he shook his head irritably. "Get going, dear lady, don't wait for the gendarmes to get us. Down the road and along the river, good-bye."

They shook hands with him, murmuring their thanks and promising to return one day under better circumstances. With a grimace Dombos disappeared into his curtained office.

The Baloghs took a suitcase each and walked down towards the main road. The Danube looked yellow and sluggish under a muslin veil of drizzle. On either side the steep mountains were covered with rust-red and yellow woods. But after a while the heights opposite receded. On a strip of flat country small houses huddled together untidily; mean little copses played at being distant in the hazy air. The view was grave and splendid. Gitta paused to rest and look around. At that moment a caravan emerged from behind a screen of trees, a procession of heavy covered wagons drawn by ungainly horses. The old women who drove them wore draped kerchiefs on their heads and sat, motionless and black, their whips erect like emaciated flags. The canvas roofs of the wagons flapped from side to side. Gitta saw piles of household utensils, dogs, children, pigtailed girls and grey old men travelling in sad chaos; now and then a head turned round as if looking for the next halt. But the horses went on relentlessly, pressing on towards the border. Even without knowing who the migrants were—perhaps German peasants from the East? —Gitta understood that this was a great exodus, a one-way journey into banishment. There was an air of terrible finality about the roped-together pots, churns, large wicker baskets and feather beds, the portable debris of abandoned homes, and the old women with their closed faces were like drivers in a funeral procession. They were the last ones to take charge, since the able-bodied men had been taken away long ago, the remaining ones were too old to hold the reins, and the young girls and small boys could only cry and shiver in the back.

With a sigh Mrs. Balogh picked up her case and began to walk. The road curved ahead gently, empty of people and traffic. Shuttered summer residences appeared behind tall garden walls, desolate with the sadness of all places that lead a heightened existence for one season and then stand forgotten for three, a graveyard of all past summers.

The steep mountain over Visegrád, crowned with ruins, sprang into view. Parts of a crumbling wall sloped down to King Salamon's wrecked tower. Beneath, the village sprawled along the main road. Leaving her mother with the luggage in a roadside shelter, Gitta began to climb the mountain. The steep path was covered with slippery red leaves; twice she had to bend down and support herself on her hands to save her foothold. She hardly paused to look at Salamon's tower. The light was beginning to fail and they had nowhere to go. But the guest house she had remembered from a past excursion was deserted and locked. The old woman who emerged from the haze said it would not open until the summer. So she hurried down to fetch her mother, and together they entered the village. The women outside the church watched them with vague hostility. One of them thought the widow at the inn might have a room to let. They went into the inn to negotiate with the widow, a hard, greedy woman habitually on the offensive. The verbal struggle lasted a long time, for the widow was not easily moved by anybody's plight and refused to haggle. Eventually Mrs. Balogh accepted the extortionate terms and at last they were in a long, low room, suddenly feeling weary because there was no immediate obstacle for them to overcome.

The room looked provincial and absurdly old-fashioned. The large oil lamp was empty; three candles stood in brass holders on the vast table. The beds were high, brown, chest-like; the chair seats were covered in bobble-fringed velours. There were a dozen pictures of St. Joseph on the walls, some printed, some drawn, others painted on glass in garish colours; a solemn portrait of Francis Joseph in the centre was undoubtedly meant to represent a secular namesake of the saint who had made good in this world. The air was heavy, the furniture and the bedclothes felt damp. One could sense the nearness of the autumn Danube outside in the dark. Mrs. Balogh lit and arranged the candles to get as much light as possible, she put their few belongings into the vast wardrobe and eventually sat down. "But what are we going to do here?" she asked plaintively. Gitta shrugged. She had no idea.

Later there was a rap on the door. The widow poked her head in and looked around avidly. "Of course you can't have an evening meal," she announced. "I only light the fire once a day, and it goes out by four. I never eat in the evenings." She shut the door. They could hear her large feet splashing about in the muddy yard. A door banged. In the silence the rain sounded tinny. "Is it too early to go to sleep?" Mrs. Balogh asked.

"Aren't you hungry?"

"No, not really. Oh God, this is dreadful, we haven't even got anything to read! Baby child, we can't sit here doing nothing, can we?"

188

"Let's talk. Oh, about anything, it doesn't matter what, we always have something to talk about, don't we? Or do you want to go out? It'll be terribly dark and wet, and there's nowhere to go, really."

Mrs. Balogh stood up. "Never mind, let's slip out for a moment. This room gets on my nerves. I didn't know such places still existed."

There were puddles everywhere. However carefully they stepped, small jets of cold slush kept hitting their calves. At the other end of the street they found a second inn and entered boldly, in search of food. There was none. The innkeeper scratched his head and said that the food situation was very bad indeed, he had stopped serving meals weeks ago, and the village shop was empty, too; Heaven only knew how long people would manage on their reserves. But there was plenty of wine, so Mrs. Balogh hastily bought a two-litre bottle of white and, amid the suspicious stares of drinking men, dragged Gitta out into the street.

"We'll have to be terribly careful," she whispered. "Obviously we're the only strangers here and we don't want the authorities to get too interested. Even though we said we'd been bombed out——"

"We'll starve to death before the police get us. At least the old witch gives us one meal a day for our money."

Back in their room they sat down with the wine bottle, ready to drink, when they discovered that they had no glasses. To disturb the widow was out of the question, so Mrs. Balogh rummaged in her toilet case and triumphantly produced a tiny gilt cup, originally intended as a brandy dispenser on long journeys. Having spent several years next to a scent bottle, the cup smelt faintly of stale perfume, but that only improved the inferior wine. Drinking on an empty stomach was depressing. Gitta recited poetry by heart to cheer them up, but she could only remember tragic poems about death, fratricide and general doom. The most topical poem, a sombre classic about King Salamon whose ruined tower stood on the hillside, came last. She scanned out the rolling lines, filling in the gaps as well as she could. She felt strongly about the unhappy king who had had to fly for his life, cursing like a fallen angel, and who had ended his days as a hermit in a dark forest.

Later she dreamt about the king, as she lay stiffly between the musty sheets. She saw him fleeing in a broken helmet, his shattered sword dripping with blood. She could even hear his voice cursing his divided people and challenging God to abandon him for ever-more. And then the raging figure stopped under the blood-red trees and turned back towards Gitta, who stood in the familiar paralysis of frightening dreams, and as her eyes met his he was no longer King Salamon, he was Pali, and he shook his fist at her and vanished.

The next morning it was still raining. They ate the meagre breakfast the widow had brought in—*ersatz* tea with saccharin and stale bread with *ersatz* jam—and then ventured out into the open. In daylight the village looked even more vacant and two-dimensional than at night, a hard-up village uncomfortably squeezed between the river and the steep mountainside, inhospitable and indifferent. They walked along the crooked streets, meeting few people, mostly women and children. At last they found a general store, an oasis where they felt they could enter and talk and perhaps buy something without arousing suspicion. So they stepped in and looked around, but there were only tins of boot polish, leather straps, balls of string, horse-whips and holy pictures to buy, no food or books. The woman behind the counter sensed their helplessness, pulled out a drawer and laid out a handful of shop-soiled articles before them. All were pretty useless but they bought a pack of fortune-telling cards in a torn box and left hurriedly. The rain was coming down hard. Returning to the inn, they spread the cards on the table. The crudely coloured pictures were badly drawn yet full of commanding force, showing a gipsy woman, a postman, old-fashioned little boys in a big wood, a dark and a fair stranger, a bosomy girl, a long toy train emitting indigo smoke, a gay green skeleton, all the symbolical rewards and dangers of life. They took turns at shuffling and dealing the cards and, not knowing the rules, made up their own in an effort to work out the future. They spent several hours playing in the damp room. The messages of Fate spelt themselves out in varying formulae under their eyes, but they could not read them and therefore tried again, hoping for a clear omen. Every time Gitta cut the pack the cards promised a long journey, a letter with joyous news, and happiness in love; and she believed them, although by then few trains were running, nobody knew where they were staying so that no letter could possibly arrive, and love in a rose garden—for that's how the card represented it, a plump couple embracing in a blossoming bower—seemed more unlikely than a day trip to Saturn.

Lunch came at two, on a none-too-clean tray. It was as unpalatable as the breakfast and hardly more in quantity. By four they were both ravenously hungry. The hours until the next morning stretched ahead like a Sahara of privation. Eventually Mrs. Balogh decided to search the village for food—surely at least a loaf of bread could be bought somewhere in this wilderness? She opened the door and shut it again. River guards were streaming into the yard, mud-spattered men in Army khaki with flat sailors' caps and square sailors' collars, the official force operating on and along the Danube. Gitta watched them through the lace curtain. They seemed to be moving into the inn, pushing and dragging their carts across the yard.

It could not possibly matter, she reasoned with her mother. The guards were probably in transit and would not bother about two quiet women living in a room. Their own documents were in order, she insisted, and how would the men know that they were wanted by the Gestapo? At last they ventured out and after an hour's search got a loaf at a price that should have bought them a three-course meal in a first-class restaurant. They crept back to the inn, hurrying past the river guards with downcast eyes, and locked themselves in. In spite of all reasoning they both felt that uniforms meant trouble while locked doors meant safety.

But later that evening there was a knock on the door, and Mrs. Balogh, cautiously unlocking it, found a river guard outside. Short, fat and jovial, he held a finger to his lips and stood on tiptoe to emphasize the secret nature of his visit.

He stepped in and locked the door behind him. "Not to worry," he said. "I understand. I've been watching you this afternoon, I know everything. Here's some food," and he took a greasy parcel from his bulging breast pocket. "Fresh sausage, cracknels, black pudding, made it myself, good for you."

Mrs. Balogh stared at the parcel. "But how——"

"It's all right, I understand. My wife's Jewish, too, she's in hiding, I know all about these things. Now there's no food in this muddy nest, I've found out that much myself, but we're carrying our own supplies and I'm the cook."

The parcel smelt tantalizingly good, oozing the honest richness of freshly killed pig and home-made delicacies. "But we aren't Jewish," Mrs. Balogh tried to explain, "we're only here because——"

"It's all right," he interrupted. "I know. You can trust me. This is a dirty world, but you must still eat. Come on, tuck in."

He watched them happily and refused to accept money or cigarettes; eventually he drank a glass of wine and told them about his home and butcher's shop in Mohács where all had been well until the world had turned dirty. They ate gratefully, nodding in assent every time his monologue required it. Unfortunately he did not know the latest news. His unit had been wandering about for a fortnight and their wireless was out of order. But he did know that within a day or two he was to slaughter Sara, the fattened sow they had brought along in a special box, and then the two ladies would get a real meal.

He rose and went to the door. "Please call me Dezsö, that's my first name and the men only call me Fatty. It'll make me feel at home if you ladies call me by my proper name." He bowed and let himself out.

"Good night, Dezsö, and thanks again," Gitta called after him, feeling moved and amused. To be fed by a fat river guard was almost as good as being fed manna in the desert, especially if one was taken for an Israelite. She glanced across the table: Mrs. Balogh was carefully wiping her greasy fingers on the shreds of a paper napkin. They had long ago used up their daily allowance of washing water.

CHAPTER TWENTY-FIVE

~~~oooooo~~Ö~~ooooooo~~~

T he room was small and sombre, half filled by a large brass bedstead and matching cabinet. The window opened on a dark well, the door was painted brown, and the air carried the stale smell of warmed-up vegetables. Pali lay back on the bed and shut his eyes. It was time to leave town. Most of his contacts had gone; his usefulness decreased every day. He could not go on like this, drifting from one small back room to the next, never spending more than two nights in the same place. He was gradually exhausting Sas's hideouts, all of which were strangely alike—ugly flats inhabited by gloomy people who pretended to ignore the fugitive, as if by withholding their smiles and recognition they could cancel out his presence.

He was travelling light, in the clothes he was wearing, with a change of underwear in his brief-case (his spare shirt was being ironed that very moment), and three books in his pocket. They were the three he had always chosen in desert island games, little knowing at the time that desert islands did not necessarily lie in the middle of the ocean. But his choice had been good: Plato, Epictetus and Marcus Aurelius were all he needed, two Greeks, one Roman, inter-related in the one-way traffic of time, since Epictetus quoted Plato and Marcus Aurelius quoted both, and he himself, at the receiving end, was free to draw consolation from all three.

He opened Marcus Aurelius at random and his eye fell on yet another cross-reference. "As Epictetus observes, nobody can rob another of his free will." Fine, Pali thought, rubbing his glasses with the end of his tie, except that after a while free will, one's last possession, turns limp and refuses to point in any direction. One starts out with so many assets—a country, a home, friends, ideas, love, a complete blueprint for life, and then, one day, having lost everything except theoretical self-determination, one ends up sitting on somebody else's brass bedstead with three dead philosophers for company and no feelings left except disgust.

It was the fourth day of all-out terror. At first he had walked about freely, rightly assuming that the storm centre was the safest point of observation. But that morning he had been caught in a street raid and pushed into a small van, together with half a dozen other men who were equally unable to explain why they were not in the Army. The van, heading for the greenshirts' H.Q., had got caught up in another street raid, and in the general confusion Pali had leapt off and submerged in the crowd, just outside one of his favourite double-fronted houses. He had dived inside, running along a series of open yards towards the other exit, flattening himself against a wall to let the pursuing greenshirts pass him. Even then he had felt calm, completely indifferent, a little dead. Death had become a minor inconvenience, life a protracted bother.

Lying on the bed he thought of death with interest and something like envy. Death was not compromised like life, it still had plenty to offer: peace, termination, escape. The moment one thought of dying in that light, the idea lost its terror. Death was horrible in terms of murdered Jews whose bodies he had passed in a street, death was monstrous to Sas who had had a lot of pain lately and in the small hours invariably thought he must have cancer, but after daybreak modified his diagnosis to ulcers ("Anybody who starts a cancer now won't live long enough to die of it" was his way of describing the situation), but to one who genuinely did not want to live, the thought of non-existence appeared infinitely desirable. Did not Diogenes maintain that the only way to attain freedom was to die serenely?

Life is a bad party, Pali thought, a children's party with tears and surprises and dreadful howls in the dark, and since one only has a child's sense of time, one never knows when they are coming to fetch one home. Some leave early, some stay late, too late, until the party gets stale, with all the lanterns burst, all the toys broken and most of the guests turning vicious. Even so, one does not quite want to go, one drags one's feet hoping that things may still pick up—but they don't, and then it is better to take a last level look at the scene and walk out into the night, shrugging off one's final disappointment.

194

If only one could lie down and die. Active suicide appeared distastefully theatrical if one wanted to make a foolproof job of it, and he hated the idea of leaving behind a terrible mess which someone else would have to clear away. He had no one to consider, no family, no relations except the chance person who would find him. Gitta—poor little Gitta, even she had become remote and not very real, a sad might-have-been, perhaps his greatest missed opportunity. He had not changed his mind about her, she still was his unique complement and matching half-kernel, except that personal happiness had become irrelevant, and he was unable to mend a situation which had gone wrong through nobody's fault. The gap that has been there from the very beginning had ruined them. Gitta was always two steps behind him, unaware of his love in March, unready for it in June, wakening when it was too late, and probably eating her heart out now, for the worst possible reasons. At first it had been good to watch her fumbling efforts to catch up with him, and she had made good progress, but her failure to do so in time had finally separated them. If they had been married or at least happy lovers, he thought wistfully, they would have been sufficiently tried and tempered to live through the present, in spite of separation and Sas's lie. As it was, he almost dreaded meeting her. What he needed—if he still needed anything from anybody—was the deep peace of a mature woman, a wise, calm mother-mistress who comforts without asking questions and loves without wanting assurances. Not quite irrelevantly he remembered the cat and dog he had owned as a child. The cat had treated him with self-contained dignity; their relationship had rested on mutual respect and controlled affection. The dog had lived in a constant storm of excitement, always wanting to be scratched, patted, talked to, taken out, brought back, fed and reassured. Ever since, he had classified his human contacts under the headings of Cat and Dog people. Most women were Dog people, even Gitta, but he thought she might eventually have graduated into the higher, wiser Cat class. Time had been too short. He could not blame her for not having matured fast enough, nor himself for letting her drift away. At a time of horror and despair it was no longer possible to work on one's private happiness.

His hostess brought in his freshly ironed shirt together with a note from Sas, describing the best route to the north-east where Pali was to join several political outlaws and wait for the Russians or whoever got there first. Pali studied the instructions. He had to pass the "Pension Dombos" before forking off into the hills.

The train was already well out of town when he suddenly began to long for Gitta. His mood was lifting. There would be no more claustrophobic nights in cramped lodgings, no more idle days spent in airless irritation. Whatever else had failed, Gitta still remained the only person capable of piercing his shell of isolation, and there was no point in punishing her for being what she was, or in breaking his promise to see her. Sas had already done enough harm with his well-meant lie, as if the poor girl had not suffered sufficiently for other reasons. It is impossible to help mankind as a whole, Pali reflected with sudden tenderness, but it is possible to make at least one person happy, and that is better than total failure.

He was the only passenger on the ferry. Few people wanted to cross the river in the early afternoon. Alone again, he thought, alone in a dangerously symbolical situation. One crosses rivers in dreams and that means a profound change; in myths, and that means death; now, in reality, it seemed to signify a step into the unknown, as if the two banks of the Danube had lain in different, hostile countries. Poor darling, he thought, contemplating the bleak, dying landscape, how on earth did she spend the day? How long was a day under this negative sky? But then how had she spent the time since their last meeting? The rain was coming down thinly. Damp pebbles screeched under his feet. She is strong, he thought, strong and healthy with colossal reserves of faith; yet he longed to see her face relaxing once more, turning happy in a glow of confidence as it had done in the past when he told her that all was reasonably well and Allah would look after the rest. So many pebbles on the road; he had long lost his half of the matching pair they had found in the summer, but she must never discover that. He walked quickly up the hill. I am coming, little one, he thought, hell and high water and Germans and greenshirts cannot separate us completely, even I can't, however hard I try out of sheer pessimism and lack of faith.

He found the *pension* dark and abandoned. Nobody answered the door, even the dog-kennel in the back stood empty, its entrance barred by a long chain and studded dog collar. The village lad coming along the road knew nothing. The day before there had been plenty of guests about, he said, but today the place was closed, and even Mr. Dombos had vanished. No, there had been no raid, no

196

Germans, no greenshirts, not as far as he knew, but these days people came and went a lot, didn't they?

Well, this is it, Pali thought, taking a last look at the *pension*. The yellow building looked back as blank as a tombstone. No footprints, no scrawled message on the door to pretend that things might continue, no forwarding address or secret sign carved into the biggest tree trunk in the garden. But then there was no continuation: things just died abruptly, never mind how burstingly alive they had been a little while ago.

He shook his head and walked away. The final stage had set in, from now on separation was no longer a matter of choice. Good-bye, little one, wherever you are, he thought, now I can't even find you any more, and yet it would have been good to be happy. He walked on evenly, effortlessly, holding his head slightly to one side. Raindrops rolled down his forehead; in the distance the jagged thin clouds began to sink over the hills. He felt so damnably alone in the grey, unresponsive landscape, all alone and cut off with only a brief-case to hold on to, and this aloneness was incurable, it closed in on one softly, mistily, so full of silence that one could not even whistle to oneself. Little one, I can't find you any more, he thought. Beginning and ending by the river, it has been a truly nautical affair.

CHAPTER TWENTY-SIX

~~⟶oocoooo○○○○oooooo⟵~~

The days were long and repetitive, the hours dragged their feet. Each trifling chore had to be spun out, fussed over and done to perfection, since it was impossible to tell when the next excuse for activity would present itself. Mrs. Balogh rearranged their belongings twice a day and cursed herself for having left her embroidery behind. Gitta toured the room straightening the innumerable pictures of St. Joseph which kept slipping into crooked positions, as if the very walls were imperceptibly shifting. Unless it was raining very hard they went for a stroll after breakfast, a longer walk after lunch. At night Dezsö brought their dinner and stayed for a glass of wine and one of Mrs. Balogh's gold-tipped Egyptian cigarettes. Last thing before going to bed Gitta laid out the fortune-telling cards. These were the fixed points of the day. The rest lay heavily on their hands.

One morning, at the end of October, they caught the small steamer and ventured over to the village opposite which from the distance seemed rich and full of possibilities. Once they were there, the imaginary amenities turned to dust. True, there was a hairdresser, but he did not possess a drop of shampoo and washed their hair with a peculiar lotion that left it stiff, hard and unnaturally shiny. The lending library only contained cheap romances and greasy old thrillers, the food shops stood empty, no newspapers had arrived for several days. They marched around disconsolately, rounding the same corners over and over again. The next steamer was not due until noon.

Turning into the church square for the fourth time, they noticed a sudden commotion. People were putting their heads together, whispering and gesticulating with amazed faces. Gitta approached a group of women. "What's happened?" she asked. "Do tell us, we're strangers here."

198

"Stalin's died," a peasant girl said. "Someone's just come from town, he says everybody knows it there, but it hasn't been on the radio yet." Gitta raised her eyebrows. "Is that good or bad?" she asked. "Everything's bad for the poor," an older woman said accusingly, "though that godless one wouldn't have made much difference either way." The others hissed and hushed, not so much by way of disagreement but because it was wrong to voice opinions to strangers.

"If it's true," Mrs. Balogh mused later in the comparative security of their room, "the Russians will go slow or retreat altogether. Oh Lord, we'll be stuck here until doomsday. If only it had been the house-painter; why can't somebody bump him off?"

"Even if it's true, the Russians won't stop. After all, he wasn't leading the troops personally on horseback," Gitta objected half-heartedly. Conditioned by history lessons, tradition and a geographical way of thinking, she was apt to regard the approaching Russian army as the modern successor of the Hun, Tartar and Turkish invasions, all of which had been catastrophic but inevitable, and in that light the possibility of Stalin's death did indeed contain dark implications. Had the victorious Tartars not returned to Asia on the death of Genghis Khan to fight over the succession? Would the Russians not . . . but this was stupid, her conscious mind interrupted, Stalin was no Genghis Khan, the Russians were no Tartars.

What were they really like, then? She could only rely on assumptions and wishful thinking. Ever since she could remember, Russia had been hidden behind a curtain of official silence. Before the war the teachers' attitude at school merely implied that Soviet Russia did not exist; if it did, its horrors did not bear describing and therefore the subject was best avoided. Later the anti-Soviet propaganda grew positive and strong, and since the occupation the Germans had been pouring it out at a deafening pitch, with the result that the pro-Germans lived in hysterical hatred and fear while the anti-Germans assumed that only the contrary of the Nazi claims could be true, and so they concocted their own kind of Soviet prototype which, besides being the angelic opposite of a Nazi, also combined the best of Tolstoy, Pushkin, Chekhov, Moussorgsky and Chaliapine. It was comforting to expect a liberating army of humanistic supermen— did not Merezhkovsky say that only a Russian could be a true European, for he had to put his whole heart and best efforts into the

199

task?—and recently Gitta had tended to feel unreservedly hopeful. The familiar urge to burrow for the truth and discard easy illusions had been dormant for some time. Theories were all very well, but what really mattered at the moment was that the Germans were after her while the Russians were not, and that (this always came as a final reassurance), if the Soviets really were so vile, the British and the Americans would not have entered into alliance with them.

"I'm going to town today," Gitta announced after a long silence. "Whether Stalin's dead or not, I can't bear sitting around any longer. Another week like this and I'll go mad. There's a train in the afternoon from over the river, I'll catch that. I must go and find out what's going on."

Mrs. Balogh's protests were vigorous but ineffectual. Something had changed now: Gitta did not plead, sulk or quarrel. She was determined to go, go she would, and all further argument was a waste of time.

In the end Mrs. Balogh removed her glasses and looked at her daughter with concern. "Are you by any chance going to look for Pali? Is it a case of the mountain going to Mohammed?"

Gitta shook her head. What a pity, she thought, that none of their differences could be resolved without a hit below the belt from her mother. It did not occur to her that anybody as immune to defeat as Mrs. Balogh could only be a bad loser. "Pali's gone away," she said, "he's no longer in the country. I've seen him only once since our release and I don't know where he is now. Please don't say you told me so," her voice sharpened, "I've been trying to avoid the subject for months and there's nothing to discuss now, anyway."

"My poor baby. I never thought he was good enough for you."

"But that's not the point!" she snapped. "You'll never understand. It's just that everything has been against us all the time—oh, he's good enough for me and I love him terribly. But although I feel we've known each other for ever, we've hardly spent any time together. Why, I believe only six or seven afternoons all told when the others weren't around or we weren't busy doing some job. And yet every hour was worth a year. Surely, if it weren't the real thing, he wouldn't have become so desperately important in so short a time!"

"All right, perhaps he is good enough for you." Mrs. Balogh sounded unexpectedly mellow. "It's only the way he's abandoned you that worries me. I know you young people are sensible and disciplined, but the way he faded out after we'd gone to jail was very odd. If that's how he behaves in emergencies, you would live a precarious life with him, darling, and I want you to be happy without regrets."

"But we don't know his reasons!" Never very good at containing her heartache, Gitta was weakening once more. "Let's wait until he returns when it's all over—it'll be all right then." This was untrue. She suspected that all was lost. Even if Pali came back safely, she sensed there would be no return for them to the boat-house, no continuation. The knowledge was purely instinctive, as weird as hearing the hoot of an owl outside a dying man's window, and equally indefensible. She only had enough strength to defend Pali against Mrs. Balogh, not against herself as well. The brief bliss of complete understanding had gone, together with her sense of trust and security. Once again men were puzzling and a little frightening, a human *terra incognita* that one could not explore without getting hurt. The first man she had loved did not love her, all he had wanted was a brief distraction; Pali had abandoned her—now there was no doubt about that—for some unknown reason, having first held out the promise of perfection; how was she to believe in anybody again?

No more was said. Two hours later she sat in the train, hardly daring to look around in the compartment. She arrived in town in darkness. The late October evening was damp. The moment she left the station the sirens burst out wailing. It was a short, stormy raid, with both the anti-aircraft guns and the bomb explosions sounding louder than usual. After the raid the remote roar of some guns continued, but as nobody took any notice, she walked out into the dark boulevard. To go home without a reconnaissance would have been sheer madness, and she hadn't the nerve to spend the night in an hotel. Hanna? The nearest public telephone was out of order; worse still, in the next kiosk there was no telephone at all, only bits of wire sticking out of the wall. To hell with manners, Gitta thought, and she caught a tram across the bridge.

Hanna received her exuberantly; of course she could stay the night provided she did not mind the couch in the bedroom, everything else being occupied by . . . guests. Hanna looked tired beneath her feverish brightness, her incendiary hair hung untidily, her eyes were redrimmed—a sad, spent giantess, she hardly resembled her old self.

"Have something to eat, you're positively emaciated, although it

201

suits you—my, your figure is first class! Not that there's anything special in the house, the food situation is simply awful," she sputtered, ushering Gitta into the untidy kitchen. "You can't get a thing and it's growing worse every day. I'm practically having an affair with the butcher and the grocer to get my basic rations. Are you all right, darling girl? Where's your mother?"

"Oh, just a little way out of town. Tell me, is Stalin dead?"

"Good Lord, I hope not. The B.B.C. didn't say anything, so I expect he's all right. But almost everybody else is dead or missing. Marta's father has been killed, plus a number of people I know. Marta never comes to see me these days, that nice young man of hers, Mihály, is away, and she's terribly depressed. Even that beastly Sas has vanished. Oh, how I hate that man."

They trailed back to the drawing-room, carrying plates of cold snacks, including a precious tin of sardines. Hanna talked on feverishly, warming a glass of brandy in both hands. It took Gitta some time to realize that Hanna was more than a little drunk.

"Thank God I've stocked up on drinks," she said, as if guessing Gitta's thoughts. "I couldn't stick it otherwise. If it weren't for my poor guests, I think I'd stay in bed all day and sip brandy. It blunts your mind until you neither think nor care—a rather low form of escape, but there's nothing else left."

The facts Gitta was longing to hear came out slowly, drowned in subjective outbursts. Emotional at the best of times, Hanna was now so racked by pain and indignation that several times she was forced to stop in the middle of a sentence, clapping her hands to her face and swaying in mental torment.

"It's murder," she said. "All exemptions have been cancelled by those greenshirt butchers. They know they won't last long, but they're determined to wipe out the Jews first. All those poor wretches who have obtained Swedish or Swiss passports or Red Cross protection or other immunities are just as badly off as the others. They're being taken away by the trainload. The only chance for them is to hide, and that's getting more difficult with all these house-to-house *razzias*."

"How many have you got here?"

"Oh, seven or so, I've lost count now. This place won't be very safe for you, angel. I'm delighted to have you here, but if anything happens, we'll all sink together."

"Of course. You don't know if our flat's been searched?"

"Let me see—no, I don't. When I last saw Pali, I asked him about it, but——"

"When was that?"

"I think two days after the proclamation. He came here to meet Sas and then they had a meal with me."

"Hanna, are you sure it was after the take-over? After we'd left town?" She spoke slowly and clearly as if Hanna had been deaf.

"Of course, my sweet. I am not that drunk."

"I didn't think you were. But this is rather important. Did Pali know where we were?"

"Oh yes, he mentioned the place but I've forgotten the name. Why, what's the matter?"

"Nothing. It's just that I don't understand anything any more. At one time I thought we knew each other's secret thoughts, now I can't even make out whether he's just trying to get rid of me or whether there's some real reason behind all this chaos. One contradiction after another."

"I don't know. Pali looked all right, rather depressed, of course, but except for not living in his flat I think he got about quite normally. I wish I could help you, but I don't know where he is. He said he would leave town shortly—I expect he's gone now."

"It doesn't matter now," Gitta said sadly. "He should have kept his promise or sent a message—never mind, Hanna, forget it. What was it you were saying?"

"Oh yes," Hanna continued, ignoring the look on Gitta's face. "What hurts me most is that all these months we haven't done anything except throw sops to our own consciences; all we have saved is our own self-esteem. Even our successes have come to nothing— why, do you remember that miserable couple and the Army officer for whom you forged those papers, so that his alleged wife could be buried? The girl's parents were deported last week, and the poor officer was killed in an air raid. How pleased we were when the documents looked genuine. Yes, we were pleased, but they're gone. The waste of it! And look at us, we've all lost something, we'll never be the same again. You can't witness all this, stay alive and continue where you left off. Gitta, my sweet, what do you think? You're young. I've always put my faith in the young, perhaps because I've no children of my own and therefore the young have something

203

rather miraculous about them—what do you say? How are we going to live on with all this in our memories? After nineteen and a half centuries of Christianity, two centuries of enlightenment and reason, after Jesus Christ and Goethe and Voltaire and the rest, how can we ever explain why women and children were murdered in the street under our very eyes?"

"I don't know. You've been alive longer than I have, you should know how it has come about. All I know is that we'll have to start all over again. But don't expect too much of us simply because we're young—do things ever change because it's the first of January? We may make the same mess of things as you've done and then hope that our children will do better. They won't. Just now I don't know anything at all, and I feel ninety years old."

Hanna drained her glass. It was time to go to bed and snatch some sleep before the bombing started. She tucked up Gitta on the couch and padded around the bedroom in a floating *négligé*. Eventually she landed in bed, cradling another full glass in her hands.

"Do you know, your ex-boss is positively pining for you?" she called out softly. "I think he's in love with you." No reply came. Gitta was either asleep or pretended not to hear.

CHAPTER TWENTY-SEVEN

On All Saints' Day, not quite twenty-four hours after her arrival, Gitta was on the move again. She left Hanna's flat voluntarily to make room for another fugitive whose need was greater than hers, because, besides possessing the wrong kind of profile, she was also expecting a baby. In any case the atmosphere of impending catastrophe which pervaded the flat was hard to bear. Hanna's tornado of emotions had weakened her own control, and now she was overwhelmed by sadness and solitude. There was no one left to help, she was alone and frightened, longing to admit her weakness and let someone tell her what to do. The last months had eaten up her reserves. Her earlier cocksureness, springing from childish confidence, was gone, together with the certainty that nothing could possibly go quite wrong. She knew now that an egg-shell of optimism was not enough to ward off disaster. Courage came from lack of imagination and its level decreased as experience grew.

Slipping out of Hanna's flat, she hurried towards Ervin's office, but the alert beat her to it. She fled into the nearest building and leant against a pillar in the hall. Two minutes later a man came in from the street. He looked at her, noticed that she was smoking and joined her with an unlit cigarette in his hand.

"May I trouble you for a light?"

She handed him her matches.

"Thanks. Unusual for a girl to have matches. Mostly they're the ones who need a light." He was thin, average. She did not reply.

"These beastly raids upset everything. Too many of them in one day. I wish it were over. When are these rotten Germans going to clear out?"

"Better ask them," she said dryly. She did not like him.

"But you do agree it's time they went, don't you? Are you on their side, perhaps? Don't you think the Arrow Cross Party is full of crooks and lunatics?"

"What does it matter what I think? I don't know."

"Of course you do, you look too intelligent to have no views of your own. In fact I can guess them!"

"Well, then, why ask me?"

"Come, come, I'm not trying to pick you up. Wouldn't you like to help me?"

Her eyebrows shot up but she did not speak. He took out his wallet and thumbed through a bundle of dog-eared snapshots. The one he gave her was newer than the others, an uncreased group photograph of men in sports clothes.

"Do you know who this is?" he whispered, pointing at the figure in the middle. Gitta did not need to strain her eyes. Even on that small print the face was unmistakable, and it wore the same warm, creased smile as on the framed double portrait the police had taken from her home.

"Yes, I do," she said non-committally. "I've seen him often enough in the papers. What about it?"

"We're working for his side. Won't you join us?"

She looked at the photograph once more. The Prince of Wales, as he then was, surrounded by the *élite* of the Hungarian hunting nobility, all of them petrified in poses of dignified jollity, looked wildly incongruous under the circumstances. The man was watching her eagerly and under the weight of surprise she was strongly tempted to nod and agree to help, provided it brought the end a little nearer. The prospect of having something worth while and exciting to do after all these idle months attracted her.

"We need people, the right kind of people. Time is so short, it may be a matter of weeks——"

Halt, her instincts flashed out a warning, this can't be true, the man is either mad or phoney or worse——

"What you do is your own business," she said gravely, "but you're very unwise to recruit unknown people like myself. Supposing I report you to the police?"

The eager look dissolved. He laughed soundlessly, showing a great many decaying teeth. "Damn funny," he chuckled, "the best joke I've heard for months. The police would simply laugh their heads off. You're all right, young woman, you're all right."

The all-clear sounded outside. "I'm glad you think it's funny. I personally don't," and with that she stalked out into the street, her heart drumming. Was everybody after her even though she was not trying to do anything dangerous?

Ervin Wass opened the door himself. His hands flew up in a gesture of surprise, he pulled her into the hall and slammed the door behind her. Thank goodness, he cried, shaking her hand at length, the worry of it all—and his joy and her timidity made them both so clumsy that it took her a little time to slip off her coat and get inside. Firing questions at her, Ervin rushed around in a flurry of hospitality. The welcome was far more overwhelming than anything she had expected.

There was little to tell. Those endless days since their departure went into surprisingly few sentences. Was it true, she asked eagerly, that the Russians were approaching the city?

"Yes, they're within shooting distance from the outskirts, didn't you know? It's really up to them when they choose to march in. The Government are busy evacuating themselves, all the brand-new Secretaries of State packing their loot and disappearing to the west. Of course the city can't be defended and the rats know it."

"And the Germans? Are they going, too?"

"I don't know. With all these troop movements one can't tell. One lot goes, another arrives; it's like a disturbed anthill only less amusing. What are you going to do now?"

"I should like to go to our flat and see if it's all right. There may be letters . . . oh, as if it mattered. But my fortune-telling cards always forecast a letter with good news, a lovely old-fashioned letter sealed in red. Every time that card came up I wondered who on earth would still bother to write letters these days."

"You must show me those cards one day, they sound more exciting than mine. I only play patience every night. I know a few complicated games that take quite some time to work out, if at all. Mostly the game collapses in the middle and I start again."

"Do you bet on the result?"

"Of course. Three weeks ago I thought, 'If I can play this game to the end, the Western Allies will get here first.' I never succeeded. Then I bet on the Russians occupying us and the beastly thing came out at the first go."

"So that's settled. And now?"

"Now I ask the cards if the Russians will get here this week. Or before Christmas. Or before the New Year. The answers are different every night which adds to the thrill. So, my dear, we're both reduced to reading the cards like a couple of demented gipsies—a fine state of affairs! But tell me, is it safe for you to return to your flat?"

She rubbed her chin. "Quite frankly I don't know. The caretaker may be dangerous, although the house commander is politically all right. But in the present situation I don't think I'm important enough to be dragged away."

"Listen to me," he begged. "Don't go home. There's another room in the back where you can stay in comfort; I'll look after you, I'll get anything you want, you'll see. Please stay here. You've suffered enough, why risk another lot of trouble?"

He was standing in the middle of the room, tall and erect in the sharp light of the standard lamp, as if posing for a sculptor; nothing softer than stone could have done justice to his strong, perfectly moulded face. His hair looked dazzlingly white, reflecting a silver light on his light blue eyes and bold nose. He looked old and young at the same time: Gitta could not decide which, because she was fully occupied with the discovery of his new and disturbing interest in her which had nothing whatever to do with her erratic secretarial services.

"Why are you so kind to me?" she asked. "I don't understand you. Ever since my troubles started you have been the only person to stand by me. Even now when everybody else has left me——"

He sat down on the arm of her easy chair and placed his hand on her hair. "I missed you," he said, "and not for official reasons. There's no work left, so I didn't have to look for papers which only you can find. I missed you altogether. You're a soothing person— even with half the police force at your heels. It's that strange detachment of yours that fascinates me—any other girl would cry and panic, but you just sit and analyse the situation as if it didn't concern you at all."

"Oh don't," she pleaded, "you don't know how near I am to howling."

"Go on, howl, my dear, you can have as many handkerchiefs as you like. You're a strange creature. When I look at you I think you're about sixteen but when you talk and act you're like an adult of thirty. What are you really like? I've spent most of my time with women who looked marvellous but didn't have enough coherent conversation or wit to last through a four-course meal, and I'm at a loss with you. I'd love to understand you, though."

She was already crying, quietly and contentedly, her fingers screening her face. He let her cry for a while and only stroked her hair. Then he pushed a large lawn handkerchief between her fingers. If only she would change her hair style, he thought tenderly.

"Now, now, everything will be all right," he murmured into her ear, "it'll be over soon and then life can begin. You poor little mite, you haven't had much fun so far, have you? Let me look after you. I'll try to make you a little happier."

She shook her head miserably and wiped her eyes. It was wonderful to be comforted like this, and the more sympathy she could extort, the better. He misunderstood the gesture in the way she had intended.

"Don't say no, say yes. It would be no trouble at all, I want to help you. No, I don't, I want you to depend on me a little. Oh, you silly girl, can't you see how fond I am of you? The trouble is, I'm old enough to be your father. You probably think I'm a ridiculous old fool."

She shook her head again, this time to refute his fears. The situation was getting out of hand; he was offering more than she had bargained for, but she had neither the strength nor the honesty to get up and go before the misunderstanding deepened. Beneath her gratitude she felt the stirrings of a challenge, the heightened equivalent of what she used to feel at a ball when an attractive unknown man approached her to claim the next dance. She stopped crying and tidied her face. He went to the cocktail cabinet.

"I'd like a brandy, please," she said. "And I think I'll still go home to see how things are. If anything is wrong, I'll accept your invitation or go back to Visegrád or something. If not, I'll fetch my mother before she dies of boredom or too much black pudding. We mustn't miss the Russians; it may be difficult to return once they're here."

He sat down again on the arm of her chair and put his hand on her shoulder. "You're so independent. Or perhaps stubborn. Wild horses won't hold you back from going to your flat—obviously I can't. What's your mother like?"

209

"She's wonderful. Pretty, elegant and very intelligent. And brave. Always knows what to do and does it rather well."

"I don't expect she would approve of me. How old is she?"

"Oh, quite young." Loyalty forbade her to disclose her mother's age. While Mrs. Balogh herself admitted her forty-three years quite freely, she often made catty remarks about women older than herself as if being fifty were a colossal error of judgement, and therefore Gitta habitually kept quiet about family statistics. Her angry revolt against her mother had ceased in Ervin's presence. This was a new situation, an opening skirmish with a member of the opposite sex, a strange man against whom (if, indeed, "against" described the situation) she automatically joined forces with her mother, entering the camp of women whom love attacks from the outside like a dangerous disease. Whatever Ervin's intentions were, he qualified as an intruder, while Pali's approach had come from the interior, as it were, their mutual recognition having grown deep before a single word had been uttered. Pali and she had been in the same camp, with Mrs. Balogh acting as an uncomprehending onlooker, and in that situation Gitta had no loyalty to spare for her. But Ervin who was now gazing at her with fond attention meant no more than a task, and all he set off in her surprised mind was a chain reaction based on second-hand material—all the information she had gathered about "love" from the wrong sources.

"I hope to God she isn't younger than I am," he sighed. "I'm forty, twice as old as you. Oh, I was born too early, or else you came too late. Why don't you tell me to be my age and leave you alone?"

Feeling treacherous and thrilled, she gave him a long, soft look. "Actually Mother's a bit older than you. Don't let's talk about age, it's neither here nor there. Six months ago I felt ten years younger than now. Another few weeks like this and I'll catch up with you."

He emptied his glass and smiled with relief. "Let's pretend all is well, shall we? Let's sit and have drinks and I'll put on a record while we talk. I want you to tell me about yourself. Start at the beginning. You were born . . ."

The trouble was, she quite liked to talk about herself, especially after all those meagre months which had forced her to hide her thoughts and opinions. But while it pleased her to present herself to this admiring audience of one (it sometimes worried her, the way she could adapt herself to the expectations of her partners), she was in

210

no position to find out about him, and that seemed a great pity. She had never tried to find out things about Pali, it had been natural to accept him as he was. The few questions she had asked had received monosyllabic answers: he was the sum total of his past, he had said, why bother with irrelevant detail? Secretive by nature, he had not encouraged prying—Bluebeard's Castle with its sealed chambers was habitable as long as guests did not tamper with the locks. That had made sense, but now she was bursting with curiosity. Obviously, a single—or divorced—man of forty with all the worldly virtues at his command would have a great deal to report about the unknown shores of adult life.

The third brandy was slowly rising to her head. Ervin had made tiny sandwiches; the royal flavour of *foie gras* spread over her palate like a caress. He had a knack for adding glamour to any occasion, and the more austere the *ambiance* was, the higher his epicurean skill ran. His motives were simple. He happened to like the best of everything and applied himself earnestly to the task of getting what he wanted, irrespective of war, occupation or shortages. Gitta, however, was unable to imagine anything as straightforward as this. To her, the brandy and the *foie gras* were only partly splendid refreshments. They represented even more an act of defiance and therefore tasted as exciting as any forbidden fruit. The Russians were coming, the greenshirts were fleeing, bombs fell from the cold sky, houses crumbled, one might die at any moment, and yet they were sipping brandy and eating *foie gras*, and Lucienne Boyer murmured seductively on the gramophone.

"I'll have to go now," she said at seven. "I want to slip into the house before the raids start and the staircase gets full of people. Of course, I won't go to the shelter."

"Won't you really stay here? You would make me very happy if you did." But she did not like the look in his eyes and rose quickly. "Not now, not tonight, I really must go home." The glow of relaxed well-being was already cooling. They reached the door together and he took her in his arms.

"When shall I see you? Tomorrow?"

"I don't know. It depends on . . ."

"If you don't return here tonight, I'll come over and visit you tomorrow afternoon. I want to see how you live. May I, please?"

"Why, of course, but——" She was out of her depth. Receiving a

211

male guest without Mrs. Balogh's presence was beyond her social experience, but she would have rather died than say so.

"Five o'clock, then. Don't prepare anything, I'll bring what we need by way of refreshment. And if there's any trouble ring me at once and I'll be along—I'm still running my car."

"If anything goes wrong I won't be in a position to ring you."

"Try. I can help you this time. The new Minister of the Interior, that lunatic, was once saved by my father who was a doctor. So there."

"I see." But she did not, really. How could he imagine that such a sentimental bond could possibly help? She tried to detach herself from his embrace, but he pressed her to his chest and kissed her vehemently until her neck muscles began to ache.

At last she was in the street and did not feel the cold. The surprises of the last few hours lay in her mind like a strange and far too splendid gift, clearly not intended for her, yet impossible to refuse. Whatever emotions she felt were purely self-centred, unrelated to Ervin: she was thrilled, amazed, flattered and confused. There was gratitude involved, too, but only to the extent to which his acts were motivated by ordinary kindness. As her mind turned over the most significant moments of the afternoon, thoughts of Pali had to be shooed away several times. Unconsciously she had already adopted Mrs. Balogh's argument: Pali had rejected and abandoned her, he had no right to interfere.

No tram came. She started off towards the nearest junction where chances of transport were better. At a street crossing she passed a ragged couple with a small child. The man turned back and grabbed her arm. It was Lázár the poet whom she had last seen in prison and not remembered since.

"Well, well," he said, "what a surprise. Isn't it refreshing to meet out here? Is your mother all right? Good. Tell me, can you put us up for the night?"

"I hardly know where I'm going to sleep," she stammered. "I haven't been home for ages."

"Where are you going now?"

"Home. But only to reconnoitre," she added hastily. "You see, the place isn't really safe."

"Safe!" he barked. "Europe isn't safe, the world isn't safe, why should your flat be any safer? Look, we've nowhere to go and Ili

212

isn't well—oh, this is Ili, and that's our little boy. Well, we've run out of places and we can't walk around all night. Please take us in— I know you're a strictly brought up girl and we're no Holy Family, but between us jailbirds—"

"Don't insist," the woman said dully. "If she doesn't want us, you can't force her." She was thin, young and faded, holding the sleeping child indifferently as if it were a parcel.

"It's not a matter of not wanting you," Gitta said, trying to sound pleasant, "but you don't want to be caught any more than I do. When did you get out?" she turned to Lázár.

"A lot of politicals were released between that stupid armistice declaration and the take-over. By the time the greenshirts recovered we were all over the place. Unfortunately the number of heroic workers who are willing to put us up is very small. The Social Democrats have made the proletariat too soft."

"Don't talk so much," Ili interrupted, "the child is heavy."

"Well, I don't mind if you come with me," Gitta said doubtfully, "at your own risk. I'll go in first to investigate. For all I know the flat may have been blitzed or requisitioned. If it's all right, you can stay the night." She pointed towards the junction. "Follow me at a distance and pretend you don't know me. Watch the top floor of the house when we get there. If I open and shut the left corner window twice, come up quickly. It's Flat 26."

She trotted away dejectedly. Oh, for a few quiet hours without being forced to participate in anything dangerous or unpleasant! Reality always caught up with her. Lázár was a grim antidote to Ervin. The atmosphere of brandy and comfort was dispelled by the problem of feeding a small child—how old was he and what did he eat?—and worrying and wondering about all the other problems that might arise.

She got off the tram near her home and glanced around. The ragged group were standing near the stop, with Ili busy adjusting the child's cap. Gitta walked down the main road and gave a wide berth to the Gestapo H.Q. before turning into a side street. She passed the park and saw the familiar street once more. Their block looked intact. Covering most of her face with a handkerchief she dived into the hall. The staircase was empty; not a sound anywhere. Up she ran at the double, knocking her case against the handrail. Eight flights up, but to use the lift would have meant summoning the caretaker, and if the Gestapo had briefed that evil creature she would alert them at once. She paused on the top-floor landing before emerging into the open passage. Still no sound. The flat door looked untouched, the key turned easily. She entered and shut the door with care before flicking on the light.

Nothing had changed. The creased and not very clean gloves she had thrown on the hall table before leaving were still there. The air smelt stale, the furniture looked discreetly dusty. Oh, thank goodness, she thought, moving on tiptoe from one room to the next, all's well, no bombs, no Nazis, no mice or spiders or other horrors—oh, the temptation of sending the Lázárs away under some pretext! But she shook her head and told herself not to be mean.

They came in on tiptoe. It flashed through Gitta's mind that with the sole exception of Pali, who always moved so fluidly that one expected him to vanish behind a wall at any given moment, people now moved according to their political creed. The Nazis strutted and threw their weight about, and all the others walked swiftly and silently, with nervous, darting eyes and studied neck movements that enabled them to look around imperceptibly. Will a change of régime bring forth a change of deportment, she wondered; but then even if the opposite camp learned to walk modestly, would our kind of person ever strut? She could not decide. The child woke up and began to moan.

Gitta lit the stove in the guest room and put clean sheets on the beds, while Ili took the boy to the bathroom. Lázár followed Gitta around, talking incessantly. He had not changed much since prison except for being even thinner and scruffier, and he still seemed to exist in a state of controlled fever, indifferent to everything beyond his ideas.

"Don't worry," he said to Gitta, "even the greenshirts don't matter. Everything that's happening now is the logical outcome of capitalist corruption, and the final agony is never pretty. It's almost over now. Soon everything will change."

"Yes, but meanwhile the deportations and pogroms go on!"

"True, but there's nothing we can do. I'm very sorry for all those wretched Jews, but it's too late to help them. The social forces that have made this massacre possible are to blame."

"Are you going to tell me that one must take a long view of history, and that the individual doesn't count?"

"Of course. The individual is only——"

"Funny, that's exactly what the Nazis are saying."

After that nobody said much. Gitta prepared a cold dinner of sorts and heated a tin of milk for the child. The Lázárs went to bed. Gitta spent ten minutes cleaning up the bathroom before running her own bath. The flat was silent, only the floor and the furniture creaked occasionally. After some hesitation she chose to sleep in Mrs. Balogh's bed, and hugged her mother's outsize pillow disconsolately. She was terribly frightened. It was impossible to tell whether the Lázárs made her fear grow or shrink; to be all alone might have been worse. Sleep did not come. She switched on the bedside lamp. The wireless did not attract her and there was no one to ring up. In the silence she could now and then hear a car pass along the street, and every time the engine noise increased, her heart began to jump. There were few cars in private use now and official cars usually meant trouble. At midnight a car approached and stopped roughly outside the house. Please God, don't let it happen, she muttered with chattering teeth, not now, not again, please take them away. Two breathless minutes later the car doors slammed and the engine began to purr. She waited for the noise to die away in the distance before getting out of bed. Padding softly to the bookcase next door, she scanned the shelves for something comforting to read. But just as in Visegrád, where she had failed to remember suitable poems to cheer them up, literature let her down once more. Not sharing Pali's addiction to philosophy, she could not think of any poet or prose writer who would have had the right answer to her growing panic. Her favourite books, read and reread under happier circumstances, looked dull and distasteful.

At last she grabbed a volume and fled back to her mother's bed. It was a leather-bound English book, *Stories of the Saints*, a Christmas present she had received from London before the war. The paper was thick, the print large, and the illustrations combined Biblical garments with unmistakably English faces. Gitta turned the pages avidly. The bigger the miracle was the happier she felt, and the legend of St. Christopher moved her deeply. God had somehow regained His beard; if all these miraculous stories were true, as she believed them to be, there was no reason why the night should not pass quietly in spite of everything.

She went to sleep at one, her mind agreeably full of miracles. In the light of the saints' trials and tribulations the Gestapo seemed a pretty poor opponent. She slept well and dreamlessly. There was no air raid that night.

CHAPTER TWENTY-EIGHT

The Lázárs got up early in the morning. Ili had remembered the name and address of a Communist cobbler in Ujpest who she felt sure would put them up; she had known him for years from the Movement. Over the improvised breakfast she thanked Gitta for their bed and board; her man kept a moody silence. Watching Ili wrap up the ugly, pasty-faced child, Gitta remembered Lázár's prison diatribe against middle-class morality. Well, free love didn't look much better. This faded girl and her unattractive love-child were a far cry from the beautiful, sensual creatures she used to visualize in that context—healthy, hot-blooded naked figures rushing at each other in sacred ecstasy, crushing *bourgeois* inhibitions under their godlike feet. There was nothing ecstatic or godlike about this group; they looked like a disillusioned married couple whose family planning had gone wrong, only worse, because they had achieved this dubious result in the name of ideological freedom and self-expression.

"I hope you'll be all right," she said to them at the door. "I hope we'll meet again when all this is over. Remember me when you're Prime Minister," she smiled wryly at Lázár. "Save me from the galleys where all the other *bourgeois* will go."

They slipped out quietly into the dark morning. She locked the door behind them and ambled back to the kitchen to tidy up, but all of a sudden the vague thought that had been bothering her from the back of her mind took clear shape. It was the second of November, the Day of the Dead, and she did not know what to do about it.

She had been trained to take the Day of the Dead seriously; it was a private day of obligation, a non-religious feast of sadness that Mrs. Balogh observed as strictly as Christmas or Easter. The day really did belong to the dead, to Mrs. Balogh's parents and husband, her few deceased friends and Gitta's little school-friend who had died of cancer at the age of twelve. It was their day when they were mourned with almost pagan pomp. In the morning candles were lit in the flat, one dead-white candle for each of the dead; in the afternoon Mrs. Balogh and Gitta, loaded with flowers and more candles, travelled out to the large cemetery in Buda. They normally got there at dusk and found the acres of graveyard in a blaze of candle-light, one or more candles flickering away on each grave under small glass bonnets, and there were thousands of white and purple asters, white and yellow chrysanthemums and pale, late dahlias around the tombstones, their faint smell turning bitter in the dampness and fog. Ever since she was a small child, Gitta had both loved and dreaded this annual pilgrimage. Dressed in black, her mother would lead her silently along the main avenue, turning to the left at the decaying figure of a monumental angel to follow the path to her parents' grave. All this was too much like a real visit to a living person, a sick friend perhaps; laden with gifts, somewhat quietly, this was the way one went to a hospital during official visiting hours, rehearsing in one's mind the pleasant, comforting things one could say without sounding silly or patronizing. Except that here the walk ended at an oblong white grave, its sodden grass surrounded by a raised stone frame, with two names in gilt letters carved into the headstone that sloped up gently, like a propped-up pillow.

But even there the similarity did not end entirely, because while Mrs. Balogh arranged the flowers and candles and then stood over the grave with bowed head, Gitta attempted a mute conversation with her grandparents below, folding her hands as she did so. Here we are, she would think timidly, Grandmother Maria and Grandfather Joseph, it's your day, I hope you're all right (by that she meant the state of their souls which she respectfully did not dare to imagine; it seemed unkind to visualize one's grandparents in Hell or even in Purgatory, doing fifty thousand years of penance, but from what she had gathered they could hardly have reached Heaven in such a short time). As she grew older, these monologues ceased or, rather, she tended to talk to herself. Here they lie, she would think, dead and gone, dry bones and no explanation. We, too—and then fear suppressed the rest. She could not, would not, contemplate the possibility of death for her mother and herself; neither of them must die

218

or, if that was impossible, they must die together. Life without Mrs. Balogh was inconceivable.

After a while they moved on, delivering the rest of their offerings first to Gitta's father, then to Mrs. Balogh's girlhood friend, to another woman friend of later years, finally to Gitta's school-friend, and then slowly they walked back to the main gate where a big stone figure of Christ held up the promise of resurrection in the middle of a desolate flower-bed. The scene was macabre and splendid; the cemetery looked like an enormous camp under the black sky, the one-night fairground of the dead where the graves gleamed and glittered and the living floated around like quiet black ghosts. Invariably the weather was cold and treacherously damp, and every year a number of elderly visitors caught fatal colds on the muddy paths, dying a few days later amid the superstitious whispers of friends who were sure that a spoilt dead person had claimed his favourite mourner. To die of a chill caught at the cemetery on the Day of the Dead was regarded as a final act of devotion.

This year the pilgrimage was out of the question. Apart from other considerations, flowers were unobtainable, and the black-out left no loophole for lit-up cemeteries. Gitta went to the pantry and dug up a packet of ordinary candles. She did not know how many to take. Candles were at a premium and Mrs. Balogh guarded her supplies jealously. Eventually she took one and planted it in a silver candlestick. This will have to do for all of them, she thought, a poor display but better than nothing. She lit the solitary candle with childlike solemnity, thinking of their dead, one by one, commending their souls to God. Soon we may be dead, too, she thought in sudden alarm, killed by bombs, Germans, Russians, soldiers, secret policemen, greenshirts—death was no longer a vague possibility, it had assumed faces and weapons and a choice of uniforms, and it was so much more real than in its peace-time disguise of heart failure or old age. Perhaps the dead, outraged at being cheated of their annual celebration, will claim us all. We may die, I may die, she whispered fearfully, experiencing the critical moment when the mental state that equals absolute youth begins to disintegrate with the acceptance of one's possible and unsensational death. It can happen, she thought; perhaps after all God isn't keeping me for some unique purpose, I am not too young to die, nobody is, not even unborn babies.

219

Hovering over the candle she noticed a deep, faint rumble in the distance. She opened the window. The rumble grew stronger. It went on fairly evenly, with an occasional explosion. The sky was clear, the sirens remained silent. It must be the Russian guns, she thought; they are now within earshot. A gust of air burst in through the open window and extinguished the candle. The dead don't want it, she shuddered; they want us. She shut the window and re-lit the candle shakily, telling herself to be sensible.

She spent the next half-hour doing the same, trying to feel more logical and less frightened, but while she succeeded in getting her terror under control, her clashing feelings merged into deep depression, and she left the house in a terrible mood, expecting to die any moment.

She toured the inner city aimlessly. The streets were drab and dirty, the people either tore along in frantic haste or ambled wearily, carrying parcels. She seemed to be the only one to saunter along with only a handbag under her arm. In these parts there was little bomb damage and yet the city looked critically ill, if not dead. All sense seemed to have gone out of it, there was no rhythm left. The activities that still went on were purely negative: taking home a few more hoarded treasures, making the deep shelters more habitable, packing, moving; and at the evil end of this negative range, in screened-off streets greenshirts broke into flats, looting and dragging away the persecuted to make them dig defences against the approaching army or be killed. The sadness of it all seeped through the surface calm, just as the firing of guns could be heard beyond the street noises.

Nothing mattered any more. Gitta entered the exclusive restaurant owned by the Officers' Casino which was nowadays only patronized by the ruling clique and where, consequently, the food was still good and plentiful. It was the safest place to visit; had not a Jewish family spent two undisturbed months in a flat right above a German military depot? She drank half a bottle of wine with her lunch. What was her mother doing? Worse still, what was she herself doing, spending the third day in town to no purpose, little wiser than she had been in the wilderness? She paid her bill and rang Marta from the nearest call box. There was no reply from her number.

There was nothing to do but slink home and go to sleep. Her eyes were heavy with wine and depression, she slept till four and then began to tear round frantically, preparing for Ervin's visit. Thank heavens the flat looked reasonably clean and there was enough fuel in the kitchen bunker for several days. But what was she to wear? None of her dresses seemed right, or rather (but she did not admit this) Ervin's visit did not seem right and therefore it was impossible to find a suitable outfit for it. Her evening things were too dressy for five o'clock, her day dresses too casual. She lifted the telephone receiver and dialled half his number, intending to cancel the meeting, but changed her mind and returned to the wardrobe. Ah, this is it, she thought triumphantly, pulling out the navy slacks she had had made for a sailing holiday—women's slacks were frowned upon except in boats and on ski slopes. But these were beautiful slacks, she told herself, and her lavender jumper would look perfect with them. She dressed in a state of cold excitement, putting on a lot of make-up and scent. From the bathroom the gunfire sounded louder. Were they coming closer all the time?

There were not many minutes left before Ervin arrived at five o'clock sharp. He put down his bulging brief-case in the hall and inspected Gitta who stood there smiling nervously, suddenly unsure of her choice of clothes. "My. my," he said, "how Amazonian you look. Isn't it a pity to hide your legs?"

"Do come in, it's cold here. Shall I make some tea or coffee?" she asked. "Oh Lord, there's no bread in the house, I'm afraid I didn't buy any!"

"Relax, my dear, I told you not to prepare anything. By the way, I have good news for you. Your caretaker and his wife won't trouble you any more; they left for the west a week ago, the assistant caretaker tells me."

Picking up his case, he followed her into the drawing-room and kissed her lightly by the door. The room must have pleased him, for he observed every detail with nods of approval. "A splendid Bokhara, that one! I like those amber-red undertones, the newer ones are horribly crude," he commented, stopping to admire a large painting on the wall. Gitta did not tell him it was only a copy of a little-known Italian altar picture. As copies went it looked utterly convincing.

"I like this place." He turned back to her, looking reassured. "I often wondered about your home and couldn't visualize it. I'm glad it's neither ultra-modern nor *fin de siècle*. Won't you show me your room?"

221

"No, no, it's rather untidy," she protested, sensing the disastrous effect her grown-out child's desk would have on him. "Let's stay here, it's the only warm room in the flat."

"I waited up till midnight, thinking you might come back or telephone. Oh, it was quite pleasant, I was thinking of you and time went quickly. You make me feel like a young student, you absurd child; a pleasant change, I must say." He opened his case and produced a bottle of champagne, a box of cigarettes and a tin of savoury biscuits from the best *confiserie* in town. He spread it all out on a low table and touched the side of the bottle. "Should be all right," he said, "it's been on ice until thirty minutes ago. May we have two glasses, please?"

She flew to the cupboard and opened it. Of course the best champagne glasses were in the cellar, but three unmatched ones, the survivors of smashed sets, stood on the top shelf. She chose the two nicer ones and watched him open the bottle; he had even brought a damask napkin for the purpose.

"Why champagne?" she asked. "I haven't had any for ages, not since my last ball, but then we drank it at midnight. Can one drink champagne in the afternoon?"

"Personally I like it for breakfast. Oh, don't worry, not every morning. Dear, dear Gitta," and he pulled her down on his knee, "this is my last bottle and my wine merchant is either dead or digging ditches in Germany, so let's have it together. Drink up!"

The cold, golden liquid made her cough. It was too dry for her taste, but she drank it bravely and reached out for a cigarette. He lit one and placed it between her lips. The smoke made her cough again.

She sat there with a stony face, an unwilling symbol of vice in her own eyes—a girl in slacks sipping champagne and smoking on a man's knee on the Day of the Dead. The situation was daring though not exhilarating. She knew from past experience that the physical aspects of mild flirtation that men seemed to relish were extremely uncomfortable from her point of view. Every time a boy had tried to put his arm round her waist she had squirmed away, not so much for reasons of modesty but because the foundation garments she had worn on account of her plumpness had been rich in hard, round buttons, and she had not wanted her partner's hand to discover them. Sitting on a man's knee was worse. She could never find an

222

elegant pose, and she felt ashamed of being so heavy. Now, too, she made a feeble effort to rise, but Ervin locked his arms round her.

"I suppose you've heard the firing," he said, "it only stopped a little while ago. They're very close now. What's worse, it looks to me as if the Germans intended to stay. If they're going to fight it out above our heads, we might just as well have champagne now."

"They can't! Why, this is literally an open city, no walls or fortifications anywhere; the Germans couldn't possibly hope to hold it!"

"Barricades," he said darkly, "tank traps, petrol barrels—oh, they're bound to lose, but not at once. You see, what worries me is that the Germans are evacuating as many civilians as they can, but they're bringing in more and more troops, which is the classical formula for a siege."

The word conjured up a hill-top fortress, walled and crenellated, all white stone and deep moats as in old etchings, and soldiers falling off ladders and cannon emitting curly smoke—but of course petrol barrels and bombs and flooded shelters were more likely, more in keeping with imminent death.

"A number of people I know have already moved to Austria," he went on, "not all of them Nazis, either. They just don't care to wait for the Russians. My brother left yesterday. He very much wanted me to join him. What do you think?"

"I think it's ridiculous. Why go? If we've stuck it until now . . . the Russians can't be worse than the Germans, and, after all, we're the ones to stay and make a fresh start. I wouldn't leave for anything."

"I wonder; I'd like to go away, at least until it's all over. I don't particularly want to be blown up or shot. Aren't you afraid of dying?"

She flushed. "I am, terribly. Especially today. I feel so cold inside, as if I were already dead. Ghosts are icy, aren't they? But I know that if I really must die, it'll happen wherever I am, so why go away?" She rose and sat down in the arm-chair opposite him, but her escape was short-lived because he immediately knelt down in front of her and put his head in her lap. They stayed quite still for a minute or two. She touched his gleaming hair that looked like a silver helmet and stroked it timidly. The gunfire began again, more loudly than ever, with colossal explosions thundering away at intervals.

223

"There's only one day left," he murmured the first line of the current defeatist hit, "there's only one day left to live. . . ." He raised his head and grabbed her hands. "Gitta, don't you love me a little? Can't you try? Is there somebody else? This is a terrible moment, we are all alone in the world. I need you, I'm so alone, there's nobody left. I've always led a pleasant life and never cared much about anything, but now I feel so empty, it doesn't work any more. I need you so much, little girl, and you need me, too, don't be logical just for once, let's keep close to each other."

"I'm alone, too." She could say no more, she felt nothing and only sensed what was expected from her, but even that not very clearly, and so she only stroked his hair helplessly and looked away.

He pulled her to her feet and began to kiss her passionately. After the first flash of panic she submitted, feeling neither pleasure nor revulsion. Without relaxing his grip he eased her slowly across the room, towards the large sofa. She sat down meekly and only began to protest when he tried to make her lie back in his arms. "No, I don't want to," she snapped, planting both feet on the carpet and pushing him away. But it was no use. His arms were around her once more, it was impossible to break out from their practised circle, and although he held her with considerable force, his voice remained gentle and pleading.

"Don't fight, I'm not going to hurt you. Tell me, is there somebody else? Am I intruding?"

"No, there isn't, not any more, it's only that I am . . . that I . . ."

"Do you know that you're very beautiful? You've changed a great deal, your eyes have become so different. Why do you struggle? I love you so much, what are you afraid of? There isn't much time left, we may be dead next week, let me make you a little happier before we die."

He talked on softly and, while she no longer listened to his words, his voice and his touch put her into a strange daze. She was overcome with desperate indifference. She still tried to push his hands away from the fastening of her jumper, but it did not really matter which of them was to succeed in the end. Her mind had become detached from her body, she listened to the distant guns and caught a glimpse of the half-burnt candle on the piano, and when he asked for the fifth time whether she loved him, she said "Yes" in a flat, dead voice. Even when he turned off the light and she renewed her half-

224

hearted struggle, she knew that nothing really mattered any more and that with so little time left she might just as well acquire this last, vital experience. But even her curiosity was as detached as that of a conscientious tourist who dashes out to see one more sight before his train leaves, knowing perfectly well that to see it or miss it boils down to very much the same thing. His skin smelt of toilet water, talc and fine tobacco; she ran her cold fingers along his strong, lean shoulders and thought: "But we hardly know each other!" Yet, feeling inadequate, she did not want to make things more awkward with such irrelevant objections.

After all the struggle, discomfort and embarrassment, the detached part of her brain registered nothing but regret. Having taken the irrevocable step, the subject of grave taboos and endless speculation, she felt mystified and cheated. In spite of their terrible physical closeness he had remained a total stranger towards whom she would always behave in an unnatural, stilted manner, like an ungifted actress struggling through an incomplete script. It had not been enough to have allowed things to happen. She was still outside it all. His whispered endearments embarrassed her because she knew she did not deserve them. She took his hand from her thigh and held it firmly, but he only responded with a quick, conspiratorial squeeze and began to stroke the inside of her wrist.

She rose and felt her way to the door. The bathroom was cold. Slipping on her blue dressing-gown, she opened the big Cologne bottle Mrs. Balogh had taken to jail and rubbed the remaining few drops furiously on her body.

When she returned to the drawing-room he was already half-dressed. The open-necked silk shirt and slim dark trousers made him look young and tremendously attractive, a divine shepherd from one of the naughtier Greek legends. He folded her in his arms and kissed her gently, almost reverently. He had collected and folded her garments over a chair; she hastily threw a cushion on the small pile.

His cuff-links were twisted knots of gold and platinum, he wore a black crocodile-skin belt and charcoal silk socks. She willed him not to put on his jacket yet; all his jackets were ultra-conservative in cut, making him look ominously adult, if not elderly.

"Anything the matter, my sweet?"

"No, no, it's only . . . I've never seen a man dress. Or shave," she

225

added thoughtfully. "All this is terribly new to me, I've always lived in a purely feminine world. I like you in shirt-sleeves. Do you ever wear coloured shirts?"

"No, only white or cream. Oh, you're so touching, such a baby. A girl who's never seen a man get dressed. I don't really think I deserve you. Will you put up with me? I'm so old and second-hand. How did you remain so untouched? What have you been doing these past few years?"

She shrugged. "Reading books, I suppose. Sounds stupid, but it's true. Waiting for life to begin, not noticing it had already done so. It's like going to the cinema in the middle of a performance and waiting for the main film which is already in full swing."

"Well, it is now, anyway." He knelt down and put his gleaming head on her breast. "I'll always stay beside you, if you'll let me. I want this to continue. When the war is over we'll do things together, travel abroad—I want to show you the places I know, perhaps they're still there—and go to shows and concerts, and meet people and go sailing in the summer. There's so much to do, and you would make everything new for me."

Stroking the back of his neck, she wondered whether all this could be true. Satisfaction seeped into her confusion. The gold and platinum cuff-links and the crocodile belt conjured up other images: she saw themselves getting in and out of international trains, arriving at famous places which she had only seen on travel posters, listening to great musicians in the flesh, not on records—and not understanding why she had been chosen for such a fascinating future, she decided that she must be possessed by some unsuspected power that had come into operation without her bidding.

The sirens began to scream. They wailed hysterically, lamenting over the series of explosions that shook the walls and made the remaining glasses tinkle in the cupboard. She buried her face on his shoulder with a little moan. If the top floor were hit and they died, she in her dressing-gown and he in his silk shirt, according to the Book they would glide straight to damnation, and she moaned again, because she felt regrettably convinced that God in His enormousness and splendour could not possible take notice of the insignificant episode she had allowed to happen.

They settled down in one arm-chair and finished the flat, luke-warm champagne. The raid was violent and brief and even the all-clear sounded like a dirge. The air may have been clear; the ground-level cannonade rumbled on.

He wanted to stay or take her back to his flat, but she would not hear of it; the felling of the greatest taboo had left the smaller ones intact. He left reluctantly, in slow stages, stopping several times in the hall to embrace her, and promising to ring later.

She returned to the drawing-room and sat down The room stared back blankly. With his innate orderliness Ervin had tidied up so well that it looked as if he had not been there at all. The silence was horrible. She ran her hands along her body to confirm her existence. Nothing has changed, she thought in amazement, everything is exactly as it has always been, I'm the same, he's the same, why did I think it would be different? She went to the bathroom and looked in the mirror. The face she saw was pale and thinner than of old, with the beginning of a hollow in the middle of her once-plump cheek, and a more tapered jaw-line. But these changes had happened gradually over the past few months. Basically the face was still identical with the one she had always had, and although she had often heard that the loss of virginity immediately left a clear mark in a girl's eyes, she was unable to detect it in her own.

Before going to bed she re-lit the candle on the piano and let it burn to the end. The Day of the Dead still had two hours to go.

CHAPTER TWENTY-NINE

~~~~ᴄᴄᴄᴄᴄᴏᴏᴏ ᴏᴏᴏᴏᴏᴏᴏᴏᴏᴏᴏ~~~~

Two weeks after her husband's funeral Countess Péterffy left town and retreated to the estate. Her staff went with her, her daughter did not. The Countess knew better than to argue. Marta's unexpected grief took the form of temperamental outbursts followed by silent gloom, and for days on end she hardly spoke a coherent sentence. It was both kinder and more civilized for them to stay apart.

The Countess departed with great dignity, marshalling the French housekeeper, the cook and the maid with eloquent eyebrows and an occasional quiet word. Widowhood suited her pale, passive character better than all the other roles she had played in her life. A failure as a wife and mother, she promised to make a perfect widow. She did not understand why her daughter wanted to stay in town where life was growing harsher and sadder every day; on the other hand she would have been genuinely surprised if Marta had meekly accompanied her to the country. They had nothing in common, nothing to talk about, nothing to share; but then the Countess had very little in common with anybody else, either, and therefore she gave the matter no serious thought. Her main task in life now was to bring up her son and keep the estate going. Her daughter, too mature for her years and therefore too ageing for her mother, would have to live her own life.

Released from every bondage, Marta immediately reorganized the flat to her own taste. Several other flats in the house stood empty and locked up, so she locked and padlocked their own front door from the outside, using the servants' back entrance instead. She curtained and shuttered the street windows and did not answer the telephone or the doorbell. One room made an ideal all-purpose home for her; she simply forgot about the others. The flat was now permanently twilighted and very quiet, the last word in privacy and isolation. She spent a few days thinking and sleeping and talking to herself. Sometimes she sat weeping for her father, sometimes she addressed angry reproaches to him as if he had been listening next door. But eventually she grew impatient and restless. Unshared freedom really meant total solitude, and she was getting tired of it.

Mihály arrived at the best possible moment. She was overjoyed and promptly invited him to stay with her in the flat, feeling certain that her mother would not return for some time. They spent a week of happy twilight and great emotional intensity that left them transfigured and exhausted; it was like condensing a lifetime into a few days, not neglecting any important detail, so that they had miniature quarrels, small arguments, brief fits of melancholy and wild reconciliations. In spite of her varied past Marta was only just beginning to discover the long-term aspects of love. It was staggering to wake up in the morning and find a sleeping head next to hers on the pillow, to have lunch and dinner with the same person, to let time flow without having to glance nervously at the clock because the end of the rendezvous had to coincide with the end of the fictitious music lesson she was supposed to attend. She was happy in a new, breathless way, enjoying the unfamiliar sensation of emotional security. Mihály knew how to turn every hour into a feast; the poems he presented to her every morning were verbal gems glittering with love and discovery. He made her feel new and virginal; the past had receded, her earlier affairs were losing even the minute significance they had once had and she emerged from her former experiences like a fresh Aphrodite, ivory-skinned and untouched. Once or twice it occurred to her that this kind of fulfilled happiness could have not come to her while her father was alive, but she did not bother to analyse the half-conscious thought. Neither did she wonder about the future. The future was the next hour; the following morning, at best. As long as Mihály was there she felt safe. It was mid-November now, with more tension than change, and the day when it was to be all over represented the watershed beyond which it was impossible to think.

Eight days after his arrival Mihály went out to look round a little and returned with the worst possible news. He was to leave the next morning with Sas and God alone knew when he would return. Naturally neither Sas nor he wanted Marta to accompany them.

Marta cried, shouted, raged and threatened suicide. Hadn't he had enough of abortive cloak-and-dagger efforts that led to nothing but frustration? Couldn't he stay put, wait and save himself until there was something worth while to do? She stormed at him and cursed Sas, hurling books on the floor and kicking rugs and footstools out of the way. She did not want to be left, it was vital that she should come first with him, that she should be held firmly until her transformation was complete. To leave her now was like throwing a partially cured invalid out in the snow or ripping the bandage off a half-healed wound. She raged at him, unable to explain her panic. Any explanation would have brought up the past, and that was to be avoided at all costs.

Her violence alarmed him, especially since there was no way out: Sas needed him badly, he could not let him down, why did Marta refuse to understand? He stayed awake all night, comforting and cherishing her till dawn. She watched him dry-eyed as he got ready to go. Folding her father's dressing-gown which Mihály had so often worn, she promised to wait for him patiently and repeated all the sad, enormous things lovers promise for the rest of eternity when they hardly know how to get through the next twenty-four hours.

After he had left she cried herself to sleep and woke up in the afternoon. The room was cold, untidy and terribly empty, with dust and neglect creeping up from every corner. All her life things had been cleaned, prepared and arranged for her by unseen hands and she knew nothing about housework. The need for self-service cast a new and unpleasant light on independence. She emptied a few overflowing ash-trays and then gave up with a shrug.

In the evening she went out for a meal—Mihály and she had been living on tinned foods for so long. Out of sheer despair she allowed herself to be picked up by a bald, middle-aged man and spent the rest of the evening with him in a café. He was a widower and talked a great deal in a fruity provincial accent, squeezing her ice-cold hand under the table. At midnight he invited her to his flat. She nodded, went to collect her coat, left the café through a side door and ran home all the way, sniffing and shivering with misery.

The next day she was picked up twice and again the day after. However much she neglected herself, her milky skin and aquamarine cat's eyes remained hypnotically beautiful. She had the icily innocent look of a depraved angel and behaved like one, letting her chance friendships reach increasingly advanced stages and then breaking away disdainfully, shaking the dust from her tarnished wings. She never took anybody home and made special efforts to avoid being followed. Faithfulness to Mihály had become a matter of geography. As long as she kept her home locked to strangers she felt free to explore bachelor suites, hotel rooms and furnished chambers in private flats that had to be approached on tiptoe along creaking corridors.

She was wildly unhappy and lonely, with no one to turn to. One day when she found herself near the City Park the memory of the convent pulled her up sharply. The last time she had visited it in March, not quite nine months ago, seemed like a recollection of a mythical age. Oh, the chapel and the white statue on the altar—why had she not thought of it before? She walked quickly towards the familiar street, wondering what to say to the Mother Superior, how to explain her private hell and what help to ask for.

The convent was gone. A wilderness of ruins covered the former garden, nothing but dead bricks, broken masonry and unrecognizable debris. All gone, nothing to salvage, not even the tiny fragment of a gilt candlestick. The very air had gone wrong, it carried a strange smell, the smell of stone dust, crumbled mortar and charred timber that had smouldered for a long time under airless pressure. It was a horrible dry odour that stayed in the nostrils for a long time, the final smell of a dying city where it was best not to look for old friends or well-known streets because one was likely to find corpses and ruins, death and no consolation.

CHAPTER THIRTY

~~~ccccccccccccccccccc~~~

"They call this coffee," Hanna said scornfully. "Liquid boot polish mixed with oak ashes to make it bitter. And the price they charge for it!"

"We're paying for the privilege of being here. So few places are open or warm or staffed. You've no idea how splendid this looks after that beastly inn at Visegrád," Gitta protested. She refused to have her pleasure spoilt.

They were sitting in the crowded café at the Lukács Baths, a sophisticated place with deep plush arm-chairs, potted palms and delicious warmth. The central heating was run on the water of natural hot springs and functioned superbly long after the fuel shortage had stopped all other kinds of heating. Apart from the horrible coffee and vile pastries the illusion was perfect. Well-dressed groups sat engaged in rapid conversation, the waiters zigzagged between the tables with friendly zeal as if the fifth-rate stuff on their trays deserved the best possible service, and in one corner four wizened musicians provided polite music. A quartet of tame Neros, they fiddled on in anticipation of the final burning that could not be very far off now. Nobody knew how far off. It was December, and while a month ago it had seemed fairly certain that the Russians would sweep in any day, the city was still tensely lying in wait. The roar of nearby guns had become so commonplace that nobody commented on it any more, and every air raid seemed to bring the end nearer. Surely, once the Russians arrived, there would be no more attacks.

"Yes, Visegrád," Hanna said eagerly. "So you went down to fetch your dear mother. And then?"

"She didn't really want to come. While I was away she'd come to terms with the place, broken it in, as it were, and that made her feel like a settler who has cleared and ploughed a piece of virgin land and hangs on to it with all his might. She had bought firewood and some flour and sugar. Also, our river guard had left her a vast amount of smoked meat and sausages before he deserted, going to look for his Jewish wife. So Mother was rather reluctant to leave."

"Marvellous woman. I think if you dropped her in the middle of the Sahara, she would promptly start organizing a model household and make the bedouin polish dates for her. I envy her," Hanna said wistfully, "she's so strong and positive, a real woman. Where is she now?"

"Sharing a flat with an enchanting woman. The funny thing is," she added in a whisper, "her hostess is Jewish with a foolproof set of documents which make her into a Protestant refugee from Transylvania, and she's hiding Mother. We've come full circle. Now it's the Jews who are hiding the Christians."

Hanna nodded. "If it weren't so sad, it would be positively hilarious. And what about you?"

"I'm staying with Ervin. And I go back every third day to the flat to see what's going on. You see, there were so many Gestapo men about in our street—a couple even came to the house, looking for someone—that neither Mother nor I can live there permanently. It would be absolutely maddening to slip up now."

"Of course. Oh, I'm very happy about you and Ervin, my dear." Hanna's face changed subtly as she assumed her special manner that was calculated to encourage intimate confessions. It was an air of total, unshockable understanding; every feature became earnest, attentive and sincere, begging to be trusted. Gitta had brusquely told her the bare facts, now she wanted to hear the details. "Are you happy, darling girl? He adores you. He told me so himself."

"Why does he?" she blurted out. "I'd be happier if I were less surprised. What on earth does he see in me? I mean, he's such a . . ." she searched for the right word in vain, "such a . . . marvellous person, so polished and so much on top of life and everything, it makes me positively dumb with admiration—how do I come into all this?"

Hanna looked away towards the orchestra. She loved Gitta and liked Ervin, and however incongruous they seemed as lovers, she wanted them to have all the happiness they could snatch. She could have told Gitta that her all-pervading innocence was her greatest

233

attraction; that Ervin, who had denied ten years of his actual age, was loving her youth as much as he was dreading his own decline, and that the less analytically she thought about the whole affair, the better it would be for both of them.

"Never mind how you come into it. You're in it now, stop asking questions. Take it for granted that he loves you and be happy while you can. I know this sounds corny, but the more you plan your life, the less it comes off. To accept things without asking why is the first stage of wisdom."

"Oh, no!" she said in alarm. "It's the why that matters! I don't want to accept things without knowing what causes them, I can't!"

"You can't go through life asking 'why?'"

"But I want to. Dear Hanna, it's in me. I can't help it. I want to understand things, not just know about them. I want to get inside and understand. That's why I want to write, too. Writing is a way of sorting out things and making them clearer. You see, ——"

"We were talking about Ervin," Hanna reminded her. "What do you think about love?"

She lowered her eyes. "I don't know. It's all very confusing and— a bit overrated. Oh, don't laugh," she said despairingly, as Hanna threw back her head and roared with such gusto that faces began to turn towards them and the conversation at the neighbouring tables ceased, "don't laugh, perhaps it's my fault, but after the colossal emotional build-up one gets from the age of five onwards, the thing itself is something of an anticlimax." She talked on bravely, but Hanna's glee was stronger. Eventually she, too, began to laugh and upset a glass of water.

Ervin arrived ten minutes later. By then they had calmed down and the waiter had changed the damp table-cloth, all was well, normal and sociable, yet Gitta's manner changed immediately. In a second she became tense and unnaturally bright, addressing most of her remarks to Hanna, as if Ervin only existed on a secondary plane. With his admirable lack of perception he did not seem to notice. He gazed at her fondly, with an occasional glance at Hanna to signal his contentment like a proud father showing off his brilliant child. She doesn't love him, Hanna thought regretfully, and neither of them knows it, and if she did love him it would be worse, because he couldn't take it in the right way and she would be much more un-

234

happy. As it is, she's only perplexed and that at least takes her mind off other things.

Being a worshipper of love, Hanna contemplated their mutual misunderstanding sadly. Unless some miracle happened, this affair would be a bad start for her and a disastrous failure for him. Nobody could help them; nobody could help anybody.

Ervin dished out his news in a low voice. He had spoken to a fresh refugee from a Russian-held district and gathered that liberation had its drawbacks, too. There were arrests, looting, rapes and other horrors going on indiscriminately. Worse still, in that particular district the Russians were not Russians at all. One local man whose mother was Russian had been chosen as official spokesman for the village, but when he began to recite his carefully prepared speech abounding in pre-revolutionary courtesies, the small Mongoloid officer yelled out that he did not understand Russian and his men punched the poor flabbergasted fellow in the face.

"Kalmuks, Tartars, Yakuts and other savages who don't even speak Russian," Ervin said scornfully. "Europe's in a fine way. The Americans send negroes to bomb us, the Russians send Tartars to liberate us—I'm beginning to wonder how it's going to end."

"The Germans of course came to do the job themselves," Gitta snapped, annoyed by Ervin's snobbery towards the rest of the world —he seemed to think that all other continents were *nouveaux riches* and somewhat comical with their vast wealth and corresponding mental poverty. What was wrong with American negroes or Kalmuks? she thought irritably. The moment they talked about subjects other than themselves, their differences showed up sharply.

Later in his flat all was well again. She enjoyed being spoilt, petted and listened to; his attentiveness was moving. As long as she switched off the major part of her mind and pretended to be small, silly and defenceless, he reacted faultlessly. The moment she tried to be herself, the contact broke, he fluffed his lines, he emerged as a conventional middle-aged man, a perfectly polished façade with nothing behind it. She did not particularly mind. The next morning she was to go home.

CHAPTER THIRTY-ONE

~~~~~~~~~~~~~~~~~~~~~~~~

Travel had become a nightmare. To get back to town Mihály had to walk, cycle, lie on the roof of an over-crowded railway carriage, sit on an open ox cart, in an Army lorry and in the moribund car of an old doctor. The distance he had covered was short, because even the slowest progress was constantly interrupted. The train ran out of fuel and had to be abandoned, a vital road had been made impassable by tank traps, a German patrol confiscated the Army lorry at gun-point and the doctor's car broke down on a rough track. It was an instructive trip and a lonely one, too. He seemed to be the only traveller heading for Budapest against the tide of people running away from it. Sas had ordered him not to return, he had used the strongest arguments against Mihály's obstinacy, but Sas did not really matter. There was no more work left for him and he was getting desperate for Marta.

He had seen too much in the past fortnight. Led and commanded by Sas who sometimes wore full Arrow Cross uniform to secure free passes and easy transport, Mihály had carried out a series of actions which in retrospect seemed impossible. Several times he had driven a stolen lorry straight at columns of Jewish death-marchers, escorted by four S.S. men towards the border to build fortifications or be gassed. He had manœuvred the ambushing lorry to enable Sas and his two assistants to shoot the S.S. men and then help the captives to disperse. On a stretch of wooded, uninhabited land that separated the big labour camp from the main road to Vienna, this simple method worked well and fast, especially since they always removed the German corpses to destroy all evidence. Unfortunately the rate of evacuation had been stepped up lately and the labour forces were being driven away in a constant flow instead of isolated groups, which made further attempts impossible.

236

But they had carried on elsewhere, blowing up a train, helping to evacuate cattle into forest hide-outs, blowing up a bridge, kidnapping three Jewish children from a small village station and spiriting them away to a Protestant orphanage twenty kilometres away, incidentally killing a few people whenever necessary. Now he could do no more. The conflict had grown too deep. Living and feeling at a high pitch of intensity, he was no longer able to reconcile his beliefs with the methods that were necessary to put them into practice. To live and die for freedom and a life worth living was one thing, to act in a real-life gangster film was another. He was no fighter; he did not feel that a noble aim justified the use of gory methods which bore no relation to the Apollonian ideal of higher order, light and ecstasy. The past fortnight had been enough for a lifetime. When Sas had run out of immediate tasks, he had taken his leave to return to Marta.

He reached town in the morning and hurried to her through the empty streets. The memory of her cool, clear voice and heady scent grew more delicious. They made such a brilliant contrast, the little-girl voice that rippled like water, and the many-dimensional scent that played on the double note of sharp citrus and deep, sensuous musk. He had often watched her using her scent spray, turning the miniature muzzle towards her white neck, an earnest Cleopatra trying out a frivolous weapon. A few atomized drops always landed in the soft hollow of her throat which he loved to kiss, and they tasted clinically bitter on his lips. But then perfume is not meant to be tasted, he thought; abuse is the death of illusion.

Marta, last refuge, perfection, shelter, gold and blue and white, the only real, true and complete one, the last life-proof casket in which to lock up one's faith and guard it until the world changed and gave more cause for faith. As long as they had each other, there was some point in waiting and hoping and starting again, in living.

Her duplicate key was still in his pocket. He ran up the stairs at the double, rang the doorbell to give her a warning and let himself in.

They almost collided in the door of the small *salon* which she had turned into her living-room. She stared at him incredulously, almost in horror. Her face was pale and tired, her once-pink dressing-gown had lost half its swans'-down trimming and the remainder looked soiled and tufted, like the feathers of a drowned chicken, and instead of basking in the aura of her scent, the untidy room smelt stale and oppressive.

237

"Sweetheart, are you ill?" he cried anxiously, crushing her in his arms. "What's the matter? Has something happened? You don't look yourself, my darling!"

"I wasn't expecting you," she mumbled. "Why have you come back now?"

Without a word he led her towards the window to see her better, but she tore herself away and fled into the opposite corner of the room. It occurred to him that she might be suffering from a breakdown; alone for a fortnight in that crypt-like flat, perhaps not eating properly, perhaps being frightened and unhappy. And then he noticed two purple marks on the side of her neck and another one just above the neckline of her dirty dressing-gown. Crossing the room, he grabbed her and tore open the front of her gown. There were a number of clear tooth-marks on her shoulders.

"Oh, my God. And I've only been away a fortnight." There was nothing else to say. He sat down and shut his eyes. His hands felt clammy, there was a strong, urgent pulsation in his stomach. This was like being suspended over an abyss on a single rope whose strands are slowly, slowly unwinding and it is only a matter of time before the last one of them will snap. The rope was turning in the same direction, jerking at every full circle, getting thinner and flimsier. She, too, was a traitor. No refuge, no shelter, no perfection, only betrayal and falsehood; the well was poisoned, the peach was rotten, the rope snapped.

"You won't understand." Her voice came from a vast distance. "I hardly understand myself, because I love you so much, so terribly, and yet . . . or perhaps because I love you and you went away, even though we've been so happy. I don't know. Darling, I've always had this. I didn't tell you, because I thought you'd ended it for me, and you did, because I didn't sleep with anybody, I swear I didn't, and if——"

"You don't want me to believe that?"

"It's true, even if I can't prove it. Oh, help me, I can't help myself any more. Perhaps I should see a doctor. Perhaps I'm mad. I don't want to do this sort of thing, it just happens and I hate every minute of it. You're the only man I've ever loved without hating myself for it or being ashamed afterwards, and if you stay with me and love me I know I'll be able to—oh, don't go, you can't go now, please, darling, stay with me and help me!"

238

"I'm a man, not a psychiatrist," he said. "You don't know what you've done. You were the only thing I still believed in and now even you have betrayed me. How can I go on like this? Oh, leave me alone!"

She pressed her back against the door, barring his way, and her hands rose in a childish gesture of appeal. But he did not see her any more, he only saw the ugly marks on her white neck which she used to spray with scent. He pushed her aside and left the flat, running out blindly into the street.

Two days later he joined a group of students, Army deserters and young Communists operating from an abandoned flat in mid-town. The group swelled from day to day. They all carried arms and fulfilled crazy—and mostly useless—missions to shorten the interminable waiting. Eventually their carelessness brought about their undoing. The large number of military-age men coming to and from a private flat was noticed by a greenshirt patrol. They went to fetch reinforcements and attacked the flat with much shouting and firing of rifles. The door was strong enough to hold out for a few minutes. Mihály ordered the men—there were some twenty of them inside—to climb up a ladder through a narrow well to the roof which offered several escape routes. He and the three eldest men stayed behind, training their revolvers on the door from behind a barricade of furniture.

The greenshirts broke in. The shooting match began. Mihály scored four times, the enemy retreated in confusion. He ordered his rearguard to withdraw. The greenshirts reappeared. Mihály felt sure he could hold them back a little longer and then get away. But the last of his men to escape suddenly panicked and pulled up the ladder from the top, so that when Mihály toppled the barricade on the enemy and made a dash for the window, he found himself stranded.

There was no time for him to ponder this final betrayal. The six shots that hit him a moment later killed him instantaneously.

239

CHAPTER THIRTY-TWO

By the beginning of December the exiled politicians with whom Pali was staying had abandoned their early hopes. Even in Budapest, at the centre of things, it had been impossible to carry out essential tasks; now, tucked away in the comparative safety and total isolation of the country, they found themselves paralysed and helpless. They knew full well what was needed; they also knew it could not be achieved. Make contact with the Allies, submit a political blueprint for the future, work out the economic problems on a national scale—how? Even cheerful pretences were running out. The brown and grey village winter, the indifferent silence, the timelessness of low clouds, muddy roads and withdrawn hills choked all ideas and intentions. There was nothing left to do but to indulge in endless discussions and keep reshuffling several possible Shadow Cabinets; to go to bed waiting for the morning and get up looking forward to the night.

Steeped in all-round frustration, Pali was careful to do no more than listen, observe and occasionally make a reserved comment. But as everybody else was talkative and emotional, his very quietness and moderation gave him authority, and once again he found himself in his pet role of chief analyst and theory-sifter. All this was vaguely amusing but it would have been more important to know where the Russians were and what the Germans were doing; and on those two subjects everybody present held widely divergent views.

One day the village apothecary's nephew brought the news that in several industrial cities the Germans were dismantling factories and removing every bit of equipment; with great thoroughness they also destroyed whatever they couldn't take away. The situation was disastrous, the nephew said, but a little organized sabotage on the workers' part would still help, and he had heard about the man who could start it, an elusive Socialist called Bakos, allegedly lying low a mere twenty kilometres away.

Within an hour Pali was on his way to find Bakos. The old restlessness had returned with a vengeance—he had had his fill of prospective elder statesmen and Party leaders, all he wanted was less talk and more action. Four hours later he reached the appointed village, but Bakos had beat him to it by a day, having moved farther east, another long walk away. This set the pattern for the next few days In the absence of transport Pali toured the region manfully in his newly acquired sheepskin coat and sturdy boots (even this rural outfit failed to conceal his urban identity and he looked as unconvincing as a badly made-up actor), but every stop brought fresh disappointment, because Bakos had already moved on eastward, presumably heading for the approaching Russian front.

Worse still, his traces were growing fainter. In one or two villages Pali's inquiries were received with stony silence. Nobody knew Bakos, nobody had seen any strangers; impassive eyes looked blank, luxuriant moustaches drooped over silent lips. But even if the taciturn peasants had been more forthcoming, time was running out fast. The unstable front line was very near now and Pali knew that it might be difficult for him—with or without Bakos—to return to German-held territory. The quest was turning into yet another quixotic failure, since the Germans worked with fast precision even when retreating, and they were too experienced in wholesale looting for any amateurish resistance to stop them.

On the fourth day of his trek Pali arrived in a small market town and decided to spend the day there. The place looked solemn and sleepy, the market square was fringed with round-headed bare acacia trees, a pock-marked grey statue of St. John Nepomuk stood guard outside the baroque church, and the barber's polished brass plate shone brightly in the grey morning. Comforted by this uneventful scene, Pali made straight for the old coaching inn that bore the name and sign of the "Marble Bride", and the first man he noticed in the taproom was Sas, a greyer, thinner Sas dressed in riding-boots and a hacking jacket.

They shook hands incredulously; Sas relieved his surprise with a string of jovial obscenities. The taproom was warm and noisy and the wireless blared over the din. Just like the good old days, Pali

241

thought, admiring Sas's choice of an isolated table by the window; and then he began to wonder why the last nerve-racking spring and summer should inspire him to near-nostalgia.

"What in the devil's name are you doing here?" Sas asked. "I knew you were around these parts, but I didn't expect such faultless navigation. What are you up to?"

"Looking for a mystery man who's supposed to be good at sabotage."

"Oh God, you don't mean Bakos?"

"Don't tell me you know him?"

"I am Bakos," Sas said gloomily. "I suppose I should feel proud of being the only famous saboteur in the area, a legend in my lifetime, you know, but it's time I made a fresh start elsewhere. All this publicity is bad for me."

Anyway, he couldn't oblige, he said, he had his orders and would be very busy quite soon. How soon? Pali wanted to know. The agent's ugly face and coarse detachment were like a tonic; he did not want their meeting to end at once.

Sas fished out a wrist-watch from his pocket. "Let's have lunch now," he said.

"But how soon will you be very busy?" Pali insisted.

"You're out of training. Do you need footnotes?"

"Does that mean that you'll be starting after lunch?"

"They have an excellent bean soup in this joint with slices of smoked bacon swimming on top. Tell me about your political hosts. Have they saved the country yet?"

No, not quite, Pali said resignedly, launching himself into a summary of political trends among his fellow exiles. He kept it brief; his first glance at flesh-and-blood politicians had been disappointing and he disliked talking about his findings. But Sas was dictatorial enough to conduct conversations on his own terms, and Pali's *exposé* enabled him to apply himself earnestly to his food. For a man with severe, if self-diagnosed, stomach trouble, he ate remarkably well.

The firing started at the very moment when the serving girl arrived with a dish of hot jam-filled cakes. Sas fished out his watch once more, grunted and went on eating. The other guests jumped to their feet; somebody turned on the wireless even louder as if expecting it to issue emergency instructions. Pali nodded appreciatively—

242

Sas had been right to order an early lunch, for momentous events were best borne on a full stomach.

"Brothers! Patriots!" an apoplectic voice boomed from the loud-speaker. "The Arrow Cross Party is guarding you against all perils. The military situation is improving. Our beautiful homeland is being cleared of the Bolshevik brigands."

"Is it indeed?" Sas said. The firing outside had suddenly ceased, only the wireless blared on.

"Our victorious German allies are working miracles," the speaker roared. "Fear nothing, the godless Reds are fleeing in panic. The day of retribution is near, the Red Army will learn what total defeat means!"

"Well, well," Sas commented, flicking up the net curtain, "here comes the crushed enemy fleeing in panic. They seem to take total defeat rather well, I must say."

The first Russians had appeared in the square. They ran around wildly, looking for Germans, but there were none and even the locals had dived for shelter at the first sight of the soldiers' round fur caps and machine-guns. Only St. John Nepomuk had remained at his post to witness the take-over, for he was too old to care. Two tanks rolled in from a side street, followed by more soldiers. A few shots popped near by; somebody shouted for help. The taproom was emptying rapidly, the landlord cursed and switched off the wire-less, leaving the words "final victory" suspended in the sudden silence. Pali looked out of the window. The short bow-legged figures in their dirty grey quilted tunics and fur-trimmed caps tore around chaotically, shouting and gesticulating like angry children engaged in a mass quarrel. This may be liberation, Pali thought, but it looks too messy to be welcomed; but then the natives, the only people with any right to be where they were, had no choice in matters of occupation or liberation.

Six Russians burst into the taproom. The landlord and a few guests went to meet them, only Sas and Pali remained seated. The soldiers tore around shouting "*Niemecki soldat*", and the landlord raised his arms and shook his head and yelled "No, no!" and the others joined in the head-shaking with an air of injured innocence. Upon that the soldiers surrounded Sas and Pali who were watching the proceedings quietly. Sas rose and handed a grey card to the most excited Russian, but the soldier kept turning it round angrily as if a

243

document had nothing to do with questions of identity. Eventually he threw it on the table and stepped forward to frisk the two civilians, but Sas broke into an unexpected hailstorm of Russian, thrusting the grey card repeatedly under the soldier's nose, and went on until the soldier nodded sullenly and led his companions from the taproom.

"Well done," Pali marvelled. "A mere change of régime doesn't seem to impair your skill, you old monster. What's that card?"

"A priority pass from the Russian Control Commission, issued by Malinovsky's H.Q. and endorsed by the NKVD. My employers think of every little thing."

"Do you mean to say it's genuine?"

"Of course it's genuine," Sas raged, "but these backward idiots can't even read or remember the names of their own generals, so I might just as well show them an old laundry list with a rubber stamp on it. I didn't expect so much ignorance. Things are getting worse, it won't be worth one's while to forge papers. The Germans at least could read."

The landlord who had followed the Russians out dashed in and bowed to Sas. "They're searching the house," he complained. "They've driven us out into the yard and heaven knows what they're up to. Can you speak to them, sir? We don't know the language."

"Neither do I," Sas admitted. "I only swore in Russian and said the rest in Slovak, and I don't see what good I can do. Which way did they go?"

They found the soldiers in the big pantry whose shelves were full of home-made preserves—tall bottles gleaming with thick tomato extract, frilly-capped stout jars holding apricot jam, whole sugared strawberries, cherries, morellos, raspberry jam and blue-black plum *purée*, a rich summer's crop briefly immortalized between glass and parchment. In spite of this luscious choice the soldiers were only interested in the giant jars of pickled gherkins seasoned with dill, fermented with leaven and slowly ripened in sun-heated containers. They had opened every jar and were fishing out gherkins by the handful, splashing themselves with sour juice and chewing noisily. Sas withdrew at once. There was no reason to interfere—the "Marble Bride" would have to get through the winter without sour gherkins, and might no bigger disaster befall her.

He did, however, seek out the NKVD captain in the square and

244

impress him sufficiently to have the inn put under his protection; and when two guards appeared outside the entrance, Sas ordered more wine and settled down in the taproom with Pali.

"Well, we've been liberated," he said. "This is my sixth military occupation to date. The first five were done by the other side but the difference is negligible. I don't think I'll stay here much longer."

"Where will you go?"

"Eventually to Putney. I have a flat there."

"Where's Putney?"

"In south-west London. What about you?"

"I'll go back to town as soon as possible."

"Why not come with me? I could probably fix you up with a job over there."

"No, thanks. I'm no great linguist and unfortunately the only things that interest me are tied up with words—writing or broad-casting or doing my thesis on the legal system of dictatorships. One of the reasons why I haven't sat for my law degree yet is that until an hour ago I've never been in a position to mention the subject of my thesis publicly, let alone work on it. I think I'll stay and tie up my loose ends."

"Pity. If I were you I wouldn't start on that thesis just now. It might make you unpopular with the next régime. That sort of subject is best tackled in a neutral place like Putney. Oh, you ought to know what I mean, there's no future in small countries, not in this part of the world, anyway, and you can't go on for the rest of your life resisting the powers that be. Resistance is a seasonal job, not a career."

"Resistance is a state of mind and as such incurable," Pali murmured, raising his glass. He did not feel like arguing with Sas who was unusually volatile though pessimistic. Perhaps his imminent return to Putney—it seemed incongruous for him to have a perman-ent address—cheered him up, or else he was simply glad to see the end of a lengthy and unpleasant job. Communication was imposs-ible, Pali thought: however much they had been through together, they were now fatally separated by the fact that Sas, to whom the past few months had only meant a job, had a flat in Putney to return to, and he himself had not.

"The place won't be the same without you," he said, and Sas pulled a sarcastic face although Pali had meant it seriously. They spent the rest of the afternoon talking and drinking and not getting anywhere; they had no common topic left, and Sas was unable to feel interested in anybody who disagreed with him.

He left in the evening after another conference with the NKVD captain who arranged for him to travel on an eastbound Russian lorry. Pali watched Sas climb in, issuing a torrent of presumably funny oaths, since the soldiers inside roared with laughter; then he turned back to Pali and made a farewell gesture, a quick downward flick of the right hand that expressed a wealth of resignation and weariness; and then the lorry drove away.

Pali left the next morning, planning to return to his hosts and then perhaps to town. On the second day of his long walk he almost ran into a German garrison, turning back at the last moment, and half an hour later he was arrested by the Russians who took him for a German spy.

They kept him in a wooden hut for a week, together with a dozen local men whom they had rounded up at random in the fields and woods. Then they packed them into an eastbound goods train. The captives travelled for twenty-four hours in the icy truck without food or drink, but then, again without explanation, they were released and told to disperse.

Pali moved away from the others and looked round. He had no idea where he was. The landscape looked unfamiliar, with high mountains in the distance, meagre fields on either side of the tracks and not a house or signpost anywhere. The goods train started moving, the soldiers shouted and the chief guard emptied his rifle in the air.

Pali folded his arms. The Russians had taken away his watch and fountain pen, but the three books were still in his pocket. He hoped his boots would stand up to another long trek. This was a bad start; perhaps Sas was right, perhaps there was no future in a small country.

The other men stood around in a daze. "Come along," Pali called out to them, "we have a long way to go."

CHAPTER THIRTY-THREE

~~~~~~rrrrrr0000000rrrr~~~~~

Mrs. Balogh returned home shortly before Christmas, on the very day when the Gestapo headquarters was being evacuated. The news of the great exodus was on everybody's lips even before the last steel cabinet had been loaded on to the last lorry. Mrs. Balogh needed no further encouragement. She packed her bag in five minutes, kissed her hostess on both cheeks and rushed home as fast as her high heels would carry her.

Having feared the worst, she was pleasantly surprised. Gitta's casual spells in the flat (oh Lord, her mother thought, she's become so independent, I hardly know anything about her now!) had wrought no havoc. In fact, the child had kept the place in amazing order. Why is she so untidy when I'm about? Mrs. Balogh wondered, not realizing that the question also contained the answer; and then she began to make up for her two months' absence.

Gitta followed her round everywhere. She was profoundly happy to have her mother back in the flat. The way she tripped from kitchen to pantry, from bathroom to linen cupboard, her air of concentration lightened by shrewd or irrelevant asides, were beginning to re-establish normality. Having grown up so fast and so jerkily, Gitta wanted to be reassured, and no one but her mother could make up for the fearful night of the Lázárs' stay, the terror of the Day of the Dead, Ervin's visit, her stay in his flat, the long telephone conversations at night when she was at home, answering him in what she hoped was a throbbing voice. All this was receding rapidly, and she was glad to let it go. Several times she stopped her mother to kiss her on both cheeks. It was the only way to tell her all the things she must never find out.

The firing came closer all the time and the air buzzed with evil noises. Nobody knew whether the Germans would evacuate the city or try to hold it, whether anybody was planning any definite move or whether the long wait was to continue. Being right in the middle of everything, people felt completely in the dark and only concerned themselves with short-term survival. Bread was the gravest problem. Flour stocks were all but exhausted. No fresh supplies came from the country, and those bakers who still had enough fuel to heat their ovens were turning out hard, heavy brown buns that were both unbreakable and indigestible.

Every morning Gitta went out with a shopping bag to hunt for food, any food. She toured the familiar shops with little result, because there was nothing left to buy, and the assistants stood about with guilty faces, as if the desperate emptiness around them had been their personal fault. Strolling down the best shopping street one morning, she saw big scrawled notices in the window of the Italian place. There was a sale on, unrepeatable bargains to be cleared, last few days, everything must go. As she entered, an explosion shook the street and broken glass cascaded on the pavement opposite. "Come along, come along, what would you like?" the saleswoman asked hysterically. "Look round, choose, name your price, take what you like before the house comes down." She nodded. The shop was so beautiful, so elegant; in the yellow niches large photographs showed the Italian seaside, Roman columns, Tuscan cathedrals with their fugue-like symmetry, the Spanish Steps, Florence; and the shelves held pottery, silks, exquisite glassware, picture books and jewellery, the essence of a country in capsule form now selling out, living its last few days, since everything must go.

Ignoring the saleswoman's patter, she chose a small gilt brooch. It was flower-shaped, with a pearl-studded calyx and filigree leaves. She refused a greatly reduced white and gold Murano vase. To buy anything so fragile seemed like tempting fate. The brooch at least was metal, and she did not go home empty-handed.

After that day neither of them went out. There was nothing to go out for and several people in the neighbourhood had been killed or badly injured by shells and falling masonry. Occasionally the electricity supply broke down. The telephone still worked and friends kept ringing up to report briefly on local events. Often they only spoke from a few streets away, but by then every house was turning into an isolated unit, quarantined by fear. Ervin rang every day. As block commander he could not leave the house. Out of deference to Mrs.

248

Balogh's presence he spoke earnestly and formally, in the manner of a solicitous uncle, and only when the conversation was drawing to a close did he change his tone to say: "and I love you, darling." "Yes," Gitta would reply non-committally before replacing the receiver. She quite liked him, especially now that meetings had become impossible.

On the morning of Christmas Eve she woke up and walked to the window to see if anything had changed overnight. The park below was bare and snow-covered. The enormous bronze figure of a bishop, holding a chalice, stood out darkly against the thick whiteness. There were Hungarian soldiers in the park, forlorn little figures huddling around an anti-aircraft gun. The scene had the stark loneliness of a winter painting by Brueghel; even the sky imitated the smoky yellow hue of an old canvas. This is bad, Gitta thought anxiously; that gun will attract a lot of attention from above.

Hanna burst in at five. She staggered in, carrying an enormous parcel, and collapsed on a chair. "I've been bombed out," she faltered. "Will you have me? There's nothing left of my flat, not a stick, and I have nowhere to go."

Mrs. Balogh patted her shoulder sympathetically. "Of course you can stay. As long as this place doesn't go up in smoke, you're very welcome." Although she was not too happy about the intrusion, she controlled her dismay: Hanna had put Gitta up at a particularly bleak moment and for that good deed she was entitled to hospitality.

Hanna did not come empty-handed. The untidy parcel disgorged a number of tins rescued from her cellar cache, some highly unsuitable clothes and the few objects the explosion had hurled out unbroken into the street below, among them the shrewd-faced jade figure of an ancient Chinese sage which she cherished as her lucky mascot. Mrs. Balogh made comforting noises and settled Hanna into a warm corner. She was busy preparing the festive meal.

"I knew it would happen," Hanna said to Gitta who was arranging her old childhood crib on the piano since something had to take the place of a Christmas tree and the shabby, helpless-looking clay figures were in keeping with the situation. "Last night I saw my white monk," she continued. "He didn't speak to me but somehow he conveyed that the flat was going to be hit, I can't explain how, I just knew. So this morning I sent my last guests away, one to Ervin, I hope you don't mind, two to another friend, and when the raid came I went down to the shelter, although I never do so as a rule." She hid her face in her hands and shuddered. "The whole floor's gone. The bomb went in through my flat and exploded next door. I simply couldn't believe it when I saw it from the street. Just gone, like that."

"But you're alive, that's what matters! Although I loved your flat dearly, it was so beautiful. Still, you've got your white monk and your Chinese sage and when it's all over we'll find you another flat which you can make just as beautiful."

She shook her head sadly. "No, my precious. It feels as if my flat had been murdered—you know, it was so personal, so much a part of me, a record of the past ten years. I'm too old to have a new one exactly like it; for one thing all the family antiques are gone. It would only feel temporary and unreal—oh Lord, listen to those windows!"

The panes were rattling behind the stout shutters, the whole house shook, a tremor ran across the floor. Mrs. Balogh raced in from the kitchen in a white apron. "Lay the table quickly," she called to Gitta, "we must eat at once before the bombing gets worse. Hurry up, the decorations don't matter!"

They ate hastily, drinking their wine in great gulps and trying to smile over the tremulous candles in the centre, and after the main course the house commander rang the doorbell to announce that the top floor was to be evacuated and would the ladies kindly move down to the shelter or at least the ground floor. Mrs. Balogh asked for thirty minutes' grace. They cleared away the table and Gitta tried to wash up, but the gas pressure was too low to heat the water.

"Anyway, it's Christmas," she said wistfully, "let's look at the crib before we go down." They trooped back to the drawing-room and placed the guttering candles behind the crib, bending over the pathetic little figures that suddenly grew big and dramatic in the flickering light. The plump Madonna, the shepherds and the wise men surrounded the pink and gold infant in adoration, the angels stood squat around them, nice solid peasant angels with straw-coloured hair and, perhaps, straw between their toes.

"Well, let's hope the next one will be better," Mrs. Balogh said.

"Come to think of it, they were all Jews, except the Magi," Hanna murmured, pointing to the crib. Gitta linked arms with them. "Oh, let's pretend," she pleaded, "let's sing something, we can't go just like this!"

The two women glanced at each other but Gitta was already intoning a carol and they joined in, not quite remembering the words.

"The Angel from Heaven came down to you, shepherds, oh shepherds," they sang uncertainly, "to Bethlehem hastily go and see, and see: the Son of God who was born in the manger, in the manger, He will be your Saviour indeed, indeed." There was another explosion. "Darling, we must really go now," Mrs. Balogh said very tenderly; if only she had been able to get a present for Gitta. Her daughter blew out the candles. "Oh, it's all right now, I only wanted to sing that one verse but it sounds all wrong, anyhow."

Still reluctant to go to the shelter, they took over a room in an abandoned ground-floor flat, a large, old-fashioned place with dark brown furniture and plush curtains. The soldiers had come in from the park and stood forlornly in the hall. "Don't worry about us," their young officer said to Mrs. Balogh who eyed them suspiciously, "we won't use that gun outside if we can help it."

They slept in their clothes in an enormous double bed. The explosions and tremors continued. At three in the morning all the windows of the house blew out with one tremendous clatter. Mrs. Balogh put her hand on Gitta's forehead. "Won't you be cold?" she whispered. But Gitta did not reply. She was fast asleep.

The shelter was very large, with thick, whitewashed walls and a double steel door leading up through the back staircase to the yard. Its eighty-odd inhabitants spent the days sitting on regulation-size backless wooden benches; at night they took turns to sleep on real or improvised beds. Each household was allowed one bed which during the day held their personal belongings, clothes, pots and pans and provisions. At night all these things were deposited on the concrete floor under the beds, until the quiet rats began to infiltrate from the neighbouring coal cellars in search of food, going as far as lifting lids off saucepans to get at their contents. This led to the appointment of a rat-watchman from among the soldiers who had moved into the shelter, leaving their gun in the charge of the bronze bishop in the park. As far as they were concerned, he could keep it.

There was one old-fashioned cooker in the shelter with enough room for three cooks at a time. The harassed house commander drew up a strict rota for every family and kept the feuding house-wives under his personal supervision. Married to a quarrelsome wife, he regarded communal cooking as one of the greatest dangers of the siege.

Beyond doubt, the siege was now in full swing. For the last five days it had been impossible to leave the shelter: the air and land duel between the Germans and the Russians did not stop for a moment, the house had been hit fifty-two times and, although it was difficult to assess its condition from below ground, everybody feared the worst. The water-tap had run dry. There was no electricity. Candles were brought out, but their number had to be strictly limited in order to save oxygen, so that each two neighbouring groups were allowed one candle only, and the dim hall broke up into a pattern of frail light and deep shadow, of clustered groups and empty spaces. Past the steel door the rest of the cellars stretched away in dank obscurity. At the far end covered buckets were spaced out to act as lavatories. For reasons of modesty the house commander had asked his flock to withdraw there one at a time, but the women insisted on going in pairs on account of the rats.

The Baloghs were reasonably comfortable on the large bedstead hauled down from the spare room. Broadened by the wooden bench at night, the bed accommodated all three of them, and Hanna was getting used to limited sleeping-space. One of the soldiers had fitted a shelf along the top of the bedstead where they kept their food and oddments. They ate their small meals at regular intervals and drank soda-water with wine from Mrs. Balogh's well-stocked cellar, since there was nothing else to drink. Most people did the same; in spite of disastrous conditions the general atmosphere was relaxed and hazy. Some people drank too much, and those who had stocked up on spirits rather than wine fared worst. But there were no serious incidents. One ugly, elderly man who never spoke a word to anybody did get out of hand to the extent of climbing up on his bed, glass in hand, and shouting out the traditional drinking cry of "We shall never die!" but the thundering explosion that followed this irresponsible statement sobered him down at once.

Mrs. Balogh poured out drinks generously. The lack of light, water, air, exercise, sanitation, decent food and hope had to be balanced with some sedative, and mild drinking seemed more wholesome than drugs. She was calm, composed and cheerful, watching the middle-class inferno around her with large, limpid eyes. Sometimes she called on two or three friendly families a few beds away. When it was their turn to light a candle, she read a little or made running repairs to their clothes. Hanna had been right about her heroic adaptability: she would have organized a household in the middle of the Sahara.

On New Year's Eve they decided to have a party. Hanna and Gitta volunteered to revel on a bottle of Hungarian whisky which Mrs. Balogh would have not touched to save her life; she said it tasted of soap and other nasty things. A small blonde woman from the opposite corner joined them on the hard bench to chat and drink red wine with Mrs. Balogh.

"Well, darling, this year is almost over," Hanna said, licking her lips after the first toast. The whisky tasted most unusual. "Some year, too. I'm surprised we're still here and I certainly dread to look back. All my life I haven't seen so much destruction as in these last few months. I mean human destruction, not just the war; changes, losses, deaths, failures. My own life is as full of debris as a res-taurant car after a rail crash, with nothing to salvage. I've lost Miklós, too. He fled to Germany a week ago. He dropped in and begged me to go with him but I refused. I couldn't have thrown in my lot with a gang of greenshirts for his sake, so I let him go. Oh well, it's over now, together with an awful lot of other things. Do you remember what we were like a year ago?"

"Yes, I do. But we're still the same. All that has happened came from the outside, I don't think we've had a choice. Circumstances were created for us and we could only react in our own individual ways. There's nothing to regret, because there's always only one possible way of acting, don't you agree?"

Hanna drained her glass and refilled it at once. "I do. We're all slaves to our individual pattern. We can't change anything. We can't alter our finger-prints, our handwriting, our desires, we're determined from birth. Everything we do or dream or feel comes from the centre, which is our karma—I rather imagine it as a greedy mollusc in a shell, a puny little ego that must relate everything to itself in order to give it meaning. We're slaves from the inside and on top of it all we happen to live in a world where there's nothing

253

but constraint and pressure. How in heaven's name is one to exist?"

"But one does. And the awful thing is that, in spite of everything, deep down I'm happy." She sounded surprised; put into words, her secret feeling of unjustified bliss sounded outrageous. "I can't help looking ahead. After all it's almost over now, isn't it, and if we survive this last bit, we can live again—oh, don't look like that, you'll see, I promise!" She pressed Hanna's hand between hers to underline her words. The horrible drink was rising to her head. The floor of the shelter thudded darkly underfoot every time a bomb exploded in the neighbourhood, but the gentle buzz in her ears filtered the outside noises and she was beginning to glow with alcoholic well-being. "Hanna, dearest, let's make plans. Tell me the best things we can do when it's all over. What was the greatest event that happened to you when you were my age?"

The round blue eyes were moist, the noble, ravaged face looked very white under the cloud of red hair. "I went to Paris for the first time," the husky voice said. "I arrived one morning in April at the Gare de l'Est and took a taxi to the Concorde. My aunt was staying at the Crillon but it was too early to wake her, so I left my luggage and walked along the Champs-Elysées. I stood all alone somewhere between the Rond-Point and the Arc de Triomphe. The sky was pearl-grey, very light and high. And the leaves on the trees looked so young, so transparent, and the air smelt different. There seemed more oxygen in it, more scent. I stood there drinking it in until I felt I should burst with happiness. I can't tell you what it was, not just what I saw—I've been back many times since and it's never been the same—it was the poetry behind it, the meaning behind every single thing in the world condensed into that one moment." She emptied her glass. There were tears in her eyes. "That morning I felt that there was nothing I couldn't do if only I tried hard enough. I felt like a young goddess with the world in my lap, all mine to play with, and Paris only the beginning. I think I fell in love with life at that particular moment. I still am in love with it. But now, if I found myself facing the 'Winged Victory' in the Louvre, I should probably turn my back on it and cry."

"Oh, don't! It's going to be wonderful. Just think of it, the Germans will go, the Russians will go, we'll be able to do what we want at last. And people won't be persecuted for something they can't help. And we'll be able to work and travel and say what we think and choose freely instead of being pushed into situations——"

"Don't shout, baby," Mrs. Balogh said over her shoulder.

"Are you going to marry Ervin?" Hanna whispered. She was reaching the sentimental stage.

"Oh, no. I couldn't. I hope he'll understand, it wouldn't work. I want to go to Paris, like you did, and write and study and—oh, lots of things."

"You really love Pali, don't you?"

"Of course." Now it was her turn to blink away the rising tears. Apart from emotion, the bitter air of the shelter irritated her eyes. "I'll always love him. Nothing can change that. He'll come back and he'll understand everything. He's bound to—we're really one and the same person."

Hanna thought she understood and nodded vigorously. Drunkenness only blunted the top layer of perception: Gitta's face was hazy and she did not know what she was doing in this awful, smelly cellar, but beneath the surface confusion she saw and felt with unnatural clarity. Whatever happened, the "Winged Victory" was right. There was no standstill, no end, the heart went on pumping blood and the soul went on churning around its hopes and needs until the puzzle clicked into position, even if it took a lifetime to do so. Gazing tenderly at Gitta she thought that this was the only real friend she had ever had, the living recapitulation of her own dead youth.

"If I die, you must have my jade figure," she said thickly. "I don't want anybody else to have him, they wouldn't understand how wise and gay he is."

The house commander approached and bent to Mrs. Balogh's ear. "The shooting's stopped. If you'd like some fresh air, come to the door quietly. I don't want the whole mob to stream out, otherwise I'll never get them back here." He favoured their group. Mrs. Balogh's tidiness and Hanna's title impressed him.

They filed out unobtrusively into the eerie silence. The yard was full of debris, chunks of frozen snow and stone dust. Timidly they picked their way to the street entrance. The street was dark but on the other side of the park the printing works were blazing in terrifying splendour; emerald-green flames shot up through the roof, while large, chemical-fed flames swooshed out of the windows like heavy curtains. The dark sky was punctured with red all about. The city was burning.

255

"God have mercy upon us," Mrs. Balogh whispered. This was the seventh pit of Hell. Even her old, familiar street looked hostile, a place of nightmare where every step might land one in a pool of blood. "Let's go back, I can't stand this a minute longer. Down in the shelter at least one doesn't see what's going on."

She tripped gingerly across the desolate yard. Sobered by the cold air and the infernal view but still unsteady from the knees down, Gitta and Hanna followed her reluctantly. As they reached the back staircase, the firing started again, flashing and thundering from one edge of the sky to the other. Gitta paused and looked up, holding on to the rough iron hand-rail. Far, far above her, beyond the blaze and the noise, the stars seemed cold, white and enormous.